W9-BGS-052

"Beastmen have raided the seacoast at the Duchy of Loguire!"

"Beastmen?" said Rod Gallowglass, frowning. "I thought they were just figments of somebody's imagination."

"Assuredly," agreed Brom O'Berin, "yet thou dost forget that on Gramarye imagination can become extraordinary durable."

And that, Rod admitted silently, was nothing but cold fact. Projective telepathy, coupled with a mysterious native substance, had produced some remarkably solid figments.

"If night-fears might become solid," Brom growled, "just such a form would they take: bogeymen, such as goodwives use to frighten children with; things half beast and half man, great shambling goblins, with ape's arms and great feet, huge clubs and witch-power. . . ."

There was no question about it. Rod Gallowglass, the Warlock in Spite of Himself, was facing a crisis that made all his previous experiences seem minor.

CHRISTOPHER STASHEFF used to be in educational television and may be again, but at the moment he is in college. He has a fondness for science fiction, theater, puns, and thinking up new answers to "How are you?"

He comes of an old and distinguished line. One ancestor had to leave Ireland in a bit of a hurry—sheriff trouble, he'd been shooting landlords out of season. Another ancestor was sent to Siberia for teaching peasants to read and write.

Consequently, Mr. Stasheff has an inborn love for freedom and public attention and, therefore, for America. His main ambition is to live up to the family traditions.

CHRISTOPHER STASHEFF

king kobold

ACE BOOKS

A Division of Charter Communications Inc.
1120 Avenue of the Americas
New York, N. Y. 10036

KING KOBOLD

Cover art by Jack Gaughan.

Also by this author:

THE WARLOCK IN SPITE OF HIMSELF (75¢)

Printed in U.S.A.

THE HEAVY CLINGING FOG lay dense, nearly opaque, over the heaving sea. The rolling, endless crash of breakers against the headlands at the harbor's mouth came muted and distant.

High above, a circling unseen bird called plaintive sentry cries.

The dragon shouldered out of the swirling mist, its beaked, arrogant head held high.

Four more like it loomed out of the fog at its back.

Round, bright-painted shields hung on their sides. . . .

Oars speared out from the shields, lifting in unison and falling feathered to the waves.

The dragon's single wing was tightly furled around the crossbar lashed to the tall, single mast that thrust upward out of its back.

Squat, hulking, helmeted shapes prowled silently about the mast.

The dragon had an eagle's beak, and a tall, ribbed fin for a crest. Two long, straight horns probed out from its forehead.

The surf moaned on the shore, as the dragon led its mates past the headland.

The child screamed, howling for his mother, thrashing himself into a tangle with the thick fur blanket.

Then the oil lamp was there, just a rag in a dish, but warm and safe, throwing its yellow glow upward on the mother's weary, gentle face.

She gathered the quivering, sobbing little body into her arms, murmuring, "There now, love, there. Mama's here. She won't let him hurt you."

She held the child tightly, rubbing his back until the sobbing ceased. "There now, Artur, there. What was it, darling?"

The child sniffled and lifted his head from her shoulder. "Bogeyman, Mama. Chasing me, and—he had a great big knife!"

Ethel's mouth firmed. She hugged the child and glared at the lamp-flame. "The bogeymen are far across the sea, darling. They can't come here."

5

"But Carl says . . ."

"I know, I know. Carl's mama tells him the bogeyman will get him if he's bad. But that's just a silly story, darling, to frighten silly children. You're not silly, are you?"

Artur was silent a while; then he murmured, into the folds of his mother's gown, "Uh . . . no, Mama. . . ."

"Of course you're not." She patted his back, laid him down in the bed, and tucked the fur robe under his chin. "That's my brave boy. We both know the bogeyman can't hurt us, don't we?"

"Yes, Mama," the child said uncertainly.

"Sleep sweetly, darling," the mother said, and closed the door softly behind her.

The oil lamp set the shadows dancing softly on the walls. The child lay awake awhile, watching the slow ballet of light and dark.

He sighed, rolled over on his side. His eyes were closing as they strayed to the window.

A huge misshapen face peered in, the eyes small and gleaming, the nose a glob of flesh, the mouth a gash framing great square, yellowed teeth. Shaggy brown hair splayed out from a gleaming, winged helmet.

He grinned at the child, pig eyes dancing.

"Mama! Mamamamamamamama! *Bogeyman!*"

The bogeyman snarled and broke through the stout wooden wall with three blows of a great iron-bound club.

The child screamed and ran, yanking and straining at the heavy bedroom door.

The bogeyman clambered through the broken wall.

The door was flung wide; the mother stared in horror, clutching her child to her and screaming for her husband. She wheeled about and fled.

The bogeyman gave a deep, liquid chuckle, and followed.

In another cottage, a bogeyman seized a child by the ankles and swung his head lightly against the wall. He lifted his huge club to fend off the father's sword, then whirled the club into the father's belly, swung it up to strike the father's temple. Bone splintered; blood flowed.

The mother backed away, screaming, as the beastman caught up the father's fallen sword. He turned to the mother, knocked her aside with a careless, backhand swipe of the club, and stove in the family strong-chest with one blow.

In the first cottage, the oil lamp, knocked aside in the beastman's passage, licked at the oil spilled on walls and floor.

Other cottages were already ablaze.

Women and children ran screaming, with chuckling beast-men loping after them.

The men of the village caught up harpoons and axes, rallying to defend their wives and children.

The beastmen shattered their heads with iron-bound cudgels, clove chests with great, razor-edged battle axes, and passed on, leaving dismembered bodies behind them.

Then drumming hooves, and a troop of cavalry burst into the village; the fires had alerted the local baron. He sat now at the head of a score of horsemen, drawn up in the beastmen's path.

"Fix lances!" he roared. "Charge!"

The beastmen chuckled.

Lances snapped down, heels kicked horsehide; the cavalry charged . . . and faltered, stumbled, halted, soldiers and horses alike staring at the beastmen for long, silent minutes.

Each beastman flicked his glance from one soldier to another, on to a third, then back to the first, holding each one's eyes for a fraction of a second.

Jaws gaped, eyes glazed, all along the cavalry line. Lances slipped from nerveless fingers.

Slowly, the horses stepped forward, stumbled, and stepped again, their riders immobile, shoulders sagging, arms dangling.

The beastmen's little pig eyes glittered. Their grins widened, heads nodded in eager encouragement.

Step-stumble-step, the horses moved forward.

The beastmen shrieked victory as their clubs swung, caving in the horses' heads. Axes swung high and fell, biting deep into the riders. Blood fountained as men fell arcing from horses. Heads flew, bones crunched under great splayfeet, as the beastmen, chuckling, waded through the butchered cavalry to break in the door of the village storehouse.

The Count of Baicci, vassal to the Duke of Loguire, lay headless in the dirt, his blood pumping out to mingle with that of his cavalry, before the thirsty soil claimed it.

And the women and children of the village, huddled together on the slopes above, stared slack-jawed at their burning houses, while the dragon ships, wallowing low in the waves with the weight of their booty, swung out past the bar.

And, as the long ships passed the headland, the wind blew the villagers an echo of bellowing laughter.

7

The word was brought to King Tuan Loguire at his capital in Runnymede; and the King waxed wroth.

The Queen waxed into a fury.

"Nay, then!" she stormed. "These devil's spawn, they lay waste a village with fire and sword, slay the men and dishonor the women, and bear off the children for bondsmen, belike—and what wilt thou do, thou? Assuredly, thou wilt not revenge!"

She was not yet out of her teens, and the King was scarce into his twenties, but he sat straight as a staff, his face grave and calm.

"What is the count of the dead?" he demanded.

"All the men of the village, Majesty," answered the messenger, grief and horror just beneath the skin of his face. "A hundred and fifty. Fourteen of the women, and six babes. And twenty good horsemen, and the Count of Baicci."

The Queen stared, horrified. "A hundred and fifty," she murmured, "a hundred and fifty."

Then, louder, "A hundred and fifty widowed in this one night! And babes, six babes slain!"

"God have mercy on their souls." The King bowed his head.

"Aye, pray, man, pray!" the Queen snapped. "Whilst thy people lie broke and bleeding, thou dost pray!" She whirled on the messenger. "And rapine?"

"None," said the messenger, bowing his head. "Praise the Lord, none."

"None," the Queen repeated, almost mechanically.

"None?" She spun on her husband. "What insult is this, that they scorn our women!"

"They feared the coming of more soldiers, mayhap . . ." the messenger muttered.

The Queen gave him all the scorn she could jam into one quick glance. "And 'twere so, they would be lesser men than our breed; and ours are, Heaven knows, slight enough."

The messenger stiffened. The King's face turned wooden.

He leaned back slowly, gaze fixed on the messenger. "Tell me, good fellow—how was it a whole troop of cavalry could not withstand these pirates?"

The Queen's lip curled. "How *else* could it chance?"

The King sat immobile, waiting for the messenger's answer.

"Sorcery, Majesty." The messenger's voice quavered. "Black, foul sorcery. The horsemen rode doomed, for their foes cast the Evil Eye upon them."

Silence held the room. Even the Queen was speechless, for, on this remote planet, superstition had a disquieting tendency to become fact.

The King was the first to speak. He stirred in his throne, turned to the Lord Privy Councillor.

This meant he had to look down; for, though Brom O'Berin's shoulders were as broad as the King's, he stood scarcely two feet high.

"Brom," said the King, "send forth five companies of the King's Foot, one to each of the great Lords whose holdings border the sea."

"But one company to each!" The Queen fairly exploded. "Art thou so easily done, *good* mine husband? Canst thou spare but thus much of thy force?"

The King rose and turned to Sir Maris the Seneschal. "Sir Maris, do you bring forth three companies of the King's Guard. The fourth shall bide here, for the guarding Her Majesty Queen Catharine. Let the three companies assemble in the courtyard below within the hour, provisioned for long and hard riding."

"My liege, I will," said Sir Maris, bowing.

"And see that mine armor is readied."

"Armor!" the Queen gasped. "Nay, nay, O mine husband. What wouldst thou do!"

"Why, what I must." The King turned to her, catching her hands between his own. "I am King, and my people are threatened. I must ride to the wreck of this village, and seek out the trail of these beastmen. Then must I build ships and follow them, if I may, to their homeland."

"Oh, nay, good my lord!" Catharine cried, clinging to him. "Have we not men-at-arms enough in our armies, but you also must ride forth to die? Oh, my lord, nay! What would I do if thou shouldst be—if thou shouldst take hurt?"

The King held her close for one moment; then held her away, tilted her chin, and kissed her lips, gently. "Thou art Queen," he said softly. "The brunt of this sorrow must thou bear; such is the office of Queens. Here in the place of power must thou bide, to care for our people while I ride. Thou must hazard thine husband for the good of thy people, as I must hazard my life—for such is the office of Kings."

She sank sobbing against his chest. He held her close for a long, timeless while, then kissed her lingeringly. He straightened, her hands clasped between his, then turned to go.

An embarrassed cough stopped him.

He turned, frowning. "Art still in this place, Brom? I had thought . . ."

"My liege," the dwarf interrupted, "what thou shalt command, I shall do—but wilt thou command nothing more?"

The King's face darkened.

Brom's voice was tight with determination. "If there is the Evil Eye in this, Majesty, 'tis matter for witches."

The King turned away, glowering, his lips pressed thin.

"Thou hast the right of it, Brom," he admitted grudgingly. "Well enough, then, we must. Send to the witches in the North Tower, Brom, directing them to summon"—his face twisted with dislike—"the High Warlock."

The High Warlock was currently leaning his back against a tree trunk with his fundament firmly founded on *firma terra*, watching the sunrise with one eye and his wife with the other. Both were eminently worth watching.

The sun was splendor itself as it rose orange-gold out of the oiled green of the pine-tops into a rose-and-blue sky; but his flame-headed wife was all that was grace and loveliness, singing lightly, as she sank her hands into the tub of dishwater beside the cooking-fire in the dry warmth of their cave home.

It wasn't just the domesticity that made her lovely, of course. Her long, loose red hair seemed to float about her, framing a round face with large, sea-green, long-lashed eyes, a snub nose, a wide mouth with full, tempting lips. Her figure was spectacular, under the white peasant blouse and tight bodice, and long, full, bright-colored skirt.

Of course, her figure was, at the moment, more a matter of inference than observation; but the Warlock had a good memory.

The memory was a little too good; his wife's beauty occasionally reminded him of his own—well, shall we say, plainness?

No, we should say ugliness—or, rather, homeliness; for there was something attractive about his face. He had the appeal that is common to overstuffed armchairs, old fireplaces and potbellied stoves. Hounds and small children loved him on sight.

And by this quality he had won her (it would be, perhaps, more accurate to say that she had won him, after an extended battle with his inferiority complex); for if a beautiful woman is betrayed often enough, she will begin to value trustworthiness, warmth and affection more than romance.

At least, she will if she is the kind of woman to whom

10

love is the goal, and romance just the luxury; such a woman was Gwen.

Such a woman will eventually be capable of loving a man with a good heart, even though his face is a bargain assortment of inclined planes, hollows and knobs in Expressionist juxtaposition; and such a man was Rod Gallowglass.

He had a receding hairline; a flat, sloping forehead; prominent bushy eyebrows; deep eye-sockets with a matched set of gray eyes; a blade of a nose; high, flat cheekbones; and a wide, thin-lipped mouth. The mouth kept a precarious perch on top of a square jutting chin.

Nevertheless, she loved him, which fact was to Rod a miracle, a flagrant violation of all known laws of nature.

Not that he was about to object, of course.

He slid down onto the base of his spine, let his eyelids droop, and let the peace of the summer morning seep into him, lulling him into a doze.

Something struck his belly, knocking the wind out of him and jolting him wide awake. He jerked upright, knife in hand.

"Da-dee!" cooed the baby, looking enormously pleased with himself.

Rod stared at the kid. Little Magnus was holding tight to the bars of his playpen; he hadn't quite learned to stand by himself yet.

Rod managed a feeble grin and levered the corner of the oak playpen off his belly. "Very good, Magnus!" He patted the baby's head. "Good boy, good boy!"

The baby grinned, fairly hopping with delight.

The playpen rose six inches from the ground.

Rod made a frantic grab and forced it back down, hands on the lid.

Ordinarily, playpens do not have lids. But this playpen did; otherwise, the baby might have floated out.

"Yes, yes, that's a wonderful baby! Smart little fella, there! *Very* good baby—*Gwen!*"

"What does thou wish, my lord?" Gwen came up to the mouth of the cave, drying her hands on her apron.

Then she saw the playpen.

"Oh, *Magnus!*" she mourned in that tone of hurt disappointment only mothers can master.

"No, no!" Rod said quickly. "He's a good boy, Gwen— isn't he? I've just been telling him what a good boy he is. *Good* boy, *good* baby!"

The baby stared, tiny brow wrinkling in utter confusion.

11

His mother had much the same look.

But her eyes widened as she realized the only way the playpen could've moved out of the cave while her back was turned. "Oh, Rod!"

"Yeah." Rod grinned with more than a touch of pride. "Precocious, isn't he?"

"But—but, my lord!" Gwen shook her head, looking dazed. "Only witches can move things other than themselves. Warlocks cannot!"

Rod pried open the playpen and took his son in his arms. "Well, he couldn't have done it by levi—uh, flying, could he?"

"Nay, he hath not strength enough to lift the playpen along with him—that he would have to do by his own bone and sinew. But warlocks cannot . . ."

"Well, this one can." He grinned down at the baby and chucked it under the chin. "How about that? I've fathered a genius!"

The baby cooed and bounced out of Rod's arms.

"Whup! Come back here!" Rod jumped and snagged a fat little ankle before the baby could float off in the morning breeze.

"Oh, Magnus!" Gwen was on them in a rush, cradling the baby in her arms. "Oh, my bold babe! Thou shalt most surely be a most puissant warlock when thou art grown!"

The baby smiled back at her. He wasn't quite sure what he'd done that was right, but he wasn't going to argue.

Rod beamed with fatherly pride as he hefted the oaken playpen back into the cave. He was amazed at his son; that playpen was *heavy!*

He got a hank of rope and started tying the pen down. "That kid!" he said, shaking his head. "Scarcely a year old—he can't even walk yet, and . . . Gwen, what's the age where they start levitating?"

" 'Levi—' Oh, you mean flying, my lord!" Gwen came back into the cave, the baby straddling one hip. "Thirteen years, or thereabouts, my lord, is the age for young warlocks to fly."

"And this kid started at nine months." Rod's chest swelled a trifle—his head, too. "What age do little witches start making their broomsticks fly?"

"Eleven, my lord, or mayhap twelve."

"Well, he's a little ahead of schedule for that, too—except that warlocks aren't supposed to make broomsticks fly at all. What a kid!" He didn't mention that Magnus was obviously a major mutation.

He patted the baby's head. The child wrapped a chubby hand around his father's finger.

Rod turned shining eyes to Gwen. "He'll make a great agent when he's grown."

"My lord!" Gwen's brow knit in concern. "Thou wilt not take him from Gramarye?"

"Perish the thought!" Rod took Magnus and tossed him up in the air. "He'll have his work cut out for him right here."

Magnus squealed with delight and floated on up toward the roof.

Rod executed a high jump that would have done credit to a pole-vaulter and snagged his errant son. "Besides, he may not even want to join SCENT—who knows?"

Rod was an agent of the Society for the Conversion of Extraterrestrial Nascent Totalitarianisms, the subversive wing of the multi-planet Decentralized Democratic Tribunal, the first and only human interstellar government in history not to be based on Terra. The Senate met by electronic communications; the Executive resided on a starship which was usually to be found between planets. Nonetheless, it was the most efficient democratic government yet established.

SCENT was the organization responsible for bringing the Lost Colonies of earlier Terrestrial empires back into the fold. Rod was on permanent assignment to Gramarye, a planet that had been colonized by mystics, romantics, and escapists. The culture was medieval, the people superstitious—and a small percentage of the population had "witch-powers."

Consequently, the DDT in general, and SCENT in particular, were immensely interested in Gramarye; for the "witches" and "warlocks" were espers. Some had one set of psi powers and some had another—but all were telepaths to some degree. And, since the efficiency (and, consequently, the viability) of a democracy varies directly with the speed of its communications, and since telepathic communication was instantaneous, the DDT treasured its only colony of espers very highly.

So Rod had been assigned to guard the planet, and to carefully nudge its political system onto the road that would eventually lead to democracy, and full membership in the DDT.

"Hey, Fess," Rod called.

The great black horse grazing in the meadow outside the cave lifted its head to look at its master. Its voice sounded through a small earphone buried in Rod's mastoid bone. "Yes, Rod?"

Rod snorted. "What're you cropping grass for? Who ever heard of a robot burning hydrocarbons?"

"One must keep up appearances, Rod," Fess reproved him.

"Next thing I know, you'll be keeping up with the Joneses! Listen, bolt-head—it's an occasion! The kid pulled his first telekinesis stunt today!"

"Telekinesis? I had thought that was a sex-linked female trait, Rod."

"Well, all of a sudden, it ain't." He put the baby in the playpen and clamped the cover down before Magnus had a chance to drift out. "How about that, Fess? This kid's gonna be a champion!"

"It will be my great pleasure to serve him," the robot murmured, "as I have served his forebears for five hundred years, since the days of the first D'Armand, who founded . . ."

"Uh, skip the family history, Fess."

"But, Rod, it is a vital portion of the child's heritage; he should . . ."

"Well, save it until he learns to talk, then."

"As you wish." The mechanical voice somehow managed a sigh. "In that case, it is my duty to inform you that you will shortly be receiving company, Rod."

Rod stilled, cocking an eyebrow at his horse. "What do you see?"

"Nothing, Rod; but I detect the sounds characteristic of bipedal locomotion of a small being conveying itself through long grass."

"Oh." Rod relaxed. "An elf coming through the meadow. Well, they're always welcome."

An eighteen-inch body burst out of the grass at the cave-mouth.

Rod grinned. "Welcome, merry wanderer of the night."

"Puck!" Gwen squealed, recognizing the quote. She turned to their guest. "Assuredly, thou art most . . ."

She stopped, seeing the look on the elf's face.

Rod had sobered too. "What's right, Puck?"

"Naught," said the elf grimly. "Rod Gallowglass, thou must needs come, and right quickly, to the King of Elves!"

"Oh, I must, must I? What's with Brom all of a sudden? What's all the panic about?"

"Beastmen!" The elf gasped for breath. "They have raided the seacoast at the Duchy of Loguire!"

14

"Beastmen?" said Rod, frowning. "I thought they were just figments of somebody's imagination."

"Assuredly," agreed Brom O'Berin, currently in his capacity as King of the Elves. "Yet thou dost forget, Master Gallowglass, that on Gramarye imagination can become extraordinary durable."

And that, Rod admitted silently, was nothing but cold fact. Projective telepathy, coupled with a native substance called "witch moss," had produced some remarkably solid figments—such as elves, werewolves, banshees, and other slightly outré developments.

"If night-fears might become solid," Brom growled, pacing with his hands clasped behind his back, "just such a form would they take: bogeymen, such as goodwives use to fright children with; things half beast and half man, great shambling goblins, with ape's arms and great feet, huge clubs and witch-power. . . ."

"Witch-power?" Rod sat bolt upright, eyes wide.

"What else would the Evil Eye be?" Brom demanded impatiently. "Evil Eye and beast-form with blood-lust—indeed, a most . . ."

"Whoa, there! Hold on! What's all this about the Evil Eye?"

Puck explained. "Rod Gallowglass, 'twas the Evil Eye! The beastmen froze both soldiers and horses with a glance, made them drop their weapons, then made them come slowly within reach of the war-clubs and battle-axes! 'Tis true, on the honor of five elves who saw it!"

Rod looked into the elf's eyes, his face unreadable.

He turned his eyes to the limestone floor, reached down, broke off a slender stalagmite. He toyed with it a moment, then spoke, without looking up.

"Any cases of Evil Eye-ism on this planet before?"

"There be legends . . ." said Puck uncertainly.

"But only legends, hm? Matins and FESSpers! What kind of witch could give the Evil Eye?"

"Why, beastmen, of course," Brom snorted, impatiently; and Fess' voice murmured in Rod's ear, "Projective telepathy would account for the phenomenon, Rod. Such a mutation is possible, in theory. . . ."

"Everything is possible, in theory," Rod growled.

"It would amount to an inborn talent for instantaneous hypnotism," the robot droned on. "There are many such cases in Terran myth and legend, and a very few in unreliable early histories; but no such case has ever been firmly established."

15

Rod rubbed his chin, nodding. "That Evil Eye must be pretty potent stuff. . . ."

"Oh, nay, surely thou dost not think so," Brom growled, dripping sarcasm, while the robot elaborated: "The compulsion would have to reach deeply enough to activate the death-wish to the exclusion of all other drives, Rod."

Rod scowled at the stalagmite. "There must be some way to defend against it. . . ."

"A counter-compulsion might be set up, Rod, if projective telepaths were available."

Rod nodded slowly, lips pursed. "They might be," he murmured, "they just might be. . . ."

"What?" Brom demanded, glowering. "What might be what? Where hast thy thoughts been, Rod Gallowglass?"

"With my wife," said Rod, looking up; and, as Brom registered shock and surprise, retreating a step, Rod turned to Puck. "Puck, go get Gwen."

"Gwendylon!" cried the elf, flabbergasted. "What wouldst thou need her for?"

"Many things," Rod said thoughtfully, "many, many things. But at the moment, I need her advice."

"Advice?" Brom thundered, recovering (but not completely, or he wouldn't have yelled). "Wouldst thou seek advice of a woman in wartime?"

"I wouldst," said Rod, his brows knitting. "This Evil Eye bit is witch business, Brom. And Gwen knows more about witchcraft than anyone else we can get hold of."

Brom opened his mouth to protest, closed it again, then nodded in reluctant acquiescence and turned to Puck. "Why dost thou tarry, elf?" he roared. "Didst thou not hear the High Warlock?"

"My lord . . ." the elf protested feebly, confused.

"Get thee gone!" Brom howled.

Puck got.

"High Warlock?" Rod said mildly, with a lift of the eyebrow.

"Aye, aye," Brom growled, pacing away. "Thou art created High Warlock, Rod Gallowglass, and summoned up to the King."

Rod sat very still for a moment.

Then he unfolded his lank length and rose to his feet. He kicked musingly at a largish stalagmite. "So I've been promoted."

Brom scowled, perplexed.

" 'High Warlock,' I mean. That has an awfully official sound. Especially considering that this morning, I woke up as Public Enemy Number One."

16

Brom shrugged. "What wouldst thou look for, Rod Gallowglass? Thou hadst struck Catharine the Queen, and felled Tuan with a most foul blow."

"Not 'felled,' " said Rod, smiling reminiscently. He rubbed his left shoulder, where Tuan's crossbow-bolt had struck him. "I gave him a bad ache in the, ah, gut, and I maybe slowed him up a little; but 'felled,' no. That kid's made of iron."

"Still, 'twas a most foul blow," Brom grumbled. "Now, thou knowest, as I know, 'twas well intended, and made Tuan our King; but wouldst thou have them know?"

"Who? Tuan and Catharine?" Rod snorted. "If I know the Queen, she'd have a divorce suit filed by morning." He held up a palm, forestalling Brom's retort. "No, I'm not blaming her, Brom. It's just—well, this, ah, promotion is kind of a sudden change of opinion, isn't it?"

The dwarf swung about, fists on hips, glaring up at Rod. "The land is endangered; there is need of thee. Thinkest thou Tuan to be so poor a king that he could not bury his own dislike for the good of his people?"

Rod nodded slowly. "Yeah, I suppose. Personal animosities go by the board pretty quick in a national emergency. . . . But I'd like to know where this particular emergency came from, all of a sudden. How come the beastmen've never kicked up trouble before?" He turned, head lifting as a sudden thought struck him. "For that matter—has anyone ever seen them before?"

Brom stopped his pacing and stood with his back to the small open fire. He looked up at the vaulting cavern ceiling, where the limestone caught the firelight in a coruscating display. His eyes took on a faraway look.

Rod sighed and leaned back against a stalagmite; he was in for a lecture.

"We ha' known o' them," Brom muttered. "For long, we ha' known o' them."

"You ever meet one?" Rod gave him a toothy smile. "Anybody you know ever meet one?"

"Nay." Brom shook his head impatiently. "How could we, Rod Gallowglass? They live o'er the sea, where none ever go—save men in exile, and they never return."

"Tuan Loguire did. Before the Queen decided she loved him, remember?"

Brom snorted. "He was took out to sea, and set adrift in a dinghy. Thereupon he turned right about and rowed straightaway back to shore."

Rod nodded. "Yeah, I should've guessed. Some men just can't resist having a price on their heads."

Brom lifted a massive eyebrow. "Rejoice that he did. Else there had been no King for you to give us."

"Well, yeah." Rod nodded judiciously. "I can see what might've happened if he'd met one of those monsters in their native habitat, and found out where their homicidal native habit's at."

"Aye," the dwarf growled, "and though they may come far from their native soil, their habits ha' not improved by much."

"Especially considering those Viking dragon ships," Rod said, lips pursed. "Not to mention the armor and weapons. Of course, I suppose you *could* call that an improvement."

" 'Tis most sad regression, from our way of looking," Brom grumbled. "Now what shall we do, Rod Gallowglass?"

Rod shrugged. "Guard against 'em. What else would you do?"

"That, the King hath already done."

"Oh?" Rod tried not to show too much interest.

"Aye. He hath sent a company of the King's Foot to each of the seacoast Lords, and hath sent the word forth for all young men capable of bearing arms to come to Runnymede, there to be trained in defense of their countrymen."

"Well, that was to be expected." Rod chewed at the inside of his cheek. "Has he set a levy?"

"Aye. He hath required of each of the seven great Lords of the inland, one hundred trained soldiers to be sent to the seacoast, and one hundred young men, never before in arms, to be sent to join the King's Foot at Runnymede."

"What about the seacoast Lords?"

Brom scowled. "What of them?"

"What sort of sentry system have they set up?"

"Ah!" Brom smiled and nodded, pacing the mossy floor with his hands locked behind him. "The King hath seen to that, and right well, to my thinking. He commands that each of the coastal Lords shall maintain sentries on the heights, not only near to the villages, but throughout the length of their coasts."

Rod nodded, frowning. "Sounds like it might work. Has the word gotten down to the people?"

Brom glanced up in surprise. "Aye, most assuredly, and thou mayst be sure they are angered."

"And scared?"

"Aye." Brom grimaced, as though at a bad taste. "Most truly afeard, and locking their doors and shutters o' nights."

"Even inland?"

"Aye, even inland. What wouldst thou have them do,

Rod Gallowglass? We know not yet the full extent of the powers of these beastmen. Art thou not also afeard?"

"Thoroughly," Rod admitted. "All right, I'll admit Tuan's set up a pretty good defense. What else is he doing?"

"He ha' took three companies of the King's Guard and rides down to Loguire, to the village that was burned, to see if he may smell out the trail to the lair of these beastmen."

"Oh? He's going to find a track across the sea, is he? Who's minding the store while he's sniffing? Catharine?"

"Aye; he hath set the Queen to care for the people."

"Poor people. . . . No, no, just a joke, Brom, just a joke!"

"Thy jests must own to a singular lack of humor," the dwarf growled.

"Well, *you* know, it's early in the day. . . . And just how, if it's not classified information, does Tuan intend to go about finding a trail over water, Brom?"

"Nay, the answer to that conundrum must needs lie deep in the realms of magic," Brom growled, glowering at his son-in-law, "and therefore hath the King sent for the High Warlock."

Rod sat immobile.

Then he cocked his head on one side, pursed his lips, and said, "Oh."

"Whom else?" Brom started pacing again. "Thou alone, of all the warlocks and witches in this land, hast magic so powerful as to find a trail where there is none, Rod Gallowglass."

"Oh, I dunno about *that*," said Rod, frowning. "Some of these telep—uh, I mean, thought-hearing witches in the Queen's Coven could do it, couldn't they? Listen for the beastmen's thoughts, then pinpoint their source. I know they don't have directional techniques, but I can teach 'em triangulation, easy enough. You take two witches, see, one in the north and one in the south . . ."

"Their thoughts cannot be heard," Brom growled.

". . . about a hundred miles apart, and each one listens for beastmen thoughts, and . . . *what?*"

"Their thoughts cannot be heard," Brom repeated agreeably.

Rod stared.

He shook his head and pressed his hand to his forehead. "You're trying to tell me these monsters don't have minds, is that what you're trying to tell me? But that's ridiculous! Take Aldis, for instance—she can read an earthworm's thoughts, and they don't even *have* any! You trying to tell me it's too long a distance? That's ridiculous too! I had her, ah, thought-hear one of the dino—uh, big lizards across the sea, once, just for a test. She wasn't herself again for three days. . . ."

"No," said Brom doggedly. "She could not hear the beastmen, even at the time they raided the village. Nor could any of the others."

Rod stared; then he turned slowly away, his eyes unfocusing. "Psychic invisibility. . . ."

"How?"

"I think this has gotten too deep for me, Brom," said Rod, rising. "This is Gwen's pigeon."

The dwarf started, then turned away, glowering, and embarrassed.

Rod frowned at him a moment; then his face relaxed into a look of weary exasperation. "Brom, why don't you just tell her she's your daughter, and be done with it?"

"Nay, nay," the dwarf muttered, shaking his head and pacing furiously. "Far better she should not know her sire, than that she should know him and be shamed of him."

"Gwen would be proud of you, and you know it damn well! Come off it, Brom! You know the truth as well as I do—you're scared."

The dwarf turned slowly, nodded thoughtfully, frowning. "Aye, thou hast it there, thou hast the right of it. Fearful am I, and quite justly so; for, as we now stand, she bears me no ill will, even honors we summat; and the risk of losing even that slight liking from my child is too great to chance the gain of daughterly love. Nay, I shall stand as I am; let her come nigh me, but only unknowing."

Rod sighed, shaking his head, and turned away. "All right, if that's the way you want it. But I'll tell you right now, you're a fool."

"I know it," the dwarf said, bowing his head. "Yet every man is a coward in some way, Rod Gallowglass, and this way is mine: that mine issue might know me."

Rod lifted his head at a scrabbling from the tunnel that led to the cave mouth. "Brace yourself, Brom; here she comes."

The dwarf turned away, pressing a fist against his mouth.

Puck burst from the tunnel, Gwen right behind him; a moment later she was in Rod's arms, and Puck engaged Brom in an animated discussion concerning a bizarre stalactite formation, until Rod and Gwen descended to the word level of communication again.

"Puck told you?" said Rod, when he'd gotten his breath back.

"He hath, my lord." Gwen's eyes were very large, a little frightened.

"Any way you can fight it?"

Gwen shook her head, looking very forlorn.

"Hm." Rod frowned. "Are you sure? Isn't there any way a witch can protect a non-witch from spells?"

"Aye, good my lord, with a counter-spell. But we know none for the Evil Eye."

Rod turned away, scowling blackly, but holding her hand. He sat down by the fire; Gwen settled herself beside him.

Rod toyed with a chip of kindling, bouncing it off a burning log. "This puts us at a bit of a disadvantage, darling. The witches can't even tell when the beastmen are coming. Brom says they can't hear the beastmen's thoughts."

Gwen's head lifted, her eyes widening with sudden understanding. "Then, that . . ."

Rod frowned. " 'That' what?"

"The dream!" Gwen cried, squeezing his hand with both of hers.

"What dream?"

"Alicia's! She came to me, this morn, in fearing and tears, from a most foul nightmare she'd had!"

Rod's eyes widened as comprehension came. He tensed, gripping his wife's hand tighter. "Just what did she dream?"

"That she was aboard of a long ship with a dragon's head at its bows, making for the shore of Savoy!"

Rod's eyes kindled. "How long was she on that ship? How much of the attack does she remember?"

"But that one instant aboard the ship, my lord, and another, when she stood in a line of fell monsters, with horsemen plunging down upon them. And a third, when she was a monster herself, and chasing a child."

"Nothing more?"

Gwen shook her head.

Rod smiled, eyes glowing. "Then this mental invisibility of theirs breaks down every now and then—*if* a witch is at her most receptive, asleep, to dream the beastmen's thoughts."

Gwen frowned. "My lord, I do not . . ."

"It's easy!" Rod crowed. "The beastmen let a stray thought slip every now and then, if they're keyed up enough. But the thoughts are so faint that a witch has to be wide-open, mentally, to 'hear' them—which means she has to be asleep! Or in a trance. . . ."

Gwen was still frowning. "A trance, my lord? What is that?"

"Something I'll teach you—and all the other witches

too!" He spun toward Brom, with a wolfish grin. "We've got our sentries!"

Brom frowned. "How . . . ?"

"Two witches—one asleep to have dreams, and another 'listening' to the first one's thoughts, to catch her dreams!"

"Aye, my lord!" Gwen had caught his enthusiasm. "Then, if a single thought slips, they shall hear it!"

"Yeah, yeah!" Rod whirled on Puck. "Off to the Queen's Coven, double-time! Tell 'em to send two telepaths—I mean thought-hearers, out to each of the seacoast manors—no, four! Four witches to each estate! They'll have to take guard duty in shifts, two hours on, two hours off!"

"Two hour watches," Puck repeated, nodding vigorously.

"And, let's see. . . ." Rod turned away, scowling and pacing, rubbing a pebble between thumb and forefinger, muttering. "Let's see, if the beastmen are projective telepaths . . . yeah!" He turned on Gwen. "Gwen, what's a projective . . . uh . . . a witch who can put her own thoughts inside a non-witch's head?"

Gwen frowned, bit her lip. "We have none, my lord . . . yet there are those who can impress their wishes on the stuff we call witch-moss. . . ."

"That's it! Puck, tell the coven to send some good witch-moss modelers to each of the coastal duchies, and tell 'em to jam the . . . uh . . . tell 'em to foul up that Evil Eye business any way they can. There's a chance they might be able to do it by working through the minds of the people who're getting the Eye—you know, think happy thoughts at 'em! And, uh—Gwen, any way one witch can add her powers to another's?"

"Aye, my lord," said Gwen, somewhat perplexed, "all they need to do is join hands. Thus we have done for games, ten witches linking their hands, and . . ."

"That many? Great! Puck, tell the Coven that as soon as they thought-hear an alarm from any one estate, all witches get to that estate as fast as they can. Then they join hands and think independent thoughts at the soldiers! Got that?"

The elf opened and closed his mouth a few times, looking rather dazzled, swallowed, and nodded bravely.

"Then git!" Rod said, and Puck broke the sound barrier.

Rod looked after him. "You don't suppose there was a touch of relief in that exit . . . ?"

"There will be great relief through all this land," Brom rumbled, "if thou hast indeed found a way to war against this most puissant, fell magic."

Rod stared, suddenly jolted back to sanity.

He turned away to stare at the fire a moment, then knelt at Gwen's side, took her hand. He smiled sardonically. "Yeah," he said. "Thanks for bringing me down to earth again, Brom."

The dwarf stared, openmouthed. "Why? What have I said?"

Rod smiled sourly. "If."

Rod's starship was buried under ten feet of clay in a meadow a few hours' ride from Runnymede. He had conned the elves into digging a tunnel to it, so he could visit it whenever he wanted.

Now, for instance. He was enjoying the rare luxury of Terran Scotch while he pored over a set of photographs at the chart table.

"I don't see anything, Fess."

"I had already informed you of that, Rod."

Fess' robot brain, a globe the size of a basketball, hung in a niche in the curving wall. Rod had temporarily removed it from the steel horse body and plugged it in to act as the ship's automatic control section. Not that he was going anywhere; he just needed Fess to operate the ship's auxiliary equipment, mainly the photo-survey file (and, of course, the autobar).

"I thought it was impolite to say 'I told you so.'" Rod scowled at the photo-map of the Gramarye coastline, the channel, and the mainland coastline opposite the island. Fess had taken the pictures during their orbital approach to the planet two years earlier.

"Any detail shots, Fess?"

"I always take a sampling of detail photos, Rod."

The dispenser slot above the chart table chuckled; Rod reached out and caught the prints.

He leafed through them, chewing his lip. "Nothing here but the tops of a lot of giant ferns, and a few primitive amphibians lying on the beaches. Wonder what's under the ferns?"

"Carboniferous fauna, I should say, Rod, to judge from the carboniferous flora."

"No bogeymen?"

"Human habitation usually occurs in a cleared space, Rod."

"You never know, they might have something to hide. Hm . . . here's a bank of cliffs around a small bay. Might have caves. . . ."

"So I had thought, Rod. But there was no sign of human or sub-human habitation."

"Sure ain't no dragon boats drawn up on the beach, anyway. Is it my imagination, Fess, or is the vegetation around that bay different from the stuff on the other side of the cliffs?"

"Totally different, Rod. Mosses and lichens exclusively."

"What, not even a fungus amongus?"

"Well, a few primitive grasses. . . ."

"So how come nothing more?"

"The vegetation would seem to indicate a small area in which the temperature is far below that of the surrounding forest. I conjecture that a cold breeze blows off the sea at that point, chilling the area around the bay. The cliff-wall prevents it from reaching the interior."

Rod tensed. "Hey! Would that indicate a cold current?"

"In all probability, Rod." The robot's voice sounded slightly patronizing.

"That could be the raiders' return route, then."

Fess' voice paused a moment, then sounded faintly surprised. "Why . . . yes, I suppose it would, Rod. I confess I do not comprehend the logic by which . . ."

"Don't let it worry you, Fess; there isn't any. That's why they send men with robots, remember? What happens to that cold current after it hits the cliff shore, Fess?"

"It is warmed just south of the cliffs by its contact with the tropical mainland, Rod. It is forced out to sea by the mass of the continent. . . ."

"And passes by the southern tip of Gramarye?"

Again, the robot paused. "Yes, Rod."

"And Loguire's in the south. So that's their invasion route."

"It would seem so, Rod."

"So they drop over to Gramarye on the southern current, raid a village or two, swing up around the island, and catch the cold current home. Fess, we've found their base."

"Circumstantial evidence would seem to indicate so, Rod."

"Then there's only one more question."

"Yes, Rod?"

"Where are they?"

The King met the High Warlock as the King's Own Guard rode south with the King at their head.

The High Warlock lounged in the saddle with one knee hooked around the cantle. The horse grazed by the roadside.

The King drew rein, his face wary. "Well met, Rod Gallowglass."

Rod gave him an affable, sleepy smile. "Long time no see, Tuan. How's Catharine?"

The innocent remark set Tuan even more on his guard. "Quite well—which I am sure thou knowest aforetime."

Rod nodded. "Well, that's what I hear from the public accounts—minstrels and so forth." He frowned, with a touch of concern. "Thing is, I have access to the Hobgoblin Information Service, too, so I get some news that doesn't trickle down to the public. I'm very sorry, Tuan."

The King jerked his head impatiently. " 'Tis lost, and we are both young yet. She shall be heavy with child again, I trust."

"I trust so," Rod echoed. "But if she starts having those cramps and headaches again, mention it to the nearest elf, will you? All she needs is some medicine."

Tuan stared, looking very confused and a little scandalized.

"Oh, I know, I know." Rod closed his eyes, nodding slightly, his mouth a cynical line. "Men aren't supposed to know anything about female trouble. But I don't have to attend her, you know; Gwen's done midwifery before. I can give her the medicines. Of course, Gwen being my wife, I don't expect Catharine would have anything to do with her. . . ."

"Nay, she most certainly shall!" said Tuan quickly. "Then, too, Gwendylon might advise the royal midwife, might she not?"

"That's the ticket!" Rod's forefinger stabbed at him. "We'll get the herbs down her throat some way, Tuan."

"Master Warlock. . . ." Tuan suddenly looked very unregal in his perplexity. "I had thought . . ."

"That I was your enemy?" Rod smiled sourly. "If I was, would I be here now?"

He leaned forward and slapped the King on the shoulder. "I'll explain it all some sunny winter morning in front of a roaring fire. But right now, I think we've got some other business to mull at. Why did you call for me?"

Tuan's smile hardened to irony. "Nay, dost thou not know?"

"The beastmen." Rod nodded. "Yes, I know. And I think I know where their base is."

Tuan gawked.

Rod nodded slowly. "All we've got to do is build the boat to get us there."

Tuan smiled. "Nay, I am the King; I may command what

I need. We shall have a fleet of fishing-boats, Master Gallowglass."

Rod raised an eyebrow. "For this many men?" He looked back along the ranks of glittering steel behind Tuan. "You're going to need one hell of a lot of boats. Those little smacks the fishermen use won't take more'n about ten men each. One hell of a lot of boats."

"We shall have them." Tuan smiled complacently. "As many as we shall need. Hast thou not heard of the King's Levy, Rod Gallowglass?"

Rod's smile hardened. He bowed his head, then looked up. "Yes, I've heard of it," he said. "Well, let's go, Tuan."

A wrinkled, gnarled old man with a very prominent, thin nose and almost no chin, huddled over a glowing brazier on the afterdeck of a dragon ship. The craft tossed and pitched as the wind moaned toward a storm, snatching at the strands of yellowed white hair that fell about the old man's shoulders, halfway down his back. He mumbled a toothless chant as he sprinkled a powder over the brazier. There was a flash of flaming smoke, then only the brazier's glow again, ruddy light on the old man's sunken cheeks and eyes, bare bony chest and arms, and the single twist of striped fur about his loins.

The hulking oarsmen had glanced at him constantly over their shoulders, till the brazier's flash sent them shuddering back to their task, muttering the words of a charm against evil.

The tall, horn-helmeted man who stood at the stern oar, chinless and beetle-browed like his crew and his Shaman, glanced warily at the old man, bit his lip, and lifted his eyes to the dots of light that sprinkled the shore far ahead of them. He barked an order and leaned on the oar. The ship turned slowly, minutely, till the shore lights silhouetted the dragon's head on the prow. He bellowed another order; the ship steadied and drove forward again.

He was a broad man, heavily muscled, standing tall and straight, but with his head thrust slightly forward from his shoulders. His long mahogany hair was bound in a thick club under the bulge at the base of his skull—better armor than iron for the vulnerable top of the spine.

A broadsword and a great battle-ax swung at his hips. He stood bare-chested to the gale, only a strip of fur about his hips. Wide brass bracelets bound his long, thick arms in lieu of armor. A great leather shield hung over the gunwale near him, the front painted brazen; and against that brass field squatted a black, potbellied, swollen-headed, spindly-limbed profile silhouette—the totem of his clan.

The old emaciated man crouched over the brazier cackled and crooned, rubbing his thin hands. "The Kobold favors thee this even', Atylem. Rich booty shall be thine this night."

"He might ha' gave us better weather for landing," Atylem growled, and hauled on the steering oar; then sketched a quick sign in the air to show he had meant no criticism of his god.

"Which wouldst thou have," snarled the Shaman, "clear skies for thy sailing, or the lightning's aid in thy battles? Thou canst not have both! Nay, but tell me!" he howled, whirling about to fling an arm at Atylem.

The tall man shrank back from the gesture.

"Clear skies? Wouldst thou have them?" keened the Shaman. He spun back to his brazier. "Thou shalt have them. The storm shall be gone in a blink, in the blink of an eye! The power of the Kobold shall snag it away!"

His arm reared up to throw powder on the brazier.

"Nay!" Atylem cried hastily. "Keep the storm!"

The Shaman chuckled softly and turned back to his brazier, nodding.

Atylem flung his head back, scowled at the leaden sky. "O Great Kobold, grant us lightning, and quickly! To shatter our enemies, to burn down their houses!"

The Shaman cackled, still nodding. "Thou shalt have it," he crooned. "Yet not so quickly, Atylem; thou must beach the boats first. The lightning must strike when you strike."

"It is fitting," growled Atylem, glowering at the shore lights. "Foul weather for fair doings, Shaman; how shall that be? Surely the gods now must smile!"

"Gods?" spat the Shaman. "Which gods? Who dost thou serve, Atylem the Eldritch? Tayr, Ydin, or Kobold?"

A warrior bent at his oar heard, and drew a shuddering gasp as he pulled at his sweep. For the half of an instant his soul clamored toward the sky, and the old gods—

But surely the Kobold might be numbered among the great gods! And therefore the gods must sanction this doing, surely. . . .

He caught himself and ground his teeth as his oar dug into the waves. If Atylem had heard that thought, the oarsman would this moment lie dead. For the war-chief had commanded that each warrior keep tight rein on his thoughts and his heart, lest he give warning to the enemy, there on the shore. Yet the Kobold was lenient this night; he had not been heard.

27

A girl, no older than fifteen surely, shot to her feet and wailed, "O ye highest gods . . . !"

Another girl, perhaps two years younger, was at her side in an instant. "Sister! Sister, hearken and waken! Why do you cry to the pagan gods so?"

They stood by an open fire in a bare earthen floor, in a hastily-built watch-shack high on the cliffs of the Romanov demesne, in the northwest of Gramarye.

"O gods!" the elder girl cried again, "preserve me from . . ."

She froze, eyes glaring; then she slumped to the floor. Lids slowly closed over her glazed eyes.

Her sister watched, tense and waiting, till the girl's eyes had closed completely; then she shook her, demanding in a low, quiet tone:

"Sister, waken! Waken, Matilda, and tell me: What is it you have seen?"

Matilda shuddered, opening her eyes. She looked about her for a moment, confused; then she saw her sister, and she relaxed, with a sigh of relief.

"I had wondered, when I did not see the stone walls of the North Tower—"

"We are here in the watch-cabin at Romanov, my sister. . . ."

"I know, I know!" Matilda said pettishly. "Wherefore dost thou waken me? Have I spoke in my sleep?"

"Aye, sister. Thou madest cry to the pagan gods, twice over. . . ."

"Aye, in truth," said the older girl, silencing her sister with a gesture. "It returns to me, Marion. 'Twas a dragon ship, with a full score of oarsmen; it drove for . . . Oh, Marion!" She turned to her sister, staring in horror. "Oh, my sister! 'Twas our nearby village they drove for; and their speech was of fire and blood!"

The usual party in the King's North Tower had a subdued note tonight, as it had had for several nights past, since the High Warlock had bade them be ready at an instant to come to the aid of those of their number who acted as watchmen. There were only a dozen or so there; they were the ones who were not exceptionally skilled or talented at hearing thoughts. Ordinarily they danced in couples; but tonight it was a great circle dance, as though the burden of merrymaking was become so great that it could only be lifted by many shoulders in labor together.

"Trip no further, pretty sweeting;
  Journeys end in lovers' meeting. . . ."

A hulking youth in his late teens led the dance with great verve and little skill.

Across the circle from him, a girl perhaps a year younger than himself stiffened with a gasp, poised as though she were listening.

The music and the dancing stopped dead. All the young folk listened with her.

Silence reigned in the room for the space of four breaths and a heartbeat, the witches listening, eyes unseeing, frozen.

Then chaos and confusion struck rampant, as the girls ran for broomsticks and the boys, for packs and weapons. Shouts filled the air:

"At the watch-cabin?"

"Aye, the watch-cabin at Romanov!"

"Did none think to stock quivers?"

"The stones I piled 'neath the east window! The slings!"

Then, one by one, the boys disappeared, like stars at the touch of the left hand of Dawn.

A moment later the girls, kerchief-packs slung on their backs, dove through the window, each clutching a broomstick. One by one they plunged out, approximately a hundred feet above the ground; and, about one second after leaving the window, each witch was about forty feet above it, and climbing.

In the village at Romanov, soldiers tumbled out of cottages by threes and fives and fell in, bleary-eyed, yawning, and scared.

The villagers, profiting from the experience of the first village, headed for the hills ahead of time.

In the watch-cabin high on the sea-cliffs, the warlocks popped into existence one by one, to greet Matilda and Marion with shouts of joyful reunion, brotherly hugs, and not-so-brotherly attempted caresses.

The girls, on their parts, were more than overjoyed. Wary, but overjoyed—especially when Toby, the eldest of the young warlocks, and the unofficial leader, materialized. Since he was all of eighteen, he was, in the eyes of the others, impossibly wise and authoritative; and it must be admitted that he somewhat shared their opinion.

In this particular instance, however, he had the bad luck to materialize just above the open fire; his dignity was somewhat dampened when his soles scorched.

And, on the beach below, the dragon ships drove in, to beach on the soft sand.

The beastmen leaped from the boats with blood-curdling, ululating warcries, shields up and battle-axes swinging.

They plunged up the beach and formed into a ragged, snarling line. They glanced from one foot soldier to another, catching their eyes.

The soldiers' jaws set; they strained to move muscles suddenly gone slack and limp, to lift their pikes and spears, to look away from the little glittering eyes.

But the control of their bodies was no longer theirs; they found they could do nothing but stare, with an ever-deepening fascination, into the red-rimmed pig-eyes before them.

The beastmen's snarls broadened into grins of victory. The war-axes swung up and back.

In the cabin on the cliffs, thirteen warlocks and two witches joined hands, wishing the other witches had had time to get there, and stared at the fire in the center of their circle. Their eyes glazed, lost focus. They fumbled without sight at a huge, soft, absorbent snowbank, a bank of black feathers, that lay in smothering density over the panicked, paralyzed minds of the soldiers on the beach below.

The witches dug under the black snowbank and heaved.

On the beach, here and there, a pike or spear slowly lifted, laboring and wavering up from their paralysis.

The beastmen lost their grins. Their eyes went wide, then narrowed as, howling, they swung axes.

But the raised pikes and spears parried with a convulsive spasm.

The beastmen wailed and waded in.

The pikes and spears came up again, much quicker this time.

Some were too slow; arms and heads struck the cold, wet sand, pumping blood. But most of the blows were parried; and, here and there, a pike labored to strike in return.

In the cabin on the cliffs, eyes squeezed shut and jaws locked, witches strained.

Thunder sounded, distant, and rain struck.

On the beach, a beastman struck a pike aside with his shield and buried his great ax in the angle of neck and shoulder. He spun about on his heel, not staying for the sight of rushing blood to answer his summons, and sprang to his ship in two loping bounds.

"Shaman," he shouted, "they swim against our full tide!"

"It is known, it is known!" snapped the Shaman. "It is that spot of light on the cliff, Atylem! Dost 'a' not see it? Call on the Kobold now, man, or die!"

Thunder shattered the night, nearer.

Atylem stared at the gaunt face glowering over the brazier for a long frozen moment. . . .

Then he wheeled, pounding back up the beach, bellowing, "To me, Great Kobold! The Kobold! The Kobold! I call upon the Kobold, to my battle and aid!"

The beastmen answered with a leaping bellow as their axes flashed in the lightning and bit. "The Kobold! The Kobold!"

"Aid me now, O my totem!" howled Atylem. His blow shattered a pike-shaft; but another pike glanced off the bracelet high on his ax-arm and slashed his flesh.

The world cracked apart in a stab of lightning and a bellow of thunder.

The great black bank of feathers heaved, lifted, and slammed down.

The soldiers froze, faces locked in a contorted grimace of churning anguish.

The beastmen's ragged, snarling howl of victory tore loose.

And the soldiers fell.

One body fell split from shoulder to hip, another with rib-cage stove in, a third with head lolling crazily from left shoulder, hanging there by a mere shred of sinew.

The tide of blood swept down the beach to the ocean, and the air filled with the howling of the beastmen as they raged in their victory.

In the cabin far above, Toby groaned and pressed against the packed earthen floor, forcing his body up till he was sitting. He drew his knees up to either side of his head, fingers kneading his temples.

He sat frozen that way for several minutes, whimpering and moaning.

Then a distant brazen howl touched his ears. He lifted his head, listening for a moment, his gaze straying over his sibling warlocks and witches where they lay senseless about him, in clumsy, grotesque postures of agony.

The howl came again, a little nearer; and, at last, its significance came home to him. His head snapped around, eyes staring in the direction of the sound.

Then he was on his knees, fingers tangled in the hulking boy's hair, snapping stinging slaps into his face. "Wake! Wake, Alvin! The beastmen mount the cliff toward us!"

Alvin's head rolled; his eyes opened, squinting. "Mine head . . . oh, let me die. . . ."

"Nay, nay! Waken, man! Rise up to flee! The foe comes hard upon us! Hearest thou not their howl?"

Alvin lifted his head, eyes widening, listening.

The full-tongued cry of the hunting pack blew on the wind.

"They come to hew and break us!" cried Toby, shaking him. "To thy feet, man! Aid me at waking the others!"

Alvin scrambled to his knees; in a moment, the two were frantically shaking and slapping their mates awake.

The howls were close, very close, when at last all fifteen were more or less returned to their aching senses.

"Now, quickly, Matilda!" Toby swung on the older girl. "Lift the roof from off of this cabin!"

As one, the thirteen warlocks shot up to the roof, backs and shoulders straining at the beams.

The girls squeezed their eyes shut, brows knitting in concentration.

The beastmen voices swelled in a roar like the thunder of an approaching tidal wave.

A nail spat out of a timber with a crack like a pistol shot.

Four more followed in quick succession; then a pause; then seven more.

And, to the seeming accompaniment of machine guns, a corner of the roof lifted, and yawned up and back with a ratcheting groan, as a crate lid yields to a crowbar, nails popping loose.

Four young warlocks shot out of the opening carrying the two child-witches, each clutching her broomstick.

"Go when I call thy name!" Toby shouted. "Xander! Giles! Basil! Dickon!"

One by one, the young warlocks peeled out from under the roof and shot skyward.

"Alvin! Miles! With me to the corner!" Toby cried.

The brawny young warlocks slid up to the corner.

"Now, on my count! One . . . two . . . three!"

The three warlocks shot out from under the eaves and arrowed skyward.

The abandoned roof poised for a moment, almost balanced; then, with a slow, wrenching groan, it leaned down, gathered speed, and slammed home.

A moment later, the clamoring beastmen stove in the door with two mammoth ax-blows. Six men tumbled into the cabin. They stood a moment in silence, their comrades howling outside.

Then the six spun about with a curse and a bellow.

The pack answered with a howl of rage, and the tall man howled and pointed as the lightning flashed.

Startled, the beastmen looked up as the thunder rolled

and a second flash followed close on the first. Eyes narrowed, lips writhed in snarls; short, tough compound bows slipped from broad, hairy shoulders. Long arrows drilled into the night sky.

High above, a fourteen-year-old warlock screamed, his back arching; then his body plummeted.

"Alvin!" Toby shouted, and dove.

Alvin swooped with him, down and around. They locked hands and took the impact of the boy's body on their arms, plunging twenty feet to ease him.

Then up, through arrow-sleet, high and higher, the two warlocks sped with the dead weight of their comrade on their shoulders.

Far below, on the beach, a village burned.

"Rod."

"Huh? What?"

Rod lay still, every muscle tense, the film of sleep clearing from wide-open eyes.

He lay on the hillside, looking out over the burned ruins of the Loguire village.

Far out to sea, a flock of small sails drifted shoreward, pale and spectral in the false dawn.

No one was near.

Rod scowled. "What'd you wake me for, Fess?"

"The boats from Burgundy are arriving, Rod."

"So let 'em arrive. The fishermen can take care of outfitting 'em, can't they? Fess, I haven't had an hour's uninterrupted sleep all night."

"My apologies, Rod. I had thought you might have special orders for this fleet."

Rod frowned. "Special orders? Why?" Then he remembered. "Oh, yeah. These are the boys with the lanteen sails, aren't they? Well, have 'em show the other fishermen how to convert their square-riggers."

"I am afraid you will have to give the order yourself, Rod."

"Oh, yeah, that's right." Rod sat up, rubbing the last sleep out of his eyes. "I keep forgetting. The folks here wouldn't be too happy about a horse giving them orders. Or even a little idle conversation."

He put two fingers in his mouth and gave a shrill whistle.

An eighteen-inch figure, wearing a green top hat, green frock coat and knee breeches, saffron weskit, white stockings and buckled shoes, and a brown forked beard, popped out of the grass just in front of Rod.

33

"Thy wish, Lord Warlock?"

Rod rolled his eyes up in a silent plea for strength. "My friend," he said. "Categorically: I am not a lord."

"My apologies, my lord."

"And furthermore, I am not a warlock."

The leprechaun nodded agreement. "Thou art not, my lord warlock."

Rod nodded, resigned. "I sort of expected that. . . . And third—who're you? I don't believe we've met."

"We have not, my lord." The leprechaun took off his hat with a flourish, bowing. "I am newly assigned to thy service my lord, the service of thyself and thy family. Until I am ordered otherwise, by Puck or by thyself, I am not to leave thy side. By name, I am one Kelly McGoldbagel."

"McGoldbagel. . . ." Rod growled, cocking his head on one side, squinting at the elf, taking in the whole of him. "I don't seem to recollect having heard of any Irish elves named 'Goldbagel' before. And for that matter, I've never seen a son of the Erse with quite that style of nose, and certainly never with a forked beard."

"Thou hast a sharp eye, my lord," said the elf, bowing again. "My forebears came to the Land o' the Green from the Holy Lands, long agone."

"From Israel?"

"Aye, my lord. And therefore I am . . ."

". . . a leprechaun," Rod finished. "Yes, I, ah, see. Well, look, Kelly, do me a favor, will you? Hop over to Tuan, and tell him that the fishermen who're just arriving have got to explain their sails to the rest of the sailors."

Kelly bobbed his head in another bow. "I will, my lord. Ought else?"

"Yeah," Rod growled. "Go 'way an' lemme sleep."

The elf grinned, bowed, clapped his hat on his head, and was gone.

Rod shook his head slowly, eyes fixed on the space the elf had occupied. "Leprecohens," he muttered, "witches. Teleporting, levitating, telekinetic—with sex-linked traits, yet. Oh, well, my country, right or wrong."

"Coffee, my lord?"

Rod turned, accepted the steaming mug. "Oh, thanks, Gwen." He turned back to look out over the sea, sipping at the coffee. "Y' know, Gwen, there's an old poem that goes, 'Lives there a man with soul so . . .' "

He froze.

"Aye, my lord?"

"Gwen," he stated.

34

"Aye, mine husband?"

He turned to her slowly. "Now, darling, don't misunderstand me. You couldn't have come at a better time. I'm delighted to see you. You have no *idea* how delighted I am to see you, *but what the hell are you doing here?*"

Gwen smiled impishly. "Whither thou goest, I will go."

"But don't you understand, darling? This is an army! We're going into battle!"

"Tush, my lord." She pressed her finger over his lips. "The battle is not yet; and even if 'twere, I ha' seen battle before, when we fought the rebels for the Queen."

She kissed him. Rod sighed, resigned himself. "I should know better than to argue with you by now. How'd you travel this time? As a bird?"

"Certes, my lord."

Rod nodded grimly. "I should kept closer watch on the ospreys, seen if maybe there was one with green eyes." He set down his mug and turned to her. "Well, as long as you're here, you'll have to accept the hazards of war."

Her eyes widened in innocence. "What hazards are those, my lord?"

"Fire," said Rod. "Steel. Looting. Pillage. *Rape!*"

He leaped at her, catching her in his arms as his weight bore her down.

She smiled, blushed, and wrapped her arms around his neck. "Thou canst not rape *me*, my lord." And she gave him a very long kiss.

"Well, there's some truth in that," Rod mused as he came up for air. "But I could try a little, couldn't I?"

"Assuredly," she murmured. But there was something constrained about her response, something uneasy.

Rod levered himself up on his elbows, frowning.

Then he smiled, very tenderly, and kissed her, very lightly. "Nice try, darling. But you can't hide it from me. What's the matter?"

Her eyes widened, lips parting, in surprise; then she was clinging to him, rolling her head in the hollow of his shoulder. "My lord, my lord! So many times, I can scarce believe thou canst not hear my thoughts!"

"I wish I could," Rod said devoutly; it was an ache within him. "But, since I can't, you'll just have to tell me. What is it, darling?"

She rolled away from him and sat up, clasping her arms around her knees. "This zeal of thine, my lord, in the carrying of the war to the home of the beastmen. It troubles

35

my heart." She bowed her head, avoiding his eyes. "Why dost thou pursue it with such fervor?"

Rod frowned, looked down at his hands. "This is war, Gwen. We have to defend ourselves, or let our people be killed."

"Oh, the defense, aye, that thou must do, I know! But why, my lord, must thou attack *them!*"

Rod was silent a moment, toying with a stalk of grass. "I could say that the best defense is a good offense; that the only way we can really stop them from raiding us is to destroy their base. But you'd know I'd only be telling you half the truth."

"Then why, my lord!" She clasped his hand between her own. "Why must thou attack them? And why, why, why must thou do it so eagerly?"

He closed his eyes, caressing her hand. "Darling . . . you know that I care for only two things: first, you, and our son; and second, that this planet should eventually have a democratic government, so that the tele—uh, witches will be working for the government that sent me out here."

"I know, my lord," she said gently, puzzled.

"All right." Rod took a deep breath. "Now, let's say we only think about defense. All we worry about is beating off the beastmen when they come raiding, right? That means Gramarye will be on a constant military alert. Sentries on all the seacoasts, that sort of thing."

"And?" She frowned, not following him.

"Well, that's the problem." Rod settled back for a long session. "Constant military mobilization causes an increase in the power of the central authority—and I'm out to weaken the power of the king, not to strengthen it."

"Well, think about it." He eyed her speculatively. "What has Tuan done already? When you boil it down, he's put all the noblemen, and all their armies, under his own direct command. He's even got his own soldiers mixed in with theirs; the Lords couldn't fight him if they wanted to, now.

"But what's more important is that none of them want to. None of them would dream of questioning Tuan's authority right now. He knows what to do, and he's doing it. They've got a good, strong, wise leader to follow, and they like it. All the seacoast Lords, and the interior Lords, too, for that matter, will be very happy to do anything Tuan says for quite awhile now.

"And even if they didn't want to obey him, they'd have to. They can't fight him now; their armies are coming very thoroughly under his command."

36

He locked his hands under his head and looked up at the stars. "What else has he done? Instituted the draft. Conscription. If the danger of these beastmen raids keeps up very long, pretty soon all the young men'll be in the army."

"And what is the harm of that, my lord?" Gwen asked plaintively.

"Nothing, as long as Tuan remains king. But what happens if he gets killed, and Catharine rules again?"

Gwen turned her eyes away, and was strangely silent.

"Yeah," Rod said with a sour smile. "Or what happens even if Tuan doesn't get killed? He's got to die sooner or later; so does Catharine. Of course, that's the next generation's problem, not ours. If they get a bad king, that's their tough luck. But personally, I can't help thinking that little Magnus is going to have enough trouble as it is; I don't want him having to fight a John Lackland, too."

"A what?" Gwen frowned.

"A John Lackland. A very evil king, in Merrie Olde Englande, as the reports go. His evilness consisted mainly in trying to centralize the authority of a small island nation before it was ready for it—for which colossal blunder, numberless generations of democrats should be eternally grateful to him."

"Why, if he sought their downfall?"

"Because he tried a good trick just a little too soon; his barons weren't about to give him an inch. They forced recognition of decentralized authority on him."

"When was that land ready for such a king?"

"About three hundred years later. But by that time, limiting the king's power was a tradition, and you never saw such a country for traditions. So the king's power never did become absolute, in that one country—and *only* in that one country. The result is that now, two thousand years later, sixty-two planets in fifty-four different solar systems govern themselves very tidily, thank you, and are able to relegate the problem of evil kings to academic debate, which is the best possible place for it—and all because John Lackland, bless his greedy little heart, wanted too much too soon.

"And *that* is why I've got to wipe out this beastman menace, *fast!* So I can be sure Tuan won't turn into a John Lackland. Because Tuan may not be the first king to scare his people with a bogeyman, but he *is* the first one lucky enough to have the genuine, real live article available. Which just might make him a *successful* John Lackland."

37

He lapsed into a brooding silence, glowering at the sunrise. Gwen wisely held her peace, and his hand.

"There is this, too," Rod admitted. "I hate to say it, but I'm almost glad this whole thing came up."

Gwen stared, shocked.

"Not the raids, of course," he went on. "And certainly not all the killing. That, I've got to stop, and stop fast.

"But the fact that this kingdom has all of a sudden discovered it's not alone on this planet, the simple fact that Gramarye has been very thoroughly shook up, that the country isn't feeling quite so fat and sassy anymore—*that*, I like in a big way. Because a country can't have too much peace—but it can have too much security.

"It's happened before. The most notable instance was four thousand years ago, a country called Rome. Rome was just starting out to conquer the whole world—or at least all the world that it knew about. It was unbeatable, and the people knew it. Any enemies it had, it could beat; it was completely secure. There wasn't anything, and I mean *anything*, to worry about.

"So, as long as the government was grinding out victories, nobody worried about it. The people just quit caring about their government. If a man looked like he could handle the country well, they let him—and he did, and they did, and his name was Caesar, and a promising democracy turned into a monarchy.

"Something like that happened in the twentieth century, in a place called the United States; only the problem was just the reverse; there wasn't quite so much security. There was a big, bad enemy called the U.S.S.R., and another one called China, and the three countries were constantly on the verge of war. It never came, thank Heaven—it would have destroyed the world if it had—but the constant threat of it kept the Americans on their toes. So the people stayed interested in the government, and democracy survived.

"Then it happened to the Interstellar Dominion Electorates, the old Galactic Union. Only this time, there wasn't any kind of threat at all. So, gradually, the people invented things to worry about, and what they worried about was each other. So they started fighting each other, and the Union fell apart, and the Proletarian Eclectic State of Terra took over.

"And it's been happening here the last couple of years. The country's been completely peaceful, and the people have begun to quite worrying about the King. They've been ready to accept any law he makes without question; in the eyes of the people, King Tuan can do no wrong.

And that's all well and good, as long as he keeps making good laws. But there's an old saying, about power corrupting. . . .

"So I'm delighted to have these beastmen appear out of nowhere. I just wish they hadn't appeared in quite so bloodthirsty a fashion. . . ."

Gwen's hands tightened on his. He looked up into glowing, long-lashed eyes.

"Fool that I was, to doubt thee," she murmured. "This talk of this strange spell, de-mo-cra-cy, my lord, I do not understand, not more than one word in eight; but that thou hast the good of the kingdom at heart, that I understand; and I was a fool ever to begin to think otherwise."

Then she was in his arms, full and warm, and very much alive. . . .

Somebody began to hum in a voice that needed oiling. Rod set his jaw and counted to ten.

"Oh, well," Rod sighed. "At least now I know what they mean by an elfin humor."

He turned to the grinning elf. "What news from U.P.I., Kelly?"

Kelly scowled. "What spell is that, warlock?"

"United Pixie Information, of course. What news on the Rialto?"

Kelly looked very grave. "Not the Rialto, Rod Gallowglass, but the seacoast of Bohemia."

Rod's face emptied of emotion. "Bohemia. That's a county in the Duchy of Romanov, isn't it?"

"It was, Rod Gallowglass."

Gwen held tight to Rod's arm.

Rod bowed his head. "Pirates again?"

Kelly nodded. "The beastmen descended at nightfall. An hour later they were fled, and the village was coals."

"Any dead?"

"All." The elf grimaced. "Romanov's troops, the King's Foot, the villagers—even one of thy youngling warlocks."

Rod's head snapped up. "Warlock!"

"Giles." Kelly looked ready to cry.

"Giles. . . ." They could scarcely hear Rod's voice. "A kid! Just a kid, scarcely a teenager!"

Gwen's head was buried in his shoulder, her body shaking with sobs.

"It was, at least, quick, Rod Gallowglass," the elf murmured.

"One of our own," Rod murmured, his eyes glazing.

Kelly nodded.

Rod grabbed the elf by the shoulders, shaking him. "All those troops, and all those warlocks ranged against them, and they still brought off a massacre? *How!*"

"By lightning," said the elf, and his voice shook. "The witches freed our soldiers from the Evil Eye; then the lightning flashed, and the witches lay unconscious. The soldiers froze, and the beastmen mowed them like summer hay."

"Lightning," Rod muttered, his eyes riveted to Kelly.

He turned away, sat still a long moment, then muttered, "That's the key, the key to this whole war, somewhere in that lightning, if I could only find it and FESSten to it."

"Here, Rod," his mentor murmured.

"Why would the Evil Eye be stronger right after a lightning flash?" Rod asked of no one in particular (ostensibly).

The robot hesitated a half-second, then answered, "Directly prior to a lightning flash, the resistance of the path the bolt will follow lowers tremendously due to ionization, thus forming a sort of 'conductor' between the lithosphere and the ionosphere."

Rod frowned. "So?"

Kelly frowned, too. "What dost thou, Warlock?"

"Just talking to myself," Rod said quickly. "A dialogue with my alter ego, you might say."

Fess disregarded the interruption. "The ionosphere is also capable of functioning as a conductor, though the current passed would have to be controlled with great precision."

Rod's lips formed a silent "O."

Gwen sat back with a sigh, patting Rod's hand. She had long ago acquired the wifely virtue of patience with her husband's foibles.

Fess plowed on. "The ionosphere is thus capable of functioning as a conductor between any two points on the earth. Signals may thus travel via the ionosphere, rather than by the more primitive method of . . ."

"Power, too," Rod muttered. "Not just signals. Power."

Gwen looked up, startled and suddenly fearful, remembering what Rod had said about power corrupting.

"Precisely, Rod," said the robot, "though the quantity of such power could not be very great."

"You don't need that much for a psionic blast," Rod growled. "Coupla microwatts, maybe."

"Uh, Rod Gallowglass," said Kelly nervously.

"All that would be needed," said Fess, "is a means of conducting the power to ground level."

"Which is conveniently provided by the ionization of

the air just before the lightning bolt, yes! But how do you feed the current *into* the ionosphere?"

Kelly eyed Rod very warily; this was beginning to sound like an incantation. . . .

"That," said Fess virtuously, "is their problem, not ours."

Rod frowned. "I thought you were supposed to be logical."

"I, Rod Gallowglass?"

"Huh? Oh—no, not you, Kelly. I was talking to my—uh —familiar."

Kelly's jaw made a valiant attempt to fraternize with his toes. Rod could, at that moment, have read a gigantic increase in his reputation as a warlock in the diameters of Kelly's eyes.

"So." Rod touched his pursed lips to his steepled fingertips. "Somebody overseas lends the beastmen a huge surge of psionic power—in electrical form, of course; we're assuming psionics is based on an electrical phenomenon. The beastmen channel the power into their own projective telepathy, throw it into the soldiers' minds—somehow, eye contact seems to be necessary there—and from the soldiers' minds, it flows into the witches, immediately knocking out anyone who's tuned in . . . only temporarily, thank Heaven."

"An adequate statement of the situation, Rod."

"The only question now is: Who's on the other end of the cable?"

"Although there is insufficient evidence," mused the robot, "that which is available would seem to indicate more beastmen as donors."

"Maybe, maybe." Rod rubbed a hand over his mouth. "But somehow this just doesn't seem like straight Evil Eye work. . . . Oh, well, let it pass for the moment. The big question is not where it comes from, but how we fight it?"

He turned to Gwen. "Well, dear, you're the local authority on witchery. Here's how it is: the lightning brings the beastmen more power for their 'spells'; their cousins at home send them the power via lightning-bolt. So how do we fight them?"

"Why . . . by . . ." Gwen spread her hands, at a loss for words. "Why, by more power, my lord! How else?"

"More power," Rod said, musing. "That means more witches. Have we got them, Gwen?"

Gwen frowned, head bowed. "Some," she said slowly, "who have not yet joined with the Queen's Coven—sour and bitter old hags and wizards, hid deep in the forests; but they have no love for humankind."

Rod frowned, lower lip protruding. "How about kids?"

Gwen shook her head and said, very low, "It has been long since I was a child, my lord; young witches seeking to conceal their witchcraft no longer seek me out. Thou must needs ask that of the younger ones."

"*Toby!*" Rod bellowed.

The air whooshed, and the young warlock floated before them. His lips were slack, his eyes hollow with grief.

Then he saw Gwen, and perked up; he even tried a feeble grin. "Gwen, lass! How dost thou?"

She smiled tenderly. "Well, Toby. And thou?"

"Ai di mi!" The boy sighed dolefully. "Lonely, lass, O! So very lonely! Pining in melancholy (sing O, a green willow!) since thou wert wed! Longing, so deeply, for the touch of thy fair satin skin. . . ."

His hand slipped out to suit the action to the word, but Rod reached out and parried it. He admired the kid for being game, but he still wasn't about to permit any liberties. "Easy on the merchandise, boy; lecher alone. That one's taken."

Gwen's being twice the age of the average Gramarye warlock had never prevented them from broad flirtations. Her marriage had been an occasion of open rejoicing and covert chagrin to Toby and his confederates. They had never slackened their hopes, mind you; but it was a little depressing to see all their passes being intercepted.

But warlock and witch-wife had very warm spots in their hearts for Junior Enchantment; so Rod tried to hide a fond smile as he asked, "Toby, do you maybe know of any young witches in the villages, who're trying to hide their witch-powers so their neighbors won't turn on them?"

Toby's face went blank; then he looked away, biting his lip.

Gwen caught his eyes, looking somber.

Rod scowled, looking from Toby to Gwen and back. "What's the matter? You don't think I'm going to turn in their names to the local witch-hunt committee, do you?"

"Oh, we know thou wouldst not. . . ." Toby's voice trailed off; he glanced appealingly at Gwen.

"My lord," she said, "good mine husband . . . we know thou wouldst not intentionally harm them, but . . ."

Rod frowned. "Revealing themselves for witches might get them into trouble, huh?"

She caught his hands, looking pleadingly into his eyes. "The day of the witch-hunt is done, my lord, that we know, but . . . still, the village folk are not over fond of we of the power, and . . ."

Rod knelt, holding her hands, nodding slowly. "Their neighbors would still turn on them, that it? Give them the cold shoulder, ostracize them? Their parents would disown them?"

Gwen nodded miserably. Toby wasn't looking any too happy, either.

Rod looked from one to the other, slowly, his face softening.

"Look," he said gently, "you don't know what this means for the witches. Maybe I'd better spell it out for you."

"My lord," Gwen cried, the words torn from her, "the day of the hunt is *not* done! The King's laws are flaunted in secret throughout the land, and disclosure of witch-hood means death!"

Rod's face turned to flint. The Queen had outlawed witch-burnings three years ago, and King Tuan had reinforced the law at his ascension, and Rod had thought it successful.

But now they were telling him the law had been about as effective as the Fourteenth Amendment in the American South.

"Why wasn't I told?" he bit out.

Gwen spread her hands helplessly, her eyes filling with tears. "So many villages, my lord, and the only sign of the King's power being a handful of King's Foot in each village . . . and if the soldiers themselves favor burnings . . . ! What couldst thou have done?"

Rod ground his teeth. That damned passive, resigned acceptance always shown by the persecuted . . . !

"A lot," he growled, "a great lot. That's just the kind of thing my warlockery can handle.

"But we don't need it now!" He riveted her eyes with his own. "Don't you see, the witches are about to become heroes! Only they can protect this land now! See it, darling! Before this year is out, witchcraft is going to become the dream of every Gramarye child! Parents will rejoice and praise God if one of their children turns out to have witch-powers! The villages will boast of their witches!"

Her eyes widened, lips parting in awe as he caught her up in the magic of the vision.

"So roust 'em out!" He whirled on a wonder-struck Toby. "Ferret them out, all the witches who've been trying to pass for normal! They can't stay at their plows and spinning wheels any longer! Their country needs them!" His brain whirled with a sudden staggering vision of a platoon of teenagers marching under a banner blazoned: "Witches of the World, Unite! You Have Nothing To Lose But Your Skeins!"

He jabbed a finger at the young warlock. "Get to it, Toby! Bring 'em out! The Day of the Witches has dawned!"

"I will, High Warlock," Toby howled, hope singing in his voice. He leaped high into the air, and disappeared.

Next, Rod gave Kelly instructions.

"Aye, warlock!" The elf popped up.

"Get down there and tell Tuan about this, tell him to set up a recruiting program; that's just the kind of thing he does well."

The elf bobbed his head and was gone.

"Now it comes!" Rod said, slamming fist into palm. "Now the witches quit being second-class citizens!" He knelt by his wife, his eyes glowing. "At last, darling! Justice! For you! For our son!"

"At the price of so many lives, my lord," she murmured, her eyes tortured. "The cost is too great, my lord, far too great!"

Rod looked into her eyes.

"Well," he said at length, "you know what it's buying better than most; you've been through some pretty elaborate witch-hunts yourself, on the wrong end."

"Aye, my lord. Yet still I say the cost is overmuch."

Rod bowed his head. "Well, if you can say that, babe, I reckon I can subscribe to it."

He picked up his mug, sipped. "Damn! It's cold."

Gwen took the cup from his hands and stared at it for a moment. It steamed. She smiled brightly and handed it back to him.

Rod took it mechanically, his eyes locked on it. "Uh . . . yes." He sipped the brew and nodded. "Very good. When did you learn to do that?"

Her eyes widened in surprise. "Why, when I was a child, my lord."

Well, it made sense, Rod supposed. After all, she was telekinetic; all she had to do was speed up the molecules.

He took a long swallow. "Hum. Yes. Wonder what other surprises you've got in store for me. . . ."

Far inland, a happening began.

It began with a tall, gaunt, hollow-eyed man. His hair and bushy beard were wild, uncut, uncombed. He wore a patched and threadbare, stained and soiled hooded robe (the hood thrown back at the moment) that might once have been the color of burned umber. The palms of his

44

hands were soft; but his naked feet were horny with callus. His limbs were as thin and hard as ancient cane. The hairs around his mouth were stained brownish-yellow. His hairs in general, along with the rest of him, were covered with a layer of mixed dust and grease that bespoke a certain lack of familiarity with the possible external applications of a general solution to basic problems of human relations.

He was a strong man, you could tell that at a glance. Or a whiff.

He had a long, gnarled, knobbed staff of mountain oak in his hand and the coals of havoc in his eyes.

Obviously either a criminal or a holy man.

He strode through the little village to the common and took up his stand by the pillory. The rays of the setting sun wreathed fire in his hair.

"Hearken unto me!" he cried, flinging up his hands with his staff stretched between them. "Hearken to my words, words of righteousness and of wrath! Come unto me, come all to Skolax, and hear the word of the Lord God of Might!"

Doors swung wide; shutters banged open; and the people of the town peered out.

"Hearken unto Skolax!" the seer shouted, eyes fixed on the darkening sky beyond his staff. "Hear ye, hear all the words of the Lord your High God! 'Thou shalt not suffer a witch to live,' saith the Lord! Thou shalt destroy them utterly!"

At the word "witch," the people shrank back within their houses.

"The land is accursed through witch-hood! Do the crops rot in the fields? Doth the brew bear no barm? 'Tis the work of the witches!"

Doors opened a crack; furtive eyes peered out.

"Doth the foeman raid and harry us?" screamed Skolax. "Is an army of half-beast goblins sent down on us? 'Tis a judgment upon us, for our harboring witches!"

The doors opened six inches, a foot; then, warily, the people began to creep out from their houses. Slowly and with halting steps, they came to the raving preacher.

The fishing boat armada sailed at dawn in the midst of cheering and martial music.

Rod was rather surprised to find that he liked it. Whenever he'd heard a bagpipe before, he'd been, to say the least, unimpressed. But here, at the head of a warfleet, and backed by a drum corps, it wasn't half bad. Just a

45

matter of the proper setting, that was all. Though it did seem a trifle incongruous to hear "The British Grenadiers" rendered on a bagpipe. . . .

Brom came swaggering up to him; the dwarf's bandy legs were eminently suited to the sea. "What is our course, High Warlock?"

Rod ground his teeth; he still wasn't fond of his new title. "Warlock," that was okay, he was resigned to that now—but "high"? Why, he'd never been drunk in his life!

Well, hardly ever. . . .

"Northwest," he answered, with a toss of his head in the relevant direction, "until we strike the western current."

Brom bellowed the order at his helmsman, then turned back to squint appraisingly at Rod. "Thou hast left her ashore?"

"I hast," Rod agreed grimly. "I'd love to have her along, but the situation promises to be a trifle dangerous, and I'd just as soon keep her head away from the war-clubs. And now that all the fuss and feathers of getting underway is over, mind if I ask you what you did with little Magnus?"

Brom glared in mock anger. "Thou callest thyself his sire, an' thou hast left off asking of him till now?"

Rod shrugged. "I was trusting to your grandfatherly pride. . . ."

"A point," Brom admitted. "But if ever thou tellest him that I be his grandfather . . ."

"I know, I know, you'll hale out my tongue by the roots. You promised me two years ago—only it was Gwen that I wasn't supposed to tell, then. And I haven't. I wouldn't subject her to the knowledge of her parentage. It's a good thing the two of you are friends, though; otherwise she might not have left him with you. So what did you do with him?"

"I ha' left him in Efland," said Brom, sounding a little surprised, "with two elvin beldames to guard him. What else should I ha' done?"

"Great." Rod lifted his eyes to the horizon, mouth tightening at the corners. "Just great. My son, the changeling."

"Hum!"

Rod scowled. "What now?"

Brom pointed over Rod's shoulder.

Rod turned, a clammy feeling in his belly.

Skimming over the waves, an osprey was following the fleet.

Rod's face congealed.

Then he sighed, and turned away. "Ah, the joys of

46

having a witch for a wife! My mistake, Brom—I only thought I left her behind."

The mud-walled, leaf-roofed huts in the cliff-walled plain on the mainland, far across the sea from the Isle of Gramarye, lay dark. In the distance, the darkness deepened into a wall of forest. Beyond it, stark white in the moonlight, white chalk cliffs thrust up toward the stars.

High in the east cliff, light glowed warm and mellow in the High Cave, where the god and his priests sat, awake; as befits the divine, they hardly slept.

The village of huts lay dark, not even sentry fires burning.

High above the waves, to the west, the moon rode toward midnight.

Its beams picked out a furtive shape, slipping between two huts.

Then, again, the village lay still, washed by the moonlight reflected from the cliffs, like a town frozen in ice.

Then, silently, a second figure slipped from a door to fade after the first, between two huts.

Then a second.

Then a third, then more, slipping away, into the forest, through the trees, to the talus slope at the foot of the north cliff.

A silent, cloaked group of earlycomers stood waiting for them at the maw of a huge, black cave, shifting nervously and muttering till more than two score had gathered.

Then, silently, by mutual accord, they turned away, into the cave, groping their way along the wall, as though none dared show a light, even though a torch could scarcely have been seen from the village.

They slid along, backs to the rough wall, the cave narrowing around them, funneling down to a sharp turn in the rock that provided a natural light lock.

As they came to the bend of the turn, they saw dim, reflected firelight flickering on the rough stone of the wall; then, turning, they saw the tunnel widening again into a cavern.

At the far side of the cavern it sat, obscene and immobile, eyes glittering with arrogant malevolence, the two snakes twisting down from its head.

The shriveled leather scarecrow at its feet leaped up, shrieking:

"Abase yourselves, Men of Truth! Down upon your bellies! Crawl unto your master, the great god, the Kobold!

47

Down, worms! Down, blind fishes! For even the strongest of men must quail before the might of the Kobold!"

The beastmen fell upon their faces, shuddering and moaning; for each had felt, at least once, the wrath of the Kobold burning through their eyes and into their brains.

Shaman sat on his heels before them, at the feet of the god, where it sat on the dais; and Shaman's eyes burned brighter than the Kobold's.

He threw back his head, his voice splitting the echoes of the cavern with a high, keening cry, wild and baleful, a stooping hawk's shriek, stabbing.

The worshipers groaned and shuddered, and answered in a moaning chant.

"The Kobold is your god!" Shaman screamed. "A strong and powerful god, a god who does not stay his power, a god of might and wrath, who will lead you across the seas, to capture all the willow-men and their island!"

"The Kobold is our god," moaned the beastmen.

"He is a god of wrath and power and might! Not like that false god, Kernel, who is nothing but a man, yet calls himself a god!"

This was not true. Kernel had never called himself a god. Moreover, he had been at great pains to tell his people, again and again, that he was only a man, like themselves, only more learned; but they had not believed him. They had referred to him as a god, spoken of him only as a god—but never to his face.

But the memories of men are short, especially in regard to their leaders; and twice more when another leader arises, calls the first one's words lies, accuses him of lies he never made. Then the second leader tells lies, and calls those lies Truth, his Truth.

The biggest of the beastmen, taller by half a head than any other, and broad-shouldered in proportion, lifted his great head from the ground and cried:

"The Kernel is false, O Shaman! For he tells us, again and yet again, that he will some day leave us, orphaned in this wilderness, in this cold, far land!"

"Indeed will he leave you orphaned!" spat Shaman. " 'Tis truth that you speak, Atylem! Having brought you here, past all hope of returning again to your home, he will leave you all lost and wailing! Oh, aye, he has brought you the corn, and the women's arts of plowing and field-care—and these, and only these, will he leave you! You, whose pride and boasting was the din of battle and the ringing of shields! This he takes from you, and leaves you,

48

belike to go to the islanders, those small, weak men, and will, belike, lead them here against you!

"Do not doubt it, men of Kobold!" he shrieked, jabbing his forefingers at them. "Be mindful! What weakling men have done to you before, they will do again! They have not the power of eye, to hold an enemy where he stands; and for this they will hate you, and will come again, with sword and with flame, to drive you from your homes, as they have done before!"

"Never again!" Atylem roared, leaping to his feet. "Seek them out, and burn them, now!"

"*Down* on your face! *Down* before the Kobold!" Shaman's voice sliced out like the crack of a whip.

Atylem paled, and fell on his face.

"Aye, grovel!" sneered Shaman. "Forget not who is master! Only through serving the Kobold shalt thou have power!"

He fell silent, nodding slowly, eyes glittering.

"Yet you speak well, Atylem, you speak well," he crooned. "We must strike them down ere they strike at us, and"—his voice hardened—"this have I already begun, children of Kobold! Have you so soon forgot?"

"Nay!" Atylem's head was up again, three or four of the others with him. Battle-lust glowed in their eyes. "That was good warring, Shaman! Our dragon boat sang through the waves, our swords drank deep! We slew, and slew well, as we shall sure slay them all! Hale out the ships again, Shaman, and carry us once more to glory! For those two battles you gave us were much too soon done! And yet"—his voice darkened with a trace of doubt—"will this battling of ours not bring the islanders, in their little boats, to strike at our village?"

"Coward! Fool!" Shaman leveled a trembling finger at the cowering beastman. "Assuredly, they will come. And what of it? Shall not all our people rise up against them? How else are we to bring all our brothers to the true worship of Kobold? Is not this as we wish it, that the islanders should come down upon us? Fool, coward! Be still!"

The beastmen ground their faces into the dust, moaning.

Shaman chuckled, nodding slowly. "They shall attack. And then shall all our brothers see Truth, see the warring, manlike Way of Life! Then shall they forge their spears and swords anew, and leap to guard our backs!"

"We cannot wait so long!" Atylem gasped. "We cannot wait so long to blood our swords again! The fire of battle roars high in me, Shaman! We must sail against the soft-bellied islanders again, and that quickly!"

"And so you shall," Shaman crooned, chuckling and nodding. "It is the will of the Kobold."

Heads snapped up, eyes eager, lusting.

"Hale the dragons forth from hiding!" Shaman shrieked, leaping to his feet. "Take up your swords and your shields, for you stride forth to battle! The ships sail at moonset!"

He waited until the clamor of the beastmen had died, then said, in a softer, droning tone, "Yet we must not abandon our brothers here; the Kobold would not have it! He would have us give them some measure, at least, of protection, lest the islanders swoop upon them while we are gone."

His forefinger stabbed out four beastmen, who shrank back, surprised, muttering.

"You four shall rest here, on the plain. You shall take your dugout boats, to float just beyond the horizon, watching for the islanders' boats. If you should see them, turn, drive back to shore to rouse your brethren, call up their arms! Turn the islanders away—to *death!*

"To battle now!" Shaman cried. "Take up your weapons! Go!"

The beastmen caught up swords and shields from where they lay against the walls of the hidden cavern, streamed toward the tunnel, howling battle-joy.

Atylem flung his sword up above his head in an arc, called as he charged into the bend.

His men followed, howling, then falling quiet as they reached the bend.

But the Shaman stayed behind, and beckoned to one beastman who lagged behind the others.

The warrior turned at the signal, came up to his master, and knelt, touching his forehead to the floor at Shaman's feet.

"You know your duty?" the scarecrow snapped.

"All shall be executed, as you have commanded," the warrior answered, and grinned. "Praise to the Kobold!"

His grin faded when it was not returned.

Shaman nodded curtly. "Go," he said.

The beastman bumped his forehead again, rose and turned away.

"And, Horgil," said Shaman.

The warrior turned again.

"Beware of your fellow sub-chief, Brellaegh," Shaman crackled. "He seeks to add your sub-chief-ship to his own."

Ragefire flared in Horgil's eyes; his lips spread wide in

a hungry grin. "I thank the Shaman," he said, "praise the Kobold."

He bowed his head, turned, and was gone.

Shaman sank down upon his heels and cackled.

Night clomped up on elephant feet as the fleet coasted past the Hapsburg estates, halfway to the western current.

Rod lay amidships with his head pillowed on Fess' saddle. The great black robot horse stood by the mast, looking down at its master. Its voice murmured behind his ear.

"Why did we not take the starship first, Rod? A preliminary reconnaissance mission might have proved or disproved the value of this makeshift armada."

"Don't say 'makeshift' when you're talking about two hundred of Gramarye's finest."

Rod propped an eyelid open and assumed a lecture tone. "It's like this, the Beast Boys may have dreamed up this Viking bit all on their own, but I doubt it. Besides which, how did they learn about the ocean currents? And on top of that, how come they didn't show up on that photo we took two years ago? All of which adds up to somebody giving them top-class lessons in camouflage, ship-handling, and practical psychology—and that somebody has to have come from off-planet, or maybe even out-time. We can't afford to laugh at the idea of time-travel anymore; it's been used on us once too often. So it's either Space or Time, but they're getting help somewhere."

"That," said the robot cautiously, "would perhaps be a warranted inference."

"Therefore," Rod went on, "if we land right in their midst in a starship, they just *might* figure that our side's got off-planet help, too."

"A point," Fess admitted.

"And if they should manage to kill or capture us (which is, although I hate to admit, lamentably all too possible), they'd have the spaceship. And I have a sneaking suspicion it wouldn't take them all that long to figure out how to use it."

The robot was silent a moment; then it said, "If the beastmen are backed by an off-planet power, Rod, why would they not use their own spaceship for terrorizing?"

"Hm, yes." Rod locked his hands under his head. "There *is* that. That's the main reason I'm inclining more toward the time-machine hypothesis, Fess. If they sent . . ."

" 'They,' Rod?"

"Hypothetical 'they.' 'They' in the abstract. If 'they' sent an anti-DDT agent through to us, and he's organized local boys into a task force, he'd have to use local materials, too: flint, bone, maybe some hardwoods. And it *is* a trifle difficult to build a spaceship with a technology that doesn't quite amount to a running start."

"True."

"Now, we destroyed the time-machine we found in the haunted section of the Loguire castle, and the one in the House of Clovis—but who's to say there wasn't a third one somewhere? Or that they haven't moved a third one in? But as I remember the two we found, they were pretty small affairs—you'd be lucky to get one decent-sized man through at a time, let alone a whole spaceship."

"It might be possible to ship through a prefabricated spaceship, Rod, and assemble it here."

Rod snorted. "*You* assemble a spaceship out of six-foot sections, without power derricks. As for myself, I've got more productive things to do with my time—like trying to solve Fermat's theorem."

"Consider me chastened," the robot murmured.

"Serves you right, too. What'd you mention a nothing idea like that for, anyway?"

"I felt obliged to point out all logical possibilities, Rod."

Rod frowned, chewing at the inside of his cheek. "Not a bad idea, as a general principle. Any other obvious possibilities I've missed? A little more feasible, though, if you please."

The robot fairly pounced. "There *is* one attitude of yours that has occasioned me some distress, Rod. . . ."

"All right, feel free to be tactless. What've I been blinding myself to?"

"You seem to have assumed that the beastmen themselves are of local origin, Rod. . . ."

"Well, isn't that the most probable solution? On this planet, that is? I mean, here we have a species that seems by all reports, to be the precise picture of the bogeymen generations of Gramarye mamas have been using to keep their kids in line; and some of those mamas must have been high-powered projective telepaths! Uh—mustn't they?"

"Given the ratio of psi powers to the total population, over a period of several centuries, it would be virtually inevitable," the robot admitted.

"Well, then, there you have it! If these projective mamas start believing in the bogeymen they're talking about, and believe in them hard enough, sometime, somewhere on this crazy planet, sooner or later, some clump of witch-moss is going to develop a pair of hind feet to stand up on, and start going, 'Ugga-blugga-lug! Me beastman! You human!' I mean, that's pretty obvious, now, isn't it?"

"It is," Fess murmured, "except that there is an even more probable explanation of why the beastmen exhibited no trace on our survey photographs of two years ago."

Rod cocked an eyebrow at the horse. "Oh? What?"

"Simply that they were not there at the time, Rod."

"Oh." Rod frowned, looked down at his belt buckle for a few minutes. "Yes, that would be pretty obvious, wouldn't it?"

"It would, Rod."

"But then where did they come from?"

"According to your own logic, Rod, they were brought in from out-time."

Rod toyed with the hilt of his dagger while he thought that one over.

"Just for the sake of argument," he said, "let's say someone shipped them in, from some weird planet where bogeymen grow. Now, from the way they've acted since establishing themselves here, and from the effects they're having on the Gramarye political system, I'd say it just might be possible that whoever brought them in has a pretty poor opinion of democracy. Which means either one of our two sets of friends from the future, totalitarians or anarchists, take your pick."

"A third party, inimical to democracy, is not impossible, Rod."

Rod gave him a sour look. "Or a fourth, or a fifth, or a sixth. Thanks, but two organized enemies will do me quite well, thank you."

"All logical possibilities . . ."

"Are just the kind of thing bureaucracies thrive on, so you can deposit them in the nearest orifice. These boys were brought in by, or are being manipulated by, somebody from out-time who's opposed to democracy, and that's all we really know for the time being. But, Fess—their scheme just might not be working."

"How so, Rod?"

"Because, by making the witches vital to the defense of Gramarye, they've made it very honorable to be a witch—which means they've made ESP a *very* favorable survival trait. And that, in turn, means that when this planet is eventually ready to join the DDT, the DDT will get many, many more telepaths than it otherwise would have."

"*If* Gramarye does evolve a democratic government, Rod."

"Well, that's what this war's for. To get the whole thing over with before it can louse up my plans."

"That may be rather difficult, Rod, in view of their power source. Especially since we'll be fighting on their home territory."

"Yes." Rod scowled at his dagger hilt. "You just had to mention it, didn't you? That's what makes the whole thing a bit chancy. But, hopefully, we'll be taking them by surprise, and we *do* outnumber them."

"But can our witches effectively counteract their power source, Rod?"

Rod frowned. "What's this business about a power source? I thought we'd decided all it was, was all the beastmen at home, lumping their power together and putting it into the ionosphere."

"Considering the level of technology available to the futurians, Rod, which is an unknown factor, but which is known to be capable of producing a time machine—there is a logical alternative."

"Which is?"

"That the psionic power source in question is mechanical in nature, Rod."

Rod scowled and picked out a star.

"Yes," he said slowly, "that *is* possible. And it would account for their being able to project psionic power through the ionosphere, when our witches can't."

"Presisely," the robot murmured.

"And the question it leaves us," said Rod through pursed lips, "is: Do all the witches we can muster have any chance against a machine?"

A flutter of wings, and an albatross landed on the gunwale next to Rod. Its form twisted, stretched, and turned into Gwen's. She smiled, flung her arms around his neck. "Doth my guise of an albatross please thee, my lord?"

"No! Uh, I mean, yes, yes! I mean . . . Damn it, quit hanging around my neck! You're choking me!"

Gwen relaxed her hold and rolled away, looking a little hurt.

Rod wrapped his arms around her and hauled her down in a bear-hug. "Besides," he growled, "mugging is the man's prerogative, remember?"

Fess gave a delicate electronic cough and turned his equine back, tactfully cutting the circuit to Rod's maxillary mike.

Rod came up for air and gasped, "Babe, you came just at the right time."

"Didst miss me so greatly, my lord?" Gwen cooed, twining her fingers in his hair.

"Uh, no! I mean, well, of course! I always miss you that much. But, well, this time, I'm glad to see you for another reason, too."

Gwen eyed him askance. "What would that be, my lord?"

Rod steeled himself and said, "Information. I need some witchcraft advice."

Gwen sighed and rolled away to sit primly, hands folded in her lap, the picture of composed spousely resignation. "What dost thou wish, my lord?"

Rod folded his arms around his knees and looked deep into her eyes. He mentally pulled back a little before he got lost, cleared his throat, and said, "Darling, I have reason to believe those beastmen can conjure up more power for that Evil Eye bit than all the teenage warlocks and witches we can recruit will be able to produce." And he proceeded to explain the theoretical mechanical psionic generator-*cum*-transmitter, doing his best to adjust the concepts to the primitive level of technology with which she was familiar. He wasn't much of a teacher, but Gwen was intelligent; she learned.

He measured the gravity of the situation by the length of the wrinkle between Gwen's eyes. "This is thy manner of witchcraft, my lord, not my own. The workings of this spell are beyond my knowing, as is its counterspell . . . and yet . . ."

"Yet?" said Rod hopefully.

"There is one who, even if the counterspell was beyond his art, might well be able to bear the weight of that awesome power upon his own shoulders, alone."

"Who is he?"

"The sorcerer of the Dark Tower, my lord; yet he would not come to our aid; he hath forsworn all dealings with mankind."

"Oh, come on, now! At a time like this . . ."

"At a time like this most especially, lord; he holds his powers aloof from mortal embroilment, and from war most of all. In his youth he was tortured for witch-hood; he will not give aid to those who once racked and burned him."

"Well . . ."

"Aye, my lord Rod. There is justice in what he will do and will not do; but there is little of mercy in him. Yet there is a woman also. . . ."

"A witch?"

"Aye, an ancient, aged, venerable woman. . . ."

"A hag," Rod interpreted softly. "I thought the old witches hated everybody, Gwen. After all, that's why all the witches and warlocks in the Royal Coven are teenagers."

"She, too, doth hate, my lord; all souls save other witches doth she loathe; for in her youth she was flogged, tried by water, racked, and would have burned at the stake, had it not been for the magic of old Galen. . . ."

"Galen?"

"Aye, my lord, the wizard I told you of but now. His white magic hath the greatest power of any sorcery or witchcraft in this land. His keep lies deep within the Forest Gellorn—a great, high tower of stone it is, dark granite; and never a light is seen at its windows. So it is that folk do name it the Dark Tower of the Wizard Galen."

"That name again!" Rod shook his head, trying to clear it. "Are you sure his name is . . . Galen?"

"It is, my lord. He chose the name himself."

"And you're *sure* he won't have anything to do with anybody?"

"He will not, my lord, most assuredly—save witches. Doth this news, then, so astound thee?"

"Oh, no, no." Rod waved a hand in denial. "It's just that . . . well, I suppose he never heard of Hippocrates."

"Hippoc . . . ?"

"Or maybe he's confusing it with Hypocrisy; it's been done before. . . . Well, never mind."

Gwen shrugged and went back to her story. "They are old, now; this took place in the days of their youth. She was a lass, scarce sixteen, and he a youth near twenty. He dwelt already in his tower—he had gone there, and exorcised it, and there had taken up abode; for the folk of his village had tortured him, till he confessed to warlockhood and wizardry. Then they threw him into water, to test the truth of his confession. He sank, as they say witches cannot do; but he did not drown, and emerged, then turned his face unto the forest and entered, nevermore to come forth.

"Then, some years later, when she had grown to witchhood, and had hidden it for four long years, the folk of her village found it out. They tortured her, with fire and whip, to have the word from her. Then they threw her into water and, when she floated, flogged her once again. Then they bound her to a stake, and lit faggots beneath her. But when smoke had hid her from their sight, Galen reached out from his Dark Tower, and snatched her clean away. He sent her out into the forest; and she wandered, lost and lone, till she came to the Crag Mountains;

and there she found a cave, where she made her home for five years.

"And soon the word had spread throughout the countryside that if a man had need of an excellent night of entertainment, he had but to seek her cave. . . ."

"Oh. . . ."

"Aye."

Rod cleared his throat. "I take it Galen was among her steadiest . . . uh, visitors?"

"Nay, lord. He would have naught of her. Naught of women, or the world."

Rod scowled, nodding slowly. "I'm beginning to get a better idea what this boy is like. . . . You say she moved?"

"Aye; mayhap because, twice in five years, the folk of the village stormed her cave with scythe and ax and fire. Whatever the cause, when she was one-and-twenty, she found another cave, high in the face of a rock; and there hath she dwelt for all these long years since."

"With gentleman visitors, of course."

"Aye." Gwen grimaced as though she had bitten into an apple and found a worm.

She sighed, and went on. "Ever and anon, throughout the long and lonely years, she would reach out with magic, to save those who were in danger."

"Only witches, of course."

"Nay, lord. Far more often villagers than witches."

"Oh-ho-o-o-o-o-o." Rod put two and two together and came up with Gramarye victorious.

"Yet notwithstanding, the folk of the villages came ever and anon to clamor for her blood."

"Didn't do 'em much good, did it?"

"Nay, lord. They could but curse her."

"That's about what I thought. The way you described that cave of hers, it sounded pretty impregnable."

"It was; and its mistress was a witch of great power, even then."

"How about her? Was she?"

"Was she what, my lord?"

"Impregnable. . . ."

"Oh." Gwen frowned, gazing at the water. "Nay, my lord. All the villages nearby knew of her; and when the mood was on them, the men would go to her cave, and find her as willing as ever."

Rod's mouth hardened at the corners. "Poor kid."

Gwen cast a brief, adoring look at him.

"Well, what can you expect?" Rod growled, lashing a

kick at the gunwale. "Her mother never told her the things a young girl should know, I'll bet. . . ."

"Aye, my lord." Gwen watched the swirl of the water. She sighed, throwing her head back, to look for the moon. It still hadn't risen.

"She saved their friends' lives," Rod growled. "You'd think that would have taught them to care for her. . . ."

"Aye, lord. But it did not. They came to her cave, by threes and fives. . . ."

"Fives!" Rod stared. "In one night?"

"Aye." Gwen looked up at him, wide-eyed. "They say she hath lain with a score of men in a night, lord."

"*Twenty?*"

"Aye. She was the bawdy jest of the countryside in her youth." Her voice hardened. "Do you not find it amusing, lord?"

"Hm? Amusing? Hell, no! Pathetic, maybe. . . ." Rod looked out over the ocean, rubbing his chin.

Gwen made no answer, but her eyes glowed as she looked at her man.

"But she does have some interest in people, Gwen? She helps when she can?"

"Aye, my lord. . . ."

"Then she might be persuaded to help out?"

"She might, lord. She would then be our shield against the power of the Evil Eye."

"All by herself?" Rod frowned. "She's that powerful?"

"Exceeding powerful, my lord. They say she hath a familiar spirit."

Rod shrugged, spreading his arms. "Well, that's a foregone conclusion, isn't it? I mean, twenty men in one night! That's not just familiar, it's downright personal!"

"Nay, nay, lord! 'Tis not that way that I mean 'familiar.' Dost thou not know? A familiar is a sort of a spirit, like an elf or a ghost, unseen and unseeable."

"Oh, horsefeathers! Look, Gwen, an esper . . . uh, that is, the kind of witches we have here on Gramarye don't need familiars. They do quite well without any help at all from the spirit world."

"Nevertheless, my lord, old Agatha hath one! And none know what manner of spirit it be. . . ."

"Well. . . ." Rod tugged at his lip. "For the sake of argument, let's say it's true. That means, if we get her on our side, we've got two allies for the price of one."

"Aye, my lord; but she hath not a price. Moreover, in her age, she hath grown to a just hatred of all men. . . ."

"So she's got this grudge against men," he said, "and

against people in general. Can't say as I blame her. But is there any chance at all we might be able to talk her into joining the war on the side of the angels?"

"A chance, my lord." Gwen looked a little uncertain. "But only a chance. . . . I shall speak to her, if thou wish it."

"I do," Rod said fervently. "Thank you, babe."

He turned away to look out over the sea. "Although, hopefully, it won't be necessary. We just might manage to clean up the whole mess with this one raid. In which case, her sympathy for the human race, or lack thereof, will be of only academic significance."

"We may hope, my lord," Gwen murmured.

"Yeah." Rod frowned. "And for the moment, I'm afraid that's about all we can do."

The makeshift fleet drifted on, silent in the night, toward the mainland . . .

. . . as three long, gaudy-winged dragon ships swung north, to put the horizon between themselves and the King's Fleet, as they sailed toward the Isle of Gramarye.

Four dugout canoes drifted, far apart, along a line parallel to the shore and two miles out from it. Four beastmen shivered, each alone, in the chill of the night. They shivered with the cold, and only the cold—or so each claimed to himself.

Four beastmen, each alone, in the dark before moonrise—

Then a touch of light on the horizon, and a stiffening in the canoes.

The light of a lantern, far away, beyond the rim of the world—then sails, dark and somber against the dusted stars. . . .

As one, the four boats whirled about, drove toward the beach on the flood tide. Double-bladed kayak paddles dipped and swung, canoes fled light, far outpacing the slow fleet behind.

"Wolves upon us!" four voices bellowed, as their owners ran up from the beach to the village, howling terror, anger, wrath. "Attack! Our foes upon us! They come from sea, they come in thousands! Awake and arm! Our foes upon us!"

Beastmen boiled from huts, calling in fear, in shock, confusion. Burning branches, yanked from cooking fires, whirled into the air about men's heads, waking the village alive with leaping light. Every man was angry, fearful, confused, calling to his neighbor—what was upon them?

"Our foes attack by sea!" someone screamed, cutting through the shouting confusion.

The crowd churned, aghast, afraid.

A figure leaped up to the roof of a hut, leather and trap-stick, parchment and bone. Two torches swung out of the crowd to throw light up into the eldritch, snarling face.

"Your foes attack!" Shaman screamed. "The Kernel has betrayed you! He had sworn there were no foes here, that none would hate you—yet here they are, upon us! Here they come upon you now, with steel and fire to slay you, when you have done nothing against them! 'Tis as it was in the lands you came from! They hate and seek your death! The Kernel has brought you into the midst of death."

And four voices took up his cry: "Death! Death! Death! Death!"

"The Kernel has betrayed you!" Shaman screamed again. He seized a torch and whirled, pointing toward the High Cave, where light glimmered behind a stocky silhouette.

"Death to the traitor!" Shaman screamed. "Death to the Kernel! Death to the false god who has betrayed you! Who has shamed you! Death!"

Four voices echoed the cry, and more took it up, till the whole crowd was chanting.

Shaman leaped from the roof, springing through the crowd. A path opened for him through the ranks, and he ran toward the west cliff, shouting, "Death to the two-faced God!"

"*Death!*" howled the crowd, streaming after him.

High above, in the spot of light on the east cliff, the stocky silhouette was joined by another—taller, leaner, cloaked. They stood together a moment; then the taller turned, calling, and four more shadows came up behind him. They stood a moment in talk; then the four shadows turned away, down the series of massive, sloping ledges that formed a giant's staircase to the ground, loping down the rock with a speed that would take them to the plain floor far before the mob could reach the cliff.

The remaining two shadows turned back into the cave, came back a moment later with packs slung across their shoulders. They turned to the right as they came out of the cave-mouth, turning away from the stone ramps, turned to clamber up the stone of the cliff-face by finger- and toe-holds.

When they came to the top, they stood a moment, looking down into the valley, silhouettes against the stars.

And far below, Shaman saw them. "They flee!" he

cried, jabbing his torch toward the top of the cliff. "They know their guilt! They know your righteous wrath! Chase them! Seize them! Trap them! They must not escape! They must know your vengeance! Run them down and rip their flesh!"

The mob behind him howled and dashed for the giant's staircase.

But, by the time they had pounded up the ledges and come, short of breath, to the High Cave, the two silhouettes atop the cliff were long gone, faded down the rock to the west, to the swamps far below, and the mob's ardor had waned somewhat with their energy.

It was, perhaps, therefore with some prudence that Shaman cried: "You have come too late, too slow; they are gone! Well, let them; they can only flee to the swamps, and the great lizards will answer for their lives soon enough."

The beastmen rumbled amongst themselves, uncertain.

"You have not time to catch two worthless cowards now!" Shaman screamed. "Have you forgot? Your homeland is invaded! Your enemies come upon you by sea! They will hack you, they will burn you! They will slay your wives and children, if you do not sail out to meet them! Therefore, to your weapons!"

A beastman at the back of the mob turned and howled, leaping down the ledges. As one, the mob turned and surged after him, howling blood-lust.

Shaman reached out a hand and caught the beastman nearest him, one of the sentries from the dugouts.

"Tell the other three that now the time is come, to haul out the dragon boats; the mob is too wrought up to wonder where the boats have come from. Set them to their oars, keep them too busy thinking of vengeance and battle to wonder, and they will do your bidding. Then bend them quickly to the great throwers; they shall wind it for you; it needs only one man to work it, and you know your work. Now go!"

The beastman raised doubting eyes to the top of the cliff above them. "But the Kernel—his men—"

"Let not your heart be troubled with that false god and his priests!" Shaman spat. "The True Kobold will soon reign here, rightfully, in the High Cave. For the false Kernel and his priests, have no care; the monsters in the swamps shall slay them. Failing that, we shall hunt them down soon enough; but there is no time for that now! We must begin this war, in earnest! Therefore, go!"

The beastman whirled and sprang away, down the staircase.

Shaman stood a moment alone, eyes glittering with the reflections of the horde of torches streaming toward the beach. He cackled shrilly, clenching his hands.

Then he turned away, toward the north cliff, to fetch his god to its new abode.

Rod looked out over the azure sea, gilded by the newly-risen sun, and sniffed the chill, early sea-breeze. "How close to the mainland are we, Fess?"

The robot cocked a sextant eye at the sun, compared the reading with the dexteriorating isotope deep within his innards that served him for a thousand-year clock, and announced, "We should sight land in a little less than an hour, Rod."

"Sail aho-o-o-o-y!"

Rod's head jerked up, startled.

A rainbow-striped sail peered over the horizon.

"The beastmen!" Tuan was at Rod's elbow, as if by alchemy—which, on that planet, was always a possibility. "The beastmen, come to raid our folk again!"

Rod, glancing sidelong at the young King, shuddered at the blood-lust in his eyes.

"Sail! Sail! Sail! Sail!"

Rod's eyes leaped back to the horizon.

Four more striped sails loomed up as the first boat reared its reptile head over the edge of the world.

Rod chewed his lip. "Uh . . . that's a little larger than the average raiding fleet, Tuan."

"Aye." Tuan scowled. "What do they here?"

Something huge and ponderous lifted off the deck of the first boat. It arced into the air, leaving a smudgy trail across the sky behind it.

"A fire-pot!" Rod glanced nervously at his horse. "It's FESSter than it ought to, too. Where's it going to land?"

"Why, they mean it for us." Tuan scowled at Rod. "But surely it must fall short, thrown from so far."

"It will land on the third boat in from the western edge of the fleet, Rod," the robot murmured.

"Clear out!" Rod sawed the air frantically with his arms, bellowing to the nearby boats. "Clear out, boys! Leave a *big* hole in the front edge of this fleet, before it gets knocked there for us! Fast! Move!"

Sails boomed about, oars struck at the waves, as the leading boats struggled frantically back against their fellows.

But they were not quite quick enough. The fire-pot arced

down, air moaning about it, to explode on the bow of one small boat. Flame sprayed over the four nearest boats.

The first boat tilted stern up and sank, as red dancing tongues sprouted on the others. The shrieks of the burned, and the hoarse, panicked soldiers who had never learned to swim, filled the air.

Rod waved off the boats that swarmed to the rescue. "Off! Back off! Throw them lifelines! You won't do them any good if you're burning, too!"

"Ready . . . fire!" Tuan had herded five archers into the bows. Clothyard shafts bounded from longbows, blazing tow bound just behind the heads. Rod had to hand it to Tuan; the kid was quick on the pickup.

The second fire-pot exploded on the stern of a would-be rescuer. The rest sheared off as the third fireball came moaning down. It blasted into clear water with the hiss of a thousand snakes; a moment later it exploded, under water, shooting a geyser and great clouds of steam twenty feet into the air.

"Witchcraft!" somebody screamed; but nobody seemed much alarmed. The form might be new, but the witchcraft itself was commonplace.

Men howled anew as the steam fell as scalding rain.

Lifelines snaked out from the boats.

Rod leaped out of the command boat as Tuan's archers launched their second volley. He hauled himself up onto a boat a dozen yards away and grabbed the first two archers he could find. "Up in the bows, quick!" he snapped. "Don't you see what the King has his men doing? Bind tow at your arrowheads and set it ablaze! Set the enemy on fire!"

An arrow had struck the sail of the first, setting the canvas aflame with a beautiful light.

"Come on, come on, men! You're still archers, you're still men! Get up there and fight!" Rod all but threw five archers into the bows. The first two had finally gotten the idea; the other three followed their example.

"Aim!" Rod bellowed. "Shoot!"

But even as their arrows shot up, the flames on the enemy sail were doused out. The beastmen had come prepared for pyrotechnical warfare.

Flaming arrows struck the other dragon ships; but as quickly as the flames sprang up, they were drowned.

"Score one for the Bogeyland Volunteer Fire Department," Rod growled, "and the fireballs are still coming!"

Rod's own men had been working frantically, dredging seawater in wooden buckets and hurling it at the decks and sails; but the exploding fireballs drenched the boats with flame faster than the sailors could quench them.

The beastmen, on the other hand, seemed to have well-drilled firemen; and their catapult teams were running a continuous barrage, staggered among the five ships.

"Spread out! Spread out!" Rod bawled at the sailors. "Don't give them such a big target! Archers into the bows! Pepper 'em with fire-arrows! Oh, for some of these telekinetic witches!"

But the witches, who could have sent the fireballs back at their masters, were a thousand miles away, at Runnymede.

"Witches" reminded Rod of something; he scanned the sky anxiously, saw the dot that was his favorite albatross. She was unhit, as yet; he hoped she had the good sense to stay high above the battle.

Then, as he watched, a fireball near the zenith of its trajectory veered widely off-course to splash sizzling into clear water, a good hundred yards from the fleet.

Rod stared; then he grinned, and waved at the albatross. Silently, he cursed the sailors' superstition that had barred the girl witches from the boats during battle.

Behind him, the archers were rallying, to fill the air between the fleet and the dragon ships with flaming arrows.

And now an occasional fireball began to reverse its trajectory completely, hurtling back on the boat that had launched it. The howls of shocked beastmen dismay came faintly over the water; and now some of the hungry fire-flowers that blossomed on the dragon ships lived, and grew.

Then, slowly, the long ships sheared off, one by one. Oars thrust out from their sides and strained to turn them. The last fireball had been launched, only to fall back on its ship; but fire-arrows fell in a torrent now, giving ample substance to inspire the beast-fleet to flight.

As their sails fell below the horizon, the helmsman shouted eagerly, "Shall we follow, Master Gallowglass?"

Rod paused with the answer on the tip of his tongue; he wasn't commanding here. He turned for a look at Tuan's boat; but the young King, too, saw the folly of following. His boat was hove to, and the other boats, one by one, were following his example.

"No," Rod shouted back at the helmsman, "heave to. We've lost too many boats and too many men; and they've probably got catapults mounted on their sea-cliffs, really *big* catapults."

The helmsman wasn't sure what manner of sorcery a catapult was, but he trusted the High Warlock when it came to witchery. He hove to.

Rod turned and dove into the water. He hauled himself up into Tuan's boat.

The King, an ugly blister on his arm where his sleeve was burned away, was bellowing orders to get the rescue work underway. The boats heeled into the former target area; fishermen plunged over the side to succor foundering soldiers.

Tuan turned somewhat angrily to Rod as the "warlock" came up. "Will you, too, now exhort me to follow this 'handful of ships'?"

"No." Rod shook his head, spattering Tuan in the process. "No, I'm with you; matter of fact, I think we ought to go home. We're not tooled up for this kind of warfare. And besides, it's not just a 'handful of ships'; we can be sure there're more where these came from, with catapults just like these, too."

"Catapults?" Tuan scowled. "What manner of enchantment is that?"

"It's—um—like a huge crossbow," Rod improvised. "It's a gadget that throws great, big fireballs. Anything else you'd like to know?"

"Nay." The King's mouth tightened grimly. "Thou hast told me sufficient. We must be gone ere they return to us with more ships and fire."

"Yeah. May I suggest we spread out, give them a lot of little targets instead of one big one?"

"Aye, that would be wise." Tuan's eyes closed; he bowed his head. "We must, then, run home, like whipped children."

"Now you've got it." Rod nodded. "Run home and haul out the carpenters, build us some catapults of our own, and some ships big enough to carry them."

"Thou knowest the contriving of these engines?"

Rod closed his eyes, nodding. "I can draw up the plans in an hour."

"Then why spoke you not of this sooner?"

Rod opened his mouth, and then closed it again. This was no time to be explaining about technological innovations and their effects on a static culture. "Because I didn't think they'd be needed. It seemed more important to get after the beastmen as fast as we could."

Tuan frowned. "Thou hadst good reason," he admitted, "though this one time, thou wast wrong. But it will take much, that is truth."

"I know. We'll have to concentrate on home defense until we've built up a battle-fleet."

"But might not the witches protect us?" said Tuan, glancing up. "Those that fell back on the enemy in this battle, that was thy wife's work, was it not? Might not more witches make their fireballs fight for us?"

"They might," Rod admitted, "but we don't have that many witches. One girl can only handle one fireball at a time, after all, and I have a strange notion the beastmen can put fire in the air faster than our girls can clear it."

Tuan stood immobile for long seconds; then he sighed, and turned away. "Thou hast the right of it once again. Captains!" He waved, signaling the other boats. "Turn about! Run for home in good order!"

The last of the burned and half-drowned were being hauled out of the water; the dead were already being wrapped in their sailcloth shrouds. The keening of the wake rose from several boats near the target area.

Gwen touched Rod's elbow, saying, "My lord, many are most horribly burned, and there is precious little salve in the fleet."

Rod's jaw clenched, his eyes squeezing shut a moment.

He looked up at Gwen again. "The Royal Apothecary has plenty of journeymen and apprentices, and most of the monasteries probably have some ointment tucked away. Call Toby."

Gwen frowned a moment, closing her eyes; then a gust of wind struck them, and Toby was hovering near.

"Gwen, lass! As beautiful as ever, as . . . Oh, good even', Master Gallowglass."

"There is great need of salve here, Toby," said Gwen, with a somber smile. "Thou must needs bid the Royal Apothecary set all his men to the making of more, as much as they may compound in the half of an hour; then more after that. And thou must send to all monasteries and convents, and bring us what salve they may have; we shall need all that thou and thy Coven-fellows can bring."

"Quickly done!" The boy grinned, then frowned quizzically. "But why such great need of salve?"

"We've hurt men here," Rod growled.

Toby turned, surprised at Rod's tone, and saw the wounded lying moaning on the decks. His eyes bulged, his jaw slackening. "Lord o' mercy, Master Gallowglass! What happened here?"

Catharine stalked into the audience chamber, knotting

the sash of a velvet dressing gown, blinking sleep out of her eyes.

The guards at the two doorways stiffened; Sir Maris, Master of the Guard, and the mud-spattered herald beside him, bowed low.

"Seat yourselves," said the Queen, sinking into one of the carven oak chairs at the table by the fire. She took a draft from the golden goblet of mulled wine that awaited her and looked up as Sir Maris and the herald sat.

"Now then, Sir Maris. What is all this coil, that is so urgent you must needs wake the Queen in the small hours of the morning?"

"It is, perhaps, not so vast a matter that it warrants disturbing Your Majesty's rest," said the old knight hesitantly. "I hope that I have not misjudged. . . ."

"Your courtesy and courtliness becomes you, Sir Maris, but it bores me," said the Queen. "Have done with it, and tell me the matter straightaway. If you have done wrong to wake me, you shall be sure of it presently. Now tell me the matter."

" 'Tis the matter of persuading the witches to come out of hiding and join the Queen's Coven, Your Majesty. . . ."

"Aye, I know," the Queen said impatiently; "the recruiting goes badly; a hundred heralds sent forth have yielded but two novice witches. What is there new?"

"The Herald Drobny hath brought the news, Majesty; perhaps it were better that he tell it." Sir Maris turned to the herald.

The herald bowed nervously, cleared his throat, and launched into his oration. " 'Twas in the east, Madam, hard by the Crag Mountains. I rode from village to village, and received everywhere a most chill reception; in truth, I fear 'twas only the royal arms blazoned on my tabard that saved me from stoning."

"There is naught new in this," snapped the Queen, stifling a yawn.

"Nay, Majesty; but by-the-by, I grew to wondering at such churlishness; and therefore I crept into the next town in peasant garb. I sat in the inns and the taverns, and heard naught amiss; but near to sundown I found mine answer."

The Queen scowled, coming a little closer to wakefulness. "Indeed? Tell me it, sirrah!"

"Why, so I do, Majesty—'twas a hermit!"

"A hermit?" The Queen gave her head a quick shake. "Have I heard you aright, sirrah?"

"Be sure that thou hast, Majesty! 'Twas a hermit, a holy man, preaching against witches!"

"What!" The Queen came fully awake.

"Aye, Majesty, preaching! 'The witches must burn,' quotha; 'they are a blight on God's earth!' Thus he spake, and . . ."

The Queen's fist slammed on the table, cutting him off. "Out upon him!" She whirled to Sir Maris. "Do thou, O Captain of Guards, dispatch men to seize him, double-quick!"

"Majesty!" gasped Sir Maris. "Seize a man of the cloth?"

"Dosta not hear me, sirrah? I command thee; have it done!"

"But the Bishop, Majesty . ."

"Time enough when the miscreant is guarded close in our dungeon to concern ourselves with his masters! Go thou, see to it!"

Sir Maris turned and departed with a rigid back and a measured stride that was as good as a formal note of compliance-under-protest.

The Queen sat equally rigid in her carven chair, fingers drumming on the tabletop.

" 'Twould be too much to ask of the Fates that troubles might brew by the pot, not the barrel," she muttered. "Now, of all times, must my Tuan be gone to the wars. . . . Page!"

A nearby page stiffened.

"Wake the cook; I wish to break my fast presently. Instruct my ladies to lay out my traveling garb!"

The page stared.

"Aye, my traveling garb!" the Queen snapped. "The authority of a recreant religious must be countered by the authority that comes nearest it—which is royalty! A renegade hermit cries that witches are evil; a Queen must pass midst the peasantry and tell them otherwise! Go!"

The page turned and ran.

"Guardsman!"

The pikeman at the door came to attention.

"Go thou after Sir Maris, and instruct him to ready the Queen's Bodyguard for a journey! We ride with the dawn!"

The soldier departed.

The Queen took a stick from the hearth, broke it, and hurled the halves into the fire.

"Swine, dog, and offal!" she spat out. "All the land knows the Queen for a half-witch, and this mockery of a monk hath bile to say . . ."

The broken stick blazed in the fire.

The Queen's eyes drank deep of the flames, as she swore, "May he choke on the cup of his own gall and die!"

By nightfall the mainland lay far behind; the dragon boats had not reappeared. The fishing-boat fleet licked its wounds, murmured soothingly to itself and, nursing its wounded, rode the current back toward Gramarye, to its lair, to lie letting itself heal—and to let a bitter, burning hatred grow deep within it.

The sun had set; the moon had not yet risen. The stars watched, uncaring.

Toby and his brother warlocks had brought salve and, for anesthesia, brandy, as a result of which the wounded lay, anointed and drunken, all about on the decks.

Rod and Gwen sat with Brom O'Berin in the bows, watching the sea foam past them.

"An evil day," Brom was muttering, shaking his head, elbows on knees, eyes on the sea. "A most evil day."

The dwarf was a most excellent mess; his clothes were burned here and there; his hair and beard were singed ragged; burn-welts and bleeding cuts were scattered over his face.

Rod surveyed his own collection of cinder-brands, deciding that he hadn't come off that much better.

"A very evil day," he agreed. "I hadn't exactly thought the expedition would end this way."

"Nay, thou mayst not take all the blame for thine own portion," Brom growled. "Thou didst not advise Tuan against this rash venture; well, so. But neither did I, nor did Tuan himself. For who could ha' foreseen this, lad? 'Twas a footman's war, till now."

"Yes," said Rod grimly, "till now. But now there's heavy artillery, even if it's only catapults. Machine against machine, and army against army, now. Not just man-to-man. What made 'em change, Brom?"

The dwarf shrugged. "We are near to their homeland now; and these war-engines of theirs are most excellent for defense."

Rod shook his head. "Catapults can be very useful for offense, too, especially when they're mounted for quick transport, the way these are. And those big dragon ships under 'em, Brom—it takes a fairly large crew to man them. And you noticed how well those crews were trained? That kind of training takes time. They've been planning this operation for a while." *But why?* "This wasn't just a bunch of raiders improvising a defense."

69

His head came up, eyes widening; then he surged to his feet and began pacing the decks. "Yes, raiders, of course! Why didn't I think about that before?"

Brom scowled up at him. "Think of what? Thou hast known they were raiders!"

"Yeah, but I forgot that raiders don't always have the government behind them! Especially not raiders who're out after loot more than destruction. That kind of boy is out on his own, just trying to get rich the quick way. Like the real Vikings, back on Terra—that was private enterprise, not a coordinated national effort! You decided you wanted to go loot England, say, so you scraped up enough money to build a dragon ship, signed on a crew of fortune hunters, and went out to build your own destiny! The government, what there was of it, wasn't backing you in the slightest!"

Brom frowned. "Dost thou say these beastmen who raided our shores, did so without the knowledge of their king?"

"I'll bet on it," Rod said, his finger stabbing out at Brom. "But I'll also bet their king does know about it now, and has decided to get into the game—with his whole people behind him!"

The dwarf shook his head, scowling. "It could not be just the one raiding party who knew of Gramarye and her riches, Rod Gallowglass. How would the king refrain from the raiding before, and be into it now? Nay, if he had those fireball-ships aforetimes, he most certainly would have harassed our shores! For how could he have lost?"

Rod frowned, brought up short. He nodded slowly, reluctantly. "A point, Brom, though I hate to admit it. . . . Wait a minute. The king had the power before, but he didn't attack, right? It doesn't make sense he'd change his mind so quick, does it?"

"With a fleet such as ours bearing down? Be sure that my own mind would change right quickly then, Rod Gallowglass!"

"No, it wouldn't! If you were the kind of a king who'd stayed out of the fight for so long, you wouldn't get into it all of a sudden! You'd send out a boat under a flag-of-truce for a parley, assure Tuan it was just a bunch of pirates who'd been doing the raiding, promise they'd be killed, and promise to pay damages! But their king didn't; he just called out the navy!"

"Aye; yet still, however unlikely, his mind must ha' changed. How else . . ."

"Revolution!" Rod grinned. "The king hasn't changed his mind, Brom. The beastmen have changed their king!"

"It may be, my lord," said Gwen, troubled. "But how will the knowing of this aid us?"

"Um," said Rod.

He stood a moment, chewing his lower lip.

"The lass hath a point," Brom rumbled.

"Unfortunately," Rod admitted, "I'm afraid she hath. Their domestic affairs may be of great academic interest; but unfortunately, the only way they concern us is one very simple, hard, cold fact: a war-fleet."

"We might wonder, though," Gwen mused, "how it was they knew of our coming. Are they thought-hearers, my lord? But if they were, surely our witches would ha' heard their thought-talk ere now."

"Aye, surely," Brom growled. "Yet they did most surely know."

Rod waved the point away impatiently. "Ever hear of sentries, Brom? A sort of a primitive coast guard? All you'd need would be a few men in small boats."

Brom nodded slowly, scowling. "True. Yet think on this, Rod Gallowglass—how knew they their need to post sentries?"

Rod slowly stiffened.

"Might it not ha' been simple caution?" Gwen asked. "Might they not ha' had such sentries posted this full year, or more?"

"They might," Rod said softly, "but somehow I doubt it—especially if this hypothetical revolution of mine really has taken place. Because if it has, the sentries would have had to have been set by the rebels—who were, presumably, a very small band, until now. And if they'd been running sentries so long, the old king would've found out about it before this."

"If," Brom growled. "If, and if, and if again. Thine house is built on weak foundations."

"Yeah, but even so, I think there's a pretty good probability I'm right. It seems to me, any way you stack the data, you wind up with the beastmen having a spy in Gramarye who told 'em we were coming."

"Mayhap . . ." the dwarf started.

"But!" said Rod, riding roughshod over the dwarf's objections. "But even if I'm wrong, it doesn't matter; 'cause the one and only significant fact we can draw out of this mess of guessing, is this: We need to know what's going on in Beastland. Right?"

Brom's eyes darkened with foreboding.

"In truth, my lord, 'twould aid us greatly," Gwen murmured, "but how are we to learn, when we cannot hear their thoughts?"

"Oh. . . ." Rod squinted sideways at Brom, measuring him. "I'll find a way. . . ."

Brom stirred nervously in his seat and barked, "Look away from me, Rod Gallowglass! Was I not ever thy friend?"

"Oh, of course, of course, Brom." Rod held one hand at the top of Brom's head, the other at the soles of his feet, gauging his length. "Of course you're my friend. After all, I'd never ask a favor like this of an enemy. . . ."

The Baronet of Ruddigore was the prudent type; he had taken some precautions above and beyond what the King had recommended. He had posted a line of dinghies just past the bar along the length of the seaward side of his estates.

The sentries in the dinghies were grumbling at the ocean, since they had nothing else at which to grumble, each being alone in his boat. They had good cause to grumble; a cold wind was blowing in off the sea, and occasional fits of lightning showed them a downpour, rushing toward them over the water.

So they growled at the ocean, and cast longing glances at the shore, and thanked Heaven they'd thought to bring their oilskins.

The storm rushed closer, and the sentry in the center boat cursed as he felt the first drops of rain.

Then the world was harsh white for a split second. The sentry looked up irritably.

Three dragon boats bore down on him.

The world went dark, and the sentry sat frozen a moment.

Then he shrieked warning as he caught at his drum, saw the battle-ax spinn'ng end-over-end toward him. . . .

He fell, his skull split in half, but the warning he'd screamed leaped from boat to boat, shoreward.

It reached the sentries on the beach, and soldiers poured out of the cottages where they were quartered.

High on a nearby hill, young warlocks began to appear around the central fire in a small hut.

A ululating war-cry rose from the long ships as they drove up on the beach.

"Down, men of Kobold!" Atylem cried, driving his warriors before him with the flat of his sword. "Down, to slaughter the cattle who hate you!"

The beastmen leaped into the surf, waded ashore.

The soldiers bellowed, "For God and the King!" and charged with leveled pikes.

The beastmen drew up on the strand in a long, open line and swung their war-clubs high. They were outnumbered three to one, but they chuckled.

The soldiers faltered, stumbled, and halted, staring at the beastmen for long, silent minutes.

Each beastman flicked his glance from one soldier to another.

Jaws gaped, eyes glazed, all along the soldiers' line. Pikes slipped from nerveless fingers.

In the cabin on the hilltop, two dozen warlocks and a witch clasped hands, squeezed their eyes shut.

On the beach, the beastmen yelled victory, stepped forward, clubs swinging.

The soldiers shuddered, gasped, saw clubs and axes swinging down at them.

All yelled; most managed to bring their pikes up in time.

Some didn't; some lay with split heads, with cleaved chests, smashed skulls, blood gushing.

But most lived, blocked the first blow and countered, countered again, and again, screaming hate.

The beastmen fell back, shields high, clubs whirling to fend off blows coming at them from three sides, fear in the faces, teeth clenched, cold sweat on their brows.

One beastman screamed. "Lightning! Send lightning, great Kobold!" and the cry went up all the length of their line, "Great Kobold, send lightning!"

And the downpouring drenched them, but no lightning came.

Slowly, they fell back toward the boats, several wounded, none dead yet, howling for lightning.

The soldiers screamed hope and pressed hard.

Horgil slipped from his place in the line, unseen in the dark. His battle-ax dropped to hang at his belt; his dagger slipped out, his shield swung to his back.

He slipped up behind one of his warriors. His forearm slapped across the man's throat, crushing the windpipe; his other hand shot out before the man's chest with the dagger, and swung.

The beastman fell lifeless and silent, and the soldiers before him cried victory; but Horgil was gone.

Gone to creep up behind another of his beastmen, with choke-hold and dagger, and gone again before the body touched sand.

All along the length of the line the traitor-chief stalked; all the length of the line, beastmen fell dead.

Eight beastmen in all, their blood spreading thick on the sands, before the lightning exploded.

Then the world turned to glaring bluish-white noon, and beastmen saw fallen comrades, and bellowing anger sprang out from their throats.

Night again, black and solid.

And high on the hill, the warlocks lay stunned.

Soldiers froze on the beach, pikes lifted high, and beastmen stepped back, roaring relief with their victory.

Then their eyes narrowed, their glares turned to very sharp icicles, and grins grew slow on their faces.

The soldiers stepped forward, stumbled, stepped out again.

The beastmen's eyes glittered, grins widening, heads nodding in eager encouragement.

Step-stumble-step, the soldiers moved forward.

The beastmen howled and swung in, clubs smashing, rebounding, ax-blades biting deep, wrenching out.

The foot soldiers of the Baronet lay crushed and dismembered side-by-side with the royal troops, blending their blood in a huge, spreading pool.

The villagers screamed and ran for the heights.

The beastmen followed, grinning.

Scarcely an hour later, the burning village lit their way out to sea.

The village morning was sunny and still as the folk wandered home, to their cottages, from the church. A herd of cows lowed in the pasture. A grumpy bumblebee stuttered from flower to flower. Children called gaily in a game of tag.

A trumpet sounded in the distance.

The villagers looked up in surprise.

Out of the dell rode three horsemen, followed by an ornate gilt coach. The horsemen wore tabards with the royal arms blazoned on them. The first bore a trumpet.

The door of the coach was blazoned with the Queen's arms.

Five more horsemen rode behind.

The villagers stared, speechless.

The leading rider lifted the trumpet to his lips and blew a blast.

Housewives came running from the cottages, leaving the roasts to burn. Young folks came running from the meadows and wood.

A tentative cheer went up as the coach approached. It

74

grew, gained certainty and volume, and caught up all the villagers, bellowing lustily.

The coach drew up in the village square; the herald blew another blast on his trumpet, and the crowd stilled, murmuring.

"Hear ye, hear ye!" the herald cried. "Bow down, bow down all, to Catharine, Queen of Gramarye!"

The footman dropped a footstool in front of the coach door, threw it wide.

The Queen stepped forth from the coach, resplendent in a crimson-and-gold crown

The townfolk gasped, flabbergasted at the sight of their Queen in a mere mud-hut village. Then, of course, they cheered.

The Queen smiled tartly in acknowledgment of their praise, waiting till the cheering slackened. When it did, she held up her hands for silence, and the crowd quieted.

"My people," she said, her voice not loud, but clear, and carrying. Her eyes bored into the crowd, and each individual in it suddenly felt that the Queen's eyes were fixed on him personally.

"My people," said Catharine, "our land is sore beset by its enemies."

The crowd sobered on the moment, and some eyed the Queen fearfully.

"Our enemies are aided by the use of the demon-given Evil Eye."

A fretful murmuring passed through the crowd.

"We have but one defense against this evil power—the power of our witches! Our witches alone may lift the black mantle the beastmen throw over the minds of our soldiers!"

The murmuring grew to a low rumble.

The Queen waited till the crowd quieted, then said, "And therefore has your Queen summoned all who know themselves to be witches to appear before the Throne in the King's Court at Runnymede!"

The murmuring started up again, the muted sussuration of a distant surf.

"A week agone," cried Catharine, "my heralds passed through your village, beseeching all witches to come to the Queen. Not a one came. So it hath been in this village, and in many other villages besides.

"Our land stands in peril!" she cried, glaring at her subjects. "And those who alone can protect us, deny us!"

The disquiet in her audience grew.

"Therefore," Catharine snapped with every bit of arrogance at her command, "the Queen herself must now ride forth to decree, to order, to demand of all who feel the slightest hint of witch power within them to come now unto me, here to my coach, and in the presence of the Queen, come to the Coven at Runnymede!"

She let the rumble of the crowd grow, dark and threatening, then cut it off with a shrill, piercing shout. "Who comes to the aid of the homeland? Will they upon whom the salvation of this their nation rests, stand idly by, to watch the enslavement of their countrymen?"

Her mouth shut with a snap. She singled individuals out of the crowd with gimlet eyes, specializing on teenagers.

For a wonder, the crowd was silent, each separate person staring wide-eyed at his Queen—or avoiding her glance entirely.

"Should there be any," said Catharine in a contemptuous, acid tone, "who know themselves to be witch or warlock, let them step forward now, to come with me—or hold themselves forever craven and coward, and traitor to their nation and Queen."

The villagers were silent, eyeing each other furtively, each one dreading that a relative or friend of his would step forward.

A girl, full-figured and pretty, perhaps seventeen, took a fearful half-step forward.

The man and woman who stood behind her gasped, horror, anger, and hatred twisting their faces. Hatred, black hatred, as the girl hesitated. The man's face darkened, stiffening with rage, and a knife flashed from his belt.

"Hold!" cried the captain of the Queen's Guard, and the man looked up, to find himself staring straight at a leveled crossbow.

The girl looked back over her shoulder, saw the knife and the face above it. She screamed and dashed forward, stumbled and fell, scrambled back to her feet. A guardsman ran forward, caught her. She thrashed about screaming in his arms.

"Calm thyself, child," said Catharine in a low, level voice. "I shall not let them harm thee."

The girl froze, her head coming up to stare at the Queen. She looked down, realized it was a guardsman who held her, and collapsed sobbing against his shoulder.

The guardsman gently led her to the Queen's coach.

"It is as thou seest," Catharine's voice rang out. "I shall not permit any to harm the witches of the Queen's Coven."

She turned her head slowly, picking out individual faces in the crowd again.

"Are there none more?" she cried suddenly. "None others with courage among you? None who find in their hearts pity for soldiers?"

Their only answer was silence.

The faces were locked to her now, hostile, defiant and guilty.

Catharine nodded once and said, "Remember, for all time, that there was in this village one soul who knew the duty her God had given her!"

She frowned then, wondering at the sudden startled shock on all the faces before her.

She dismissed it, gave the crowd a look of withering scorn, and whirled about. The footman slammed the coach door behind her and the girl.

Inside the coach, it was Catharine's turn to be confused and uncertain, for a girl nearly her own age was sobbing on Catharine's shoulder; and Catharine began to realize the fullness of what it meant to be Queen. Yet, all she could do was to pat the girl's back and make soothing noises until the sobs quieted.

When they did, Catharine said, in as gentle a voice as she could reconcile with her royalty, "Who were that man and woman, child?"

The girl looked up at the Queen, and horror wrote itself on her face again. "My mother," she gasped, "and my father!"

The tears burst forth afresh, and the coach rolled on, with the Queen cursing herself for a fool.

Brom laughed.

"Oh, cut it out," said Rod peevishly, daubing with the paintbrush.

"That," said Brom, grimacing, "hath already been done. In truth, a great deal of me seems to have been cut away. But if thou meanest, cease, why, I cannot—hee hee!—till thou hast ceased thy doings, Rod Gallowglass. Desist in thy pricking of—haw!—my foot soles!"

"Patience, Brom; just a little more blood here, and we'll be all set."

Brom lay on a table in a ship's cabin, Rod bending over him with a brush and a pot of thick, crimson paint. Between Rod's efforts and a batch of cornstarch-water dough, several paint-pots, and a few leather straps, Brom had begun to look uncannily like the top half of a beastman. He was encased in dough from the chest down, legs and feet immobilized, the fake flesh just under his feet sculpted into an excellent likeness of meat hacked through by a

77

sword. Rod was applying the fake blood to this "wound."

"Why?" Brom sighed. "Why, indeed? Why me?"

"Because you're the only one ugly enough to pass for a beastman, that's why." Rod applied a last judicious blob and stood back to survey his work critically. "Besides, you're the only one with broad enough shoulders and enough other muscles to look like one of 'em."

"The top half of one," Brom reminded.

"Well, naturally. I mean, you're naturally foreshortened, so we make you look like a beastman who's been accidentally cut off from all hope."

"And all else below the waist," Brom growled. "Dost thou imply something in that, warlock?"

"Now, Brom!" said Rod, injured. "Would I do a thing like that? Especially in view of the last time I wrestled you? And lost?" He reached for an iron that had been heating in a brazier.

"True, true," Brom mused.

Rod took the iron away from the "wound" and stepped back, head cocked to one side. "It'll do. Not all that well, but it'll do. You could pass for a corpse that accidentally got cauterized. Remember that, Brom, if the beastmen stop to wonder how you could get chopped like that and still be alive."

"Oh, be assured, I will not forget it!" said the dwarf fervently.

Rod looked up, surprised. "Why, Brom! You, afraid? I thought you were immortal."

"But half-immortal," Brom growled, "only half. Hast thou forgot? I am half man and half elf, and there is the cause of my kingship."

"Oh, yeah, that's right." Rod frowned slightly, and Brom turned to a magenta shade in half a second.

"Nay!" he wailed. "Hast thou no heart, Rod Gallowglass?"

"None," Rod assured him, working up a rich lather in a shaving bowl. "All the reports say the beastmen are beardless, Brom."

"Why, the lesser men they, then! But thou would'st not serve *me* so? Thine aid in disaster, the shield on thy back? Thine own father-by-law?"

"Oh, come off it." Rod daubed on the lather. "A lot of men in Gramarye go clean-shaven. Including the King, as a matter of fact." He lifted the tip of Brom's beard and started cutting.

"A boy, a beardless boy!" the dwarf howled, but carefully holding his head very still. "A youth, scarce into the domain of manhood! A puling, infantile . . . yii! A pox on thy palsied paw!"

"Well, if you wouldn't gripe so much, I might be able to tell where the beard leaves off and you begin. Look, let's check through your cover story again. What happened to you?"

Brom sighed with massive patience and recited, "I was thrown in the water in the midst of the battle, clambered aboard the ship I find myself on, whereupon one of King Tuan's soldiers espied me supine, there in the thick of the fighting, and I was sectioned by a Gramarye sword."

"Right. And the top half of you fell into a fire, which nicely cauterized your waist."

"And therefore am I still alive," Brom finished. "Well, it might do. Still, it stretches the bonds of belief!"

"A point," Rod admitted. "But then, any good spy has to take a few calculated risks, Brom."

The air whooshed nearby them, and Toby floated above the deck. "Master Gallowglass, there is grave news!"

Rod whirled, dropping the razor. "What . . . ? Oh, it's you, Toby! What happened?"

"The beastmen again," the boy said in a hollow voice. "They fell upon the village called Basingstoke, in the Baronetcy of Ruddigore. . . ."

"Basingstoke?" said Rod, unbelieving.

"Basingstoke," said Toby. "Many of the villagers are dead, and all of the soldiers. By great good luck, our warlocks escaped; but they did little good at the battle, for a thunderstorm raged, and the warlocks were struck senseless, all in a moment."

Rod nodded, his face hardening. "So," he murmured, "the new king likes to run two projects at once. But what was this third raid supposed to accomplish? For that matter, what were the first two for? Aside from booty, of course. Maybe just to make the war develop FESS-ter?"

"The major result of the raids, Rod," murmured Fess' voice, "was undeniably the creation of a national emergency on Gramarye. Presumably, it had the same effect in Beastland."

"Yes!" A glitter came into Rod's eyes. "The rebel leader used the raids to create a national emergency, to get the people behind the war party! And this third raid is supposed to clinch the deal!"

Brom and Toby were looking at him, a little strangely.

Rod spun on Toby. "Toby, do me a favor—set somebody

79

to trailing that raiding party, and keep me informed of their whereabouts!"

Toby frowned. "But why, Master Gallowglass?"

"So we can meet them in mid-ocean with our full fleet!" He spun back to Brom, started shaving again, with quick, sure strokes. "After all, we have to create an occasion for smuggling the half-corpse, here, aboard—now, don't we?"

"Hearken to Skolax! To the words of the preacher, hearken and heed!"

The doom-prophet stood atop a boulder in the middle of a meadow, staff held high, horizontal.

Peasants from twelve villages clustered around the base of the rock. More peasants streamed through the trees that bordered the meadow.

"Hearken to the words of the Lord thy God! 'Thou shalt not suffer a witch to live,' saith the Lord! Our land is infested with witches, and none seek to bar them! Is this as the Lord hath commanded?"

"Nay. . . ." came halfhearted murmurs, from various places in the crowd.

Behind them, the Crag Mountains shouldered above the treetops, dark and lowering against the evening sky.

"Hale them down!" the preacher roared. "Trample upon them! One witch cannot withstand a hundred and more of good folk! Hale them down! The Lord hath commanded it, drag them down! Rend them! Raze them! Send them! Send them back to the flames whence they came!"

A building mutter ran through the crowd.

"Will we suffer these witches to live?" Skolax cried, jabbing his staff at the crowd.

"Nay, nay!"

"So thou sayest!" Skolax leaned on his staff, sneering down at his audience. "Yet, in a cave on the mountain nearest to here"—his voice rose, his staff rising with it—"high in the crags of that very peak dwells a hag, most depraved, most evil of witches!"

The crowd gasped and cowered, eyeing the mountain behind them fearfully.

"Hale her down!" stormed the preacher, striking the rock with his staff. "Down and down, to the lowest of Hells! Smite her, strike her, most licentious of women! Hale her down."

"Master Gallowglass!"

Rod's head snapped up as Toby popped into being before him, dark against the paling sky.

"They come, Master Gallowglass! They are near to thee now, three ships of them!"

Rod nodded, smiling tightly. "We're ready, Toby. Let them come."

All night the fleet had quartered across the wind, to reach the northern current at the position the raiders should be in by dawn. They had had an hour to rest, riding at sea anchor, waiting for their prey. Now the beastmen lay just over the horizon, running toward the Gramarye ships; and calls went from boat to boat, as footmen readied their pikes, and archers fitted arrows to their bows.

Rod looked down to the deck beside him, felt a momentary surge of pride at his skill with cosmetics. Of course, there wasn't really enough light to tell yet; but Brom. *did* look very much like the top half of a beastman.

"Cease thy grinning," Brom growled. " 'Tis not thy painting, but mine own skill at playacting."

Rod snorted. "You're ready, though?"

Brom, lying on his back, spread his hands helplessly. "What more might I do? In this guise, I can be but the football of fate."

"True enough," Rod agreed. "I'll go tell the King."

Tuan stood, tousle-headed, sword in hand, with eyes on the horizon.

"Let them come," he said grimly, as Rod came up. "Now let us revenge."

A chill ran down Rod's spine, and he opened his mouth to mutter something a little less bloodthirsty; but just then the lookout cried, "Sai-il!"

Rod spun about.

A square sail loomed above the horizon, silhouetted against the false dawn.

Around them, the air buzzed and rattled with discordant shouts, the clank of arms, as the Gramarye men saw the enemy.

Then the dragon ships were tacking across the wind toward them, bearing down on the fishing-boat fleet.

"The best defense is a good offense, and they know it," Rod growled, "especially when we've got better rigs for sailing into the wind."

"Archers!" Tuan shouted.

Most of the archers and crossbowmen were already in place, touching flame to their arrows.

A flight of arrows arced up from the dragon ships, fire-arrows.

"Buckets!" Rod bellowed. "Stand by to douse fires!" And to Tuan, "I hope this means they don't have catapults."

81

The arrows slammed deep into decking and sail, bouncing off armor and shield.

"Give them their own fire back again!" Tuan cried, and fifteen hands wrenched the burning shafts from the decks.

"Pull!" bawled the King. "Loose!"

The arrows leaped into the sky, a moment before the second volley flew from the dragon ships.

"Loose!" the King cried again, and a flight of crossbow bolts shot high over the beastmen arrows.

Gouts of water sloshed from buckets over the decks of the fishing-boats.

Flames sprang up on the dragon ships, and were drowned.

A man screamed as the second flight of beastmen arrows landed.

"Soldiers!" Tuan shouted. "Light arrows for archers!"

The footmen jumped to obey, and a steady stream of fire began to pour into the dragon ships.

The hail of arrows from the beastmen slackened and died; matchstick figures raced about the decks in frantic haste to put out the fires.

Rod grinned savagely. "They've all got to fight the fires now; they can't spare anyone for archer duty. And they're raiders; they have to travel light and fast; they can't mount catapults. We've got 'em, Tuan."

"Aye." The young King bared his teeth. "Now let them learn how well their cripple can fight. Helmsman! Turn to port!"

The royal fleet swung about, quartering across the gale toward the dragon ships.

Too late, the long ships sheered off, laboring to turn. But a full belly never made a fast runner.

The King's fleet bore down as the beastmen fought to get to windward. Grappling hooks flew out, caught, and held; and with murderous cheers, the King's Foot clambered over the gunwales.

Rod caught Brom up with a whoop, shoved him firmly up onto the deck of the dragon ship, leaped up after him, drawing his sword. His feet hit the deck, and he spun about, swinging a vicious overhand slash that slammed into the decking five inches below Brom's "belt." The dwarf let out with a bloodcurdling shriek, gasped, coughed, rattled, struggled to rise, and collapsed, spread-eagled on the deck.

Rod grinned and shoved him over to the gunwale, where he'd have at least some protection. Beyond that, he had no qualms about leaving Brom unguarded; anybody attacking the dwarf with less than a cannon was in for a bad time.

Rod swung about, sword at the ready, a perverse curiosity clamoring within him for a look at a beastman in the flesh. But he struggled to keep his mind on business, and shouted, "Don't look in their eyes! Stare at their helmets! 'Ware Evil Eye!"

And, of course, half his warriors immediately looked the enemy full in the face.

They froze, pikes upraised.

Rod froze, too, but for another reason. For the first time, he found himself looking at a beastman.

And he recognized it.

Neanderthal.

There was no mistaking the sloping forehead, the brow ridges, the chinless jaw, the lump at the base of the skull. . . .

He had an overwhelming desire to look one in the mouth, to check the dentition. . . .

Then a chill hand clutched his belly.

Neanderthals. Chinless jaws.

Brom had a chin.

And a recent shave.

He swung about, to find Brom again, and toss him back into the King's Fleet, and safety; but two huge beastmen blocked his path, with two huge war-clubs.

All the beastmen had felt a sudden surge of confidence as the Evil Eye took hold on the soldiers; they were grinning again (yes, the dentition *was* right), and swinging their war-axes high.

Rod was saved from the Evil Eye by his fascination with Neanderthal dentition; but one fascination is as good as another, and two clubs were swinging at him.

Half the King's soldiers had heeded Rod's cry, though, and looked at the beastmen's helmets or, more to the point, their axes; their pikes swung up to block the heavy Neanderthal blows.

Rod shook his head, coming out of his daze just in time to see an ax coming edgewise at his sinuses.

A broadsword swung in front of him, lopped off the ax-head.

The next swing lopped off the axman's head.

Rod lifted his shield to guard position, glancing out of the corner of his eyes, yelled, "Thanks, Tuan," and started chopping.

The Neanderthals were just beginning to realize how

badly they were outnumbered. They were thick and powerful, far beyond the average; but three foot-soldiers were still more than a match for one beastman.

"Gwen!" Rod shouted, skewering an enemy, "lift the Evil Eye!"

On the deck of a fishing-boat, Gwen grabbed whatever junior warlocks could teleport to her in two seconds and closed her eyes.

The frozen pikemen came out of their trance with a shudder; then scarlet anger boiled up in them, and they waded in.

It was hopeless slaughter, all over the decks of the dragon ships, as sixty beastmen fought like bears at bay against the whole of an invasion force of thousands. The sky was clear; the beastmen could look for no aid from their Kobold.

Rod hewed his way toward a bull-shouldered beastmean who stood at the tiller, still laboring to turn his vessel.

A wall of Neanderthals formed up in front of him. Rod fell back. "To me!" he yelled, "to the High Warlock! For the honor of Gramarye!"

A squad of spearmen popped up in back of him. Rod waved his arm, bellowing, and advanced, his sword darting and flickering before him.

They chopped a hole in the Neanderthal line and plunged through. Rod lunged for the steersman's heart; but the beastman, still clinging to the tiller with one hand, plucked a club from his belt with the other, beat aside Rod's lunge and, before Rod could recover, whirled the club into Rod's shoulder.

The blow was only from the wrist, but it smashed into muscle and bone like a wrecking ball, whirling Rod around and throwing him to the deck. He ground his teeth against a scream of pain, and threw up his sword to parry whatever blow might be coming.

The steersman towered over him, screaming and swinging his club for the death-blow.

Five soldiers jumped him.

He threw them off, bellowing, as Rod struggled to regain his feet, his head whirling.

Then huge arms caught him around the middle of the body, crushing the breath from him; the ships, the sky, and the sea whirled before him; then a huge splash filled his ears as water struck him like a break-away wall; and water closed over his head.

He fought his way to the surface, one-handed, his left shoulder still throbbing from the blow. His head broke surface, and he gasped. A wave struck him full in the face. He fought to the surface again, a spasm of coughing racking his body; he looked up to see a dozen Gramarye men falling from the dragon ship, behind them a momentary glimpse of the Neanderthal steersman, a long spar in his hands.

Howls filled the air, and another dragon ship vomited soldiers as the crew of beastmen caught up spars and pikeshafts, in imitation.

On the third ship, the few surviving beastmen tried to rally; but, between the dead and the lost-overboard, there were far too few of them. Tuan's men crowded the decks, with their shouting King at their head; and, one-by-one, the beastmen began to abandon the ship.

Rod swam as best as he could with one arm, and tried to clamber up the sleek, mossy side of the dragon ship. A soldier fell into him, knocking him back.

As he surfaced again, spewing water, the long ship turned, her stern lumbering around to the wind, and the great striped sail filled.

Rod shouted something incoherent, but the ship glided away, picking up speed, long oars coming out to add their push to the wind's.

The second dragon ship glided after it; but a howling rose from the third, and Rod turned to see the last of the beastmen leaping from its decks, shedding their armor in mid-air.

The second dragon ship sprouted ropes, flung into the waves; the swimming Neanderthals caught them and clung, scrambling up the sides; then she was gliding away, with all the survivors of its crew, and all the living beastmen from the third ship aboard her.

The third ship, decks awash with blood, loomed above Rod. He looked up, saw Tuan standing in the bow, behind the great dragon head, soaking wet with as much blood as seawater.

The prow loomed up and glided by; a rope fell near Rod. He grabbed it and clung one-handed, as the men on deck hauled him up, bumping against the side.

Up and over the gunwale, onto the blood-soaked deck. He thanked the men who had fished him out and turned away to find the King, wincing as every other step jolted up to his shoulder.

"Well, we ha' taken one of them, Rod Gallowglass." Tuan had a very black look about him.

Rod frowned. "That's a victory."

Tuan whirled away and spat, slamming his heel against

the deck in fury. Then, calmed a little, he turned back to Rod, rage glowing deep in his eyes.

"Victory! Thou speakest victory when, with a fleet against three, we can take but the one? Victory, aye! Victory for them! Count our dead, and count theirs! If thou canst find more than five beastman corpses, I shall pay thee a bounty for the sixth! And we, if we have lost but a score, we may cry thanks to Heaven! Victory! Aye, twenty lives for a boat and six beastmen! Great victory is ours!"

"They're trained for sea fighting," Rod said gravely, "and your boys aren't."

Tuan's eyes narrowed. "Seek not to soothe me, Rod Gallowglass! 'Tis deeper by far, as thou knowest! These beastmen are fighters such as never this land ha' seen, even though stripped of their Evil Eye!"

He turned away, pacing, fist slapping thigh, eyes roving the sea.

"If they come," he said softly, "to Gramarye, full force, not mere raiders—if they come, why then, Heaven help us; for sure, we shall not be able to give aid to ourselves!"

"Come off it!" Rod snapped, and the King turned, perhaps as much in surprise at being addressed in anger as anything else.

Rod thrust his face within an inch of Tuan's and said, low and hard, "They're brave fighters, Majesty, but not brave enough. We outnumber them, ten to one—or had you forgotten?"

A sour smile played about Tuan's lips. "Outnumber? Why, so we did today; and praise Heaven for it, or we might all lie dead."

"But we did," Rod said, "and we don't."

"Oh, aye, aye," the King admitted. "Yet bear in thy mind, this—the sky was quite clear. If they come to our land, thou mayst be certain that they shall choose the time of their coming for weather more suited to their manner of fighting; and against that Evil Eye, Rod Gallowglass, we are powerless."

"There wasn't any lightning; so we haven't really faced the Evil Eye one single time on this whole expedition," Rod said tightly. "We've proved nothing about our abilities against it, either way. All we've proved is that they've got a weapon we didn't have, but will soon—the fireball catapults—and that, man for man, they're fiercer fighters. But that last we can counter with numbers of soldiers, and the first we can counter with witches and catapults of our own."

The King stared at the deck, scowling, lips pursed.

"Thou hast reason," he said, lifting his head slowly. "And I had forgot. Mayhap we may yet all live; yet in my deep heart of hearts, I do doubt it."

"Now to another matter," Rod said, setting his fists on his hips and flinching as pain lanced his shoulder. "Is Brom on this ship?"

"I ha' not seen him," said Tuan, looking up in surprise. "Nay, I am sure; he is not among us." He frowned. "There is concern in thine eyes, Rod Gallowglass; yet is this not in accord with thy scheming?"

"It was," said Rod grimly, and opened his mouth to say more; then he reflected that the King had enough to worry about as it was. He turned to watch the beastmen's sails disappear over the rim of the world, fervently hoping that Brom's immortal genes were dominant.

The hooves of the horses of the Queen's Guard struck hollow on the drawbridge, then clattered on the paving as they passed under the portcullis and into the courtyard.

The Queen slipped out of the coach with a gusty sigh, and turned to catch up the goblet of wine a page offered her. She drained it at a breath, and patted her lips with the napkin the page proffered. "Thou hast performed thy duties well, lad," she informed him as she flicked the napkin back.

The page flushed with pleasure and embarrassment, ducked his head in a bow, and turned to run back to the kitchen.

Catharine turned to frown at Sir Maris, who hovered anxiously in the background.

"Who of the Queen's Coven is present?" Catharine demanded, looking sternly about her.

Alicia, one of the older witches (she was all of seventeen) stepped forward.

"Ah," said the Queen. Well."

She turned about, holding out a hand toward the coach door. Hesitantly, the village witch-girl stepped out.

Catharine took Alicia's hand, placing the village girl's within it.

"Greta," she said, "this is thy sister, Alicia; she shall teach thee thy lessons of witchcraft, show thee thy lodgings, and join thee with the rest of thy sisters and brethren. If thou art troubled in thy heart, Greta, and hast need to speak of thy cares to one older than thee, thou shalt come to see me."

A startled gasp ran through the assemblage; personal interest in one of her subjects was very rare in the Queen.

Then to Alicia, "I give to thee the care of this child. See that she wants for naught."

When the two witch-girls had turned away, Catharine turned her head, seeking out the old Master of Guardsmen. "Sir Maris."

"Majesty!" The bent, black-robed figure hobbled forward, leaning heavily on his staff.

"Now, Sir Maris—what news of the fleet?"

"Majesty," said the old knight hesitantly, "they were driven from the homeland of the beastmen by a witchcraft with balls of fire." At the look of alarm in her eyes, he rushed on: "Thine husband is well, though they ha' fought a second battle since then, and have taken one dragon ship."

Catharine relaxed, her eyes glowing. "Victory!" she murmured. "And he whole. Praise God!"

"The warlock who brought us the news," Sir Maris continued, "gave word that the fleet shall beach this very night at Loguire; and with good fortune, the King shall return in two days to the castle."

Catharine's eyes kindled; but she said only, "Sir Maris, when they are returned, do thou wait one night, then summon the High Warlock, Rod Gallowglass, to mine audience-chamber."

The old knight's eyes widened in surprise; what weighty business was this, that the Queen must bid him to it so far ahead?

Brom felt naked without his beard. He knew that if he had not shaved it, he would not have lasted a moment among the beardless beastmen. Still, the bush of black beard had clothed his cheeks since earliest manhood, and he felt strangely emasculated without it.

And having been seemingly cut off at the waist didn't exactly diminish the feeling. Even though he knew his own legs were still with him, firmly encased inside the ersatz flesh of his "belly," he somehow felt weakened, and very, very defenseless.

It was a bad feeling, especially since he was thoroughly at the mercy of his beastman "rescuer." He lay inside the creature's hut, on a bed of furs, a pallet on the floor, and the bark walls and leafed roof towered over him. The hut was, moreover, filled with the rancid smoke of a tallow lamp, one which gave much more smoke than light.

Brom lay alone in the hut. The woman and children who had been there, when Brom was brought in, had gone to join in the crowd that milled about outside; the howling of angry voices came clearly through the thin bark walls.

Brom shuddered, thinking how quickly that pack could turn to tear him, limb from body. Yes, he was immensely indebted to his rescuer.

So far. His squat, shambling host was up to something, and whatever it was, Brom had a nasty, nagging suspicion that it boded no good for himself. At the moment, though, Brom supposed he was safe, for only he and the beastman knew the monstrous extent of the lie.

At least, Brom hoped no one else knew yet.

And a fantastically huge lie it was, for the beastman had claimed Brom as his relative.

"Be still!" the beastman had hissed in his ear, as he clutched Brom to his huge chest, after stumbling over him near the gunwale. "Thou must needs appear all but a corpse; and thy face must needs be hid, or they will know thee for what thou art!"

Brom froze.

The beastman had wailed, "Oh, kin to my blood, and my flesh! How they have racked thee!" while he strode away down the deck to deposit Brom on a folded cloak underneath his own rowing bench, instructing Brom, in a whisper, to groan and moan deliriously if anyone came by and, above all, to keep his face out of the light.

Brom had followed the instructions with a verve and a zeal uncommon even in him, all through the long voyage back to Beastland.

And now Brom lay here, in his "cousin's" hut, once again on the verge of asphyxiation—he had a feeling that fresh air was going to be a decided rarity for the next week or two.

More to the point, how could he find out what was going on in Beastland if he had to stay cooped up in the hut?

Of course, the voyage home had been instructive, in a way. He had overheard some very strange talk; now, if he could only find out how to make sense of it, he might have something worth reporting.

The warriors had scarce settled into the rhythm of the oars after escaping from the Gramarye fleet when the steersman turned his great sweep over to his second and strode down the deck, between the ranks of oarsmen, to the great dragon head at the prow.

There he whirled about, fists on hips, facing the crew, and bellowed, "Who doubts now that they hate us?"

The crew looked up, startled. Then a few muttered, "None, Atylem." "None." "All know that. . . ."

"They slew us on the beach," Atylem bellowed, "eight of us, all their fleet against ours. Indeed, they must have known of our raiding, known our ship's path, for they sailed against the current to meet us!"

Ugly growls rose here and there among the crew.

"Destroy them!" Atylem hissed, his eyes narrow coals. "Destroy those who hate us for being stronger than they, who hate us because they have not the Eye! Rend them! Tear their limbs from their bodies! Split the bones of those who would crush you!"

The crew roared, rising from their benches.

"Down to your oars!" Aylem thundered. "They may yet pursue us!"

The beastmen subsided, turning back to their rowing with ugly growls.

In the blackness under the bench, Brom shuddered.

The ship was relatively quiet for a while. The crew talked in low growls, the waves lapped at the sides, the oars chopped into the long swell.

Then Atylem began to talk with his second, in a low muttering voice which nonetheless carried to the bows, clear and angry. The crew fell silent, eavesdropping.

"It is in my belly, Dalzin, to wonder if Shaman has misled us in this raid."

The crew stiffened and feathered their oars.

Dalzin murmured something in a shocked tone.

"Nay, I dare indeed say it!" snapped Atylem. "Three of the men on this ship have died, eleven amongst the other two ships—eight in the raid, and six in the sea fight! Is this the victory Shaman promised us from the Kobold?"

Brom caught a few words from Dalzin's answer: "Surely . . . not yet . . . openly show . . ."

"Aye, aye," Atylem growled, "when the Kobold may openly show his great power, we shall in all truth be unbeaten, aye. And, to that, how could Shaman have known their fleet would seek us out? . . . Still, the Kobold must ha' known; why did he not tell Shaman?"

After a moment, Atylem said, slowly, "Or it may be the Kobold did tell him, and Shaman considered, then thought it best not to tell me. May it not be so?"

And before Dalzin could answer, Atylem went on, "It is enough to make a man heed this murmuring talk I have heard, that Shaman will not deal fairly with us, his chiefs and sub-chiefs, for fear we might gain too much of his power. And that other gossip, that Grakild seeks to destroy

90

me, so that he may have both his power and mine, and . . . Phaugh! I tell you, Dalzin, I have no stomach for this ruling of Shaman, that there must be a war-chief for each thousand of warriors, and myself chief of the war-chiefs. A plague of boils upon it! Why not one war-chief over all the tribe, as was ever the way of our peoples!"

Dalzin's answer carried clear this time: "It is the will of the Kobold, Atylem!"

Atylem was silent a moment. Then, grudgingly: "Aye, that it is, it is the Kobold's chosen way of ruling. . . . Aye, it must needs be right then, for who dares question the Kobold?"

And Atylem lapsed into a moody silence, maintained for the rest of the voyage.

That had been all Brom had learned so far; still, it might be enough. There was some discontent among the beastmen; but what good did that do Gramarye?

Of course, if Brom could find a way to foster that discontent . . .

The hide hanging at the door swung away, showing a massive, cloaked silhouette against the light of a blazing bonfire outside; then the skin swung to behind the beast-man, and the tallow lamp illuminated him dimly as he threw off his fur cloak. Powerful, swollen muscles rippled under leather-strap armor, dwarfing even Brom's mighty arms. The beastman strode to the center of the hut and sat on his heels, stirring up the embers of a cook fire with a massive forefinger, warmed his hands at the flames with a huge sigh. He dipped up a bowlful of ale from a great tub that stood near, drinking it off in one breath.

Wiping the back of a huge paw across his mouth, he rose and moved slowly toward Brom, a huge, shambling shadow with the light at his back.

Brom's stomach curled in on itself. He tensed his muscles, gathering himself for a leap at the monster's throat.

"I am Kroligh," the dark, towering form rumbled. "Be at peace in my home."

Brom blinked.

Kroligh sat down with a gusty sigh, near Brom but looking a little away from him; nonetheless, the dwarf was sure the beastman was watching him closely out of the corner of his eye.

"It was well for you I was first to stumble upon you," Kroligh growled, "for 'tis plain at a glance that you are not of us; and therefore, you must be of our enemy."

Several questions clamored in Brom's mind; the first one that got out was, "How is it so plain?"

The beastman turned, touching a great splay fingertip to Brom's chin. "This; this knob, here. We none of us have it. Only you of the island have it."

It was true, Brom saw, looking at Kroligh's face with a new understanding; the beastman had no chin, the jaw sloped back toward the neck. Brom's heart sank as he realized how close he had come to death.

"Why didst thou, then, give me succor?"

The beastman nodded ponderously, musing. "You are the enemy of we who fight for the Kobold," he said, "and for Shaman. And Shaman fights Kernel. And therefore you fight for Kernel."

"Kernel?" Brom frowned.

"Kernel, aye. While we were raiding your nation, Shaman was to have roused the people against Kernel, to chase him and slay him. But I know the Kernel, as all here do, and know him for what he is—a god, though he denies it; a god, or a half-god at least, with a god's strength and power. It was in my belly to hope that Kernel had escaped Shaman's vengeance; and on the chance of that, I saved you and sheltered you."

Brom lay quiet, stray thoughts spinning through his mind.

"Thou dost no longer wish to fight for the Shaman?"

The beastman shook his head, his eyes hardening.

Brom felt a strange dread welling within him; but he asked the question anyway.

"Why?"

Kroligh's eyes glittered frozen fire, and his breath hissed out in a razor-edged whisper. "Because I have seen on the beach in this raid, a chief stabbing men of his own in the back!"

He bowed his head, eyes hooded in shadow, great shoulders hunched, a line of muscle standing out between jaw and temple; and somehow, Brom knew the grief, the confusion, despair, rage, and clawing revenge-ache in the huge, hulking form.

Slowly, then, Kroligh lifted his head, bleak eyes searching out Brom's. "It is true, little man; I have seen it. While we battled your soldiers, Horgil crept amongst us with his blade, and slew eight."

He turned his eyes away. "I have no stomach for this, guest of my house. Such treacherous evil was never amongst us before, not in our Old Land, nor even in this, while Kernel ruled over us."

He straightened, shoulders squaring. "I will not have it, my guest. I will have Kernel back though I die for the doing of it. For my hope was well-founded, and Kernel has fled with his captains, fled over the cliff to the swamp! I would go there to join him myself, but . . . I have a wife and three children. . . ."

Brom cleared his throat, a little hesitantly. "Good mine host . . . Might not your leman and bairns enter, and hear us?"

Krolight lowered his head, turning it slightly; a quirk of a smile touched his lips. "Nay, guest of mine, they will not come. They are there"—he tossed his head toward the door—"in the war dance."

Brom's stomach bounced downward. "War?"

"War dance, aye." Kroligh surged to his feet, and paced the hut. "For when we came to the beach, we raiders, and the tally of our dead was made known, there was wailing and keening, and Shaman crying out our blood-debt, whipping the people all to a fury." He bowed his head, shaking it slowly. "Till now, there was hope for stopping this war. But with this landing, with the tale of our dead, it is blood-feud. Now our peoples must fight till one of them falls."

"And still thou wilt protect me," Brom murmured.

Kroligh's head snapped up, furious. "Aye! For I know, I alone, with whom our blood-feud must be. With Horgil, with his masters Atylem, and Shaman, and above all the Kobold! But how may I strike, I with my woman and children here in the village, here where Shaman rules hard? How!"

And he strode to Brom, his shoulders hunched, his eyes burning, finger jabbing out like a sword. "How? I shall tell you. Through you! This much may I do to call Kernel back here, to rule us! This much, to keep you alive, that you may bring word to your island, that there are those here among us who would fight by your side, were we able!"

He straightened abruptly. "For I am not alone in this! Not I alone wish the Kernel back! For scarce had the people fought off your fleet when some among them began to—have second thoughts. The dragon ships, for one—where had they come from? None had seen them before; how had they chanced to be ready?

"And the Kobold is a monstrous god; that, they learned when they were brought, one by one, to its worship.

"But more than all, it was Shaman's chiefs, the ones under Atylem, like me. But few were as I am, willing and ready to work long in the fields; that may be due to few having wives, as I do. The most of them, they were great lazy louts, leaning against trees, talking battle, speaking against Kernel—aye, he allowed it—speaking against our plowing and hoeing, calling it women's work, unfit for a man. The only work fit for a man, said they, was hunting and warring; and what manner of god was Kernel, if he gave them little enough of the first, and none at all of the last? Why, a woman's god, was he not?

"Yet few paid heed to them. And now we wish that we had, that we had at least suspected them of secret doings, for these men are now Shaman's under-chiefs, and under-under-chiefs, and they swagger about insulting whom they wish, pawing men's wives and daughters, bragging and boasting of their glory in battle, calling all other men less than male—and that alone is enough for the people to wish Kernel back."

Brom frowned. "Are there many such in this village?"

Kr#oligh snorted, mirthless. "Who can say? For each man keeps his thoughts in his own belly, alone. They have seen what happened to those few who did dare speak in anger to the under-chiefs; so none speak against Shaman, where others may hear them.

"But I have seen for myself that five families are no longer here, in the village. And news travels quickly among us, news that one family was caught climbing the cliff, and was slain out of hand. Aye, slain, all! Man, wife, and children, aye, even children!"

He swung about, his eyes burning down into Brom's. "No, you may be sure of it—seven families are there now in the swamps with Kernel. And you must now join them."

Brom lurched up on his elbow. "I?"

Then the dwarf frowned, looking away, nodding his head thoughtfully. "Aye, thou hast the right of it, good mine host; for if it is so easily seen that I am not of thy people, I die if I set foot past thy door. I have therefore two roads—the one back to Gramarye, with near nothing learned; or the other, over the cliff to the swamp, to the men free to fight by my side."

Kr#oligh nodded grimly. "You will be welcome there; aye, be sure of it. For they will be plotting already to bring Shaman low; there is blood-feud between his clan and Kernel's now."

He swung away to snatch up his cloak. "I shall take you now, through the crowd and the war-cries, when with you under my cloak I shall be least remarked. I shall set you down on the beach with a hollowed-log boat; then you must paddle your way past the cliffs to the jungle-beach, find a river, and make your way inland to the swamps. This much can I do for you, and no more."

94

He fumbled at his belt for a broad-bladed knife. "There are great, crawling lizards in the swamps," Kroligh muttered. "You may have great need of a blade. Farewell, and tell this to the Kernel: that there are those in this village who will fight at his call."

The Queen sat at the fireside with a cup of mulled wine, fighting a losing battle with her eyelids; she had had precious little sleep in the last few days.

"Majesty," said the page, materializing in the doorway, "I present the High Warlock."

Catharine looked up—slowly; her head felt a little on the heavy side. "He may enter."

The page disappeared; Rod marched in. He gave a perfunctory bow, notable for its lack of sincerity. "What does Your Majesty require of your humble servant?"

"A little less sarcasm, for one," said the Queen. She waved at a chair. "Be seated, Lord Gallowglass."

"I'm not a lord," said Rod automatically, but he sat anyway.

Catharine's head snapped up, eyes flashing. "If the King His Majesty hath said thou art lord, then lord thou art!"

"Received," said Rod wearily, "and acknowledged. I'm noble."

"A point of contention," said the Queen tightly, looking into her wineglass. "Yet thou shalt be addressed as 'Lord,' for mine husband hath said it."

Well, he'd managed to wake her up, anyway. Rod sighed, and asked, "What did you want to see me about, Your Majesty?"

"I have been sniffing out witches," said Catharine, her voice carefully controlled, "and have found one within twelve miles of this castle."

"One, on the first try?" Rod's eyebrows went up. "Not bad, not bad at all. Your Majesty is to be commended— but if the kid was that close to Runnymede, how come she didn't come in on her own, a little sooner?"

" 'Tis that that I wish to tell thee," said Catharine impatiently. "I had some converse with the lass as we drove back to Runnymede."

Rod hazarded a guess. "She didn't come in because she was afraid of royalty."

"Nay. She had not come forth, Lord Gallowglass, due to the authority of parents and village, which had more place in her heart than royal decree."

Rod sat silent for a moment.

He stirred, turning to look into the fire. "She was afraid

95

of her parents, and what her neighbors would think of her?"

"Aye, and how they would treat her parents for begetting a witch."

Rod nodded, brooding. "I thought public opinion was turning in favor of the witches."

"Mayhap it was," said Catharine, "and mayhap it would have continued to do so, had there not been a voice raised against it."

"Whose?" said Rod softly, with incipient murder in his voice.

"A holy man," said Catharine, sitting back in her chair.

Rod's mouth slowly opened, then snapped shut. He sat back, a touch of disgust in his face. "I should have known," he murmured.

" 'Tis a renegade friar," said the Queen, toying with her wineglass, "or seems to be. I ha' spoke with My Lord the Archbishop, and he disclaims all knowledge of the recreant, as do his abbots."

"A self-appointed Jonah," said Rod, smiling tightly, "living in a cave in the hills on berries and bee-stings, calling himself a holy hermit, and a prophet, and never, ever, washing."

"He preaches against me," said Catharine, her hand tightening on the glass, "and therefore against the King also. For I gather the witches to me, here to the castle, and therefore am I unworthy of mine royal blood, and mine husband of his crown, though he be anointed sovereign of Gramarye; for mine own slight witchcraft, says this preacher, is the work of the devil."

Progress, Rod noted silently. Two years ago, she wouldn't have admitted to her own telepathic powers, rudimentary though they were.

"And therefore," said the Queen, "are we agents of Satan, Tuan and I, and unfit to rule. And, certes, all witches in our land must die." She released her wineglass, striking the table with her fist.

Catharine let her head drop into her hands, massaging the temples with her fingertips. "Thus is all our work, thine, mine, and Tuan's, our work of two years and more, 'tis brought low in a fortnight; and this not by armies or knights, but by one unclean, self-ordained preacher, whose words spread through the land faster than ever a herald might ride. It would seem there is no need of battles to unseat a King; rumor alone is enough."

"I think," Rod said slowly, "that this is one little virus that had better be quarantined and eliminated but fast.

Where's he operating—uh, preaching? Do you know, Your Majesty?"

"Our new witch ha' said that the news had come from the south," said Catharine wearily. There was a certain hopeless quality about her.

"Stumping villages in the south." Rod nodded. "And his voice is so loud they hear his sermons in the north."

He slapped his thigh and stood, turning away to the door. "Sir Maris and the King can take care of everything that has to be done here, Your Majesty. And Toby can whip the warlock forces into shape, with your help. For myself, I'm going to take a week off and go snake-hunting."

Gwen edged her way along a narrow rock ledge, telling herself there was nothing to be afraid of; but herself wasn't listening too well.

It wasn't the half-mile drop below that was worrying her; she had her broomstick clenched firmly in one hand—if she fell, the broomstick would have her back up on the ledge in almost no time at all.

The black cave-mouth to her left, however, was another matter. Gwen knew that, as a witch herself, she had nothing to fear from old Agatha; but in her childhood, she had heard as many fairy tales about wicked old witches as the next child; and all the cradle epics came flooding back as she sidled toward the dank darkness of the witch's lair.

Also, the fact that Angry Agatha had been mentioned by name in many of those stories, in a featured, popular, but not entirely sympathetic role, did not aid Gwen's tremors at all. A comparison of the relative weights of logic and childhood conditioning in determining the mature human's emotional reactions makes a fascinating study in theory; but firsthand observation of the practical aspects can be a trifle uncomfortable.

She stumbled; her foot went off the ledge, and she plunged forward. She snapped a thought at her broomstick; her elbows cracked as it jerked upward, to deposit her safely once more on the ledge.

She could, of course, have simply flown into the cave on her broomstick; but in approaching a witch's den, the utmost circumspection is highly recommended, especially if you happen to be another witch, with conflicting political views. . . .

A hideous, bony face thrust out of the hole in the rock, wisps of smoke streaming from it, grinning like a gargoyle, cackling.

Gwen plastered herself back against the wall in a paroxysm of terror.

Agatha's smile faded a bit, then hardened with irony. She nodded, slowly. "Eh, then, thou too, eh? Even thou, Gwen Gallowglass, who art thyself a witch, and wife to a warlock—even thou fearest old Agatha, dost thou?"

She held Gwen's eyes for a moment. Gwen stared back, fascinated; for here was the witch of her childhood, come before her. The body was wasted, emaciated; the leached and mummied skin was a fantastic netting of wrinkles. The long, greasy hair was white, stained toward yellow a bit. A long, thin blade of a nose protruded between bloodshot, rheumy eyes of a faded blue, the whites also yellowed a bit. There were huge, yellowed-white tufts of eyebrows, and a gash of mouth between sunken, wrinkled cheeks. A few straggling hairs sprouted from a great mole on her lantern jaw.

Her blouse, shawl, skirt, and the kerchief that bound her hair might once have had some coloring of a sort; but only varying shades of gray could now be seen through the dirt and grease that encrusted the cloth.

Yet there was something about the old woman, something in the way she carried herself, in the way she held her head on her thin, hunched old shoulders, some lingering shadow of pride and womanly wariness, that told you she once had been beautiful.

She shook her head, mouth tight with exasperation and contempt, and turned back to her cave. "Nay then, come in, lass. I'll not harm a witch, and a mother."

Gwen stayed rooted to the rock for a moment, staring at the spot where old Agatha had been. Then, swallowing an enormous lump in her throat, she sidled into the cave.

The rock flared out just inside the doorway, widening into a domed chamber perhaps twelve feet high and twenty-five across. Gwen picked her way through an obstacle course of stalagmites and stalactites, ducking now and then to avoid a sharp point. She shied away from the three black bats that hung in a row at her left.

She was more than a little ashamed of herself when she realized she was watching for stray bones.

Before her, the cave narrowed, forming a yard-wide archway. Ruddy light glowed through the moth-holes in the tattered old blanket that hung across the constriction in lieu of a door.

Brushing through the rotting wool, Gwen came into a smaller cavern. The walls had been hewn away on either side to make deacon's benches. A rough wooden table stood in the center of the room; behind it, in a huge firepit, a bonfire blazed.

Cobwebs filled the corners, festooned the ceiling. Jars and bottles of vile-looking stuffs lay all about, on the floor, on the table, on the benches, filling two vast shelves on the far side of the firepit. The floor was carpeted with patches of anemic-looking moss, liberally sprinkled with toadstools.

A huge, steaming black caldron hung over the firepit, chuckling with malevolence. The witch stood hunched over it, her back to Gwen, stirring with a long wooden paddle.

And a gleaming, polished skull sat on the table.

Gwen shuddered and braced herself against the wall.

"Come in, come in," the old witch snapped impatiently. "There's a chair by the table there."

Gwen nervously picked her way between patches of moss (which, upon closer inspection, looked more like mold) and sat down at the table, keeping as much distance as possible between herself and the skull. She kept her broom clutched tightly in her hands.

Agatha frowned, looking up at Gwen's silence. She watched the girl for a moment, then smiled bitterly. "Aye, 'tis scarcely a pretty kitchen, is it? One scarce might credit it, but in my youth, I was diligent in my housekeeping. But now . . . Things lose importance in age, child, in long, lonely age. One neglects things. . . . My life is like this room now, moldering and garbage-strewn. . . ."

She turned back to the pot, stirring with a vengeance. "And have no fear of Iyorika there; she'll not hurt you."

"Iyorika . . . ?"

"The skull," said the old witch; and, with an ironic smile, "My mother. My mother in witchcraft, at least; she who dwelt in this cavern before me, and welcomed me here in the first days of my banishment."

"Thy . . . teacher?" Gwen ventured.

"Aye, in a measure; but more than that, too. I came, in the bloom of my youth, still at an age when I should have been innocent, but knowing already the abusage of men. I clambered along the ledge, seeking a refuge redoubtable; and I came to this cave. 'Eureka!' I cried; and a crackling old voice from within quavered, 'Who calls my name?' "

"And . . . and it was this skull?"

"Nay; there was flesh on her bones yet, albeit precious little. She lay on a couch, palsied with ague, near to death —quite near; she was gone in three hours. Yet in that short time she taught me the mission and anguish and glory of witch-hood—to give, and give more, and ever more of yourself, though your wages are never but pain and exile, persecution and agony."

" 'Tis the work of a saint," Gwen whispered wide-eyed.

"Nay; 'tis but the age-old work of all womankind, though intensified thousandfold by the denial of those consolations and comfortings which are woman's by right. Not the work of a saint, lass, but nobility; for we are a kind of nobility, we, born with gifts denied to the many; and in those gifts we are cursed. That is just cause for bitterness, true; yet the knowledge of nobility is great consolation. To us it is given to aid and to guard, and that is great gifting. We are of the Blood, thou and I and Iyorika; but birth to the Blood brings obligings withal; nobility is obliged, in truth; yet it hath the great comfort of knowing itself to be noble."

Agatha was quiet a moment, stirring the brew.

"All this she taught thee, in so short a time?"

"Aye, this and more, many powerful spells. 'Twas her last act of giving. She died." The old witch heaved a convulsive sigh. "Aye, she died; and I set myself to live in her cave, setting her skull on the table, as she had bade me, that she might speak and warn me when my life was endangered; and she has spoke often, down through the years." She glanced at Gwen over her shoulder. "Rejoice, girl, that you live in the new day which has dawned upon us, when the Queen protects those of witch-power, and a witch may find out a warlock to wed her."

Gwen blushed, and lowered her eyes. "In that, I know, I am most fortunate, reverend dame," she murmured.

"Most excellent fortunate, to be sure," the old witch agreed. "Yet I doubt thou knowest the true extent of thy fortune. There was no tall young wizard for me, but a horde of plowboys from mountain villages, who came by ones and by fives to me for a moment's pleasure, then came threescore all together, with their mothers and sisters and wives and their stern village clergy, to flog me and rack me, and pierce me with hot needles, crying, 'Vile witch, confess!' till I could contain it no longer, till my hate broke loose upon them, smiting them low and hurtling them out from my cave!"

She broke off, gasping and shuddering. Alarmed, Gwen clasped Agatha's hands in her own, and felt the chill of them creep up to her backbone. She had heard the tale how, long years ago, the witch Agatha had flung the folk of five villages boiling out of her cave, how many had broken their heads or their backs on the slopes far below. No witch in Gramarye, in all the long history of that eldritch island, had been possessed of such power; most witches could lift only two or three at a time. And as for hurling them about with enough force to send them clear of a cave—why, that was flatly impossible.

Wasn't it?

Therefore, if a witch had indeed performed such a feat—why, obviously, she must have a familiar, an invisible, helping spirit.

" 'Twas then," panted old Agatha, "I came to this cavern, where the ledge without was so narrow that only one man could enter at once; and so that, in my wrath, I might never injure more than a few. But those few . . ."

The scrawny shoulders slackened, the back drooped; the old witch slumped against the rough table. "Those few, aie! those few . . ."

"They sought to burn thee," Gwen whispered, tears in her eyes, "and 'twas done in anger, anger withheld overlong, longer than any man might contain it! They debased thee, tortured thee!"

"Will that bring back dead men?" Agatha croaked, darting a whetted glance at Gwen.

She thrust against the table, came to her feet again, brushed Gwen roughly aside, and took up her paddle to stir the brew again; but her shoulders still trembled.

The caldron bubbled and seethed. Softly, softly, the old witch crooned an incantation into it, calming herself.

Gwen flinched from the stench that rose from the caldron. "What . . . what dost thou brew?"

"Brew?" The old witch looked up in surprise. "Why, it is naught but the year's laundry, girl." She smiled sourly. "Belike thou bethought 'twas a compound vile, of adder's tongues and two-tailed lizards; didst thou not? Eh, thou wouldst still hark to the old wives' tales, wouldst thou not? Even thou, who hast witch-hood within thee, thyself!"

She turned back to her work, shaking her head. "Child, child!"

Gwen stared at the old, gnarled hands, fascinated. "Agatha . . ." Gwen bit her lip, then rushed on. "Dost thou wish to repay the lives thou hast taken?"

The hag lifted her head, blinked old, rheumy eyes. "Ah, then," she crooned, and cackled. She nudged the skull with her elbow and cackled louder. "I had pondered the why of thy coming," she said, nodding and wiping her eyes, "for none come to old Agatha lest they have a wish, a wish that may not be answered by any other. And this is thine, is it not? That the folk of the land lie in danger;

101

they stand in need of old Agatha's power. And they have sent thee to beg me the use of it!"

Her gaunt body shook with another spasm of cackling. She wheezed into a crooning calm, wiping her nose with a long, bony finger. "Eh, eh! Child! Am I, a beldame of threescore and more, to be cozened by the veriest, most innocent child? Eh!" And she was off again.

"Nay," Gwen said, "I have come of my own, to beg of thee . . ."

"Of thy own!" The witch glared. "Hast thou no stripes to thy back, no scars to thy breasts, where their torturers have burned thee? Hast thou not known the pain of their envy and hate, that thou shouldst come, unforced, uncajoled, of thy own, to beg help for them!"

"I have." Gwen felt a strange calm descend over her. "Twice I was scourged, and thrice tortured, four times bound to a stake for the burning; and I must needs thank the Wee Folk, my good guardians, that I live now to speak to thee. Aye, I ha' known the knotted whip of their fear; though never so deeply as thou. Yet . . ."

The old witch nodded, wondering. "Yet you pity them."

"Aye." Gwen lowered her eyes, clasping her hands tight in her lap. "Indeed, I do pity them." Her eyes leaped up to lock with Agatha's. "For their fear is the barbed thong that lashes us, their fear of the Great Dark that stands behind such powers as ours, the dark of Unknown, and the unguessable fate that we bring them. 'Tis they who must grope for Life and for Good in midnightmare, they who never ha' known the sound of love-thoughts, the joy of a moonlit flight. Ought we not, then, to pity them?"

Agatha nodded slowly. Her old eyes filmed over, staring off into a life now distant in time. "So I had thought once, in my girlhood. . . ."

"Pity them, then," said Gwen, sawing hard at the reins of her eagerness. "Pity them, and . . ."

"And forgive them?" Agatha snapped back to the present, shaking her head slowly, a bitter smile on her gash of a mouth. "Nay. Thou knowest not what thou speakest, child, and I pray Heaven thou never wilt. Will they forgive me, child, will they pity? Never. They will come again, with their torches and steam and sharp, heated knives. Pity them? Aye; and for that pity, they bleed us."

"Nay, nay! It is *not* so! No longer, old Agatha; that day is gone, buried, never to rise again!"

"Is it, indeed?" the old witch mocked her, and spat. "Nay, child; forget not that ghosts do walk, in Gramarye.

As it was once, it will be again; for those in the darkness shall ever hate those in the light."

"Nay, Agatha, nay! The past dies, and is dead! All things change, all must change; that law alone stands enduring!"

"Aye, child, all things must change, Man most of all, and we are the proof of it. Indeed, that law is old, enduring, as unyielding as the cry of the belly; and therefore does Man yearn for the safety of changelessness, that the staff of hard-garnered knowledge may not crumble to dust in his hand. He desires most dearly that constant world which he may not have; and therefore will he ravage and rend all that which changes."

She glared down into Gwen's eyes. "And we are Change, child of my craft; we are the Mankind that is changed; and *therefore* they hate us! Not for your puling fear and envy, but simply and clearly for what we are, which is what they are not. We are, after all, but the strange bird in the flock, which must die, or fight and so rise. Or flee. *There* is the evidence of your law, the law of the earth and the trees and the sky, the law that they must hate us. 'Tis born into them, 'tis akin to the Belly and Loins, all parts of the Way of the World. There is your law, enacted in the Parliament of the Ages, the Changeling Law, and its text is most plain: 'Thou shalt Hate!' "

"But in this day come upon us, the witch shall be honored, not hated!" Gwen protested.

"And thou, child of thirty, hast still in thee innocence to believe it! 'Tis a lie! They shall hate, they shall always hate, for they must!"

She thrust her face close to Gwen's, and crooned, "Dost not know the fate of a Changeling, lass? The mother hurls it out from the cradle, leaves it in the midst of the forest, a meal for the wolves! For even the mother must hate it!"

She wheeled, stumping away down the length of the room. "Changelings we are, and for Changelings they hate us." She spun on her heel, finger stabbing at Gwen. "And we must therefore hate them also!"

She sobered suddenly, her anger deepening into midnight musing as she came back up the room, slowly. "Yet, still, in my heart, I might forgive them. The stripes and the blows, the burning needles, the chains and the flaming splinters under my nails—aye, even this might I forgive them. . . ."

Her eyes glazed, gazing back down the years. "But the abuse of my body, my fair, slender, girl's body and my ripe-blossomed woman's body, all the long years, my most tender flesh and the most intimate parts of my heart, the tearing and rending of that heart, and again and again, to feed them, their craving, insensible hunger . . . no!" Her voice was low and guttural, gurgling acid, a black-diamond drill. "No, nay! That, I may never forgive them! Their greed and their lust, their slavering hunger! Forever and ever they came, to come in and take me and hurl me away, to come for my trembling flesh—then spurn me away, crying 'Whore!' Again and again, by one and by five, knowing I would not, could not, turn them away; and therefore they came and they came. . . . Nay! That, I may never forgive them!"

Gwen's heart broke open and flowed; and it must have shown in her face, for Agatha transfixed her with a shimmering glare. "Pity them, if you must," she grated, "but never have pity for me!"

She held Gwen's eyes for a moment, then turned back to the caldron, taking up her paddle again. "You will tell me that this was no fault of theirs," she muttered, "any more than it was of mine, that their hunger forced them to me as truly as mine constrained me to welcome them."

Her head lifted slowly, the eyes narrowing, filling with poison. "Or didst thou not know? Galen, the wizard of the Dark Tower. He it was who should have answered my hunger with his own. The greatest witch and the greatest warlock of the kingdom together, is it not fitting? But he alone of all men would never come to me, the swine! Oh, he will tell you he hath too much righteousness to father a child into a Hell-world like this; yet the truth of it is, he fears the blame of that child he might father. Coward! Churl! Swine!"

She dug at the caldron, spitting and cursing. "Hell-spawned, thrice misbegotten, bastard mockery of a man! He"—she finished in a harsh whisper—"I hate most of all!"

The bony, gnarled old hands clutched the paddle, so tight it seemed the wood must break.

Then she was clutching the slimy wooden paddle to her sunken, dried breast. Her shoulders shook with dry sobs. "My child," she murmured. "O my fair, unborn, sweet child!"

The sobs diminished and stilled. Then, slowly, the witch's eyes came up again. "Or didst thou not know?" She smiled harshly, an eldritch gleam in her rheumy yellowed eye. "He it is who doth guard my portal, who doth protect me —my unborn child, Harold, my son, my familiar! So he was and so he will ever be, now—a soul come to me out of a tomorrow that once might have been."

Gwen stared, thunderstruck. "Thy familiar . . . ?"

"Aye." The old witch's nod was tight with irony. "My familiar, and my son, my child who, because he once might have and should have been, bides with me now, though he never shall be born, shall never have flesh grown out of my own to cover his soul with. Harold, most powerful of wizards, son of old Galen and Agatha, of a union unrealized; for the Galen and Agatha who sired and bore him ha' died in us long ago, and lie buried in the rack and mire of our youths."

She turned back to the caldron, stirring slowly. "When first he came to me, long years ago, I could not understand. 'Out of tomorrow,' it was, he said he had come; my full-grown son of twenty years of tomorrows had come to protect his old mother, to guard her until she should be wed to her man, so that the son might be sure his mother might live to bear him. It seemed lo, full strange to me, most wondrous strange; but I was lonely, and grateful. But now . . ." Her breath wheezed like a dying organ. "Now, I know, now I understand." She nodded bitterly. " 'Twas an unborn soul that had no other home, and never would have, for I never could do the greatest duty a mother owes to her child."

Her head hung low, her whole body slumped with her grief.

After a long, long while, she lifted her head, and sought out Gwen's eyes. "You have a son, have you not?"

There was a trace of tenderness in Agatha's smile at Gwen's nod.

But the smile hardened, then faded; and the old witch shook her head. "The poor child," she muttered.

"Poor child!" Gwen struggled to hide outrage. "In the name of Heaven, old Agatha, why?"

Agatha gave her a contemptuous glance over her shoulder. "Thou hast lived through witch-childhood, and thou hast need to ask?"

"No," Gwen whispered, shaking her head; then, louder, "No! A new day has dawned, Agatha, a day of change! My son shall claim his rightful place in this kingdom, shall guard the people and have respect from them, as is his due!"

"Think thou so?" The old witch smiled bitterly.

"Aye, I believe it! The night has past now, Agatha, fear and ignorance have gone in this Day of Change; and the Changelings may wa'k, proud and tall, in the sunlight! And never again shall the folk of the village pursue them in anger and fear, and red hatred!"

The old witch smiled sourly and jerked her head toward the cave door. "Hear thou that?"

Gwen turned slowly, hearing the low, distant rumble now, and realizing it had been there for some time, coming closer.

Her eyes widened. "What . . .?"

" 'Tis these amiable villager folk of thine," said old Agatha, with a sardonic smile. "The folk of twelve villages, gathered together behind a black preacher, come to roust old Agatha from her cave and burn her to ashes, for once and for all."

Fess swept down the road to the south in the easy, tireless, rocking-chair canter possible only to AC engines. Rod sat back in the saddle and enjoyed the ride; Fess' gait was very easy on the rider.

"Of course," he was saying, "it's possible this revivalist is just what he seems to be, nothing more—just a neurotic, unordained, religious nut. But somehow I find myself able to doubt it."

"Coincidence is possible, Rod," the robot murmured, "though scarcely probable."

"Especially since his activities are weakening the war effort very nicely—for the beastmen, that is. And why else would he start operating at just this particular time? He must have begun preaching a week or two before the Royal Heralds started recruiting; otherwise we would have had at least a *few* volunteers."

"We may assume, then, that there is some correlation between the two phenomena—the war and the preacher," Fess opined.

"Correlation, hell! He's working for 'em, Fess! How else could you explain it?"

"I do not have an alternate theory prepared," the robot admitted. "Nonetheless, the probability of direct collusion is extremely low."

"Oh, come off it!"

"Examine the data, Rod. The Neanderthals and the preacher are separated by approximately eight hundred miles of ocean. Moreover, there is no physiological resemblance apparent from the reports we have received."

"A point," Rod admitted. "Still, I say . . ."

"Master Gallowglass!" An elf leaped up to Fess' back. "Thy wife is in Agatha's cave. She is in danger most foul, for a band of peasants led by a preacher assault the cave!"

Rod stared, frozen a moment; then he howled, and Fess leaped into the air, jet engines extruding from his flanks.

"Hear!" Agatha snorted, nodding toward the cave-mouth. Her mouth twisted with bitterness at the corners. "Hear them clamoring for my blood! Aye, when an unwashed, foaming madman drives them to it!"

"Yet thou must not blame them for that," Gwen murmured, beseeching—and a little sheepishly. "They are half-mad with his shrieking, and the clamoring of their neighbors. Come to their senses, they would not . . ."

"Aye, well I know it." Agatha turned her head, hawked, and spat. "They are like chaff on the threshing-floor, blowing this way and that at the will of the wind."

Agatha gave her a sardonic smile. "Now my fowls come home to roost. Hear you the glorious titles they give me? 'Killer of Swine!' 'Eater of Children!' 'Spoiler of Harvests!' The fools, three thousand times fools! The 'Bane of the Valley,' they call me, when not once, but a score of times and more, only I, I and mine unborn son, have held famine and plague from this valley. Every one amongst them has taken his life from me and mine again and again and again. And this is our thanks!"

She spat out the door and cackled harshly. "Look at them, rippling down below us! They cry that my witch-hood is sin, and the wages of sin shall I have; and quite certain of it they are, for they come now to pay me my wages. My creditors, come to pay. . . ."

Gwen's eyes had grown slowly rounder as she listened. "And yet thou wilt tell me thou hatest them. . . ."

"Aye," Agatha agreed, "and now and again I may even witch myself into believing it. But let a child be lost in the wood, or a soul cry out in the torment of sickness, and I know the true folly of my falsehood. For hark, young witch-wife"—she speared Gwen with a glance—"learn now the true curse of witch-hood. Blest are the warlocks, for they do be men, and may harden their hearts, as old Galen ha' done, there in his Dark Tower; but a witch bears the double curse of witch-power and womanhood. They hate us, and we ought by all law to hate them, to return them their hate. Yet we are women, and must not only be having love, but giving it, too; such is our nature, and such our fulfillment; and in this act of giving, we know we are women, and know that we live. We must give of ourselves, or else wish to die. We ought to return them their hate, and so be truly witches; but one curse of our witch-hood is the power to hear souls in torment, and one single such cry is more than enough to make us women again."

She looked down at the swarming mob, climbing ledge by ledge toward them. Steel winked in the sun.

Gwen felt the clammy touch of fear; but fear of what, she did not know. "Thou speakest almost as though thou hadst known this beforehand. . ."

"Oh, to be certain, I did." The old witch smiled. "Has it not come often upon me before? It was bound to be coming again. The time alone I did not know; but what matter is that?"

The ledges narrowed as the horde surged higher. Gwen could make out individual faces now. "They come close, Agatha. What must we do against them?"

"Do?" The old witch raised shaggy eyebrows in surprise. "Why, nothing, child. I have too much of their blood on my hands already. I am tired, old, and sick of my life; why then should I fight them? Let them come here and burn me. This time, at least, I will not be guilty of the blood of those I have saved."

Agatha turned away from the cave-mouth, gathering her shawl about her narrow old shoulders. "Let them come here and rend me; let them set up a stake here and burn me. Even though it come in the midst of great torture, Death shall be sweet."

She stopped, looking over her shoulder at Gwen. "Fly, lass. Thou'rt young, and a-love; thou hast a bairn and a husband. Thou hast many years left and they will be sweet, though many bands like to this come against thee. Fly."

Gwen looked at her broomstick; then her eyes strayed to the clamoring horde rising up toward her. Her hand went out to the broom; but she paused, and turned to look at the old witch.

"Fly, fly!" cried Agatha, her face twisting in a grimace of contempt. "Thou canst not aid a sour old woman in the midst of her death-throes, lass. Thy death here with me would serve me not at all; indeed, it would deepen the guilt that my soul is steeped in."

There was a clicking, a rattling, from the back of the cave.

Both women turned to look.

The skull skittered, chattering, on the rough wood of the table.

"Nay, I will *not* leave you!" Gwen said. "What of this message of evil the skull bears to thee? Belike thou shalt need more witch-power than thine own!"

"*Thou* must needs be away from this cave, and right quickly!" Agatha snapped, her hands like iron on Gwen's wrist. "Rarely indeed hath Iyorika spoken, scarce ever in the sixty long years of my life here. I know not what this portends; but 'tis evil, most evil, and thou shalt not bear it with me!" She slapped the broomstick into Gwen's hands and threw her bodily out the cave door.

"*Oof!*" Gwen said intelligently, and bounced back into Agatha's hands.

"What . . . ?" The old witch stared over Gwen's shoulder.

The air at the cave-mouth shimmered.

The old witch's face darkened with anger. "Harold! Begone! Withdraw from the cave-mouth, and quickly; this lass must be away!"

The shimmering intensified, like a heat haze.

A huge boulder just outside the cave-mouth stirred.

"Nay, Harold!" Agatha screeched. "Thou shalt not! There ha' been too much bloodshed already!"

The boulder lifted slowly, clear of the ledge.

"Harold!" Agatha screamed, and fell silent.

For, instead of dropping down onto the toiling peasants below, the boulder lifted out and away, rising swiftly into the sky.

It was twenty feet away from the cave when a swarm of arrows spat out from the cliff above, struck the boulder, and rebounded, falling away into the valley below.

The old witch stood frozen a long moment, staring at the heat haze and the boulder, arcing away into the forest.

"Harold," she whispered, "arrows. . . ."

She shook her head, coming back to herself. "Thou must not leave now, lass."

"He ha' saved my life," said Gwen, round-eyed.

"Aye, that he hath; there be archers above us, awaiting the flight of a witch. Mayhap they thought I would fly; but I never have, I ha' always stayed here and fought them. It would seem they know thou'rt with me. A yard from that ledge now, and thou would most truly resemble a porcupine."

Gwen's lips parted, horror in her eyes.

"Come!" Agatha turned away, dragging Gwen with her toward the back of the cave. "Thou, at least, must not die here! We shall see what ill news it is that Iyorika ha' brought me! Then we shall brew witchcraft, thou and I, for a storm of magic such as hath never been witnessed in this land! Harold!" she called over her shoulder, to the heat haze. "Guard the door!"

The old witch paused, her hands poised over the now-silent skull. Then, slowly, her hands fell to her sides, as her wrinkled brow knit in a whorl of concentration.

Gwen scarcely dared stir. Witch though she was, it chilled her to the marrow to see the dead speak—perhaps more than a normal woman, for Gwen had been able to feel the presence of the dead, ancient witch.

And now, equally, she felt the lack of the presence. She summoned her courage, and whispered, "The spirit is fled."

"Aye, fled and gone." Agatha scowled blackly. Her bony hands contracted slowly, like the claws of a dying raven.

"But why?" Gwen breathed. "Why would she speak, and then flee, ere we could understand her meaning?"

"The ways of the dead are beyond the knowing of us mere mortal witches," answered Agatha. "We may know only that it is a deep and chill, sable barrier that sunders our worlds. Great power, indeed, must a witch needs have to speak through that curtain, even for so short a while. She came to us for as long as she might, I doubt not; when she could no longer withhold that dark gauze, it fell again between us."

Gwen had a lost look about her. Witch-hood she knew, and knew well; but the spirit world and its workings were miles beyond her.

Agatha's brow furrowed again as she glanced back at the skull. "Might it not have meaning that she faces the back of the cave . . . ? But nay, there be naught there but good solid stone."

She turned away briskly, stumping over to the shelves of bottles. "All we may know is that she came from the dead to speak briefly with us; and her message must needs have great import, to bring her so untimely again to the living."

She hauled a small iron pot from the shelf, and gasped as its weight plunged against her hands. She heaved, thrusting with her whole body, to throw it up onto a small tripod that stood on the rough table. "I grow old," she growled as she hooked the pot onto the tripod, "old and weak. Long years it ha' been since I last stewed men's fates in this."

"Men's fates . . . ?" Gwen was at her elbow. "What doth thou, Agatha?"

"Why, a small cooking, child." The old witch grinned. "Did I not say we would brew great magic here?"

She turned away and began pulling stone jars from the shelf. "Kindle me a fire, child, for certain it is that old Iyorika ha' spake; and whatever dark news she brought us, the end of it all is that old Agatha may not yet let
110

herself die. Great tribulation comes upon this land shortly, and the people shall cry out with one voice in their need. And"—she set the jars down on the table with a series of very solid thuds—"the witch's curse it is that, when the people cry out in their terror and horror, the witch who was never a mother must hark to the cry of the lost and the fearful. We shall live, lass, for we must; this land hath not yet given us dismissal."

A spark fell from Gwen's flint and steel into the tinder. Gwen breathed on the resulting coal till small flames danced in the kindling. As she fed it larger and larger wood scraps, she ventured, "Thou art strangely joyous for a witch who ha' been deprived of that which she wanted, old Agatha."

The old witch cackled and rubbed her thin, bony hands. "It is the joy of a craftsman, child, that doth his work well, and sees a great task before him, a greater task than ever his trade yet ha' brought him. I shall live, and more joyous and hearty than ever before; for there is great need of old Agatha, and great deeds a-doing. The undoing of this war thou hast told me of will be old Agatha's greatest work.

She took a measure from the shelf and began ladling powders from the various jars into the pot.

"I told thee of this war, and the people's great need of thee, and thou spake that thou cared naught; yet at half of a word from old Iyorika, thou'rt halfway and more to the battle," Gwen said, musing.

Agatha snorted. "Thy power is scarce that of an eighty-year-old witch, child. How much less is it of the power of old Iyorika who, dead though she be, still is a witch of far greater power than you, or I?"

Agatha took a small paddle and began stirring the brew.

Gwen flinched at the stench that arose from the heating-pot. "What is this hideous porridge, Agatha? I have never known a witch to use such a manner of bringing magic, save in child's tales."

Agatha paused in her stirring to fasten a pensive eye on Gwen. "Thou art yet young, child, and know only half-truths of witchery."

She turned back to stirring the pot. "It is true that our powers be of the mind, and only of the mind. Yet true it also is that thou hast never used but a small part of thy power, child. Thou knowest not the breadth and the width of it, the color and the warp and the woof of it. There be deep, unseen parts of thy soul thou hast never uncovered; and this deep power thou canst not call up at will. It lies too far buried, beyond thy call. Thou must needs trick it into coming out, direct it by ruse and gin, not by will." She peered into the smoking, bubbling pot. "And this thou must do with a bubbling brew, compounded of things which stand for the powers thou doth wish to evoke from thy heart of hearts and the breadth of thy brain. Hummingbird's feathers for strength, speed, and flight; bees, for their stings; poppyseed, for the dulling of wits; lampblack, for the stealth and silence of night; woodbine, to bind it to the stone of the cliffs; hearth-ash, for the wish to return to the home."

She lifted the paddle; the mess flowed slowly down from it into the pot. "Not quite thick enow," the old witch muttered, and went back to stirring.

Gwen lifted one of the stone jars and looked at the label. "Powdered mummy," she murmured. "What was this put in the brew for?"

"What . . . ?" The old witch looked up, frowning. "Oh, that? To give the brew body. Put the jaws back on the shelves, child; a tidy kitchen makes a good brew."

Gwen picked up a few jars, but as she did, she glanced toward the cave-mouth. The clamor was much louder. "Old Agatha, they come!"

The first of the villagers stormed into the cave, brandishing a scythe.

"Their clamor shall but help the brew's flavor," said the old witch, with a delightedly wicked grin. She bent over the pot, and crooned.

The peasant slammed into the invisible haze barrier, rebounded, knocking over the next two behind him. The fourth and fifth stumbled over their fallen comrades, adding nicely to the pile. The stack heaved, as the ones on the bottom tried to struggle to their feet. The top layer shrieked, leaped up, and fled smack-dab into the arms of their lately-come reinforcements. The resulting frantic struggle was somewhat energetic, and the ledge was only wide enough for one man at a time; the peasants seesawed back and forth, teetering perilously close to the edge, flailing their arms for balance and squalling in terror.

" 'Tis a blessing the ledge is so narrow, they cannot come against me more than one at a time." Agatha wrapped a rag around the handle of the pot and hefted it off the hook, strands of muscle straining along her arms. "Quickly, child," she grated, "the tripod! My son Harold is summat more than a man, but he cannot hold them long, not so many! Quickly! Quickly! We must prepare to be aiding him!"

She hobbled into the entryway. Gwen caught up the tripod and ran after her.

As she set down the tripod, and Agatha hooked the pot on it again, two sticks of wood thudded against the ledge, sticking two feet up above the stone.

"Scaling ladders!" gasped Agatha. "This was well-planned, in truth! Quickly, child! Fetch the bellows!"

Gwen ran for the bellows, wishing she knew what old Agatha was planning.

As she returned—handing the bellows to Agatha, where she crouched over the pot in the middle of the entryway—a tall, bearded figure appeared at the top of the ladder, clambering onto the ledge. The man leveled his dark, polished staff at the cave-mouth. The staff gave a muted clank as he set its butt against the stone.

"An iron core!" Agatha pointed the bellows over the pot at the preacher and began pumping them furiously. "That staff must not touch my son!"

But the forward end of the staff had already touched the heat haze. A spark exploded at the top of the staff. Skolax howled victory and swung his staff to beckon his forces. The peasants shouted and surged into the cave.

"Bastard!" Agatha screamed. "Vile Hell-fiends! Murrain upon thee! Thou hast slain my son!"

She glared furiously, pumping the bellows like a maniac. The steam from the pot shot forward toward the mob.

They stopped dead. A deathly pallor came over their faces. Little red dots began appearing on their skins. They screamed, whirling about and flailing at their comrades, swatting at something unseen that darted and stung them.

For a moment, the crowd milled and boiled in two conflicting streams at the cave-mouth; then the back ranks screamed and gave way as the phantom stings struck them, too, and the mob fled back along the ledge, away from the cave.

Only Skolax remained, struggling against the flock of phantom bees, his face swelling red with ghost-stings.

The old witch threw back her head and cackled shrill and long, still pumping the bellows. "We have them, child! We have them now!" Then she bent grimly over the pot, pumping harder, and spat, "Now shall they pay for his death! Now shall my Eumenides hale them home!"

With a titanic effort, Skolax threw himself forward, his staff whirling up over the witch's head. Gwen leaped forward to shield her; but the staff jumped backward, jerking Skolax off his feet and throwing him hard on the stone floor. Agatha's triumphant cry cut through his agonized bellow: "He lives! My son Harold lives!"

And indeed it seemed true, for the preacher lifted, struggling and howling, into the air, and dropped again from a height of five feet.

He pulled his chin in as he landed, taking the impact on his shoulders; but before he could struggle to his feet, invisible hands lifted him slowly into the air again.

With a thundering roar, the back wall of the cave fell in.

A swarm of dark, hulking shapes shouldered through the billowing dust of the shattered cave wall.

"Beastmen!" Gwen screamed; then she dropped to her knees, her eyes narrowing, and chunks of rubble flung themselves from the rock-heap at the Neanderthals!

"Aye, lass!" Agatha screamed. "Take as many to death as thou may!" She sprang to the other side of the pot and began pumping the bellows again.

But the beastmen had thick skins, and were well-armed. They warded off the pummeling stones with their shields, and snarled in anger at the faint prick of the bee-stings. They plowed forward through the rubble, and the leader swung up his club.

Thunder rumbled outside the cave, and the first drops of rain struck.

Suddenly, a young, gangling form appeared between the Neanderthals and the witches, chopping at the beastmen with longsword and shouting, "To me, brave hearts! To me, now!"

"Toby!" cried Gwen.

Suddenly it was bargain week, for a dozen more young warlocks appeared at one moment, swords in hand, forming a wall between witch and Neanderthal.

But a maniac voice shouted glee at the back of the cave, and the beastmen stepped back, grinning.

Toby and his Coven Corps scowled and jumped forward, blades whirling.

The beastmen lifted their shields, warding off the blows almost negligently, chuckling, and through the ruined wall at the back of the cave came a hunched, gnarled, twisted figure, seeming almost to be compounded of stick and parchment—the Shaman.

He cocked an eye at the cave-mouth and stood poised a moment.

Then his arms flung up, and he shrieked.

Lightning split the air of the valley outside the cave.

Gwen's head split with a screaming, whistling explosion and a glare of light; something pressed clenching at her brain. Something hard struck her side, then rolled to her back. The glare over her eyes lessened for a moment, and through it she could see the Shaman pointing at her, heard her name called, saw three beastmen coming toward her with a net, saw the young warlocks collapsed on the stone, and the net coming down at her. . . .

Light, blinding light, a sunburst, a nova, silent light, everywhere.

It dimmed slowly, and the keening wails of the terrified beastmen rose.

Very slowly, the red afterimage haze cleared from the beastmen's eyes; they were able to see again.

They could see the cavern, the Shaman, and each other; nothing more.

The witches and warlocks were gone.

At the cave-mouth, Skolax lifted his head, shook it, groped about for his staff, and hauled himself to his feet.

Wind-demons howled, steel hooves clattered, something struck Skolax in the back and sent him spinning.

Rod reined in the great black horse and looked wildly about him.

The beastmen moaned and backed away.

Skolax slowly picked himself up again.

Rod took it all in at a glance—whatever else was in the cave, Gwen was not.

He fixed on the Shaman, his eyes growing hard and very, very cold.

"You foul, dunghill bastards!" he hissed.

The dagger whirled up in his hand, poised for throwing.

"Down, Rod!" Fess' voice snapped, and the great horse collapsed beneath him.

Rod threw his arms about the robot's neck, and heard the air sizzle above him.

He whipped about in the saddle as the horse lurched to its feet again, the dagger reversing in his hand so that the great, glowing ruby in the pommel pointed straight ahead of him.

It pointed straight at Skolax.

And Skolax's iron staff was pointed straight at Rod, a gaping, black maw in its end, still glowing from the laser-beam it had just fired.

Rod's thumb rested lightly on the firing stud in the hilt as the two men looked long into each other's eyes, each knowing the other for what he was.

Then Skolax's forearm tightened, and Fess whirled aside. Rod's hair singed as the bolt spat past and his thumb tightened, the jewel in the hilt tracking Skolax as the man leaped for cover.

The bolt tore into his shoulder. He fell, howling, behind a boulder.

Rod lowered his aim, and the beam tore through the rock. Skolax howled again; his cry ended abruptly.

Fess whirled about, and Rod found himself staring at the Shaman, who cried, " 'Tis the greatest prize of all! Take him! For the Kobold, now take him!"

The beastmen shifted uneasily, looking at one another out of the corners of their eyes.

Rod leveled the dagger-hilt at the Shaman and pressed the stud.

The Shaman dived, screaming.

The dagger spat a brief bolt, fizzled, and died.

Rod cursed the miniature powerpack and jammed the blade back in its sheath. His sword whirled out as he kicked Fess into a plunge for the Shaman.

The beastmen yelled and jumped into his path. Their clubs swung up . . . and held, poised, wavering.

Rod reined back, growled, and kicked Fess. The horse shouldered through the beastmen in a bound that sent them spinning. Rod's blade swung down at the Shaman.

The little man sprang aside, screaming, "Take him! You fools! His magic is spent! Take him!"

Rod caught a glimpse of the beastmen as Fess reared, wheeling about. The Neanderthals were still uncertain, eyeing one another. Rod heard mutinous murmurings.

Fess leaped forward again as the Shaman zigzagged, blocking his path. The little man dodged aside, and Fess sprang again. Rod chopped; his blade whistled by an eighth of an inch from the Shaman's back as the old man made a frantic dive.

He rolled, and came to his feet, and turned to run.

The stone wall loomed up before him.

He pivoted, and saw the great black warhorse rearing, turning, above him.

He backed against the wall, arms outstretched, screaming, wild-eyed; then dropped to one knee, caught up a stone, threw it, hard.

Rod ducked, and the stone whistled past his ear as his arm drove forward in a thrust.

Hands caught his arm and dragged back, huge ham hands caught his shoulders and waist and reins, hands dragged him from the saddle as more hands immobilized the plunging robot, biting hard hands forced him back-downward to the stone floor, two more knotted hands drove a great war-club down at his face, and—

Light, glaring and blinding, all about him, and silence, deep and sudden, and falling, falling. . . .

Then blackness, total, unrelieved, all about him, and cold that drilled to his bones. . . .

And something struck his heels, throwing him back. Something hard, heels, hips, and shoulders, and he tucked his chin in from reflex.

And fire burned in the blackness.

A campfire, only it burned in a small iron cage, black bars slanting up to a point.

Rod's eyes fastened on that cage for the simple reassurance of solid geometry in a world suddenly crazy. It was a tetrahedron, a fire burning inside a tetrahedron.

But what the hell was it doing here?

And for that matter, where was "here"?

Rephrase the question; because, obviously, the fire and cage belonged here. So—

What was Rod doing here?

Back to Question Number Two: "Where was 'here'?"

Rod started noticing details. The floor was stone, square, black basalt blocks, and the fire burned in a shallow circular well, surrounded by the basalt. The walls were distant, hard to see in the dim light from the fire; they seemed to be hung with velvet, some dark deep color, not black; Rod squinted—it looked to be a rich maroon.

Looking around, he saw the great black form that lay about ten feet from him: Fess.

Rod knelt and felt for broken bones, taking things in easy stages. Satisfied that he didn't have to be measured in fractions, he clambered carefully to his feet and went over to the horse.

Fess was lying very still, which wasn't like him; but he was also very stiff, each joint locked, which was like him when he had had a seizure. Rod didn't blame him; after being confronted with that pseudo-LSD nightmare journey, he could do with a seizure himself—or at least a mild jolt; bourbon, for instance. . . .

He groped under the saddlehorn and found the reset switch.

The black horse relaxed, then slowly stirred, and the great head lifted. The eyes opened, large, brown, and bleary. Not for the first time, Rod wondered if they could really be, as the eye-specs claimed, plastic.

Fess turned his head slowly, looking as puzzled as a

horsehair-over-metal face can; then turned slowly back to Rod.

"Di—dye . . . chhhab a . . . zeizure, RRRRRodd?"

"A seizure? Of course not! You just decided you needed a lube job, so you dropped into the nearest grease station." Rod tactfully refrained from mentioning just how Fess had "dropped in"; since that nightmare passage obviously couldn't have happened, and equally obviously had, the mere recollection of it would probably be enough to give the robot another seizure.

"I . . . fffai-led you innn . . . duhhh . . . momenduv . . ."

Rod winced at the touch of self-contempt that coated the vodered words and interrupted. "You did all you could; and since you've saved my life five or six times before, I'm not going to gripe over the few times you've failed." He patted Fess between the ears.

The robot hung his head for a moment, then surged to his feet, hooves clashing on the stone. His nostrils spread; and Rod had a strange notion his radar was operating, too.

"We arrre inna gread chall," the robot murmured; at least when he had seizures, he made quick recoveries. "It is stone, hung with maroon velvet curtains; a fire burns in the center, in a recessed well. It is surrounded by a metal, latticework, tetrahedron. The metal is an alloy of iron, containing nickel and tungsten in the following percentages. . . ."

"Never mind," Rod said hastily. "I get the general idea." He frowned suddenly, turning away, brooding. "I also get the idea that maybe my wife isn't dead; if she was, her body would have been there. So they've kidnapped her?"

"I regret . . ."

" 'That the data is insufficient for . . . ' " Rod recited with him. "Yeah, yeah. Okay. So how do we find her?"

"I regret. . . ."

"Skip it. I've got to find her." He struck his forehead with his fist. "Where would they have taken her? Back to Neanderthal-land? Where is she?"

"In the next room," boomed a deep, resonant voice. "She is unharmed, and quite well, I assure thee. Agatha is there also; but thy troop of young warlocks is already fled back to Runnymede."

A tall old man, with long white hair streaming down over his shoulders and a long white beard down his chest, in a long, dark-blue monk's robe with the hood thrown back, stood by the fire. His robe was sprinkled with silver zodiac signs; his arms were folded, hands thrust up the wide, flaring sleeves. His eyes were surrounded by a network of fine wrinkles, under white tufts of eyebrows; but the eyes themselves were clear, and warm, gentle. He stood tall and square-shouldered near the fire, looking deep into Rod's eyes, as though he were searching for something.

"Whoever you are," Rod said slowly, "I thank you for getting me out of a jam, and incidentally for saving my life. Apparently I also owe you my wife's life, and for that I thank you even more deeply."

The old man smiled thinly. "You owe me nothing, Master Gallowglass. None owe me ought."

"And," Rod said slowly, "you owe nothing to anyone. Hm?"

The wizard's head nodded, almost imperceptibly.

Rod chewed at the inside of his cheek and said, "You're Galen. And this is the Dark Tower."

Again, the old man nodded.

Rod nodded too, chewing again. "How come you saved me? I thought you ignored the outside world."

Galen shrugged. "I had an idle moment."

"So," said Rod judiciously, "you saved two witches, all the young warlocks of Gramarye, my horse, and my humble self, just to kill time."

"Thou are quick to comprehend," said Galen, hiding a smile deep in his beard. "I had no pressing researches at the moment."

"Rod," Fess' voice murmured, "an analysis of vocal patterns indicates he is not telling the whole truth."

"For this I need a computer?" Rod muttered dryly.

"Come," said Galen, turning away, "thy wife is without the chamber."

Rod stared after him a moment, surprised at the old man's abruptness; then he shrugged and followed, and Fess followed Rod.

The wizard seemed almost to glide to the end of the cavernous room. They passed through the maroon hangings into a much smaller room—the ceiling was only fifteen feet high. The walls were hung with velvet drapes, cobalt blue this time, and one huge tapestry. The floor boasted an Oriental carpet, with a great black carven wood chair at each corner. Roman couches, upholstered in burgundy plush, stood between the chairs. A large, round, black wood table stood in the center of the room, before a fair-sized fireplace. Six huge calf-bound volumes lay open on the table.

Rod didn't notice the splendor, though; at least, not the splendor of the furnishings. The splendor of his wife was something else again.

Her flame-red hair didn't go badly with the cobalt-blue drapes, though. She stood at the table, bent over one of the books.

She looked up as they came in. Her face lit like the aurora. "My lord!" she cried, and she was in his arms, almost knocking him over, wriggling and very much alive, lips glued to his.

An eternity later—half a minute, maybe?—anyway, much too soon—a harsh voice grated, "Spare me, child! Pity on a poor old hag, who never was one-tenth as fortunate as thou!"

Gwen broke free and spun about. "Forgive me, Agatha," she pleaded, pressing back against her husband and locking his arms around her waist. "I had not thought . . ."

"Aye, thou hast not," said the old witch, with a grimace that bore some slight resemblance to a smile, "but such is the way of youth, and must be excused."

"Bitter crone!" Galen scowled down at her from the dignity of his full height. "Wouldst deny these twain their rightful joy, for no reason but that it is joy thou never knew? Hath the milk of love so curdled in thy breast that thou canst no longer bear . . ."

"Rightful!" the witch spat in a blaze of fury. "Thou darest speak of 'rightful,' thou who hast withheld from me . . ."

"I ha' heard thy caterwauls afore," said Galen, his face turning to flint. "Scrape not mine ears again with thy cant; for I will tell thee now, as I ha' told thee long agone, that I am no just due of thine. A man is not a chattel, to be given and taken like a worn, base coin. I am mine own man to me alone: I never was allotted to a woman, and least of all to thee!"

"Yet in truth thou wast!" Agatha howled. "Thou wert accorded me before thy birth or mine and, aye, afore the world were formed in God's own mind. As sure as night was given day wert thou allotted me, for thou art, as I am, witch-blood, and of an age together with me! Thy hates, thy joys, are mine. . . ."

"Save one!" the wizard grated.

"Save none! Thine every lust, desire, and sin are each and all alike to mine, though hidden deep within thy heart!"

Galen's head snapped up and back.

Agatha's eyes lit with glee. She stalked forward, pressing her newfound advantage. "Aye, thy true self, Galen, that thou secretest veiled within thy deepest heart, is like to me! The lust and body weakness that ever I made public

120

thou hast in private, mate to mine! This thou hast hid for three-score years, thy secret shame! Thou hast not honesty enow to own to these, thy covered, covert sins of coveting! Thou art too much a coward. . . ."

"Coward?" Galen almost seemed to settle back, relaxing, smiling sourly. "Nay, this is a cant that I ha' heard afore. Thou wanest, Agatha. In a younger age, thou wouldst not so soon have slipped back upon old argument."

"Nor do I now," the witch said, "for now I call thee coward of a new and most unmanly fear! Thou, who cry heedlessness of all the world without the walls of thy Dark Tower; thou, who scornest all the people, fearest their opinion! Thou wouldst have them think thee saint!"

Galen's face tightened, eyes widening in glare.

"A saint!" Agatha chortled, jabbing a finger at him. "The Saint of Hot and Heaving Blood! A saint, who hast as much of human failing as ever I did have, and great guilt!"

"Greater!"

"Aye, greater, for in thy false conceit thou hast robbed me of mine own true place with thee! For thou art mine by right, old Galen; 'twas thou whom God ordained to be my husband, long before thy mother caught thy father's eye! By rights, thou shouldst be mine; but thou hast held thyself away from me in cowardice and pompousness!"

Galen watched her a moment, with shadowed eyes; then his shoulders squared, and he took a breath. "I receive only the curse that I have earned."

Agatha stared for a moment, lips parting. "Thou wilt admit to it!" Then, after a moment she fixed him with a sour smile.

"Nay. He means only that he hath saved mine life six times and more; and thus it is his fault that I do live to curse him."

She lifted her head proudly, her eyes glazing. "And in this thou mayst know that he is a weakling; for he cannot help himself but save us witches. It is within his nature, he who claims to care naught for any living, witch or plowman. Yet he is our guardian and our savior, all us witches; for if one of us should die when he might have prevented it, his clamoring conscience would batter down the weakness of a will that sought to silence it, and wake him in the night with haunted dreams. Oh, he can stand aloof and watch the peasant and the noble die, for they would gladly burn him; but a witch, who hast not hurt him, and would render him naught but kindness—had he the courage or the manhood to be asking it—these he cannot help but see as part and parcel like him; and therefore must he save us, as he ha' done a hundred times and more."

She turned away. "Thou mayst credit him with virtue and compassion if thou wishest; but I know better."

" 'Tis even as she saith," said the old man proudly. "I love none, and none love me. I owe to none; I stand alone."

Old Agatha gave a hoot of laughter.

"Uh . . . yes," said Rod. The fight seemed to have reached a lull, and Rod was very eager to be gone before it refueled.

And, since Galen's brow was darkening again, it behooved Rod to make haste.

"Yes, well, uh, thanks for the timely rescue, Galen," he said. "But now, if you'll excuse us, we really gotta be getting back to Runnymede, uh—don't we, Gwen?"

He paused suddenly, frowning at the old wizard. "I don't, uh, suppose you'd consider coming back with us?"

Agatha's head lifted slowly, fire kindling in her eye.

"I thank thee for thy kindness in offering of hospitality," said the old wizard, in a voice rigid with irony. "Yet greatly to my sorrow, I fear that I cannot accept."

"Oh, to thy sorrow, to be sure!" spat Agatha. "Indeed, thou art the sorriest man that e'er I knew, for thou hast brought me sorrow deep as sin!"

She spun toward Rod and Gwen. "And yet, fear not; thy folk shall not go all unaided! There lives, at least, still one old witch of power three-score-years-and-ten in learning, who will not desert her countrymen in this time of need! There lives still one, aye, be assured; though this old gelding"—she jerked her head toward Galen—"will idly stand and watch thy folk enslaved, a power strong as his will guard thy land!" She stretched out her hand. "Come, take me with thee, get us gone, for my stomach crawls within me at his presence! He thinks of naught but himself."

"And thou dost not?" Galen grated, glaring at the old witch. "Is this aught but a sop to thy thwarted wish for mothering of a child thou never hadst?"

Agatha flinched almost visibly and turned, hot words on her tongue; but Galen raised an imperious hand and intoned:

"Get thee hence, to Runnymede!"

White light flared, burning, blinding.

When the afterimages faded, Rod could see, as well as feel, Gwen in his arms, which feeling had been very reassuring while the sun went nova.

He could dimly make out Agatha, too, leaning, shaken, against a wall, a gray granite wall.

And a high, timbered ceiling, and a knot of young witches and warlocks gathered around them, staring, eyes and mouths round.

Their voices exploded in clamoring questions.

Yep, home, Rod decided. It was obviously the Witches Tower in the King's Castle at Runnymede.

He wondered what would happen if Galen ever got mad enough to tell someone to go to Hell.

Brom woke with the sun in his eyes. He stretched, yawned, and was about to leap to his feet when the gentle rolling of the wood beneath him reminded him he was still in the canoe.

He grasped the gunwales and sat up carefully; the dugout was fully as treacherous as it looked.

He had a sneaking suspicion that the same could be said of the land.

The white sand beach looked innocent enough, except for the huge lizard, looking to be mostly teeth, that sat half in the water, blinking sleepily at Brom, as if trying to decide whether he represented a big enough mouthful to be worth a morning swim.

Brom caught himself eyeing the lizard with similar sentiments. Lizard meat wasn't the most appetizing in the world, but it had been a long night, and there hadn't been time to provision the canoe before Brom's rather sudden departure.

He was also thirsty; perhaps finding fresh water was more important than debating the proper way to cook lizard steak. In fact, it was definitely more important, a parched throat informed him; it had already been making indignant noises the night before, when Brom had reached the swamp-coast; but the verdant jungle hadn't looked especially safe by moonlight, so Brom had dropped the anchor and himself, and snored.

He pulled the anchor up now, and slid out the paddle, turning the head of the canoe toward the mouth of a large stream. He eyed the jungle warily as he paddled toward it; it didn't look all that much safer by day.

In fact, he thought as he paddled under the great, moss-hung trees, it looked about as trustworthy as a diplomat agreeing to a compromise; he felt as though, any minute, something with very sharp claws and maybe a war-club, might leap out from behind a tree, and . . .

"Hail, my lord Brom O'Berin!"

Brom snapped about, dropping the paddle, hand going to the knife at his belt.

But the beastman who stood on the bank, not ten feet away, was holding up open hands; the shortsword was sheathed at his belt. His face was open and friendly, and he was grinning.

He was also short, broad-shouldered, bull-necked, naked except for a leather loincloth and a sword-belt, with a hunting bow and a quiver slung over his shoulder. His hair was a shaggy black thatch, his face wide, with high cheekbones, his nose short and broad, and his chin missing.

Brom scowled, relaxing a little—but only a little. "Thou knowest my name, 'twould appear. Have the goodness to tell me thine own."

"Oh, sorry, I keep forgetting my manners. I'm Yorick, my lord, and I'm your guide."

"Guide?" Brom glowered. "To what?"

"To the government-in-exile. The nation-in-exile, too, for that matter—what there is of it, anyway. Isn't that what you're looking for?"

"Who told thee that?" Brom all but roared. "Who sent thee to find me?"

"Kernel, of course," said the beastman, with an indulgent smile. "I take my orders straight from him; y'see, I'm sort of his right-hand man. Shall we go?"

Greta elbowed the thick oaken door open and glanced at the old woman in the rocking chair by the fire. Agatha sat slumped, her head lolling against the padded chair-back, seemingly asleep.

Greta bit her lip and tiptoed up to the little table next to the rocking chair, to set down the tray of bread, cheese, and wine she was carrying.

The old witch opened one eye and came dangerously close to smiling.

Greta straightened with a gasp, hands flying to her mouth. "Thy pardon, most excellent Agatha! I . . ."

"Nay, nay!" The old witch waved a languid hand. "Thou wert most excellent silent, child, have no fear; but even a mouse could not pass me unnoticed. My thanks for thy serving."

"I had not meant to trouble thee. . . ."

"Nay, thou didst not!" Agatha snapped, glowering. She stirred impatiently, turning to glare at the fire. "Why must all here revere me like unto a queen!" She smiled covertly, cocked an eyebrow at the girl. "Though if truth were told, 'tis a most pleasant alteration of circumstances."

Greta started a tremulous smile.

She took a sip of the wine and sank back in the chair with a weary sigh. "Sit now by the fire, if thou must—though why thou and thy siblings art so determined that I shall never lack one in attendance upon me, I cannot at all see."

Greta did notice, however, that the old witch hadn't really been displeased with the reverence shown her by the young members of the Coven.

"Sit by the fire, and be still," Agatha said, closing her eyes, "for I must listen for thoughts from the Beastland."

Greta sat on the low stool by the fire, hands folded in her lap, watching old Agatha with a touch of foreboding.

The old witch rocked herself slowly, scarcely seeming to breathe.

After a while, Greta's eyes wandered to the fire.

The room grew very still, silent except for the rhythmic creak of Agatha's rocker.

The old witch looked up suddenly, frowning, as a vagrant sensation brushed the fringe of her consciousness. The frown turned to a scowl as she scanned the girl's face; there was something strange there. . . .

And something strange in the mood of the room, all about her. . . .

She looked into Greta's face again. The girl's eyes were on the flames, but they were unfocused; she had a faraway, dreamy, almost intoxicated look to her. . . .

Suspicion formed in Agatha's mind.

She smiled covertly, and her voice lashed out:

"Child, what ails thee!"

Greta's whole body jerked as though someone had slapped her; her eyes leaped to Agatha, staring wildly, confused.

Then horror crept over her face, and she burst into tears.

It felt good to be walking again.

For that matter, it felt good to have legs again.

Of course, the meal Yorick had shot on their way to the exile camp did contribute to the feeling of well-being a bit. It seemed lizard meat wasn't half bad at all, if you knew how to cook it.

Yorick didn't seem half bad, either—but Brom was reserving judgment for a while. There had been altogether too many surprises lately.

The camp had been a surprise, too. One moment there had been just the usual wall of vines and brush ahead of them, like any other wall of vines and brush they'd encountered that morning; then Yorick had shouted, and the

125

wall swung away, revealing a shallow valley, and a clump of brush huts.

"Welcome to home," Yorick said, "my lord. 'Tain't much, but we like it. For the time being, anyway."

"Hum," said Brom cautiously. "Hrrumph, yes."

He turned his head slowly, surveying the valley. "Thou hast builded thyselves a most thriving town."

"Village," Yorick corrected modestly. "Yeah, it's not too bad, considering we're all refugees, and the thing got thrown together in one hell of a hurry. But then, we're all pretty much used to making home out of nothing. After all, most of these kids came from nomad cultures. Hunting-and-gathering types. And the few of us who came from sedentary cultures, like the lake-dwellers—well, they picked up the nomad ways quick enough when we were on the run. Before we came here, I mean. Back on Terra."

Brom's head snapped up. "Thou art not of this world?"

Yorick frowned quizzically. "Well, that was pretty obvious, wasn't it?"

"Hm. Um, aye, certes." Brom turned away, with the vague feeling that he'd given away information. "Um, speak thou, and tell to me—why dost thou post so many watchmen?"

A good third of the exiles, at least, were patrolling the perimeter of the camp, with short, heavy, recurved bows in their hands, eyes roving restlessly over the swamp about them. They were very businesslike, and grim.

"Well, that's why we can't talk Kernel into letting us take raiding parties back into Shaman's territory," Yorick said cheerfully. "You haven't seen half of the fauna that frisks in that forest, my lord. . . ." He stopped as Brom cleared a rusty throat. "Something bothering you, my lord?"

"Aye," Brom growled. "Thou hast spoke several times of this 'Kernel,' and I do wonder greatly who, or what, he may be. Take me to him."

"Uh—yes." Yorick tugged at his ear, looking a little embarrassed. "Well, I'm afraid I can't quite do that, my lord. You see, we *can* spare enough men for one occasional riding party, and of course Kernel leads it himself, and I'm afraid he's out harrying the foe at the moment. That's why he sent me to meet you, 'stead of coming himself. I, uh, was meaning to get around to telling you that, my lord . . ."

"I cannot meet thy master?" said Brom, thunderclouds gathering.

"Yeah, I'm afraid not." Yorick smiled weakly. "We could only spare about twelve of the boys for guerrilla work, y'see, and those twelve have got to create the maximum havoc with the minimum effort, so Kernel has to be there to run things, and . . ." His voice trailed off at the glitter rising in Brom's narrowed eye.

"He said to tell you hello, anyway, my lord," the Neanderthal finished feebly. "And said to tell you he was sorry about the poor accommodations, but we'll try to make you comfortable. . . ."

Brom nodded slowly, still gimlet-eyed.

Then he swung away toward the mountains. "Come, Master Yorick, let us go."

"Go!" Yorick yelped, jumping to catch up with him. "Go where?"

"Why, to the mountains," said Brom, lifting an eyebrow in languid innocence. "If thy Kernel will not come to me, I must needs go to him, must I not?"

"But you *can't!*"

Brom smiled sourly. "Dost thou think I cannot endure such a climb, Master Yorick? Mark my word, I could walk the legs off of thee any feast-day in the calendar!"

"Yeah, sure, all right, you're a champion hiker, but you don't know those mountains, my lord! And, look, we've only got twelve men against five hundred, so they've got to stay hid, and hid but good! Stay hid from Shaman's scouts, and those scouts *do* know the mountains! So if you go stumping your way around up there, chances are one of their patrols'll spot you, and . . . well, there goes the war."

Brom's brow furrowed. "But wouldst thou not guide me?"

Yorick shrugged. "Would that change things much? You're not used to the mountains, you'd leave a trail. And you might kick a pebble, or something like that, that'd tell them where we are. No, I'm sorry, my lord; we just can't take the chance."

Brom gazed at the beastman shrewdly, feeling for the flaws in his story. It rang as hollow as a smuggler's bootheel.

Of course, he couldn't really blame the beastmen for their reluctance; after all, any man from civilization is bound to be lacking a bit in scout-craft. But Brom wasn't all that civilized, and he *was* half-elf, which implied a certain bond with nature. And, somehow, Brom was very sure that Kernel knew about the elf half—along with everything else pertaining to Gramarye.

No, Brom decided, he did not like this Kernel. He knew too much that he could not possibly know.

And he obviously did not want to be seen.

Brom turned his back on the mountains, strode toward the village. "Tell me this, then, at least, Master Yorick: What is this 'Kernel'?"

"Oh, he's our leader," said Yorick, with massive relief at the change of topic. " 'Course, some of the folks have begun calling him a god, but he doesn't take to it too well."

Brom stopped short, turned to frown up at the Neanderthal. "He is a man, then?"

Yorick frowned. "Sure, just a man, like any other man—well, not *quite* like any other man, but you get what I mean, he's not immortal or anything like that. Why?"

Brom cocked his head on one side. "If he is but a man, why dost thou, then, call him 'Kernel'?"

"Oh!" Yorick's face cleared to a grin. "That's 'cause he brought us maize."

Brom's brows furrowed. "Maize? What is that?"

Yorick opened his mouth, then paused, "Well, uh—you know wheat, my lord?"

"Aye, certes," said Brom impatiently.

"Uh, yes. Okay, then, my lord, uh—imagine a great stalk of wheat, five feet tall, with an ear as long as your—uh—as long as *my* foot, that is. And each of the grains is the size of the tip of your finger."

Brom's face darkened with anger. "Oh, aye, to be sure, and next thou wilt have me believe in the ram of Darby, whose horns brushed the sky!"

Yorick shook his head stoutly. "No, it's true, my lord, and I can show you some of the kernels, to prove it. Not the whole plant, of course, we haven't been here long enough to get any growing yet, but we do have the kernels. And that's why we call him 'Kernel.' "

Brom's eyes held on the beastman's open, honest face, while Brom weighed the man's words.

Finally, he turned away, nodding. "And whilst thy king is gone to the wars, who governs here?"

Yorick shrugged. "Oh, me, I suppose, as much as anybody does. We don't really worry about it too much."

They strolled down the main "street" of the village. Women knelt in the doorways, grinding corn between stones, singing lightly; babies slept in cradle-boards, strapped to their mothers' backs. The men who were off duty dozed in the sun, or sat cross-legged in the shade, making weapons.

A lot of weapons. More than so few men could possibly use.

The people looked up and called cheery greetings to Yorick and welcomes to Brom as they passed by; Yorick answered in kind, and Brom responded with a stiff nod, trying to smile. He felt ill-at-ease, thrown off his guard by the friendliness and sincerity of the welcome; he would have felt more comfortable with hostility.

"How is it," he growled at Yorick, "that I am so well-liked so quickly?"

"Oh," Yorick said. "Well, you're hope, don't you see, my lord, you're promise of help from overseas to overthrow Shaman. We figure, with your espers to back up your armies, you might have a chance against the psionic generator. Then we could attack from the back, and between us, we could mop 'em up. Sound like a good plan, my lord?"

"Um—to be sure." Brom was frantically trying to remember what an "esper" was. He was sure he had heard the word before, but where . . . ?

Yes. From Rod Gallowglass.

And if this beastman used the same word for "witch" that Rod had used . . .

He stored the datum away in a niche in his mind, and made sure it was tagged for very quick reference.

He strolled down the street, studiously casual. "Indeed, it hath a most excellent sound, Master Yorick. And what is the strength posed against us? The number of soldiers thou said thy raiders opposed? Five hundred, was it? Why, that should be naught . . ."

He jerked to a stop, the realization hitting him. He wheeled on the beastman with a bellow.

"*Five hundred?* It cannot be so few! Thou hast at least that many souls in thy camp here already! And if these be but moiety of thine host, then the soldiers of Shaman must number by legions!"

"Yah. Yah," said Yorick, nodding. "Right, my lord. They've got about three thousand troops, total. But most of them are out of town at the moment."

"Out of . . . ?"

"Yeah, with the expedition."

"And what expedition would this be?"

Yorick turned, frowning. "Oh, you know, the expedition. With the fleet, remem— Oh! Damn it, that's right! I haven't told you yet, have I?"

"Indeed, thou hast not," Brom assured him grimly. "What is this talk of fleets?"

"Damn!" Yorick looked away, lips tightening with self-disgust. "And I was going to tell you that first thing, I made a mental note, I was so sure I wouldn't forget, and . . ."

"Wilt thou tell me!" Brom roared. "Or must I reach down thy throat and hale it out for myself! What is this fleet!"

"Why, an invasion fleet," said Yorick, faintly surprised. "They sailed for Gramarye this morning."

Rod cracked his eyelids open, frowning. What had wakened him . . . ?

The moonlight, channeled by the window, painted a swath across the stone chamber and the bedclothes, and Gwen's head, where it rested on his shoulder.

She turned restlessly toward him.

Her eyes were open.

There was a furrow between them.

That was what had wakened him, then. His wife had troubles.

He set a fingertip against the furrow in her forehead. "Quit that. It's bad for the complexion."

She looked up, startled, then smiled very tenderly. "Aye, my lord, if thou wilt have it so." And she kissed him—a long, moist, enveloping kiss.

Rod surfaced with a satisfied sigh, and a firm, deep conviction that the world couldn't be all bad, after all.

"Any particular reason for this sudden gush of tenderness?" Rod murmured.

She looked up, startled.

He smiled indulgently. "Wouldn't have anything to do with what's worrying you, would it?"

Gwen lowered her eyes again, sighing. " 'Tis this new-found witchling of ours, my lord."

A wrinkle tucked into Rod's forehead. "Greta, you mean? On the noon-to-four Agatha shift? What about her?"

Gwen smiled up at him, with a touch of regret. "What is it ever troubles young girls, my lord?"

Rod squeezed his eyes shut. "Oh, no! An acute case of love? Quarantine her, quick!"

Gwen punched him in the navel.

"All right, all right, I surrender! Love's a blessing, a treasure, a joy! But why can't you convince *her*?"

" 'Tis a matter of whom she has fallen in love with, my lord," Gwen murmured, nestling back into his shoulder.

"Oh, come on, it can't be all *that* bad! The worst that could happen is, she's fallen in love with a kid who isn't a warlock. And, admitted, it's pretty bad for a witch to

130

have a thing for a boy who doesn't have a witch-power to his brain, but . . ."

She punched him again.

"Nay, my lord."

Rod raised an eyebrow. "Unrequited love, chronic dosage?"

"Nay, my lord. He requites her completely."

Rod frowned. "What's the trouble, then? Bundle 'em off to bed, and let 'em work it out there!"

"That would, I doubt not, be quite the best, my lord," she murmured, "save that he has no body."

Rod stared.

Gwen nodded, eyes huge.

"No," Rod choked out.

"Aye," Gwen commiserated.

"No. It can't be. It's impossible. Unthinkable. It can't happen." He broke off, shaking his head slowly, eyes tragic. "The poor kid. The poor, poor kid." He scowled. "Poor both of them, come to think of it."

"Aye, poor indeed," Gwen murmured. "She came bursting in whilst I sat in study, and fled to my arms, weeping a deluge, shuddering as with the ague."

Rod raised an eyebrow. "Old Agatha'd found out about it?"

Gwen nodded.

"And cussed her out?"

"Nay, though the child had feared that she would, but Agatha was joyful, delighted; for now, quoth she, she would have a relation embodied, as soon as the young folk were wed; but then she stopped a moment, and thought, and turned to Greta to ask, as gently as she might . . ."

"Which isn't saying that much," Rod grumbled.

"Yet she meant well, my lord. She asked Greta how they might in all truth bring this marriage about, since Harold her son hath no body."

"A point," Rod said, very softly. "Oh, yes, a most relevant point." He looked at Gwen out of the corner of his eye. "And the kid bust out bawling, and ran for you?"

"Aye, my lord. It would seem she had not thought of that side of their loving before. . . ."

"I take it the whole thing got started when she got assigned to Agatha?"

"Aye, my lord. A young, giddy girl-witch and the son of a witch and a warlock. . . ."

"A *possible* son," Rod murmured, "of a marriage that didn't occur. An immigrant from a world of If. . . ."

"Still, my lord, one living and vital, though he hath

131

no body. Yet he hath great powers, and thought-speaking and -hearing he numbers among them."

"But of course," Rod muttered. "Love at first thought. . . ."

" 'Tis even so, my lord. But 'twould seem, neither of them had given a thought to a more—shall we say, tangible form of communication? And now they are both most distraught."

"Yes, I can see how they would be." Rod nodded judiciously. " 'Course, I know some girls who'd think it was ideal. . . ."

"But Greta may not be numbered among them," Gwen murmured. "Nor may I. . . ."

Rod stiffened suddenly, startled; then he glowered at his wife. "Quit that! We're not done talking yet."

She looked down, toying with the hairs on his chest. "I will own to thee now. I have, now and again, been angry with my God, for the man he destined unto me could not hear my thoughts, nor I his; for that touch-and-caress of the minds is God's great blessing to witches. . . ."

Rod's stomach sank; a sheet of cold wrapped itself round his spine. His eyes hollowed.

"Yet now," Gwen went on, a purr coming into her voice, "these two world-crossed lovers have taught me anew the great blessing thou art; for thou, at least, hast a body."

The purr was full-bodied, and the glow in the eyes was voracious. Her breasts caressed him as she stretched up to nibble his ear.

Rod caught his breath, then let it out in a gusty sigh. "Yes," he said. "Well, I *suppose* that's a compliment."

"It is, be quite sure," she murmured. "For, my lord, if I must be made to choose between the higher love and the lower, be assured that the higher would never be my choice."

"Um," Rod said. "Well. Uh. Yes. So much for Plato," he sighed. "*Cam*mere, kid!"

He lunged, and Gwen shrieked, and they went down in a churning tangle of blankets. The tangle heaved, surged . . . then settled, and began to emit languorous murmurs. . . .

A delicate cough broke.

Rod froze.

Somebody began to hum in a voice that needed oiling.

Rod sat on his heels, grinding his teeth.

Gwen nodded, commiserating.

"Sometimes," Rod mused, "I get to wishing that elves could understand the concept of privacy."

He turned to face the grinning elf. "What's got you, gob-hoblin?"

Kelly extended a folded, sealed paper. " 'Tis word from my lord, Brom O'Berin."

Rod sat very still for a very long moment.

He said, very softly, "This couldn't have waited till morning?"

"I fear not, Rod Gallowglass." The elf held the letter up to the moonlight. "For, look you, Lord Warlock—the substance and gist of the letter is this: the beastmen invade."

"He is a viper, a scorpion, a poisoned thorn in the flesh of our land!" Skolax hissed.

The faces of the men of the peasant household stared wide-eyed about him, lit by the fire, loose-jawed and fearful.

"Our God has commanded that he should die!" Skolax snapped. " 'Thou shalt not suffer a witch to live,' saith the Lord! Yet here, near to here, stands that sable stronghold of menace where Galen, most arrogant of wizards, plies his nefarious arts! And what will you do, you who call yourselves men, Christian men? Wilt thou hale down that tower, as the Lord hath commanded? Nay, surely not! 'Thou shalt not leave one stone upon another,' saith the Lord! But you, who call yourselves men of God, will not bring down that tower; for, out of fear, you worship that black wizard!"

"But—but, holy man," said the eldest, his voice quavering but reverent, "if we do as thou sayest, who shall guard us from that darkling sorcerer?"

"Why, I!" thundered Skolax. "Have I not prevailed 'gainst the Witch of the Mountain, black Agatha? Even 'gainst she whose name means dark death, have I prevailed!" He winced at a twinge of pain in his bandaged shoulder. "Thou hast heard the tale, for it ran here before me, how I and my stout peasant band fought our way to her cave and drove her away! Shall I not give to thee as much of protection? The power of the Lord is strong here, within me! Stronger than the powers of that wizard's Hell-magic!" He glared at the four faces around him. "Who dares say me nay?"

He glared into the four faces around him, one by one. Each man cowered back.

" 'Tis well," Skolax nodded, satisfied.

"*Who will march with me 'gainst him?*" He surged to his feet, staff whirling above his head.

The four men sat, staring, dumb.

Then, all together, they began to clamor, nodding their heads, pathetically eager.

"I, Skolax, I!" "I too, Skolax, I too!" "I also!" "And I!"

" 'Tis well," nodded the preacher, leaning on his staff, lids drooping sleepily.

Then the eyes gleamed with fire. "Go now," he commanded, "and tell others!"

" '. . . and therefore do I adjure thee in all haste to prepare, for the beastmen shall soon be upon thee! And look you, Rod Gallowglass—do thou not squander time in thy seekings and ponderings; but be quick!' Then his name, and that's all. He didn't sign even one of his titles. That worries me."

"Perhaps it is merely an indication of the degree of his concern, Rod," Fess murmured.

"Of course it is! That's what worries me; things must be worse than I thought." Rod folded the letter, stood up, frowned, and kicked the bale of hay he'd been sitting on.

Fess chewed a mouthful of hay thoughtfully. "What preparations is Tuan making?"

"He's sending all his troops to the mouth of the Fleuve, except for a few left to guard the castle and maintain order on the Royal Estates," said Rod, frowning, "and commanded all the barons within a day's march to do the same. The rest of the lords are supposed to send their troops to Runnymede, so Tuan can have them on tap." He kicked at the wall of the stall.

"A practical measure," the robot murmured, "but scarcely likely to be of much value. Has he any plans for dealing with the reinforced Evil Eye, Rod?"

Rod shrugged. "Only Agatha and her familiar. She should improve our chances some . . . uh, shouldn't she?"

"The probability of successful defense against the invaders is now point three-one-seven, Rod."

"Pi in the sky," Rod growled. He felt as though his stomach were looking for a dropshaft. He spoke sternly to it, and it huddled back; but it scrunched up as small as it could.

"And what precautions have been taken against the fireballs?" Fess murmured.

Rod shook his head. "I don't think they'll even try to use them here. They know we'll have TK witches waiting, to throw them back—or at least, whoever's bossing them probably knows that. But I'm having the witches stand by, just in case."

" 'Whoever's running them,' the robot mused, "yes."

134

"Shaman," Rod growled, "through Atylem. Or maybe the Kobold, whatever it is, is running Shaman, who's running Atylem, who's running the show. This Japanese usurpation gets complicated. . . . Anyway, whoever it is, he's got a psionic generator, which would seem to indicate he comes from off-planet."

"Or out-time," Fess reminded.

"Well, yes, out-time, too; it comes to pretty much the same thing—we're fighting boys with a high technology. At least as high as DDT's. Maybe higher. And, worse, they're smart. The way Brom describes that revolution, it was anything but an amateur job. They know how to organize. And infiltrate."

"Infiltrate?" The robot's voice sounded puzzled.

Rod looked up, surprised. "Of course. Skolax. You didn't think he was working on his own, did you?"

"I have encountered no data that would effectively repudiate that theory, Rod."

Rod scowled. "What do you call the ambush at Agatha's, then? He and Shaman worked together very tidily on that—managed to lure the bulk of our available witch-power into the trap before they sprung it. Tried to take Gwen alive, too, to use as a hostage against me. Skolax in front and Shaman behind. Only reason it didn't work was old Galen, and you couldn't have expected them to know about him; I certainly wouldn't have thought he was relevant to the situation. No, it was a very neat setup, very well-planned —and that kind of coordination has to be the result of collusion."

"Not necessarily," Fess demurred. "Shaman might have deduced Skolax's intentions, and have laid his own plans to take advantage of Skolax's actions."

Rod frowned, chewing at the inside of his cheek. "Possibly," he admitted. "But it would imply that Shaman has an almost impossibly efficient intelligence system. After all, tunneling up to the back of Agatha's cave took some time. No, I find it much easier to believe they've got some sort of alliance going. And Skolax's part in the alliance is apparently to soften us up for invasion, by getting us to fight one another."

"He is also executing a rather effective program of limiting Gramarye's ability to resist the Evil Eye," Fess ruminated, "by obstructing the campaign for recruiting of espers."

"Much too effective," Rod agreed, "which rather galls me, since I had—well, still have—hopes that this Evil Eye war would turn the witches into national heroes, 'guardians of the homeland,' that kind of thing. Make esper powers a positive survival factor. But Skolax has very nicely muddied up my Big Plan."

"Which would seem to suggest," murmured Fess, "that Skolax is also aware of the 'Big Plan.'"

Rod waved the suggestion away impatiently. "He couldn't unless he's got a pretty clear idea of how Gramarye's going to affect the future of the DDT, like our friends the futurians, the Councillors and the House of Clovis, but we cleaned them out, and destroyed both time machines. . . ."

"You mentioned a few days ago, Rod, that they might have managed to introduce a third time machine. . . ."

Rod stood immobile for a few seconds, staring at the straw on the floor.

He lifted his head, nodding slowly. "Yes, I did say that, didn't I? And, now that I think about it, Skolax's *modus operandi* does look familiar—rabble-rousing against the government, like the House of Clovis. . . ."

"The totalitarian futurians," Fess interjected.

"Ye-es. And, speaking of M.O.'s, Shaman's power-behind-the-power-behind the throne bit looks suspiciously like the councillors' techniques. . . . Fess, I think our old friends are back."

"But certainly that would obviate any possibility of collusion between Skolax and Shaman, Rod."

Rod shrugged. "Haven't you ever heard of a rogue's alliance? Or of uniting in the face of a common enemy? No, they could be in cahoots easy enough. . . ." His eyes began to glow. "And, keeping with M.O., and thinking about how Brom says Atylem was haranguing his crew, planting doubts of Shaman in their minds . . . Fess, I think Skolax has an agent in Shaman's camp!"

"If that is so," the robot murmured, "any alliance between them must be highly unstable."

"Yeah, but I'll bet it'll be stable enough to last until they take Gramarye—until and if. At which point, if Skolax's plans work out, Atylem should lead an uprising to overthrow Shaman. . . ."

"As Shaman did to Kernel," Fess mused. "Extremely poetic."

Rod's head turned slowly toward Fess. "Yes, Kernel," he said, nodding slightly. "I'd forgotten about him. Where'd he come from, Fess? And who's he working for? If his lieutenant knows what a psionic generator and an esper are, doesn't Kernel? So he's out-time, too—or off-planet."

"Out-time would seem more probable," the robot interjected, "in view of the presence of Neanderthals."

Rod nodded. "A point. But where'd he get 'em? And how'd he get 'em here? And can we trust him to keep faith with us, if we call him 'ally' and invade Beastland? Sure, his hammer-and-pincers idea sounds great—but can we trust him? After all, Brom hasn't laid eyes on him—couldn't this whole business about Kernel and the exiles' camp be one of Shaman's ploys, to lull us off-guard?"

"Rod," Fess sighed, "your paranoia is showing."

"Oh, all right, so I'm not being logical! But neither is Kernel—is he?"

"I wouldn't know," said Fess thoughtfully. "I never met him."

"Yes, that is sort of the core of the problem, isn't it? We don't know anything about him. Specifically, we don't know when he came from, which means we have no idea about what kind of powers he can command."

"It might be advisable, Rod, to bring in some additional forces of your own."

Rod laughed—one inner spasm. "How? Tell SCENT to send reinforcements? All right, go ahead! Send a 'gram!"

Fess hesitated, then said doubtfully, "They will comply, Rod; but the minimum transport time from the nearest base would in all probability exceed the duration of the current crisis."

"I *never* would have guessed." Rod leaned back against the wall, folded his arms, let his head fall back against the wood, closing his eyes. "Take a note, Fess—after this is all over, we send home for more agents. Chances are we'll need some, some time in the future."

Fess hesitated a moment, then said doubtfully, "They will reply that, due to a chronic shortage of personnel, they are unable to supply you with additional . . ."

"I know, I know," Rod grumbled. "I can have all the equipment I'd need to make a mountain come to Mohammed, even if he was on Terra at the time; but no men—not until the situation becomes critical, anyway. Like it is now."

"*As* it is now, Rod."

"Oh, shut up. Anyway, by the time they sent men, the war would be over and done with."

"Again, as it is now," the robot murmured, "or nearly. *Sic transit gloria mundi.*"

"Our transit isn't all that sick yet, Pollyanna," Rod growled. "All I'd need to round out this war would be to have you in charge of morale. Okay, I think we've covered all the major factors. Add 'em up and tell me where that puts us."

"In a somewhat untenable position, Rod."

"The wonders of cybernetics," Rod groaned.

"However," the robot mused, "I do have some random correlations that might be of interest. . . ."

"Oh?" Rod pricked up his ears. "Ramble on, Robot Roan."

"Since there seems to be a correlation between Skolax's and the House of Clovis' *modi operandi*," said Fess, chewing thoughtfully, "and a similar correlation involving Shaman and the councillors, a resemblance in method . . ."

"Resemblance!" Rod's eyes snapped wide. "Yes, now that you mention it—Shaman even looks like the councillors! You know, shriveled and skinny. Of course, he's got the Neanderthal brow and chin—or lack of chin, that is. But surgery could do that. A little fantastic, I'll admit, but that far in the future, plastic surgery should be as common as cosmetics. And if Kernel, whoever he is, could bring Neanderthals here (assuming they're the genuine Terran article), presumably via time machine, there's no reason why the futurians couldn't have pulled off the same trick. After all, they had to get their first time machines here somehow, didn't they? And what they did once, they can do again!"

"And again, and again, and again . . ." Fess murmured.

"When I need encouraging thoughts, I'll ask for them. Now, how about Skolax and Atylem? If they're from the future totalitarians, then . . ." Rod broke off, staring. "Fess! The House of Clovis leader, the Mocker—we've got him and his lieutenants in the dungeon, right?"

"We have, Rod. They were placed there at your orders . . . against my advice, I might add. The logical move would have been to execute them."

"Yes, well, you didn't have the misfortune of being built with a conscience, Fess. But, look—how did the Mocker get his name?"

"Why, by his ability to change his appearance, Rod. So that . . ." The robot's voice trailed off.

"Just what I was thinking," said Rod grimly.

He spun around and strode out into the courtyard, shouting, "Jailer! Warder of the dungeons! I want an inventory!"

Rod stumped up the last few stairs and out into the sunlight. The great iron door crashed shut behind him. He took a deep, grateful breath of fresh air, and turned to find Fess standing patiently by the dungeon entrance.

"You heard?" Rod mumbled.

The black horse-head nodded once. "I did," said the voice behind Rod's ear. "Eavesdropping through your microphone, Rod."

Rod nodded. "Well, looks like we were right, Fess. There should be four men in that dungeon, and there're only three. Sure, one of them looked like the Mocker, but a little cold cream and soap and water changed that. Besides, he was about three inches too short, and a shade too heavy."

"Then Skolax is, indeed, the Mocker," the robot murmured.

"Was," Rod corrected him. "I *think* I killed him at Agatha's cave. If I didn't, we'll be hearing from him pretty soon, you can be sure of that."

"Master Gallowglass!"

Rod swung about, scowling, to see a page running toward him breathlessly. "Word from the witches, Master Gallowglass! The beastmen attack!"

Brom lay among the rocks above the talus slope, watching the quiet dance of the watchfires in the village below, small, vibrant pebbles of warmth and light in the dark, moonless night. The silhouette of a sentry occluded one fire for a moment; then all was still again.

"But I do not understand," Brom muttered. "Here, in thine enemy's mouth, with so small a force? What canst thou hope to gain?"

"A small force travels light, my lord." Yorick grinned wolfishly in the night beside him. "Light, and fast—very fast. So fast that we can destroy their storehouse and be back in the heights before they can get troops out against us."

"But their storehouse! What gain is that? They will only build it again. And these jars of fire-oil, that thou sayest lie within it—will they not fetch them more? So, at great risk of life for all of thy men, thou wilt destroy their ability to make fireballs for their catapults—for a matter of days only!"

"True," Yorick agreed. "But, well—if you had an army, my lord, and a bunch of bandits burned your armory, and you couldn't catch them—and as soon as you built it again, they burned it again, and this kept happening every time you rebuilt it— How would you feel?"

"I would become exceedingly wroth," Brom admitted.

"Yeah, and it'd bug the hell out of you, too. And way down deep, my lord, you would become just the teeniest, tiniest bit afraid—now, wouldn't you?"

"And that is what thou wouldst do to them?"

"Mostly," said Yorick judiciously. "It's called breaking down morale. Though of course, every gallon of, uh, fire-fluid, every gallon we burn is a gallon that doesn't burn us—if you follow my meaning."

"Most assuredly. But tell me, Master Yorick—where is thy Kernel throughout this? And how is it I have not yet seen him?"

"Oh, he's up at the High Cave." Yorick jerked his head in the relevant direction. "He's lurking in the rocks up there, in case any of the sentries happen to notice one of our boys taking out one of theirs, before the big blowup."

"In which case . . . ?"

"In which case, he has a loop of very hard wire that does an excellent job of canceling any feedback of information, from the sentry to any of the boys guarding the Kobold. He wouldn't trust that job to anyone else."

Brom scowled. "Why dost thou not take the High Cave and the Kobold, rather than burning the storehouse?"

"Because the guards in there outnumber us about five to one. And we're very good fighters and all that, but there *are* limits."

In the valley below, a sentry crossed in front of a fire. A silhouette rose out of the ground behind him, slammed a judo chop into the base of the sentry's neck. The sentry stiffened, then slumped, dropped, and the attacker faded into the night, toward the storehouse.

"It's starting," Yorick said grimly.

"Why dost thou not slay?" Brom growled—insincerely.

"You don't kill men who used to hunt with you, my lord. Not if you can help it, anyway. . . . But they don't really leave us much choice, sometimes. See you in a little bit, my lord." He crawled to the lip of the ledge.

"I ha' fought well in my day, and that day is not yet done!" Brom said angrily. "Why may I not lend my knife to this work?"

Yorick shook his head regretfully. "You don't know this village, my lord. And you're not immune to Evil Eye power. Besides which, we can't risk losing you; you've got to take word of this back to Major Gallowglass. Give him a few ideas, remind him about a chapter in military history he's forgotten about."

He looked quickly toward the village, saw another execution silhouetted. "It'll be a little tougher this time. They've doubled the guard, and they're really alert—kind of edgy, in fact. But then, that's what this whole shenanigan's about, isn't it?"

He dropped out of sight, over the ledge to the talus slope.

Brom lay silent on the rock, watching the black bulk

of the storehouse against the night sky. His pulse beat unnaturally loud in his ears.

A chorus of howls exploded; a moment later, the storehouse burst into flame.

Its ruddy, wavering light picked out the prone, unconscious bodies of a score of guards, and a dozen hulking forms leaping away into the night.

The dragon ships moved up the river, manned by skeleton crews. The bulk of the beastmen force stayed ashore, flanking the fleet on either bank, and moving with it inland. They burned the villages and the crops in the fields as they went; they slaughtered the cattle and ate them. Where they had passed, only smoking desert remained.

But the villages they burned were empty; for elves ran a day's march ahead of the enemy forces, warning the peasants to flee.

With the enemy on either bank of the river, the King must needs split his army to fight them; but the beastmen were all of one force, for the dragon ships formed a moving bridge between them.

Several times, Rod and Tuan beat them back to the river banks; but they could drive them no farther, for whenever they paused in their march, the beastmen threw up huge, steep-sided earthen walls, behind which they sat and waited, impregnable.

So the King drew back his forces, and waited too.

He waited until the next thunderstorm.

Then, with the power of the Evil Eye behind them, the beastmen broke out, howling for blood.

At the first distant rumble of thunder, Tuan ordered his men back, and dispersed them in good order.

After the third such encounter, he was forced to admit that the elves were already doing all that could be done.

So the people of the Kobold bored into Gramarye unhindered; and the people of King Tuan fled before them unhampered, taking only their wives, their journey-bread, their children, and whatever antiques they chose to glorify with the title of "weapons."

Up the River Fleuve moved the invaders, like a hot spit thrust into meat.

Near the headwaters of that river stood Runnymede—the King's Town, the capital of Gramarye.

For a week the people had camped in the meadow, their numbers growing daily.

Before them, at the edge of the meadow, towered the dark wall of the Forest Gellorn.

But the sky was blue and clear, and the sun beat down warmly; and Skolax, aware that the forest looked menacing, had sent hunting parties in the first day, had sent messengers to tavern keepers in the nearby towns, saying that kegs would be rewarded by the holy man's blessings and prayers.

So, for a week, life in the meadow had been one continual party, with a deer always roasting on a spit, and the kegs flowing freely. Now and again a peasant would notice the dark, brooding trees, and would stop, jaw slackening, color draining from his face; but a wench would catch him away, laughing, to a dance, and the forest would sulk alone.

Alone till this day; for Skolax counted noses and nodded, satisfied, then clambered to the top of a huge rock that stood at the east edge of the meadow.

"Harken!" he roared, brandishing his staff. "Harken to Skolax!"

A few peasants, nearby, turned their heads at his voice, sobering. They took up the cry till it rang through the meadow, while Skolax leaned, nodding and satisfied, on his staff.

Slowly, the meadow quieted. All faces turned to Skolax, expectant.

"Now comes the hour for which we all have longed!" Skolax cried, his staff whirling high, his voice carrying clear to the edge of the forest. "Now comes the day of the Right, the failure of Evil! Thou hast drunk, thou hast fed, thou hast been joyful in the eyes of the Lord! And rightly hast thou rejoiced, for the laugh in thy hearts has been the clamor of the victory of Right!"

Peasants scattered throughout the crowd began cheering. The crowd took it up, howling the joy of their wine-fed courage.

" 'Tis the hour!" Skolax shouted, " 'Tis the day of the Lord! Ere this sun sets, we shall hale down that bastion of Evil, the Dark and Fell Tower of the Sorcerer Galen! And the strength of our arms is the Right!"

The crowd roared.

"Reason, rationale, logic— Faugh!" Agatha spat into the fire. "A pox on thy logics, I say! I know what I know!"

She hitched her stool closer to the hearth and held her knobby old hands out to the blaze.

"But it can't be organic—uh, alive!" Rod paced the packed

142

earth floor of the peasant hut like a leashed cheetah. "I tell you, I know these boys, and organics is not one of their tricks, damn it! Either that extra psionic—uh, witch—power that comes with the lightning bolts comes from hundreds of collective beastmen minds, or from one big machine, a thing of cold iron, hear me? It can't come from one mind!"

"Yet it doth," said Agatha complacently, chafing her hands. " 'Twas in my mind, not thine, arrogant youth, and I tell thee, I felt it! Dosta hear me? With my mind, I did feel it! My mind and my soul, and it weighed down and near rent them asunder! 'Twas I who bore the brunt of that hideous force, I who held mind-touch with it, and I tell thee, I know what I know! 'Twas but one mind, and living!"

She scowled, mumbling almost to herself. "Although it was, in all truth, a most unhuman mind, and of most horribly huge and vast power; yet it had not a thought of its own! I tell thee, it was a mind such as three of mine could not equal, yet it had no more soul than a haystalk! Gross and distorted, most hideous grotesque; one would almost think it more animal than man, yet still less than animal. . . ."

"Cold?" Rod ventured. "Almost mechanical, you might say?"

Agatha shook her head decisively. "Thou might say it, but I never would. Had it been mere and only lifeless, there had been naught of the eerie about it. But to have life without the simplest sort of a soul . . ." She shuddered. "I could strongly, devoutly, pray 'twere but a machine."

"Look—the beastmen are just five miles away, down by the riverside. In just one stormy night, they've managed to carve their way twenty miles into Gramarye. They're camped down there at Gilpin's Ferry, and"—his arm swung ninety degrees—"Bogeyland is a thousand some-odd miles off that way. Now, how the hell could one living mind, no matter how strong it is, send a blast of power all that way?"

"That," said Agatha smugly, "thou hast already made known to me. This weird brew of ironic-spears, cat-toads and ant-odes, potent-shells, and all manner of recipes like to make the most hardened witch blanch. . . ."

"All right, all right, so it's theoretically possible," Rod snarled. "But I tell you it's just not their style!"

He started pacing again. "They don't use living things, I tell you, they use machines! Copper! Plastic! Steel! Oil! Resistors! Isotope batteries!"

"May they not ha' changed their 'style,' as thou wouldst have it?"

"Changed?" said Rod stupidly.

"Aye, changed. Because thou art too aged to change, Rod Gallowglass, is no reason that they must needs be so."

"Too old!" Rod gawked, scandalized. "Me? Why, you old, ossified, ornery, unprintable octogenarian!"

"My lord!" Gwen burst into the cottage, caught up her husband's hand. "Good my lord, thou must needs go, and go quickly!"

Rod's head snapped up. "Why? Vigilantes?"

"Nay, my lord, 'tis the false preacher Skolax. He ha' raised a mob of poor peasants, and moves to attack the Dark Tower! Thou must ride, my lord, to the rescue, right quickly!"

Rod stood a moment, then whirled to the door, muttering into his mike, "Fess! Warm up your jets!"

He stopped dead with his hand on the door, whipped about to his wife. "Wait a minute! What should I go for? To help the most powerful wizard in Gramarye? Sure, lady, sure! If he can't handle a simple little rural riot all by himself, who can?"

"He can, my lord, but he doth not!" Gwen ran to him, clutched his doublet. "Oh, my lord, the elves ha' brought word! The mob doth march unopposed through the Forest Gellorn; the wizard doth naught to obstruct them!"

Rod stood quiet a long moment; then his eyes narrowed. He turned to glare at Agatha. "Thanks!" he spat, and whipped the door open.

Agatha sat up stiffly, brows lifting. "Thou art most assuredly welcome! Yet may I inquire the cause of thy gratitude?"

"For putting ideas into Galen's head!" Rod barked over his shoulder. "Apparently he's decided to copy your bit and die, rather than kill anyone else."

Agatha's shoulders shrugged once with a contemptuous inner laugh. "Nay," she said, settling back into her rocking chair, "nay, be assured, 'tis not that. That could not be the cause of his lack of defense of himself. He could not be a man of such courage."

"Then why else would he—" Rod broke off, staring. "Hey! Wait a minute . . . you don't suppose . . ."

Agatha frowned.

Gwen took Rod's hand. "My lord . . . ?"

"This business about dying, Gwen. . . . You don't suppose he's . . ."

"Dead!" Agatha sat bolt upright, blanching. "Nay! It be

144

not so, say not so, he must not . . ." She broke off, her face becoming a mask, and sat back in her chair deliberately. "Well, mayhap so. And if 'tis, I rejoice. The world is rid of a coward and cheat, of the scum of the earth! I rejoice."

She sat a moment, glaring at the fire.

Then her eyes snapped around to Rod's. "And what dost *thou* stare at, thou great loon? Begone, fool of warlocks! To Gellorn! To thy work!"

"Yeah," Rod said, nodding slowly. He cleared his throat, nodded again. "Yeah. Sure, Agatha. Sure."

The peasants burst howling into the narrow strip of land around the base of the brooding, black monolith, the Dark Tower.

Skolax, at their head, shouted, "Find doors! Seek out portals!" and the peasants, bellowing lustily, fanned out in a circle around the Tower.

The clamoring slackened, then stilled. An uneasy, fearful muttering grew in its place; for the Tower had no doors.

"Holy man!" cried a peasant. "Venerable Skolax! No doors hath this keep! No way of admittance!"

" 'Tis the work of the devil!" someone screamed, and the crowd's murmuring rose toward a roar. A few edged toward the forest.

Skolax surveyed the crowd with a look of disgust.

"Silence!" he roared, his staff lashing out; the crowd took on a notable resemblance to a graveyard in a vacuum.

"Well, then," Skolax said calmly, "the keep hath no portal.

"*What of it!*" The staff chopped down in exasperation.

He glared at the crowd. "Will not the power of the Lord breach these walls? The Lord hath brought thee here unto this place, the Lord shall protect thee! The Lord shall defend thee! The power of the Lord shall be in thine arm, as it is now in mine!"

He held the staff in both hands, pointing it at the granite wall. A lance of fire sprang from the tip, smashing into the stone.

The crowd gasped; the nearest fell back, pushing against their fellows to open a small clearing around the preacher.

Molten rock began to drip down the wall under the relentless boring of the laser.

A moan of awe swept the crowd. As one, they fell to their knees, hands uplifted in prayer.

Lava oozed down the wall.

Skolax scowled, realizing that if the granite blocks were

145

as thick as those usually used for castle masonry, he would be hours carving a door large enough to admit his army.

The beam went out, the staff swung up to the vertical. "Now dost thou know the power of the Lord!" Skolax thundered. "Now thou hast seen, dost thou believe?"

A groan of ecstasy, almost a roar, swept through the crowd as the peasants surged to their feet, shaking their fists at the tower, bellowing their faith.

"Be sure," Skolax howled, "that the power of the Lord lies here to defend thee! Here by thy side, should it be needed! Yet—" The staff jabbed out, and the crowd fell totally silent.

Skolax swept them slowly with his eyes.

"It is the will of the Lord," he intoned, "that thy tribute to Him, thy victory over this evil, be of thy doing! Thine, without benefit of his aid—if thou hast strength enow! He would have thee breach this loathsome edifice by thine own effort! He wishes that thou shouldst show him thy courage, thy faith, and—*thy manhood!*"

The crowd screamed with him in a cathartic display of true zeal.

"Thou must rise above it!"

The crowd roared its approval.

"Ladders!" Skolax howled. "Cut saplings! High above you, there"—his staff jabbed up at the walls—"above you, scarce fifty feet, there are breaches in this wall!"

Half a hundred feet off the ground, the high, thin embrasures of windows looked down upon them.

"We shall go up through these windows of this Dark Tower; we shall scour this keep of its loathsome dark master!"

"That's it, just ahead, down there." Rod leaned forward in the saddle, pointing at the black obelisk rising from the center of the clearing. "But what's all that activity about two-thirds of the way down?" He frowned, squinting, then jolted back in his seat. "Ye gods! The Preacher's Pogrom is coming through already!"

Fess adjusted his eyes to electron telescopy and murmured, "Their ladders appear to be rather insecure, Rod. But while they last, they will undoubtedly prove effective."

"Well, we can make 'em real ineffective, real fast," Rod said grimly. "Prepare to dive, Fess."

On the ground, a peasant glanced skyward, then glanced

again, and screamed, pointing at the flame-tailed dot driving toward them.

"Flee!" he shrieked. "We are doomed! *'Tis a flying sorcerer!*"

The direction of swarming on the ladders reversed, heading toward the ground at full speed. The peasants on the lowest rungs had gotten the message, too, and were treading toward the tall timber at triple time; so there was comparatively little jamming at the bases of the ladders. There was more confusion on the rungs; but even so, relatively few bodies plummeted forty feet to the ground.

So, by the time Fess dived down to burn through the ladders with his exhaust, most of the peasants were well out of the danger zone. Those who were still twenty feet in the air when the ladders came crashing down were bruised, with a few broken limbs, but alive. And the hundred or so peasants who were already inside the tower were temporarily safe.

But those in the middle, the few still fairly high up on the ladder, were out of luck. Also life.

"Rod," the robot murmured as it boomed around the tower, "I detect human voices calling inside the tower."

"Oh? What are they calling for?"

"Warlock blood."

Rod nodded grimly and hauled back on the reins. "Head for the top window, Fess. The skylight with the telescope."

"I am quite capable of estimating the sizes of windows," Fess replied a trifle huffily. "The observatory is the only window wide enough to admit me."

The roof of the tower formed a four-sided peak; one of the triangular sides was open. Fess leaped through it, killing his engines.

"Down the stairway, Fess." Rod pointed. "And turn your eyes up to infrared. The old boy must be the economical type; he doesn't seem to believe in keeping extra torches burning."

They racketed down the spiral staircase—and down, and down, and down, till Rod was dizzy, and a little nauseous.

Then the stairway widened to a huge arch, cloaked by dark velvet hangings.

The robot burst through and jerked to a halt, paying just enough lip service to the Law of Inertia for Rod to be able to stay in the saddle.

The chamber was about the size of your living room, deeply shadowed, dimly lit by a smoking oil lamp. The walls were hung with deep purple velvet. A thick candlestick, guttered, stood on a small table next to the low, velvet-covered couch, where the old wizard lay, his head on a gold brocade cushion, a burgundy-red blanket pulled up over his thin, laboring chest. His eyes were closed, his face drawn and pale, drops of cold sweat on his brow. Hard, wheezing breaths rasped through his throat.

Rod swallowed, hard. "Did we get here in time, Fess?"

With a howl, the mob and the preacher burst through the hangings on the far side of the room.

With a shout of triumph, Skolax leveled his staff at the wizard.

"I would say we arrived at precisely the correct moment, Rod," the robot murmured.

"Havoc!" Rod bellowed.

The dart of fire from Skolax's staff shivered aside, missing Galen by inches, as the preacher jumped, startled by the ancient war-cry. He looked wildly about; his eyes fastened on Rod.

Then the maw of the camouflaged laser-rifle was fastening on Rod, too.

Rod shouted again and dived from the saddle; the beam stabbed through the space where he'd been. Rod sprang around the head of the couch, charging the preacher. Fess leaped into full gallop around the foot, ears laid back, alloy teeth bared.

Skolax stood in momentary confusion, unable to decide between the black horse charging down from one side, and the man with the dagger leaping in from the other.

The peasants stood rooted, staring, jaws slack.

Skolax whirled, staff swiveling toward Fess.

Rod froze, pointing the hilt of his dagger at Skolax, thumb on the rigger button.

A peasant jolted out of his stupor and shouted, hurling a mattock.

It struck Rod's hand just as the ruby beam spat out from the hilt. Rod scowled an oath that would have taken the scales off a snake, barely managing to hold onto the dagger.

The ruby beam sizzled over Skolax's shoulder.

The preacher glanced quickly at Rod, and Fess dodged. Red fire hissed from the end of the staff, missing the robot by inches. Skolax thundered an oath that should have completely disillusioned his congregation, and took fresh aim.

The mattock-throwing peasant grabbed up a scythe and charged Rod, bellowing.

Fess swerved, charging the peasant. Skolax's staff snickered again, and missed again. Skolax cursed, swinging the staff over to cover Rod.

On the couch, old Galen's eyelids flickered.

Skolax's staff snapped out of his hands, whirling end-over-end to the far side of the room.

Fess jerked to a halt between Rod and the peasant, shuddered, convulsed, and froze, knees locked stiff, head swinging gently between fetlocks.

The peasant hesitated a moment, confused, then sprang to go around Fess' south end.

Rod set his hands on pommel and cantle, executed a side-vault that did credit to his gymnastics teacher, and clubbed the peasant on the nape of the neck with his heels.

He landed clear, spun about to dive under Fess, switching his dagger to his left hand, and turned back toward his attackers just in time to see Skolax racing to his staff at the far end of the room.

Rod snapped a shot at him; but he wasn't too dexterous left-handed, and the beam sizzled past a few inches in front of the preacher's face.

Skolax, however, had a certain amount of inborn caution and intelligence amounting to the better part of valor. He skidded to a halt as the reek of charred velvet curtains hit his nostrils, and whirled about.

"Retreat! For the love of thy lives go! Get back, get away! One wizard the power of the Lord might defeat, but not two! Back to the ladder, now flee!" Skolax bellowed.

The peasants obeyed in a concerted surge, clearing the room with a dispatch that was a model of efficiency. Their leader was hard on their heels, bursting through the curtains milliseconds after them.

The curtains swayed together, then stilled.

Rod stood staring at the velvet, massaging his right hand, listening to the fading sounds of the routed mob. He had time; the ladders were fallen. The peasants would probably be able to clamber down the masonry—slowly and painfully, for the blocks of granite were smoothly cut, and large; but there were finger- and toe-holds where the blocks were joined. They just might make it. But it would take them a while to nerve themselves to it. Rod could be back in action before Skolax reached the ground.

He sighed, shaking his head, and turned to Fess. He groped under the pommel, found the reset switch, threw it.

Slowly, the robot lifted its head.

"You had a seizure," Rod said quickly, to forestall the

robot's usual questions. Then, slowly and clearly, "You—had —a—seizure."

Fess was still a moment, puzzling over the statement, then nodded slowly, bemused.

"Now," Rod said reluctantly, "I hate the idea of fighting a cornered quarry, and taking the risk of some panicked peasants jumping out of a window fifty feet in the air. But, nonetheless, I think we'd better make sure of our Mocker-cum-Skolax while we can. If we let him run loose, there's no telling how much damage he'll manage to do . . . or how many deaths he'll manage to cause."

He sighed, and swung into the saddle. "Down and upon them, Old Iron!"

"Down . . ." Fess murmured, shaking his head. He turned, and managed to trot through the curtains.

But, when they reached the windows, they found them empty, and the yelling was going on outside. A makeshift rope, made of torn velvet curtains, straggled through the window and down the wall, its inner end secured to a scythe-handle set crosswise against the embrasure.

Rod ground his teeth. "Of course, I should have guessed the lower chambers would have curtains, too!"

Fess lifted his head slowly, ears pricking up.

Rod frowned. "What do you hear, Animated Alloy?" He cocked his head, listening.

Faintly, Skolax's voice came to him. But he couldn't make out the words.

"Heee . . . egggzorrrtsss themmm . . . Rrrawd-d-d."

Rod scowled. "Trying to whip them up to another attack?"

"Prrr . . . eee . . . ciseluh—ly."

Rod's head snapped bolt upright. "Sure, why not? With the rope still there, he can get back in easy! Fess, can you get through that window? No, of course not, that's why we had to come in through the roof. Okay, back up to the observatory, and fast, Fess! . . . Uh, I hate to push you this way right after a seizure, but . . . for God and Gramarye, Fess!"

"I . . . ammm agnoss . . . tic . . . Rrrawd."

"I don't care what your hobby is, just get upstairs. Come on, gee-up!"

Skolax had gathered a small crowd again. More stragglers were stepping uncertainly from the forest as Rod and Fess dived out from the observatory.

The jets coughed to life as the robot horse plunged

down. Then, with a roar, it pulled out of the dive and rose, to circle the tower.

Skolax looked up wildly, then screamed blasphemies, shaking his fist at the flying horse.

But the peasants, being of a slightly more practical bent, were already disappearing into the forest as rapidly as their legs and superstitions could take them.

Fess took a nose-dive at the screaming preacher; Rod leveled the laser-hilt.

Skolax dove frantically aside as the beam spat out.

Then, before Fess could turn for another pass, the "prophet" disappeared into the forest.

"Shall we pursue, Rod?"

"No," Rod said reluctantly, "we'd burn down the whole forest in the process. Besides, we've let old Galen go long enough. He's still alive, anyway; that's the only way Skolax's staff could have gotten away from him. Uh . . . Since we have to get back up to the roof, you might as well fly a few circles around the Tower on the way."

Fess flew a woozy, climbing spiral, leaving a trail of black smoke that looked like a snake with the ague.

"That oughta keep 'em from coming back, no matter what Skolax tries." Rod grunted, satisfied. Fess dived in through the roof.

Rod closed his eyes and spoke sternly to his inner ear as Fess clattered down the spiral stairway at full speed; but it didn't work, by the time they hit bottom his stomach was mutinously maintaining that down was up, and was trying to handle his last meal in accordance with the belief.

Rod swung down from the saddle with a sense of distinct relief. "You better stay here, Fess. After all, if the old man's feeling poorly, there's no sense confronting him with something that's thaumaturgically impossible, like an iron horse."

"I am constructed of a nonferrous alloy, Rod."

But his master had already stepped through the velvet curtains.

Rod told himself it was, of course, just his imagination; but it *did* seem as though he could hear the old man's heartbeat rattling even as he pushed through the curtain.

The wizard's head turned a fraction of an inch; one eyelid lifted, showing a dim blue, bloodshot orb. It rested on Rod a moment, then swiveled away, the eyelid coming down to cloak it. "Thou hadst . . . thought to . . . save mine life?"

"So far, I seem to have done a pretty good job." Rod

151

smiled sourly. "You don't seem to think it much of a favor."

The old body convulsed with a shuddering, racking spasm of coughs; then Galen lay back wheezing, giving his head a feeble shake.

"Tough," Rod growled. "I stand in your blood-debt, and I won't be beholden."

Straining, the wizard lifted his head. "Canst thou not . . . let . . . me die . . . in peace, alone?"

"No. Matter of fact, I can't let you die at all."

A faint smile touched Galen's lips. "Thou hast scant choice." He closed his eyes and settled back into his pillow with a weary sigh, a sigh that became another coughing fit.

When the spasm passed, he drew a rasping breath and asked, "How camest thou . . . within . . . this keep, Master . . . Gallowglass? . . . Oh, aye, I . . . had forgot . . . Thy horse is . . . cold iron, is he . . . not? . . . He might, then, pass through my . . . spells with . . . great ease."

Rod fought to keep his face from reflecting his shock at the old man's wasted condition. "How'd you know my horse was iron?"

Galen managed something like a sour smile. "The elves were ever my friends, Master Gallowglass, and they ha' known all thy secrets since first thou camest to this land. But now, tell me, why hast thou come?"

"To save—uh, to get you back on your feet, if I can," said Rod, advancing to the bed.

"Save thy efforts," Galen muttered as Rod sat. "There is no curing this final illness of mine, tho' devoutly I wish it. Our good Lord summoneth me home, and this is His sign—that my illness hath never before been known in this land."

Rod snorted an obscenity as he took up the old man's wrist, feeling for the pulse. "God never made an illness that couldn't be cured." He frowned suddenly, looking deep into Galen's eyes. "You want to die, don't you?"

"Nay!" Galen stared, trembling, his body stiffening with indignation. "I wish to live, Master Gallowglass! I am, in these my last days, stalking close after the greatest wisdom. . . ."

"Come off it, old man." Rod laid a hand on Galen's forehead, estimating the temperature. "If you wanted to live, you'd be trying every poison in the books in hopes that it'd be a cure. But you've resigned yourself to death, with scarcely any fight at all. You want to die. You always have, haven't you?"

For a moment, he thought the old man was about to go into apoplexy.

Then Galen relaxed, sinking back onto his pillow with a sigh. "Nay, thou hast the right of it, lad. 'Tis too late, now, for falsehood. Thou hast it aright; mine life was ever a burden. Yet let this be said in my favor, that I ever fought off the thought for a sin."

Rod interrupted him with a tongue depressor from his medkit. "Stick out your tongue and say 'Ah. . . .' Had to fight it off quite often, did you?"

Galen looked into Rod's eyes, frowning a little as Rod removed the depressor. "I had thought thou couldst not hear thoughts, Master Gallowglass, that thou wast . . ." He broke off into a sudden spasm of coughing, great hoarse bass barks that racked his whole body.

"Been doing that a lot?" Rod asked as the spasm passed and the old man sank back with a low moan. "Coughing, that is?"

Galen nodded faintly, without opening his eyes.

"Hm." Rod chewed his upper lip. "Sneezing a lot, a few days back?"

"Aye, that I was indeed, for a week and more." Then Galen opened his eyes a crack, frowning faintly. "Thou hast, then, knowledge of this illness?"

Rod nodded. "Tough luck, old man. It looks like I may be able to cure you."

Galen closed his eyes and sighed, with the weariness of a lifetime, letting his head roll to the side. "Why?" he murmured. "Tell me, why? Canst thou not allow me . . ."

"No, I canst not," said Rod shortly. "Your God must be the merciless type, old man. Apparently he's got a few things he wants you to do yet. So grin and bear it, *mon vieux,* and set your mind to recovering." He frowned, rubbing his chin. "How long you been like this?"

"Since a few days after thou, with Agatha and thy wife, had quit this Tower." Galen sighed. "A week, and several days."

Rod nodded, frowning. He'd seen the common cold in the land before, but few of its successor diseases. "Well, whatever you've got, it's gone beyond a mere chill." He scratched behind his ear. "Been working along any new lines of research lately?"

Galen's eyes opened with a guarded look about them. "How dost thou mean . . . ?"

"Any experiments on, uh, animals, anything alive, anything like that?"

153

The old man relaxed again, smiling. "Nay, naught of that, sort, Master Gallowglass."

"Oh?" Rod lifted an eyebrow. "Then what *have* you been doing? 'Cause whatever it is, I'll lay five against ten that's how you caught this thing."

Galen's lips tightened, his eyes closing. There was something dubious about him, unresolved.

Rod decided the situation justified a little dirty pool. "It's your duty to your God to get well," he growled, "and your chances are much better if I know how you caught this thing." That was the nice thing about the concept of Fate—if you were a good persuader, it could be a very useful tool. "Come on, let's have it."

The old man was silent a moment longer, his lips turning in and pressing tight.

Then he relaxed, with a grimace, and nodded faintly. "I ha' gone fishing."

"Fishing!" Rod stared. "I thought you never left this Tower."

"Fishing in a pool that cannot be seen, Master Gallowglass. Fishing with the mind, in an ocean of pure thought, in a pond of stars and damnable chill, in a place barred to Man but free to his soul."

Rod's eyes widened slowly as his brows pulled down. "A dimensional nexus . . ." He breathed. "What . . . ? How . . . ?"

Galen lifted his lids a little, smiling faintly. "How chanced I upon it? I had thought it was haply thy doing."

"Mine?" Rod gasped, aghast.

"Thine." Galen closed his eyes again, folding his hands on his chest. "I ha' found a key, and I found it where it had not been a moment before; I will swear to that, if thou wishest. Nay, more—I found it the day that I saved thee, but a moment or two after thou hadst left this place."

"Oh?" Rod raised his eyebrows, thrusting out his lower lip and nodding.

He clasped his hands around his shin and leaned back, rocking. "Well, I didn't put it there. But, uh—what is it, this, uh, 'key'?"

Galen squeaked an eyelid open and nodded at a curtain opposite Rod. It opened slowly, as if drawn by an invisible hand. Rod realized, with a shock, that the old wizard had the power of telekinesis. He was the only warlock, aside from Magnus, who did.

Beyond the curtain, a lump of clay sat on a pedestal.

Rod frowned, looking up to glance at it—and glanced away, quickly.

It was a mass of turns and flowing angles, the kind of thing a schizophrenic sculptor with a background in topology might turn out. "This is, uh, a 'key'?"

"Aye." The old man nodded, wearily. "Trace its curves with thine eye, Master Gallowglass; seek to understand where they lead to, and thy soul shall shoot away from thee, into a pool churned by a wind that never ha' blown on earth."

"*You* trace its curves. *My* soul might not come back." Rod set his jaw and shifted in his seat, his eyes carefully averted. He began to realize just how much grit and determination, and moral courage, Galen had. "And this thing takes you to that, uh, 'pool,' as you call it? Where you go fishing?"

"Aye."

Rod chewed the inside of his cheek, musing. "What do you catch?"

Galen stirred restlessly. "Bits of rack, wreck, and rubbish, Master Gallowglass. A morsel of some stuff like wood but not wood; a thing shaped like a carpenter's square with a strange, small lever in its angle; gauds of false jewelry; a long thin wire with a knob on the end that folded in on itself; a half of a book with no binding, writ in strange characters; bric-a-brac and rubbish, naught of any worth. . . ."

"Not what you were after, anyway," Rod interpreted.

Glalen hesitated a moment, then admitted, "Nay."

Rod waited for him to enlarge upon the statement, and, when he didn't, Rod prodded, "Uh . . . just what were you after?"

The pause was longer this time; then Galen sighed and said, "A living creature, Master Gallowglass, a thinking soul, that could tell me whence he came and what the nature of his world was. And, live or die, I shall pursue that plan—if it is allotted to me that I may, beyond the grave."

"Oh, quit talking about graves," Rod griped. "You'll be back on your feet in a week, maybe less." He rose, pivoting, and slapped his way through the hangings.

The great black horse stood, stolid and impassive.

"Been listening, Horseface?" Rod murmured.

"I have, Rod. The symptoms would seem to be those of a form of influenza."

"That's what I thought." Rod pressed a hidden catch, opened a small panel in the horse's flank, and hunted in the small pharmacopia within. "Good thing we haven't needed very much of this stuff; don't know when we'll see more of it. . . . Uh, where'd you put the universal antibiotic?"

"There is no such thing as a universal antibiotic, Rod; it is a logical impossibility."

"All right, all right, so where's the general purpose gook?"

"Third vial from the right on the second rack from the top, Rod."

"Got it." Rod shook a large gelatin capsule out of the vial, eyed it skeptically. "Well, either it'll cure him, or he'll choke to death trying to get it down, which just might be more merciful. What'd you think of that story of his, Fess?"

"I would say that one or more of the objects he 'caught' was the source of the virus, Rod."

"I would *never* have guessed. You'll buy the general concept, then?"

"That a virus may be contracted from a contaminated object? Of course, Rod."

"No, no! This business about fishing in a mental pool."

"It is plausible," said the robot judiciously, "if one grants the primary assumption of the validity of parapsychology."

"To say nothing of downright mysticism," Rod agreed. "But whatever condition his main hypothesis is in, I have to believe him."

"Why, Rod?"

"I had a look at that 'key' of his. So what is his 'pool'?"

"I would say the effort to comprehend the topological forms of the 'key' guided his mind to a condition in which it could perceive a dimensional nexus, Rod. It is an indication of the extent of his esper powers that he is able to extract artifacts through the nexus."

"Yeah, that's pretty much what I figured," Rod mused, nodding. "But where'd the key come from?"

"By his account, Rod, it appeared just after your own visit to this Tower. It follows that a member of your party left it."

"Yeah, I'd agree that was logical, except that neither Gwen, Agatha, or me had the damn thing on us at the time—I mean, it's a little on the bulky side, you know; it's not the kind of thing you can just slip in your vest pocket."

They were silent for a moment.

"Rod . . ."

"Um? What do you deduce now, Brother Watson?"

"That a fourth person—aside from Galen, of course—must have been present at the time."

"That's logical, Fess; but wouldn't we have noticed? Or even if somebody stopped by a little later in the day, wouldn't old Galen have had some notion of it? Besides, with all the spells the old boy has around the place, who could have gotten in? Even Skolax had to have cold iron, in that staff-cum-laser rifle of his. Therefore, the key must have been magicked in here the same time we were."

"It is the only logical alternative, Rod."

"Hey!" Rod said suddenly, brightly. Then he frowned, knocking the side of his head against the heel of his hand, as though clearing water from his ear. "No, no. That's just *too* impossible."

"What is, Rod?"

"Well . . ." Rod turned away, stamping his foot. "It's ridiculous, damn it!"

"Most of your intuitive—uh—'deductions' are, Rod. But you have a disconcerting record of accuracy."

"Well . . ." Rod bit his lip; then the words spilled out. "There *was* a fourth, um, entity allegedly present that day, Fess. The, uh, 'familiar,' remember?"

There was a deathly pause.

"Rod," said the robot, "do you refer to the witch's—uh—unborn 'son'?"

"Yeah, yeah, Agatha's son Harold, remember?"

Another small pause.

"Bbbuuddd . . ." said Fess. "Thaadddizz imbozzib . . . Rrruddd. . . ."

Rod frowned. "What? I can't understand you, Fess."

"Alll . . . immmbozzi . . . Rrruuddd . . . Awwweee . . ."

Rod leaped for the reset switch, suddenly realizing what the robot's incoherence meant.

But he wasn't quite quick enough. The robot stiffened, legs locking, head plummeting for the floor, jerking as it hit the end of the neck, muzzle swinging between fetlocks.

Rod sighed, shaking his head sadly as he thumbed the reset switch. Fess just couldn't adjust to Gramarye's alogical structure.

Well, it could be worse. He *could* be *grand mal.* . . .

Galen choked, making gargling sounds, but he did manage to get the huge capsule down.

"There, you look better already." Rod slapped him on the shoulder. "You should be back on your feet by the end of the week. But rest at least that long, will you? Your system needs to recover in a big way."

Galen fastened a glittering, if bloodshot, eye on him. "Thou knowest, Master Gallowglass, that I do not . . ."

"I know, I know." Rod turned away to hide a look of

mild disgust. "This just balances the score for your saving my life. You're not under any obligation to me."

He turned back to the wizard, managing to keep a poker face. "Or, to put it a little more succinctly—you're not about to fight the beastmen just because I saved your life. But, damn it, you could relax your damn stiff-necked grudge just for a week, at least! Agatha can forget her injuries long enough to help us when we need her—why can't you?"

" 'Tis not in my nature," the old man rasped, his hands trembling as he clasped them on his chest, "as it is in Agatha's. 'Tis her nature to aid when needed, as 'tis mine to shun all human company."

"Oh?" Rod smiled, with more than a touch of sarcasm. "You're self-sufficient, then?"

Galen's eyes closed wearily. "No man is that, Master Gallowglass. All souls need other souls; give an old fool credit for that little wisdom, at least. Yet a man may make shift with the pursuit of knowledge in lieu of companionship; 'tis a poor substitute, but sufficient, as a man may make shift with bread and water when he hath no meat and wine."

His eyes opened again. " 'Tis of my nature to seek the pallid delights and barren embraces of scholarship for the safety of its companionship, to prefer this safety to the risks encumbent on human society; and art thou, then, so perfect that thou mayest sneer at me for a coward?"

Rod straightened slowly, gazing at the old man. "No," he said gently. "No, I have no right. Heaven knows my failings are as heavy as yours. But, damn it, old man, we need you!"

"Thou hast my sadness, Master Gallowglass," the old warlock said faintly, closing his eyes.

Rod sighed and turned away. "Well, every man has his own load of guilt to bear. Mine is the men that I've killed; yours is the lives you haven't saved. If there is a God, and if he ever brings us to judgment, he'll probably damn us both equally."

He lifted the curtain, turned back in the doorway. "When you get back on your feet, scrub down every inch of this Tower with alcohol. If you don't, you'll probably catch this sickness all over again."

He lapsed into silence, frowning at the old man.

Galen opened his eyes, smiled faintly. "Why dost thou tarry, Master Gallowglass? Thy dealings here are done."

"Tell me," said Rod, "what're you gonna do when you get well again?"

"Do?" The old man's eyebrows lifted slightly. "Why, certes, I shall go a-fishing."

Rod nodded, with a trace of a smile. "Just be careful you don't hook into something that's bigger'n you. I'd hate to think you were hanging over a fireplace somewhere, stuffed and mounted."

The old man's eyes widened at the joke, and there was quivering terror in their depths. "The thought occurred to me," he said in a voice oddly stiffened, "and I will own to thee, Master Gallowglass, I am mortal afeard."

Rod was silent for a count of three, eyes widening under scowling brows. "But you're not about to stop fishing."

Galen nodded assent.

"You won't let your fear of the unknown keep you from seeking knowledge, but you'll let your fear of people drive you into total hermitage."

Again, Galen nodded.

"But *why?*" An intense whisper. "Why, old man? How can you be courageous and cowardly at the same time?"

"Why," said the old man, with a bleak smile, " 'tis my nature."

Rod turned away in disgust.

"Mayhap I fear a threat to my life less than a threat to my heart." The old wizard's voice was gravel, crunching under approaching giant feet.

Rod muttered under his breath and turned away, letting the curtains swing together behind him.

He crossed the stone floor, shaking his bowed head, glowering at the paving blocks. "I don't understand him, Fess. I just don't understand him."

"It should not distress you, Rod. Competent psychiatry was not, after all, the primary goal of your training."

"True, true." Rod swung into the saddle. "But it still bugs me. . . . Well, home, Fess."

As the horse roared away over the treetops, Rod swallowed huge, grateful gulps of the clean, chill air, very welcome after the dankness of the Dark Tower.

He frowned then, glaring at the back of Fess' head. "*Damn,* but he gripes me!"

"Because of his refusal to lend his support, Rod?"

"No. . . . Well, yes, that bugs me, too, of course. But that's not the main thing."

"What, then?"

"His going on with that 'fishing' business, even if it's got him scared stiff. *That* gets me."

The robot's voice had a note of perplexity. "Why, Rod?"

"Because," Rod growled, "I've got a strange feeling the old coward just may have more guts than I ever had."

Brom O'Berin sat glowering at the fire, hands clasped, elbows on his knees, muttering to himself about irresponsible sons-in-law who were never at home when a crisis was brewing.

He turned at the door's opening, and the glower sharpened to a glare as Rod drifted in.

"And thou art right quickly come to my call!" Brom snapped. "And where hast *thou* been—tickling fish?"

"No, just Gwen," Rod said, smiling. "Just reassuring her."

Rod pulled up a chair, then frowned slightly, eyes focusing on Brom again. He leaned forward, clapping his hands. "Now! To business. . . . Good to see you back, Brom. What's the word?"

"The word is that thou haply mayest ha' killed me," Brom growled. He ran a hand over the bristle on his jaw. "Oh, there was nothing for it but thou must needs shave me, was there not? Didst thou never pause to think these beastmen might not have chins?"

"No," said Rod, sobering. "As soon as I found out, I tried to get you back. But there was a small forest of bogeymen in the way; and by the time I'd gotten to where you'd been, you weren't there."

"Naetheless, I lived—small thanks to thee!" Brom rose to pace the room. "And my sojourn in that foul Beastland is ended. I have learned all that I may, and return bearing news."

"Oh?" Rod's ears pricked up. "What news? That Kernel still wants to join forces with us, when and if we invade?"

"Aye, that is a part of it," Brom grumped grudgingly, "yet be assured, there is more. They ha' showed me a new form of warfare, which I fain would term cowardly; yet I find that I cannot, for it pits twelve men against, mayhap, twelve hundred. Nay, it doth require great courage, and greater skill. And, though it costeth the enemy little in men, it naetheless doth indeed strike to the heart of his army."

Rod frowned. "Sounds good enough to compete with peyote. What is it?"

"A form that thou knowest," the dwarf said, frowning, "or so they say."

" 'They'?" Rod lifted an eyebrow.

"Kernel." Brom's mouth tightened at the corners. "Or so I assume; though it was his henchman, Yorick, who told me. He saith that thou knowest; that I have but to bring

160

it to thy mind again; that I shall say to thee but two words, and thou shalt dash out to conquer the beastmen."

"They're not much on exaggeration, are they?" Rod smiled sourly. "All right, what are the two words?"

Brom scowled, perplexed. "There is no sense to them; still, here they are: 'guerrilla raids.' "

"Sure . . . we can't break through their defenses. And we can't hit 'em when they're on the march, because they only march on stormy nights, so they can fall back on the Evil Eye if we attack. But if we send in small bands while they're dug in at camp, ten or twenty men to charge over the breastworks, do as much damage as they can, and get out, *quick*—well, in a long enough time, we could wipe them out."

Brom frowned, musing. "Mayhap," he said slowly. "But I do not think we have so much time as that, Rod Gallowglass. . . . Yet, in truth, we can do nothing more." He turned about, facing Rod. "But what of these small bands of thine? Will they not be frozen by the Evil Eye, and chopped down?"

"No, not at all. We put a small band of witches and warlocks, see, on a hill nearby, to protect the soldiers." Rod's eyes glittered. "And we only raid on clear nights, so the beastmen won't be able to knock out our witches with their extra-power Evil Eye."

Brom nodded, slowly, frowning. "It might prove feasible, Sir Gallowglass. . . . Aye, it might indeed. Only clear nights. . . ."

Rod dashed out to conquer the King's approval.

"Well, it worked." Rod collapsed full-length into the stack of hay at the side of Fess' stall. "Took me a while to talk him into it, but he finally saw the light."

Fess chewed thoughtfully at a mouthful of oats. "I would have thought that a trained warrior would have seen the advantages of guerrilla warfare rather quickly, Rod."

"Oh, it didn't take him long to see it would work. *That* was the easy part." Rod bit reflectively into a wisp of hay. "It was getting to it that took the time—about two hours, in fact; just persuading him that it wasn't dishonorable for twelve men to sneak up on a whole army." He shook his head despairingly. "I suppose chivalry served a function at one time . . . but I can't quite believe it."

"When will we stage the first raid, then, Rod?"

"About a week—on a clear night, of course." Rod shrugged. "If it worked for Kernel, it should work for us."

He frowned. "That reminds me—Yorick. What do you make of him, Fess?"

The robot's eyes lost focus. "I would say, from Brom's report, that there can be little doubt Yorick is an authentic Neanderthal."

"The name would be enough to make me doubt it. . . . But I suppose . . ." Rod looked up at Fess. "You're forgetting knowledge. He definitely knows too much to be just one of the Beast Boys . . . unless Kernel's got one hell of an education program going. And, from what Brom says, there didn't seem to be quite so high a level of knowledge among the other Neanderthals. So might we be justified in saying Yorick is atypical?"

"We might," the robot said judiciously. "Certainly, his vocabulary would indicate that he is not native to this time-space locus."

"And I'd bet you two to one he's not native to the time and place the Neanderthals came from, either." Rod scowled. "Of course, he *could* just be one of the local boys, whom Kernel singled out for special attention and education. . . ."

"This, however, merely transfers the problem, Rod."

"Yeah." Rod nodded. "Then Kernel knows too much. And that makes him an agent from an outside power. But then, we were pretty sure he was a time-agent, anyway."

"What is your opinion of the alliance Kernel proposes, Rod?"

Rod shrugged. "Why not? Presumably he's on our side, anyway, since we're both fighting the same enemies."

"But what will happen when the problem posed by the existence of those enemies has been eliminated, Rod?"

Rod winced. "I wish you wouldn't be so cold-blooded about it—but you've got a point. A common enemy isn't really a very good basis for a lasting friendship, is it?"

"It *does* tend to make for an unstable reciprocal relationship. . . ."

Rod sighed and broke a stalk of hay between his fingers. "So it comes back to the old question, doesn't it?"

"The issue cannot be long avoided, Rod."

"Yeah." Rod grimaced. "Wonder why he doesn't just come out and tell us. It'd sure be a lot easier making up my mind if I just knew who he's working for."

"If he did, Rod—would you believe him?"

Galen sat in a great wooden chair before a small, flickering, open fire. Across the fire from him, on a slim four-foot pedestal, sat the Key, its weirdly-contoured form ever-changing in myriad shifting shadows from the firelight.

The only sound in the room was the ticking of the clock-work mechanism that rotated the Key slowly, so that Galen's eye might follow its feedback curves all about its form.

The old wizard sat immobile, every iota of his strength pouring into his staring, concentrating eyes.

He seemed almost lifeless; but fear of the unknown was heavy upon him. Therefore had he fallen back on the superstitions so long associated with his craft. His great oaken chair sat in the center of a chalked pentagram; his loose robe and tall, pointed cap were both dark blue, both blazoned with cabalistic symbols.

His whole body was like wood, his breathing and heart-beat slowed tremendously. Only his eyes had any life in them, twisting, probing into the lightless gulf the Key had opened to his mind.

A misty shape formed over the fire. A form within it coalesced, fluxed for a moment, hardened, and a hollow cylinder of very thin metal, painted in a swirl of bright colors, fell at the side of the firepit.

The noise of its falling failed to disturb the wizard; he sat as lifeless and detached as ever, his eyes staring through the Key into the dimensional nexus, his mind flexing and groping like a blind, spasmodic hand within the lightless pool.

Mist appeared over the fire again. Colors faded in, swirl-ing within it, sorted themselves out to definite areas of the great egg-shaped fog, dark at the bottom, royal blue for the bulk, tan at the top.

The mist coalesced, gelled, hardened, and a young man floated over the fire, descending slowly.

The flames touched his bootsoles, and he yanked them away with a muttered oath. He leaped aside, landing light-ly on the balls of his feet; a long shudder shook his body. He knelt, resting his forehead against clasped hands for a moment, then lifted his head, shook his shoulders as if to settle them back into place, and rose, turning toward the old man in the blue robe who sat in the great oaken chair.

The young man was tall, broad-shouldered, deep-chested, with sandy-blond bowl-cut hair. His eyes were light brown, his skin deeply tanned. His ears were a little too small, his mouth a little too wide, his face a little too square, his nose a little too flat for him to be called handsome; but the tawny eyes were honest and open, sparked with more than a hint of mischief and merriment.

He wore a royal blue, Roman-collared shirt, royal blue

open jacket, and skintight royal-blue trousers with a gold stripe down the outside seams. His boots were black and wide-topped. Gold letters were blazoned over the chest pocket on the jacket.

The boots were high enough to hide a knife of respectable length, and wide enough to make it readily accessible. The jacket bulged a trifle at the armpit.

He studied the old wizard, and his face was a curious mixture of affection and contempt.

He knelt by the chair, cradling Galen's hand in his own, feeling for the pulse, then squeezed the palm lightly, in counter to the heartbeat.

"Wake up," he murmured in a soft, rich bariton. "Wake up, old man. Waken, Galen, great wizard, excellent esper. Return to the living."

He muttered those words, and many like them, in a steady, monotonous chant, as the old man slowly withdrew himself from the pool between the worlds.

Slowly, Galen's head bowed forward, eyes closing, a puzzled expression coming over his face.

Then the old head lifted, turning to the young man who knelt there beside him. Slowly, the rheumy old eyes focused. . . .

And widenened in horror.

Rod was poring over a map of the river, planning the first raid, when the door opened a crack, and Gwen peeked in.

"My lord . . . ?"

Rod looked up, exasperated. His frustrated concentration cross-faded into a tenderly lecherous smile. "Hi, babe."

Gwen smiled and glided in to rub his shoulders. "My lord, there is word for thee."

Rod sagged in his chair. "What now?"

"Thou must needs go to the Dark Tower, my lord."

"What?" Rod sat upright, craning his head around for a look at his wife. "What's the matter with the old coot now? Triple pleurisy?"

"Nay, my lord. He hath 'succeeded in his fishing,' so he said, and standeth in great need of your counsel and aid."

A small frown bent Rod's eyebrows. "So the big one didn't get away after all. . . . Well," he sighed, lurching to his feet, "I suppose I'd better go. If I do him enough favors, he must might start feeling grateful."

"And someday," murmured the robot in Rod's ear, "Mount Everest might move."

Rod strode through the purple hangings and stopped dead, staring in amazement at the tableau before him.

Galen sat in an oaken armchair before an open fire, head buried in trembling hands. A tall, broad-shouldered young man in an informal military uniform stood with his back to the old man, running his fingers through his sandy hair and looking exasperated.

"Well!" Rod set his fists on his hips.

Both heads snapped around to him, startled.

"You *did* catch a big one, didn't you, Galen? Does he speak our language?"

"Oh, yes," said the young man, with a quirk of a smile. "As well as if I were born to it—which I was."

He had a faint accent; but it was the accent of a dialect, not a foreign language.

Rod frowned, studying the young man suspiciously. There was something vaguely familiar about him. . . . The uniform and the face, both; they were almost right, but not quite.

The uniform, especially. It wasn't *quite* military. And that by itself struck a chord within Rod. . . .

"I hate to seem impolite," the young man said, "but might I ask your name?"

Rod transferred his frown to Galen. "Didn't you tell him I was coming?"

The young man stared. "You can't be Rod Gallowglass!"

The frown switched back to the young man, deepening in the process. "Why can't I?"

The stranger looked vaguely appalled, his hands floundering in confused gestures. "Rod Gallowglass is a warlock. . . . Or so the legend says."

"Legend?" It was Rod's turn to look appalled.

"Yeah, sure, the legend. And if you were a warlock, I would've been able to hear your thoughts as you came in." The stranger frowned. "Unless you're a really good warlock. In which case you'd be able to hide your thoughts. . . ."

"I am not at this time, never was, and never will be, a warlock," Rod answered in a very careful, measured tone. "I may bear the title of High Warlock, but that was wished on me; it doesn't change the fact that I'm not one. But, with equal certainty, I am now, will always be, and have always been, Rod Gallowglass, scion of one of the oldest and most noble families of the Terran Sphere."

The young man frowned. "You don't know any magic?"

"Never touch the stuff."

"Don't have any magic powers?"

"Wouldn't be caught dead with 'em."

165

"Very few warlocks ever are . . ." the young man said. "I was expecting someone of a slightly more noble aspect. . . ." Then, hastily, "Sorry, I didn't mean to say that out loud. It's been a rather trying day for me; I forget my manners. Of course you *look* aristocratic enough, I didn't mean that, it's . . . well, you just talk like a tramp deckhand, that's all."

"I *was* a tramp deckhand," Rod said, very evenly, "for quite a few years. That doesn't change the fact that I was born a nobleman. But you're right on one thing—you have forgotten your manners. Would you mind telling me who *you* are?"

The young man's face snapped into official neutrality. "Captain Harold Galenson of the Service, Colonel Gallowglass."

"Major," Rod snapped absently while a dreadful suspicion grew in his mind. He looked the question at Galen.

The old man nodded with a shaken, sardonic smile. "Thou hast it aright, Master Gallowglass. He claims that he is mine unborn son."

Some hours later, Galen was taking some much-needed rest in an adjoining chamber while Rod was taking some much-needed wine in the main hall.

Harold chugged his third cup. Rod smiled bleakly. "Little better now?"

Harold shrugged, pouring himself a refill from the capacious pitcher. "Oh, I s'pose. I feel fine, in a way. Must be kind of hard on the old man, though. Must kind of shake you to meet a man who isn't even born yet."

"I don't think he quite believes you."

"Yes, you might say that." Harold gave him a wry smile. "At least the legend's right about your proclivity for understatement."

"Oh, don't sweat it. He'll believe you eventually." Rod lifted his cup in a toast.

Harold lifted his cup in response but not in enthusiasm. "I sure hope so." He shook his head despairingly. "You see, I'm kinda used to his not believing me. He always told me I had one hell of an imagination." He looked up, a sudden brooding frown on his face. "Although, strictly speaking, I suppose today is the first time he's ever told me that—objective time, of course. In my own subjective time, I've lost count."

Rod was beginning to see why Galen had yelled for help.

And, finally, the other half of the correlation hit him.

"Captain, uh, Galenson, uh . . . you're, um, Agatha's son, too?"

"Agatha's and Galen's, yes."

Rod squatted and began to sketch geometrical figures in the hearth ashes. "And you don't remember seeing me before?"

"No." Harold smiled wryly. "When you're a pure spirit, you don't see so good."

"Pure spirit . . . uh, independent of your body, I take it?"

"Yeah, Dr. McAran's First Technique. Spirit can travel in time independent of the body. We'd always wondered what would happen if there wasn't a receiving body on the other end of the line, and . . . well, now we know."

"You become a familiar?" Rod lifted one eyebrow.

"Not so familiar as all that," said Harold grimly. "Matter of fact, it was damn disorienting for the first few hours. Being pure spirit, you see, you don't have any eyes, so you can't physically see at all. You have to feel your way around by thought perception; all you can see are people and other life-forms. And . . . well . . ."

"My thoughts were a lot more noble than I am." Rod nodded grimly.

"No-o-o . . ." Harold pursed his lips. "To tell the truth, General Gallowglass . . ."

Rod looked up, frowning. "General? I was a colonel a few minutes ago. What's with all the promotions?"

"Oh yeah, of course, I forget, you haven't been promoted yet." Harold raised a hand, eyes closing in chagrin. "My apologies, Colonel."

"Well, if you want to get technical about it," said Rod, rising, "my official SCENT rank is major."

"Yeah, yeah, Major! Sorry, I'm not quite so far up along the time line as I thought. Well, anyway, Major, you're psychically invisible, in case you didn't know."

"I'd heard some indications of that sort, yes."

"Yes. Well, anyway, I couldn't see you—neither mentally nor physically, that is—so, I didn't know what you looked like at all, you see, and . . . well, the way they describe you in the legend . . ."

"You were expecting me to look noble as hell. I see. Yes." Rod glanced at the Key and as quickly glanced away. "I take it you left that thing here for your father to find?"

Harold nodded.

"The logical deduction from that, Captain, is that you

167

were deliberately trying to get your body back to this time."

"Right," Harold admitted. "There wasn't a time machine available in this section of the Galaxy—you see, they're still rather bulky, where I come from, and infernally expensive, mostly because McAran won't let too many trade secrets out of his hideout back in the twentieth century, and we had to get somebody back here, because . . . well . . ." He studied the palms of his hands, and, a trifle sheepishly, announced: "Well, the fact of the matter is, Major Gallowglass, you need my help."

"Oh," said Rod brightly. "Do I?"

He looked into the fire. "Well, that's an honest opinion, anyway." Then a connection closed in his mind. "Wait a minute! If you're the son of Agatha and Galen, you should have . . ."

". . . a very great deal of inborn witch-power, otherwise known as ESP, yes." Harold looked up, meeting Rod's eyes. "But unfortunately, inborn aptitude counts for a lot less than professional training, Master Gallowglass. And, being only twenty-two, I haven't had all that much training."

"So?"

"So I can't do you all that much good. Not enough to make a significant difference, anyway. The one you really need is . . ."

"Your father." Rod nodded, with a sourdough smile (which is to say, a rye grimace).

"Frankly," Harold said, "when I first came back here, I expected to find my father working frantically on your side. But, for that matter, I expected to find my parents happily married, too . . . though I admit I couldn't understand why they'd come forward."

" 'Come forward'?" Rod frowned. "Oh. To the future, you mean."

"Yes." Harold rested his lower lip against his clasped hands and glowered at the fire. "It's . . . a little confusing, Major Gallowglass. At first it was just an experiment, to find out what would happen if spirit time-travel was tried without a receiving body. I met my mother, about middle-aged, and . . . well, I was a little surprised to find her still, uh, single. Then, when I met my father, here in the Tower a few weeks back, all three of us together, I began to understand some things, like why they weren't married, but I was a little more confused about others."

Rod kept his face very carefully expressionless.

"And," Harold went on, "by this time, I had grasped something of the political situation; and it didn't take all

168

that much logic to see that someone was trying to twist history—the history I learned in school, anyway. I figured you might be able to use some help, so . . . and, of course, I had some personal interest in the situation. . . . Well, the upshot is that I used TK to sculpt the Key out of some river clay and left it here. I'd learned some things about my father that I hadn't liked too well. . . ."

Out of the corner of his eye, Rod saw the hangings part behind Harold, saw Galen standing in the opening, and was very surprised to see hurt wash through the old man's face—hurt quickly and carefully masked by a look of cold defiance, but hurt nonetheless.

". . . But at the same time," said Harold, "I'd learned a lot of other things about him, too. It was almost like meeting a completely new person. . . . Well, seeing him in his own environment, as a master warlock, and I all of a sudden realized just how much power the old man had, in his own right, and . . . well, I learned a hell of a lot of respect for him, too. I mean, sure, I'd always respected him as my father, but . . . well, respecting him as a man, in his own world, that's something else again. And I knew that, if I left the Key, he'd use it. He'd have to; that's the way he is." He looked up at Rod. "He's different from us, Major Gallowglass. But he's got more guts than either of us, in a lot of ways."

"Yes," Rod said slowly, "I've noticed that."

He eyed Galen over Harold's shoulder. The old man stood frozen, his face flint.

Harold took a deep breath. "So," he said, "I stayed around for the first battle, when the Neanderthals invaded. Thought maybe I could help you all turn history back onto its proper track. But—I—just—don't have the power. Or I may have it, but I don't know how to use it yet—which comes to the same thing. So I didn't know what I could do to help out, but I figured I better get my body back here, especially since it looked as if my mother and father were going to get themselves killed without having had a chance to get me born . . . and that, I didn't like at all. And, well, here I am."

"Nearly having killed your father with flu in the process," Rod observed.

Harold smiled ruefully. "Lucky for me you were around, Major. Anyway"—he spread his hands—"I'm here to do what I can. My, uh, excellent father doesn't seem to be able to see his way clear to help out, so it looks as if I get to put in the military duty in his stead. 'Fraid I won't be much more help than I already have been, as my mother's familiar; but here I am, such as I am—if you'll accept me in your command, that is."

Rod was careful not to let his surprise show.

He sifted a handful of ash through his fingers and watched it drift to the floor. "How come you're willing to take orders from me?"

Harold lifted his head, surprised. "I'm a captain," he said. "You're a major."

Rod looked up slowly. Military discipline, he decided, did have its uses, after all. Because this was a kid who could be very, very much trouble, if he'd wanted to be.

"Join the force," he said. "You're welcome six times over."

He came to his feet. "Which reminds me, there's a war on. We ought to be getting back to it."

Harold's eyes lit up like arc lights. "Yes, by all means, let's get back to Runnymede! Uh—after all, I came to help out, didn't I?"

Rod frowned, then shrugged. "I've got transportation in the next room. My horse—uh, robot, that is—can carry two as easy as one."

"Robot?" Harold frowned. Then his face cleared with a beatific smile. "Of course, you've got old Fess."

"You know him?"

"Yeah, sure, he's the grand old robot of the Service. You'll be glad to know he's still faithfully serving your descendants."

Rod opened his mouth, taking a very deep breath, which he expelled on one word: "Yeah. Well, I'm quite reassured to know I'll have descendants." He turned, lifting the hangings. "Shall we go, Captain?"

"Sure." Harold jumped to his feet, then hesitated. "Maybe I oughta check with my father. He might have had a last-minute . . ."

"I know thee not," Galen snapped from the far side of the room.

Harold spun about; their eyes met, Galen's showing more desperation than hate.

Harold's face slowly congealed. He drew himself to attention, snapped a quick, formal bow to his father, turned, and marched out through the hangings.

Rod shot a commiserating look at the old wizard, receiving the same glacial glare as Harold had, shrugged, and turned away, shaking his head.

The hangings swung to behind him; their swinging stilled as, muted by a little distance, there came the coughing roar of two small jet engines, a roar settling to a bass drone as it faded away.

Slowly, old Galen relaxed, slumping down into his chair, his face sagging into lines of deeper misery than any man should ever know.

The firelight fluttered shadows over his face.

Harold had a definite case of the fidgets on the trip north.

Finally, he brought it out in the open. "Uh, Major—would you mind if I went on ahead? By teleport, of course."

Rod frowned, glancing back over his shoulder. "This bus too slow for you?"

Harold hesitated, caught between politeness and truth. Rod raised one eyebrow. "Little bit eager, aren't you?" Harold's eyebrows shot up.

Then he smiled, shrugged. "Well, why shouldn't I be?" And disappeared.

"On the other hand," Rod mused, "why *should* he be? I mean, I've heard a lot about 'warriors impatient for battle'—but isn't this taking it a bit far?"

"Rod," Fess murmured, "you have a disgustingly suspicious personality."

"Well, yes, but that's just a description of the true scholar."

"The true scholar, Rod, must also possess something of a logical faculty."

"Most of the faculties I've met weren't all that logical. . . . Which reminds me, you ought to be teaching."

"I am, Rod. Constantly."

Rod ground his teeth. "All right, if you're so logical, *you* tell *me*—what do *you* think of his story?"

After a moment, Fess admitted, "There *are* a few discrepancies. . . ."

Rod grinned, with great satisfaction.

"After all," the robot mused, "his powers were just as much at Gramarye's disposal without his body, as with."

"Precisely." Rod frowned. "So, in terms of advantages for our side of the war, all he's accomplished by bringing his body back here is making it possible for the beastmen to kill him. Wherefore, we come to the critical question: Why is his corpus so crucial?"

"And the inevitable answer, of course," said the robot, nodding. "When the proclivities of the human male in that state of emotional dissonance commonly referred to as 'love' are taken into consideration, the only possible con-

171

clusion is that his principle motivation for transporting his physical components back to this time-space locus is—"

"Greta," Rod agreed. "So the whole thing adds up to an increase in their happiness, and a decrease in his efficiency."

"If that is the case, Rod, why did you not command him to return his body to his own time?"

"Well, for one thing, military discipline not withstanding, he just might have refused to obey."

"True, true. . . ."

"And for another"—Rod grinned wolfishly—"I think I foresee a way in which Harold Galenson is going to make a big contribution to the war effort. . . ."

The robot said, "Rod, I believe you are considering unethical conduct."

"Oh, no, no, nothing like that." Rod pushed his tongue against the inside of his cheek. "Just a little mild treachery. . . ."

Rod stepped back and eyed Harold critically. "Well, it's a little tight across the shoulders and chest, and a little long in the sleeves, but it'll do. Good thing we're more or less of a size."

Harold squirmed inside the beige and saffron doublet. "If you say so, Major. Uh—kind of itchy, isn't it? Say, can I at least wear an undershirt?"

Rod closed his eyes, shaking his head with great finality. "Totally *trayfe*, Captain. You might get away with a singlet, if you wanted; but that wouldn't help the shoulders and arms much. Of course, you *can* wear just a plain white shirt under that, if you want; but believe me, the way they make linen here, it won't be much of an improvement."

Harold gave a martyr's sigh. "Ah, the price of patriotism. . . ."

"Those uniform pants'll do for hose until we can get the castle tailor to make you up a good wool pair." Rod turned back to the closet quickly, before Harold could see his smile. "Here's a cloak," he called, taking a deep red cape off a hook. He tossed it to Harold, who swung it about his shoulders, fastened the frogs at his collarbone, and immediately began strutting. "Say, now, that's got some flair to it! Wouldn't have a full-length mirror, would you, Major?"

Rod smiled behind his hand. It never failed; put a cloak, doublet, and hose on a man, and he strutted like a bantam in April.

"Catch!" he called, tossing the captain a rapier and dagger.

Harold fielded the swordbelt, and buckled it on without comment—well, verbal comment, anyway. The swell of his chest and the lift of his shoulders were quite eloquent.

There was a knock at the door, and a muffled, "Lord Warlock, may I enter?"

Rod frowned. "Sure, come on in."

The door burst open, admitting an agitated Greta. "Lord Warlock, 'tis a cataclysm! Old Agatha is struck in the heart, for—oh, 'tis news too horrible for the bearing! Lord Warlock, her familiar hath left her, and she . . ."

She caught sight of Harold, and froze. Her eyes widened, rounding to poker chips.

Harold's eyes burned into hers.

Rod looked from her to him and back again, and grinned toothily. "Ahem! Greta, may I introduce Captain Harold Galenson, currently on detached duty with the Warlock's Auxiliary Platoon of His Majesty's Foot. . . ."

His grin faded; for the look in her face had turned to horror. She was pale as ivory, and trembling.

Rod frowned, glanced quickly at Harold, who looked deeply concerned, almost fearful. Slowly, he held out a hand to her.

She shrank away.

Rod whirled back to the girl. "Don't you understand, kid? This is your disembodied lover! Now embodied! He's yours, all yours! Take him! Or be taken, whichever you prefer; preferably both. . . ."

Harold's lips parted, his eyes widening.

Rod suddenly realized there might be a telepathic conversation going on, from which he was very effectively excluded.

Harold held out his arms to Greta.

She burst into tears and whirled away, fleeing through the door.

Rod stood transfixed.

Harold let his hands drop to his sides. His head bowed, eyes closed, lips pressed in.

Slowly, he looked up, saw Rod, and smiled sardonically. "Close your mouth, Major. You look like a sturgeon."

Rod started, then looked away. "I didn't think I went that much toward Gothic. . . . I mean . . ."

He broke off, frowning at the look on the young man's face. "Would you mind telling me what that was all about, Captain?"

173

"Oh . . ." Harold turned away, eyes drifting toward the door. He scowled. "Nothing, Major."

Rod let a beat or two pass, then shrugged, turning away. "I suppose not. You don't look all that shook about it, anyway."

"No." Harold smiled bitterly. "No, I . . . sort of expected it. No, well . . ." He frowned, musing. "Not 'expected,' really. But you might say I was afraid this would happen."

"Oh?" Rod said quietly, lifting an eyebrow.

"Yeah." Harold turned away, glowering at the fire.

Well, Rod mused silently, any man who puts his beloved to the acid test deserves what he gets—or loses.

Aloud, he said, "We might drop by Agatha's suite, Harold. Your mother seems to be worried about your not being home on time."

"Huh? What?" Harold looked up, frowning abstractedly.

"Your mother," Rod reminded. "Got to let her know a new factor has materialized. Let her know she isn't losing a familiar, just gaining a son."

Agatha sat by the fire, gripping the arms of the straight-backed hard chair, stiff, immobile, glaring at the fire. She was dry-eyed, but the paths left by a torrent of tears added new grooves to her wrinkled old face.

The door opened quietly, almost secretively. Gwen crept in and knelt by Agatha's side. "Agatha," she said, taking the old woman's hand, "Agatha, hear me, Grandmother. Hear me."

"Leave me," croaked the witch, eyes fixed on the fire. "Leave me to my misery, witch-girl, and pray, not for me, but for thyself, that thou mayest never know the pains of desertion."

Gwen bit her lip, stared into the old woman's face for a moment, then tugged gently at the old, dry hand. "Agatha, attend me! Thy son has come!"

The old witch sat rock-still a moment.

Her head snapped to the side, her eyes glowing coals, searing into Gwen's. "Wilt thou mock me, Gwen Gallowglass? Must thou make sport of . . ."

"Mother," said a rich baritone from the doorway.

Agatha's head snapped up as though she'd been slapped, something akin to fear and horror creeping into her eyes. Her lips parted. "Who . . . ? What—what art thou?" she croaked.

Harold stood, flint.

The old witch seemed to lift and swell in the chair, mouth and eyes widening.

174

Then, with a single, keening cry, she threw herself from the chair and staggered a few steps toward the doorway.

She stood swaying, eyes glazing, shuddering like a tree at the blows of an ax.

Then, slowly, she leaned forward into another stumbling step toward her son. . . .

But his arms closed about her, he was there beside her, folding her in his arms, pushing her old head into his shoulder. She stiffened slowly, drawing in a long, shuddering breath, then heaved out a great sob, and the torrent of tears broke.

"Very strange sight, when you come to think of it," Rod muttered to Gwen. "First time I've ever seen a mother reunited with her son before he was even born."

Gwen smiled slowly, calmly. "Yet it touches thee, my lord. Do not seek to tell me it doth not."

"Touches me?" Rod looked surprised. "Whatever gave you that idea? I'm not touched, I'm just glad."

Gwen looked at him out of the corner of her eyes. "Thou art rejoicing, my lord? Who would not?"

"True," Rod admitted. "But I'm rejoicing for military reasons."

"Military?" Gwen frowned.

"Yes. I think that little tableau in there is our victory in embryo."

He looked up at an approaching, jangling clatter. Tuan strode toward them, down the dark, torch-lit corridor, flanked by two pikemen.

"Rod Gallowglass . . ." he called, breaking off at Rod's frantic shushing motions. He came close and said, in a low, conspiratorial tone, "What is this news I have heard, that we have gained a warlock in the fullness of his years?"

"Uh . . . yes," Rod said, putting an arm around the young King's shoulders and leading him aside. "That news is right, but a little misleading. He just *looks* like 'the fullness of his years,' to our teenager witches; actually, he's twenty-one."

"Why, that is full," frowned Tuan, who was aged twenty-three.

"Uh . . . yes, middle-aged." Rod was thirty-four. "But we're not really all that much stronger than we were before. You see, Sir Harold in there is just old Agatha's familiar, come to life." He answered the King's appalled stare by saying, "Don't try to figure it out, Tuan. Mere mortals like you and me can't question the ways of witches."

Tuan smiled, with a touch of irony. Rod noted the touch

approvingly; the kid was growing up. "Thou, Master Gallowglass," said the King, "art scarcely true mortal."

"Oh, but I am! That's the trouble."

Tuan frowned. "How . . . ?"

"Yes. Uh, you see—we've got Sir Harold with us in the flesh now, and that means he can be killed in battle—like you, and, uh, like me. So, actually, we're potentially worse off now than we were before."

Tuan's face fell. "I like this not."

"But I do." Rod grinned, glee breaking loose. "Oh, I do."

"How so?" The young King swam in confusion.

"Oh, you'll see, you'll see. But for now, well—his chances of getting killed in battle aren't all *that* good—but then again, of course, there's Finagler's Law. . . . But this is our first real, *trained* warlock; and he also happens to be a knight, a *trained* knight, I might add." He didn't have to cross his fingers *too* hard; after all, karate and judo, and strategy and tactics, were martial training, even if they weren't all that kosher by the laws of chivalry. . . . "A trained knight, forged in skirmishes and tempered in guerrilla raids."

A slight frown knit Tuan's brow. "But thou art thyself both knight and warlock, Master Gallowglass."

Rod opened his mouth, remembered his failures to convince Tuan he wasn't a warlock, and said instead, "Yes, well, let's just skip that point for the time being, shall we? The main point is that, just by being here, Sir Harold should improve morale tremendously. Now, let's strike while the iron is hot, as the Steelworker's Union used to say, and hit them triple strength, three raids at once, tonight, with Sir Harold in charge of one of the Warlock Operations, Extramilitary, groups."

"Three raids at once?" Tuan's voice held a touch of awe.

"Yeah. I wouldn't try it unless morale was really riding high. But, I think our boys can do. Uh, it will be a clear night, won't it?"

Without waiting for an answer, he turned and called at the empty air, "Duty elf! Front and Center!"

"Aye, Rod Gallowglass." Kelly seemed to tumble from the ceiling, landing in a crouch.

Rod frowned. "What do you think *you're* doing? Eavesdropping? Say, how's the weather tonight?"

" 'Twill be a fine night!" The elf grinned. "The moon shall be bright as a shilling, new-minted. The stars shall besprinkle the sky like clover, in meadows of spring!"

Rod thought about mentioning the virtues of conciseness in military reports, but contented himself with asking, "Where's their army weak tonight, Eldritch?"

"In Wayairdie Glen, hard by the village of Tarnhelm." The elf grinned. "Yet they are weaker still at Wyndon Creek, where it flows into the Fleuve."

Rod eyed Kelly sidewise. "Weak? With their backs to the river?"

"Aye, should we spring up the riverbanks to attack them. Then would they fall back amazed and confused, and elves might happen upon them and trip them in flight."

Rod grinned. "While our men relieve their camp of everything that can be carried away, huh? Not such a bad idea, after all."

He turned to Tuan. "Let's assign, uh, 'Sir' Harold to Warlock Support for the Riverbank Raiders."

Slowly, the King grinned. "It should be quite amusing, Lord Gallowglass."

The woodchopper trudged down the forest path, his back bent under a heavy load of wood, cursing the Fates, and dreaming of the day when he might be able to afford a donkey.

A tall, spare figure stepped out of the brush behind him, light-foot and quiet, long hair, tangled beard, streaming in the wind.

The green wood staff lifted and swung, cracking against the peasant's skull. The woodchopper gave a single, choking gasp, and fell, face-down in the dust of the path.

Skolax dropped his staff, and bent to strip the peasant, throwing the rough homespun into a pile by the path.

He stood, shrugged out of his robe, naked but for a knife swinging by a thong at his neck. He threw the robe over the woodcutter with a contemptuous snort, took up the pile of clothing, and turned away into the wood.

The staff lay by the peasant's bundle of firewood.

Rod snagged a chicken leg out of the air a foot above his head with a nostalgic smile. "Just like home. . . . Son, quit playing with your food!"

The peas, chicken pieces, and mashed potatoes settled back onto Magnus' plate; but the child was looking rebellious.

"Excellent babe"—Gwen patted Magnus' head—"to obey so promptly when thou art told." She smiled fondly, with some motherly pride.

The child's look of truculence metamorphosed into a one-toothed grin.

"Such joy," Rod sighed, "having dinner with the family again. . . . What's it been, Gwen? A month?"

"Three weeks, four days, and nine hours, my lord."
Gwen managed to combine a smile and a frown. " 'Tis a
wonder the child doth comprehend thy words; for I would
ha' sworn he was yet too young for ought but thought-
speaking."

"Oh, I dunno. . . ." Rod shoved the food over to one
side of his mouth so he could chew and talk at the same
time. "His physical coordination hasn't progressed far enough
for him to be able to talk, sure; but he understands fine.
After all, you talk to him aloud whenever you talk to him,
and he's, uh, 'hearing' your thoughts at the same time,
every time, isn't he? So he'd connect thought with sound
a lot sooner than most kids. . . . Son, put that down!"

The globe of milk fell back into the glass with a splash.
Magnus thrust his lower lip out, and sulked.

"But he comprehends only witches and elves," Gwen
mused, frowning. "Only thou, of all those who cannot
thought-speak, doth he comprehend. . . ."

"Well, yeah; but he's been around me a lot more than
most folks. Probably gets a lot of it from my tone. . . ."
Rod watched the peas disappear from Magnus' plate, reflecting that, two years ago, it would have unnerved him
fantastically to watch someone teleport food directly to
their stomachs. "Son, I keep telling you—*chew* the food
before you swallow it!"

Gwen sighed, sitting back, and fixed the baby with a
motherly glare.

Magnus pulled his head down between hunched shoulders, watching Gwen warily out of the corner of his eye.
His mouth bulged with a sudden mouthful of food.

"After all," Rod went on, "you've got to develop your
jaw muscles, boy. In this family, you'll need it."

Magnus chewed, swallowed, and opened his mouth. A
pea shot into it from the plate.

Rod frowned at his wife. "What's the matter, hon?"

Gwen looked up, smiled quickly.

Rod smiled gently. "Greta again?"

"Aye, my lord." Gwen's smile turned sad. "She will
never know the joy of a man and a babe."

" '*Will* never' is the right phrase," Rod said reflectively. "There stands Harold, hers for the taking; but she won't
take." He shrugged, smiling sourly. "Nothing new about
that, actually. That's the way it's always been with most
women. When they can't have the man, they want him;
but as soon as they can have him, they don't want him
anymore."

"Is it not that way also with men, good my lord?" Gwen said softly.

"A point," he admitted. "If I ever quit feeling you were just about to slip out of my grasp, you'd probably have to start wondering."

"As 'tis also with myself," Gwen admitted, ruefully.

Rod's eyes widened a little, mainly because his wife had the look of deep immersion in a very dark mood, not too far removed from a rage.

Rod frowned. "Look, girl, if Greta doesn't want Harold, she doesn't. Why should she get uptight about it?"

Gwen stirred impatiently, tossing the ceiling a look of exasperation. "Men!" she sighed. "So blind. . . ."

"Oh-h!" Rod lifted an eyebrow. "She doesn't want him, but she really does, hm? She found out he wasn't quite as handsome as she'd pictured him?"

"He is so horribly warlike!" Gwen glared at Rod as though it were his fault.

"Ah, so!" Both eyebrows went up. "How unreasonable of a knight, to wind up looking like a fighting man." He smiled sadly, shaking his head. "Well, it's always bound to be a little painful, bumping headlong into reality."

Gwen nodded sadly, looking away. "She needed but one look at him, my lord, to fall out of love. . . . But, such is the love of children. . . ."

Rod nodded, commiserating. "First sight does wonders. . . ."

A tall, thin peasant in ill-fitting homespun tunic, leggings, and buskins, with bushy sideburns and a long, drooping moustache, hair bound at the nape of his neck in a sailor's pigtail, strode into the seaport town.

He stood a moment at the door of a tavern, listening to the clamor from the docks, where the chandlers and shipwrights were building long ships for the King's Fleet.

The tall peasant's face twisted into something that might have been a grim smile.

He turned, and strode into the tavern.

Rod chuckled.

Tuan frowned thoughtfully at him. "Thou art strangely joyous, Lord Gallowglass, for one who ha' but now consigned twelve squadrons of men to their deaths."

"Deaths?" Rod stared, surprised. Then his lips split into a grin again. "Crocodile tears, Tuan. Only that."

The young King scowled blackly. " 'Tis the enemy thou

art intended to devour, Lord Crocodile, not men of thine own."

"Oh, they won't be hurting." Rod squelched another chuckle. "At least, no more than usual. Matter of fact, I think their chances'll prove a little better than ordinary."

A blast of wind hit them, whipping their cloaks about.

"Dost thou not smell the rain in that wind?" Tuan grated. "Dost thou not know the lightning comes with it? The lightning, to strengthen the black Evil Eye of these beast-men? Shall not my men then be overwhelmed? And, nay, not twelve squadrons alone, but the whole of mine army, which thou hast bid me hold near!"

Rod quirked up an eyebrow. "If you're so sure they're headed for doom and destruction, how come you're going ahead with it?"

Tuan turned away, growling.

Rod grinned, barely managing to keep from laughing. "You . . . trust . . . me . . ." he sang, taunting. "You should know better; you're the King."

"And thou art a warlock," Tuan snapped, turning. "High Warlock have I named thee, so that thy powers are at the call of this nation! For I know there is a geas on thee, that binds thee to the guarding of the welfare of my and mine, of myself and my kingdom! Deny it if thou canst!"

Rod sobered, turning his head from side to side. "No, I can't deny it. You're right."

Tuan smiled sourly. "And is my faith in thee, then, not warranted?"

"Very," Rod admitted.

He turned away, his eyes going to the hastily-built shack on the nearby hilltop.

Tuan smiled, eyes glittering. " 'Tis there," he murmured. "Therein lies the vindication of my trust in thee. There lies thy geas: only a woman."

Rod looked back over his shoulder, smiling bleakly. "A witch-woman," he said. "Don't forget that. But you forget she's not in the cabin; she's at Runnymede, with the reinforcements. Still, you were part right." He turned back toward the cabin. "That shack also holds the justification of my plan, Tuan. My main reason for confidence."

Tuan scowled at the cabin. " 'Warlock Operations, Extramilitary,' as thou hast named them? Assuredly thou dost not trust in them only!"

"No, not them alone," Rod admitted. "But you forget, Harold's one of them this time."

"As he was before!" Tuan stiffened, alarmed. "In our last battle, was he not with us? Aye, not in the body, most surely; yet his powers were linked with Agatha's! Were they not? And are we, then, now stronger?"

"True, true, all very true," Rod said. "But this time he's here in the body."

"And may thus be slain!" Tuan cried, falling back a step. "Is *this* the source of thy power, by which we shall defeat the beastmen?"

"Yeah, I suppose you could look at it that way," Rod said judiciously. He turned away, sinking his eyeteeth into the inside corner of his mouth to keep his face straight. "Indirectly, you'd be right. Indirectly. . . ."

Thunder boomed in the distance. The first drops of rain fell.

"Give the orders," Rod said quietly.

" 'Tis near time, is it not?" growled a beastman.

They squatted about the watchfire, cloaked against the chill, muttering and grumbling, chafing their hands near the flames, waiting for the signal to assemble for the charge. When storms came, the Kobold men moved upriver.

A second Neanderthal pulled his cloak tighter about him, shivering. "The nights grow cold," he growled. "Did not Atylem tell us we would be done with battling ere now?"

"Aye," growled his mate, sticking his great splay feet out toward the fire in vain hope of warming the soles. "The summer ha' tarried and gone. We should be roistering, warm and cozy, in the inns of Runnymede now."

"What are these puny, pale creatures," snarled another, "that they mock at the power of the great Kobold so? Shaman ha' told us . . ."

"Aye, aye," interrupted the first impatiently, "Shaman ha' told us we would be in Runnymede ere the winter took hold of the land, safe and warm in the King's Castle ere the harvest came. But how was the Shaman to know of these skulking, fleetfooted cowardly bands of the Slender Folk, that strike us and run ere we have the time to strike back?"

"And the goblins . . ." muttered the third.

"There are no goblins," snapped the first. "The Shaman ha' shown us. Each time these coils were bred, 'twas our own careless doings. We had let the milk spoil, we had let the tent-ropes rot, we had let the beer sour."

"Aye, aye," swore the third. "But will carelessness lay a fire to a tent?"

"Aye, if you light the fire too close to the tent."

The third snorted. "Will carelessness fill a man's boots with water?"

181

The first grumbled some sort of retort and was silent.

The second Neanderthal howled, grasping his foot.

"What is it, brother?" said the first, alarmed.

"Mine foot, oh mine foot!" groaned the second, his hand carefully away from his sole. The round welt of a burn showed on the ball.

"Goblins!" gasped the third.

"Nay, nay!" the first said, too quickly. " 'Twas a cinder that flew from the fire." But there was fear in his voice.

"I care not the cause," moaned the second. "Bring me cold water for the burn! Bring me . . ."

He broke off at the sound of throaty chuckling.

The three Neanderthals looked up and saw a tiny, foot-high shape flit out of the firelight.

"Goblins!"

"There *do* be goblins!"

"Nay, nay! The Shaman ha' sworn not!"

The first, recovering from his shock, growled, "Goblin or not, I'll crush the life from it!" And, catching up his great war-club, he lunged after the elf, ignoring the cautioning cries of his mates.

They saw him lumber away toward the river bank, saw him stumble down the bank with a cry of vengeance . . . heard the cry cut off sharply.

The other two men sat frozen a moment, shivering with more than the cold of the wind.

"What ha' become of him?" whispered the second.

"The goblins ha' taken him," whispered the third.

The second threw himself to his feet, wincing at the pain of his burned sole. "Are we to let goblin-magic slay our brother, and not take revenge? Hai! To me!" he bellowed, swinging his club in a beckon to the other, nearby men of the camp.

They looked up from their fires; a murmur passed through the camp. Beastmen leaped to their feet all about the watch-fires, collected their clubs, and shambled toward the second.

"Be wary!" bellowed that worthy. "There is magic afoot!"

He turned away and, in a long, growling line, the beastmen followed him—to the brink of the river bank. Cautiously, warily, the long line bowed, peering over the bank.

They gave sudden, barking grunts. One howled; the cry was cut off, quite quickly.

Then, slowly, the bodies leaned forward, toppled over the bank.

The beastmen nearby, who'd been watching, sat frozen by their fires in shock for one moment. . . .

And in that moment, a clamoring horde of demons poured over the bank, howling and yelling, "For God and the Island of Gramarye!"

Fifteen beastmen fell dead in that first rush. The others came to their senses with a jolt, leaped up and fled howling in superstitious terror.

The soldiers howled too as they chased the Neanderthals. Lightning split the sky, and thunder tumbled brawling in its wake.

The beastmen came to a halt, reminded of the power of their god.

The instant's hesitation was all Atylem needed.

He rose up in the middle of the battle line, flailing the air with his club and howling, "To me! Form for battle about me! Shall a score and a half of these slender fellows now rout us? To me, Hai! By the Kobold!"

The beastmen wavered; then, as Atylem leaped through them toward the charging Gramarye raiders, the Neanderthals whooped with a return of battle-joy, and turned to receive the Gramarye charge.

Thunder rolled, coming nearer.

The raiders hit the Neanderthal line with a crash like a broken beehive in a percussion section. Beastmen caught soldiers' eyes; soldiers froze in their tracks.

In the hilltop cabin, warlocks and witches joined hands, squeezed eyes shut, as old Agatha cried, "Now!"

In the valley, the Neanderthals waded in with their clubs, to take advantage of the cold snap.

Three seconds was about all they had before the thaw hit. The black blanket lifted from the soldiers' minds, and pikes shifted to parry, then swept in quick chops.

The Neanderthals lifted their shields to ward off the pikes and swung their clubs like wrecking balls, snarling horrible oaths. But, fortunately, their clubs had not only the force of a wrecking ball, but also its maneuverability; and the beastmen still hadn't learned how to guard against thrust and lunge. And the soldiers knew their backs would eventually be to the river.

Beastmen fell, their blood pumping out through slits in their bellies and rib cages, and planes where their throats had been.

Lightning slashed the night; darkness bled thunder.

Soldiers froze.

In the cabin, all the witches lay senseless except, at the head of the circle, Agatha, and beside her, Harold. Their hands were locked, the muscles of their necks bulging taught under strain.

In the valley, soldiers began to move.

But Atylem was pointing up at a hilltop shouting, "There! The light of the Kobold revealed it! The lair of the strength of our enemies! To the hill! Hai! To me, and up!"

The beastmen whirled away from the Gramarye soldiers to bound up the hillside.

They raised shields against a sudden hail of arrows. Beastmen screamed and fell, slamming the earth; but Atylem had more than a hundred men at his back for the charge. They plowed remorselessly through the volleys to the high, lonely cabin.

The door crashed open, shattered to kindling.

Harold leaped up, dropping Agatha's hands, whipping out his sword, leaping to the door as a broad, gorilla-shaped beastman shouldered through the splintered doorway. He swung up his shield to catch Harold's cut . . . and his eyes caught Harold's.

Harold felt the black pall flowing down over his mind, weakened by the Kobold's blasts. The black cloud settled, chilling. . . .

On the floor, Agatha's shoulders hunched, trembling, with a surge of effort.

Harold threw off the cloud with a wringing wrench of his mind and, glaring, threw it back into the beastman's eyes.

The Neanderthal froze, his eyes glazing. Harold thrust him away with a twist of his shoulder, swung his sword at the head with a great two-handed chop. It clanged off the helmet, denting it nicely, and the beastman jerked, awaking from his trance just long enough for a half-scream before Harold's next cut slit his throat.

Atylem stepped over the senseless body, his huge lead-weighted club dropping like a meteor.

Harold swung up his sword to parry.

Lightning screamed outside the cabin.

The muscles between Agatha's neck and shoulders knotted; her teeth ground, face twisting into a grimace of agony.

Harold's sword met the club, and held against it for an instant. . . .

Lightning flared again.

Agatha cried out, once, a scream ripped out of the lining of her throat, and fell senseless, sprawling on the floor.

Harold's mind congealed as the black cloud engulfed him.

Atylem's club smashed the blade of the sword crashing

down into Harold's shoulder. The bone cracked and the left knee gave way; Harold knelt, slack-mouthed, on the floor.

Atylem grinned and whirled his club up for the death-blow. The cudgel whistled down. . . .

And struck rebounding off the thin, bony hand upraised a foot above Harold's head.

Atylem's head snapped up, face contorting with anger and horror; he stared into the clear eyes of a tall, old, blue-cloaked, white-bearded man, towering over the fallen knight.

Desperately, Atylem tried to drive his glare deep into the old man's eyes, tried to catch the wizard's brain. . . .

A volcano exploded in his mind. With a howl of pain he dropped back, stumbling away with his singing head in his hands.

The Neanderthals closed around their wounded chieftain, warding off the wizard's Eye by turning their backs. None dared confront the old man who had felled Atylem.

They fled from the cabin, then turned a hundred yards away, growling and cursing, pouring looted brandy between Atylem's lips, struggling to wake the chief, and to work up their courage to attack the cabin again.

Lightning slashed the sky.

Inside the cabin, Galen fell to his knees, hands clutching his temples. His back bowed under the strain, but held.

Harold shook his head, the numbness ebbing from his mind. . . .

He screamed as the pain from his shoulder bit through.

On the plain below, battle raged raw and scarlet between Neanderthals and soldiers.

In a copse of woods near the cabin, Rod sat clutching his sword hilt till the knuckles stood white. Sweat beaded his upper lip.

"Shall I not send word now, Lord Gallowglass?" Toby pleaded. "The King's band stands taut and ready! At thy word, these beastmen die!"

"Not yet," Rod snapped, and cursed the quaver in his voice. If he was wrong, Atylem might yet take the cabin, and Gramarye would lose half its witch-power. . . .

But if he was right . . . and he'd been right so far . . .

He cleared his throat and said again, "No. We wait till Atylem's awake, and they charge the cabin again. We wait."

Within the cabin, Harold sat beside Galen, clutching the old man's hand, teeth clenched against the pain in the shoulder.

Agatha lifted her head slowly, looked about, and saw Galen and her son.

Her jaw knotted; with a sudden heave she forced herself to her knees, clutched Harold's hand.

One of the boy warlocks lifted his head.

Outside the cabin, the beastmen broke howling from their huddle, charging the cabin, Atylem at their head, war-club raised high.

"Now!" Rod shouted, and Fess leaped forward.

They burst out of the copse, fifty horsemen at their back, thundering down on the charging Neanderthals.

From the other side of the cabin, a war-cry split the air as Tuan and fifty more horsemen swooped down.

Atylem jerked to a halt, bellowing a curse and a command. His men formed up behind him as he set himself, legs wide apart, club raised high.

A huge black horse bore down on him, black lips lifted to reveal steel teeth.

Atylem leaped aside, but Fess followed the movement, slammed a shoulder into the beastman's chest.

Atylem slammed back into five of his men.

Fess raced through the line, scattering beastmen like a bow-wave.

Rod leaned from the saddle, swinging his sword like a scythe.

Fifty horsemen followed them, cutting the beastmen line to ribbons.

Rod pulled up and turned about, his men falling into line with him, readying another charge.

Fifty yards on the other side of the beastmen, Tuan's squad bore down.

But the Neanderthals had had enough. Lifting the body of their wounded leader on their shoulders, they raced for the wooded slope below, the forest where the horsemen would lose advantage.

Rod raised a hand, signaling his men to stand fast.

Tuan's horsemen slowed, cantered up to join Rod's men.

"Shall we not follow, Warlock?" Tuan cried, reining in beside him.

"No," Rod sighed. "They'll run now, and keep on running. I thought this'd do the trick. They saw their chief fall once, and they rallied; but not after he'd fallen twice. With any luck, they'll keep on running all the way back to Beastland."

Tuan frowned. "They might yet rally, 'tween this field and the coast. . . ."

"They might," Rod agreed. "But we've beaten them at

their own Evil Eye game, in their own kind of weather. I don't think they'll try to stand against us again." He turned, looking toward the sounds of distant battle from the plain below. "I hope. . . ."

In the cabin, all the warlocks and witches sat upright now, weary, nauseous, but bearing the load, and bearing it without strain. The crisis was past; and the storm was moving off. . . .

Harold was trembling.

Galen looked up, feeling the shiver of his son's hand, concern in his eyes.

The air popped in the middle of the circle, and Toby stood a moment, singling out Agatha. He glanced at Galen in the process, his eyes widening with awe and fear; then he quickly glanced away.

He turned to Agatha, knelt by her, touched her hand.

She looked up, bleary-eyed.

"They flee," Toby murmured, voice not quite steady. "We must follow after, to guard the troops."

Agatha closed her eyes, nodding wearily. Then she lifted her head again, a single sharp command snapping from her mind to those of the younger espers.

The warlocks looked up, surprised, then nodded, and disappeared.

The girls rose, reaching for their broomsticks.

Harold's form wavered.

Agatha's fingers sank into his shoulder like calipers. "Thou shalt rest here!"

"Aiieee-yah!" Harold nearly went through the roof. "Mom . . . the shoulder, Mom. . . ."

Agatha released the shoulder with a gasp, her eyes rounding hugely. "Child! What ha' they *done* to thee!"

"Naught that I cannot tend," Galen rumbled. "Get thee hence to tend thine army."

Their eyes locked, venom and fuming acid spitting between them.

Agatha broke the glare, turning at a sound, and saw the last of the witches soaring out the door on her broomstick.

She glanced back at Harold, her resolution wavering, torn between the injured child who would live, and the children in mortal danger far away.

"Thou mayest entrust him to my care," Galen informed her in a voice like a jet of liquid air. "I have some skill at healing, and mine own concern for him is in no wise less than thine."

"Go on, Ma," Harold sighed. "I'll be just fine."

Agatha glanced at the door, bit her lip, glanced back at Harold, and decided.

"Well enow, then," she said, touching his shoulder—the good one—lightly. "I shall return as soon I may, to tend thee."

Agatha transferred her gaze to Galen for one last brief glare, then caught up her broomstick and was gone.

Galen sighed, relaxing, brought out a penknife, and cut away the cloth around the shoulder. He touched the bone lightly, feeling out the break.

Harold gritted his teeth in stoic silence.

Galen wrenched the broken bones back into alignment with a sharp, quick twist.

Harold howled, and would have gone six feet straight up if Galen hadn't snapped a restraining field around him.

A roll of bandage appeared in the old man's hand. He wrapped it about the shoulder quickly, secured it, then frowned as Harold said, between gasps and clenched teeth, "I'd appreciate it if you'd help me up, too. I could use some fresh air."

"Nay," the old wizard started to protest, but Harold was already struggling to his feet.

Slowly, Harold stood, clutching at his father a moment to steady himself till the world stopped spinning. Then they hobbled to the door. Harold took a deep, long breath of the cold, wet wind, coughed, and lifted his eyes to Galen's. "Thanks."

Galen nodded slowly.

Harold freed his arm from the old man's shoulder. "How come you saved me?"

Galen smiled bitterly. "How could I fail to? Thou art mine son, by what witchcraft I know not, yet still, thou art son to me, mine to me."

Harold's eyebrows lifted a little. "Oh, you believe me, then?"

"How might I believe ought else?" the old man said sourly. "Thou art my son; it is stamped on thy face; for so I looked ere my beard grew; and thou hast done deeds I should ha' done."

Harold smiled, with a touch of bitterness, and nodded.

Then he frowned, his eyes drifting away toward the battlefield.

"What moves in thy heart?" Galen muttered, apprehension in his voice.

"I should have been down there," Harold said loud. "I could have done a lot of good in the front ranks."

"Nay!" Galen fairly cried. Then, angrily, "Hast thou not

yet learned enow of why the High Warlock ha' forbade the young warlocks combat physical?"

Harold frowned, bowing his head. He bit his lip, nodded. "Yeah," he said. "I was kind of forgetting that, wasn't I? Simple conservation of vital military resources. You see, we don't have that problem where I come from. The whole planet's full of warlocks; they're a dime a dozen, about as valuable as students at a big university. I keep forgetting there're only a few of 'em here."

"Then thou wilt not march to battle?" Anxiety underscored Galen's words.

"Oh, I wouldn't say that. . . ." Harold pursed his lips. "A warlock has a lot of advantages over an ordinary soldier, you see. I just might be able to make the vital difference, get this war over with for good, before I was killed. . . ."

"Nay, nay!" Galen thundered his anger that was two-thirds fear. "Naught of good wilt thou do in such fashion! What gains thou madest would quickly be lost after thy death! Thou knowest naught of the force of that Evil Eye!"

"True; but I do know that the Evil Eye is only unbeatable during thunderstorms. And winter is icumen in, so there won't be many more thunderstorms." Harold frowned over the late Neanderthal camp. "Of course, that won't make much difference when we invade Beastland. . . ."

"Invade!" Galen gasped, his face a mask of horror.

Harold turned, frowning. "Of course. If we don't, they'll just be back next spring. And by that time, they'll have figured out a better way to deal with us witches."

He turned toward the battlefield again. "No, the only way to get them off our backs is to invade them—and I'm sure we will. Of course, right there on their home territory, they probably won't need thunderstorms. . . . Oh, well, all the more reason to have a warlock in the front lines."

"Thou must not!" Galen's fingers bit deep into his son's arm. "I will not permit . . ."

"Permit . . . ?" Harold turned slowly, a slight smile touching his lips. Galen could almost see the chip settling onto the young man's shoulder.

Slowly, he released his hold on his son. "Aye!" he thundered, with all the weight of his years behind it. "I will not permit! I am thy father, am I not? And thou must needs be subject to me!"

Harold shook his head, slowly. "No. Father. I'm not a child—in case you hadn't noticed. And moreover, you didn't raise me. I owe you no debt of thanks; in fact, I don't even owe you the starting of my life, yet. The man to

189

whom I owe fatherhood is five years in my past, and quite a few lifetimes into the future. True, I owe you my life for your having saved it just now; and I'm grateful, but not grateful enough for you to have any control over me."

He looked away, out over the battlefield, again. "For, when the last word is said, a man must be subject not to his father, but to his God. . . . When you die, you'll die with honor; for you've followed your own God, no matter how much fear you had to conquer to do it."

He bowed his head, avoiding his father's eyes. "But your God and my God are two very different beings; and I have to follow mine every bit as much as you have to follow yours."

The old man nodded slowly. "Aye," he said quietly, with the strength of despair.

Galen's eyes burned into Harold's. "Go to thy death, then; and when I chant the coronach over thy grave, I shall have this cold comfort: that I fathered an honorable man."

Harold bowed his head, and disappeared.

Galen stood alone, listening to the moaning wind and the distant sound of battle.

"Had I not been so new to fatherhood," the old man murmured, "I might not ha' brewed with him this coil, and I might yet have hope of swaying his will."

"Precisely on schedule," Fess murmured. He stood, with Rod astride, on the next hilltop, their eyes on Galen.

Rod lowered his lorgnette—a disguised pair of electronic binoculars—and loosened his collar. "Not quite on schedule, Fess. The old boy cut it a little bit fine, there. I was expecting him to show up the moment the Neanderthals smashed down the door."

"Still, it was, all in all, an excellent exploitation of an emotional vulnerability, Rod. Congratulations are much in order."

"Yeah, well, thanks. Too bad you have to call a father's love a 'vulnerability,' though." Rod winced; he'd forgotten that a loosened collar would let the rain in. He fastened it again, muttering, "Still, the old boy came damn close to being as hardhearted as he claimed."

"Close," the robot echoed. "In the final analysis, however . . ."

Rod shrugged. "Blood will tell. . . ."

"Even if it has not yet been transmitted," Fess murmured.

"Objective time, of course," Rod interjected.

"Of course. . . . At any rate, once again, congratulations, Rod."

"Yes," Rod muttered, "since it worked."

With the whole of the King's Army as an incentive, the beastmen fled back to their long ships.

Then Tuan brought up his archers, and a steady stream of fire-arrows began to pour into the wooden dragons. Neanderthal forms scuttled madly about the decks with hide buckets, dousing flames; but no sooner was a fire extinguished than five more cropped up in its place.

Then, with things in a fine state of disorganization, Tuan called for a charge.

Atylem looked up from a freshly-quenched bonfire and saw a small horde of horsemen thundering down on him.

It was just too much.

The big Neanderthal called up his own archers and, while they held the cavalry at a precarious bowshot's length (for as long as the ammunition lasted), Atylem called orders, hatchets thudded on mooring cables, and the long ships turned their bows to the east, drifting downstream. Sails spread and filled.

But the army kept pace with the fleet, and the storm of fire-arrows slackened but never ceased. And the Evil Eye wasn't too effective when the enemy was too far off to see the whites of his eyes.

Also, Atylem had better sense than to land and try for another battle; even he had lost confidence in the Eye now.

So, even though Rod had sent a few squads of witches along with the army, they weren't needed. Still, they stood by, watchful and ready, while the dragon ships sailed down the Fleuve, all that night, all the next day, with horsemen going in relays to keep them moving, till they came to the sea.

There the ships paused, hove to near the horizon, as though considering another try. But a line of archers assembled on the sea-cliffs, with telekinetic witches behind them, and the resultant fire-arrow trajectories were long.

The dragons raised sail again and disappeared toward the west.

In the midst of the cheering and drinking, Rod shouldered through to Tuan. He grabbed the King by the neck and shouted in his ear to make himself heard.

"Your Majesty! You better send word to the shipwrights to get back to work!"

"Um?" Tuan blinked owlishly, then turned away, scowling in deep concentration.

"Nay," he said at some length, "now I bethink me, I never did give order that they should cease labor. Belike they are still at their building." He turned back to Rod, frowning. "But why dost thou wish it?"

"Because," Rod yelled over a particularly joyous toast, "we'll need 'em for the invasion!"

"Invasion?" Tuan went egg-eyed. "Nay, assuredly thou dost not mean that we would sail with our armies to Beastland!"

"Why not?" Rod shouted in his ear. "We've done it before! And this time we even stand a chance of winning! Besides, you don't think they're just going to sit there minding their own business for the rest of recorded history, do you? They'll be back here next spring, soon as the thunderstorm season starts! And they'll have figured out something to do about the witches! Besides, Galen might be dead by then, maybe Agatha too, you never know!"

Tuan scowled furiously, then slowly nodded. "Aye," he muttered thickly, "thou hast much reason. The time to strike them is now."

Rod expelled a vast sigh of relief.

"Tell the shipwrights to step up the pace," he shouted, "and get the armorers busy making catapults. Oh, sure, I know the real battle will be between the Evil Eye and the witches; but there's no sense taking chances!"

"Rod," murmured a voice in his ear, "I have an interesting article on sun dances on file. . . ."

The low beams of the tavern ceiling were dark with years of smoke and grease. So was the air.

The place really had atmosphere; smog control, after all, requires a fairly high technology. The bracketed torches along the walls made a brave effort to cut through the suspension of dark particles, and failed. The torches in the narrow street outside were having a little more success with the night; but not too much of their light managed to make its way inside.

Nonetheless, the place was cheerful. Loud voices lifted in cheerful conversation and raucous laughter, liberally accented with the clink of beer mugs and the squeals of pinched barmaids.

But things were a little more serious at the table in the back corner.

". . . sin and blasphemy, the works of Satan!" The lean, moustached man thumped his beer mug for emphasis.

"But assuredly our King and Queen would not . . ." a young man interjected.

"Assuredly they would!" snapped the lean man, cutting him off. "Do those in power care for ought save more power? Nay, surely not! And will they not do anything they must to gain more power? Aye, surely so!"

"Then all is lost," growled a heavy-set bullet-colored sailor in the shadows, "for what may mere mortals do 'gainst witch-folk?"

There was a chorus of muttered agreement from the other sailors at the table.

"Not so!" snapped the lean man. "The power of the Right, the strength of the Lord, these may strengthen mortal arms till they may hale down witches!"

"So many witches as the King doth harbor?" snorted a scar-faced sailor.

"Aye, so many, and more!" the lean man all but shouted. "Hast thou not heard the wondrous works of the holy man Skolax? How he hath forced Old Agatha to flee her cave, how he hath forced entry even unto the Dark Tower of the wizard Galen?"

The sailors shifted and muttered, some crossing themselves.

"The power of the Lord can win against these witches!" the lean man declaimed. "And His power is in me, for the holy man Skolax hath laid his hands on me!"

He fell suddenly silent, his dagger-gaze seeking out each man about the table, one by one.

"In the coil of the battle, when these blasphemers attack the beastmen," he breathed, "I shall rise up and hale these witches down, and the names of all who strike with me on that day shall live in holy glory!"

Once again, his eyes made the circuit of the table.

"Then that day comes," he hissed, "whose arm will strike with mine?"

"No," Rod said without even looking up from his writing.

Harold pressed his lips together, forced his voice to sound pleasant. "But look, Major, I could really accomplish something in the lines. . . ."

"You could accomplish your own death," Rod spared him a glower, turned back to his writing. "Sorry, Captain."

Harold ground his teeth, counted to ten, tried again. "Look, Major, I've gone to a lot of trouble on this already. I even told my father to go to hell because . . ."

"You *what?*" Rod spun around, aghast.

Harold's eyes widened with faint surprise. "I told him

193

where to go. What the hell else did you expect me to do?"

Rod stared, openmouthed, appalled.

He surged to his feet, pacing angrily about the chamber. "You fool! Idiot! Imbecile! Moron! You colossal bungler! Do you realize you just may have lost us this war?"

Harold looked at him sidewise. "Major, are you sure you feel all right?"

Rod's lips thinned. "Yes, *Captain*, I feel excellent—or I did, until you told me about this hare-brained, numb-skulled . . . Look! You tell your father to go to hell, you alienate him, do you realize that? Get him mad enough at you, and next time, he just might not come to help you! And if he doesn't help *you*, how's he gonna help *us?*"

He turned away, pacing the room in a simmering fury.

Harold started to say something, then remembered military discipline and clamped his jaws shut.

Rod whirled, forefinger jabbing out. "*Next* time, you will be in the witches' hut, no matter *what* manner of excuse you manage to dream up to get into the fighting! Is that clear—*Captain?*"

Harold slowly rose, his eyes turning to ice. "Why? Just because the old man tells me to? And we can't take the chance of putting him against us?"

Rod stopped, rolled his eyes up to the ceiling. "No, Captain," he said, very quietly. "That's not the only reason, no." His jaw tightened. "Such colossal military stupidity has not been seen since Custer mistook a buffalo harvest for a war party! You idiotic, shlemiel, meshugganah blockhead!"

He spun about, his forefinger jabbing out at Harold. "You could've got yourself *killed!* And I can't afford to lose warlocks! Like it or not, boy, you are a vital military resource, and as such you will henceforth take all possible measures to preserve, conserve, and protect yourself! Kapiche?"

Harold sat slumped with his elbows on his knees; but his mouth was a tight white line as he reluctantly nodded.

Rod relaxed—but only a little. He wondered how long Harold's obedience would last. Oh, not that he doubted the kid's sincerity; he was sure Harold had fine intentions. . . .

The captain's head lifted again. "But if you'd like some judo practice, Major—strictly off the record, of course. . . ."

Rod fought down a grin and nodded slowly. "Sure. What's your belt?"

"Black. Third dan. And yours?"

"Black," Rod said agreeably, "fourth dan."

"Well, well, well!" Harold came to his feet with a grin. "This should be a most interesting match!"

"It should," Rod agreed. "I haven't had an easy win in a long time."

He took a stand by the doorway, bowing. "After you, Captain."

Harold stood opposite and bowed, mimicking Rod. "No, after you, Major."

"No, I insist, Captain!"

"Military etiquette, Major!"

"I'm not worthy of the honor, Captain!"

"Experience before innocence, Major!"

"Glad you admit it, Captain!"

"Go to hell, Major!"

"After you, Cap . . ."

The door slammed open, almost pinning Rod's hand to the wall.

"Thou slimy curmudgeon, thou!" Agatha stormed, thrusting her face within an inch from Rod's. "What dost thou think thyself? How hast thou the colossal gall to chide mine only child! Thou swine, thou ingrate! Thou offal, thou crow's meat—"

"Captain!" Rod snapped. "Are you going to stand there and let her use that kind of language on your commanding officer?"

"Sorry, Major," said Harold, whose look of shocked horror had run through the emotional spectrum to his present look of keen enjoyment. "Sorry, but you heard what she said. A dutiful child can't contradict his mother, can he?"

"He could try a little," Rod growled, in the midst of trying to climb backward into the wood of the door.

"Okay, so I'll try," Harold said affably. "Uh, Mom—we've already settled this whole thing between us."

"Oh, hast thou, indeed?" crooned the witch, the glint in her eye sharing many implications with the overload light on a generator.

Rod spoke up before she could say anything else. "Yes, we were on our way to formalize our agreement with a friendly wrestling match."

"Wrestling!" Agatha spun on him, aghast. "Then thou wouldst offer him corporal harm? Nay, thou shalt never lay hand to my boy, thou miscreant magus!"

"Thou shalt hold thy tongue!" bellowed a voice with the leaden ring of self-appointed authority.

Agatha whirled, staring.

Galen stood in the middle of the room, bony forefinger

pointing at Agatha. "Go thy ways, woman, for men have matters of import that must be debated here!"

"Oh, have they, now?" purred the old witch, and Rod ducked in sheer reflex.

Agatha stalked forward, fists on her hips. "And what wouldst thou have to speak of with these two bold warriors? Thou, who hadst never the courage to so much as bid a good morning to thy fellow man, and still less heart to offer a fair greeting to any woman alive! Thou dast bid *me* to silence?"

Galen drew himself up to all the height he could muster, looking down his nose with every iota of arrogance at his call.

It had startlingly little effect.

"Aye," said Agatha, fairly purring, "but I must give thee thy due; for thou hast, after / all and at long last, had the courage to come forth from thy Tower." Her voice deepened in exaggerated mockery of the wizard's pontificating. "What cataclysm of destiny could be so vital as to draw the great, honored, virtuous and much-revered Galen"—and her voice hardened—"from beneath thy moss-covered rock? Speak, salamander! What danger could draw thee? What charm, aye, what peril?"

"The life of thy son!" the old man grated, "the life of thy son, and mine!"

The old witch took a step back, shocked into silence, eyes widening, hand coming to her lips.

Then she burst into a tearing rage.

"*Thy* son and *mine!* Slander, malediction intolerable! Unspeakable!"

"Be still!" thundered Galen; and, for the first time, there was a touch of genuine, unalloyed anger in his words. "Hold thy tongue, queen of bitches! Feast of the slavering pack! Wife of a thousand thousand husbands who ever were nameless. . . ."

"Sir Gallowglass," said Tuan, coming into the room.

"Sh!" Rod waved him to silence. "You're interrupting one of the choicest battles of the century!"

Tuan frowned, and turned to contemplate the two wailing, howling furies before him.

"Major!" Harold's face was drawn and pale; his knees shook a little. "You can't let them keep on like this!"

"Why not?" Rod grinned. "Let them bellow themselves out. Then they'll both be manageable."

Harold stared, aghast.

Then his mouth firmed.

He spun toward the battlers. "Shut up! Both of you!"

"Know they not their nation is this moment at war?" Tuan murmured to Rod.

"I think they're above such mundane matters at the moment, Majesty," Rod answered.

"I bethink me, then, that I must needs remind them," said Tuan. He turned to the yammering trio, took a deep breath, and bellowed in his best orator's voice:

"*Silence!* In the name of the King your liege lord, *be still!*"

Omelet silence splattered over the room.

The witch-family turned to stare at the source of the voice that had managed to outshout all three of them.

Agatha was the first to return to her vocal cords, as the joy of battle flamed anew in her eyes. "So, Your Majesty wouldst bid a grown witch to silence? Shall I tell thee the folly of . . ."

"Peace!" snapped Galen, and old Agatha whirled to start in on him again; but Galen was speaking before she could get her pharynx in phase.

"With all due respect, Royal Majesty," the old wizard said, bowing gravely, "dost thou seek to command witches?"

"I do," said the King.

Tuan turned to Rod. "I do not know this venerable ancient, Sir Gallowglass. Wilt thou do us courtesies?"

"Gladly," said Rod, bowing his head while he wiped the smile off his face. Lifting his head, he gestured to the old wizard and said, "Master Galen, His Majesty Tuan of Gramarye," and, turning to Tuan, whose eyes had already widened a trifle, "Your Majesty, Master Galen, Lord of the Dark Tower."

Tuan stiffened, his eyes emulating saucers.

Then, recovering himself, he inclined his head slightly in a very formal bow. "I thank thee, great wizard, for having lent us thy great aid, in ridding our land of these fell beastmen."

Galen returned the bow.

"I am honored by thy presence in my castle, august witch and great wizard. Yet forgive my lack of hospitality, that I must now inquire, so soon upon thy coming, honored Galen—it is a question that presseth me greatly, or I would not neglect courtesy so; therefore tell to me: Hast thou come to aid us when we invade our enemies' homeland?"

Galen opened his mouth to answer, but Agatha forestalled him.

"He hath not the courage," she snorted, turning away.

197

Galen glared at her back, drawing himself up to his full height.

With almost ponderous dignity, he turned and bowed to the King, straightened, and said, "Majesty, I have. And I will."

Three weeks later, Rod and Gwen stood atop the sea-cliff on the Loguire estates, looking down at the refurbished King's Fleet, ready to embark again. As before, the bulk of the Fleet consisted of small fishing boats; but this time, the vanguard consisted of twenty long ships, on the beast-man model, with the captured dragon boat at their head. The Neanderthal boat had a dragon-figurehead, of course; but the other long ship bows sported heads of hawks and eagles.

"A bird-headed fleet," Rod mused darkly. "That strikes me as a bitter omen, somehow."

"Nay, my lord," Gwen chided gently. "I ha' seen the eagle slay the serpent ere now. Be not so troubled in thy heart; we may yet win."

Rod cocked an eyebrow in her direction. "Take your own advice, darling. You're not looking exactly exuberant yourself."

The air popped, and Toby appeared right in front of Rod. "My Lord Gallowglass!"

Rod leaped back, arms flailing for balance.

Then he recognized Toby and regained his composure, if not his breath. "Ye gods, kid! Haven't you ever heard of manners?"

"Your pardon, Lord Warlock." Toby was instantly contrite, for an instant. Then he was all exuberance again. "There is word from old Galen, Lord Gallowglass! He sendeth to tell thee he shall hold himself in readiness to come to the fleet, if he should be needed."

"Very good," Rod said, nodding, "and I'll keep my part of the bargain: Harold won't be in the battle line. Of course, no point in telling the old man that was my original intention, anyway."

He turned away as Toby disappeared in a slight implosion, to deliver Rod's reply to Galen.

Rod gathered his wife into one arm. "Well, babe, that insures us an even fight, anyway. The psionic generator'll be a lot stronger on its home ground; but we'll have Galen along. It all goes to prove the value of face."

"I would I knew thy meaning in this term, 'sigh-yon-ik,'" Gwen said frowning; "and even more, at this moment, this 'value of face.'"

"Face? That's simple." Rod grinned. "Galen knows he's going to take part in the battle anyway—it's the only way he can be sure his son'll stand a fair chance of surviving. So rather than have it look like someone's manipulating him, he volunteers and gets a little credit for being a hero." His grin widened. "I love human vanity, darling—it's so dependable."

The fleet sailed at dawn amidst cheers, song, and laughter.

The laughter lasted about as long as it took the men to realize what "the high seas" meant.

It was late October, and the water was cold. The sailors had ample opportunity to verify this theory; winter waves tend to run high, and usually over the decks.

There was nothing in view but gray, foamy sea, and a sky that was usually cloudy.

The waves tossed higher and higher, building to a full winter storm. The fleet ran before the wind, and prayed.

Rod sat shivering, his hands spread over a brazier in a makeshift cabin that had been quickly added to the lead dragon ship.

He rubbed his hands over the glowing coals and growled, "I thought this whole planet was supposed to have a tropical climate."

"It does, Rod," said Fess' imperturbable voice. The robot was in a stall in the hold, but this was no obstacle to conversation. "The planet as a whole is equatorial, much as Terra may have been during the Carboniferous Era; but there are small ice caps, and a current from one of the caps . . ."

". . . brushes the northwest tip of Gramarye. I know," Rod growled. "That's why the Romantic Emigres selected the island for their colony; it required less terraforming to give it a temperate climate, like Medieval Europe."

"Precisely," the robot agreed. "But the terraforming itself lowered the winter temperature of the arctic current pronouncedly; therefore, the weather is temporarily disagreeable."

"All so they could have white Christmases, probably," Rod growled. "These romantics!"

The robot paused for a moment, then corrected, "Available data indicates that the majority of the early colonists were more concerned with a white Thanksgiving, Rod."

Rod rolled his eyes up to Heaven.

"However, Rod, there is cause for hope."

"Oh?" Rod said, skeptically.

"Affirmative. Although the peninsula which, as indicated by available data, is the prime base of the Neanderthals, normally has a prohibitively high mean temperature, it was selected because it is touched by the northern current, from Gramarye, which lowers the temperature to a bearable maximum. Since the peninsula, our final goal, is quite a few degrees south of our present position; the climate should become warmer as we near our destination."

Rod frowned at a sudden sound, distinctly resembling a pair of soprano castanets. He looked down at the brazier.

Puck rose up, seemingly out of the floorboards, huddling low over the brazier, hands spread to the heat. His teeth clicked like a triple salvo of popcorn.

Rod stared, his jaw dropping. He picked it up, shoved it back into place with an audible pop, swallowed, and tried to sound authoritative. "And just what the hell do you think *you're* doing here?"

The elf grinned, which is not easy with chattering teeth. "Why, thou didst not think I could be held off from the end of this tale, didst thou, Master Gallowglass? And shall I not be useful?"

"Well, I dare say you will be," Rod admitted. "Why didn't Brom tell me he was bringing you along?"

"He doubtless will tell thee ere long," said the elf cheerfully. He bent low over the brazier. "Cha-a! 'Twill be a cold passage, Rod Gallowglass."

"Well, cheer up," Rod said, with a dry smile. "It'll get warmer as we go south."

" 'Tis a consummation devoutly to be wished," the elf said fervently. "Will this Kernel keep faith with thee, Rod Gallowglass, if thou dost accept his proffered aid?"

Rod's jaw sagged again. "How did *you* know about that?"

"I ha' long ears," said the elf, grinning. "If he doth indeed aid us, our chances of victory are fair, are they not?"

"Uh," said Rod. "Probability of victory . . . uh—"

"Without Kernel's aid," Fess murmured, "probability of victory is point one-seven-four. With Kernel's aid, point three-one-seven-four."

"Well," Rod said judiciously, "let's say the Kernel's help increases the circumference of our hopes. Or the diameter of our despair. . . ."

The elf's eyebrows shot up. "So bad as that?" And he turned back to the brazier, murmuring, "Well, *well*. . . ."

"Our chances would be much improved," murmured Fess, "if we could shift the decimal point one space to the right."

"Just a matter of a decimal point," Rod assured Puck.

"It must indeed be a most dismal point," Puck agreed. "Thou art not looking overly cheered, Rod Gallowglass."

The fleet fled on toward the south, through many hours of leaden skies and churning sea, sudden snow flurries and bursts of freezing rain.

But, slowly, the rain warmed, and the air warmed, like a spring thaw. The sailors doffed their cloaks and shouted their joy as the sun shouldered through the clouds.

Rod looked decidedly gloomy, and waited.

"Hail to the sun!" the sailors cried. "Hail!"

"Boys, can you call your shots!" Rod muttered that night, as he listened to the hailstones bounce off the cabin roof.

The door opened, admitting a howl of wind, a clatter of hailstones, and Brom O'Berin. Brom shivered and stumped up to the fire, holding out his hands to the blaze.

Puck sat cross-legged in the air a foot above the brazier, held up by nothing but his own idea of humor. " 'Tis a good omen, is it not, Majesty?"

"Indeed," Brom admitted grudgingly. "Hail comes rarely, in winter. 'Twill be summer again, ere we reach Beastland."

"Well, at least we don't have to worry about the weather," Rod mused. "Thunderstorms, even, won't make much difference on the Kobold's home territory."

"Let not the loss of that care concern thee," Brom growled. "Thou hast another in place of it, which thou knowest not of."

"Oh?" Rod said. "What?"

Brom chewed his moustache (which was back to respectable size, along with a jaw-line beard). "I ha' told thee that I commanded some among mine elves to Beastland, to spy out their doings. . . ."

"And a miniature messenger managed a missive?"

"He did." Brom hunched his shoulders, shivering. "A plague upon these chandlers! Were they so pressed for time they could not lay down a decent hearth? . . . 'Tis this talk of the chieftain Atylem's I told thee of. . . ."

"Oh? New developments?"

Brom nodded. "It would seem that he hath swayed a very fair number of beastmen to his faction—which his titular liege, Shaman, knows not of; and when our men invade, in the midst of battle, Atylem will cry out against Shaman, calling him false priest and traitor; then will he and his men arise to overthrow both priest and god. Then will they sue for peace with Tuan. Then will they avow that all this long war is the doing of Shaman, and none of their own; and they will swear fealty to Tuan and Gramarye."

"Well!" Rod's eyebrows were lifted. "That works nicely to our advantage, doesn't it? If we could trust them. . . ."

"If," Brom agreed. "They are sure that we will, that Tuan will leave but light force there to guard them."

Rod nodded tightly. "And Tuan's just young enough, and trusting enough, that he might do it. . . ."

"Then, when Tuan and the bulk of the army have left," Brom went on, "the beastmen will slaughter the Gramarye garrison, then rebuild their strength at their leisure, till they shall have power to bring war to Gramarye once again."

"So. . . ." Rod nodded, lower lip thrust out. "Well, we just might do well to let Tuan in on this little plot, mightn't we? And spread the word among the soldiers—if any beastmen start yelling surrender in the thick of the battle, we don't believe 'em. . . . And, of course, if Atylem's planning a little surprise, we might do well to assume Skolax will manage a few licks, too."

Brom looked up, scowling. "How might he trouble us here? Bides he not back on Gramarye?"

"I wouldn't put it past him to find a way to cause us some trouble. Anyway, it can't hurt to expect it. . . . And, come to think of it, I did hypothesize Atylem's playing a double game between Skolax and Shaman, awhile back. . . ."

He smiled brightly. "Anyway, Atylem's breeding a small civil war among the beastmen, which should weaken them nicely."

Brom nodded, a slight, savage smile on his lips. "And I shall weaken them further for thee. Or rather, this merry wanderer shall."

He jerked his head toward Puck, who bowed in polite acknowledgment.

"Oh?" Rod smiled covertly. "What're *you* figuring to do, mannikin?"

Puck spread his hands, looking his most innocent. "Why, what do I ever do, Lord Warlock?"

Rod nodded, chewing at the inside of his cheek. "True, true. All you ever had to do to cause havoc was follow your natural impulses."

Puck nodded, grinning. "Oh, we shall have them slashing at shadows ere thou dost come."

Rod let an amused smirk show. "So. You soften them up a little, then we land and charge up the beach, with the witches supporting us from the shipboard cabins. The beastmen manage to pull themselves together and scrape up something resembling defense with the Evil Eye and anything else they have handy. Our witches fight the Evil

202

Eye, and we fight the 'anything else.' Then, whenever he figures it's appropriate, Atylem cuts loose, overthrows Shaman, and tries to fool us into a false peace. . . . Skolax'll probably be mixing in there, somewhere. . . . It sounds like a delightful royal mess, Brom."

"Thou hast forgot that Kernel and Yorick, with their men, shall attack when thou dost—if thou dost wish it."

"If," Rod said softly.

"*If* we take Kernel up on his offer, Brom."

"Thou wouldst be a capital fool not to," the dwarf growled.

The air *whooshed!* and Harold stood in front of Rod, saluting. "Permission to speak, Major."

Rod managed to scowl and stare at the same time. "What's with the military etiquette all of a sudden?"

"Thought you might be holding a council of war or something, so I figured I ought to look professional." Harold turned to the brazier, dropping to his knees, holding his hands out over the coals (and under Puck). "Just wanna get a few things straight about the Auxiliaries, so I can make sure we've all got our briefings straight." He looked up, saw Brom on the other side of the brazier. "Oh! Uh—my apologies. Didn't mean to interrupt. . . . My Lord O'Berin, I assume."

Brom inclined his head gravely, gestured toward Puck. "Thou knowest Puck."

"Only by reputation." Harold's voice held steady enough, but his eyes rounded.

He looked over his shoulder at Rod. "Do I salute, or shake hands?"

"Bow," Rod confided. "In this culture, that's always safe."

Harold threw him an askance glance, turned back to Puck, and Brom. "Pleasure to meet you, gentlemen," he said, bobbing his head.

Puck hooted laughter.

"Uh—'gentlemen' has a rather specific meaning in this culture, Captain." Rod bit his cheek to keep from laughing at Harold's confusion. "What're the questions about the Aux'liaries?"

"Well, the way I understand it, all the witches are in the one cabin, aboard the flagship. Right, Major?"

"Right; no back-up units. After all, where would they escape to? It's all or nothing this time, Captain. We'll need every bit of power we can scrounge to fight that generator. If we lose, we lose flat."

Harold raised his eyebrows, shaking his head. "Let's hope we win. . . ."

"Our chance of victory would be greatly improved," Brom growled, "if this snuff-brain would but admit the virtues of alliance."

Harold frowned. "Alliance? With who?"

"With Kernel, whom I hold to be worth our trust. Yet tell it to this mop-head here. . . ."

"Kernel?" Harold scowled. "That's the head honcho in Beastland, no?"

"The exiled head honcho," Rod corrected. "And he's offering to attack the High Cave with his partisan force. And, since the High Cave holds Shaman, the Kobold, and, presumably, the psionic generator—well, Kernel's help *could* be a sizable boost."

"Hm!" Harold raised his eyebrows, thrusting his lower lip out. "Sounds like a good deal to me, Major. What's he want for his help?"

"That's the hitch," Rod said grimly. "Nothing."

Harold stared. "Nothing?"

"Nothing." Rod nodded. "No strings attached; gift free and clear. That's enough to make me mistrust him right there."

"Then let thy heart know rest," Brom growled, "for he hath sent word that he doth seek recompense."

"Oh?" Rod's head snapped up. "What?"

"Clemency." Brom scowled, glowering at the fire. "Pardon and citizenship, for all beastmen save Shaman and the Kobold."

Rod's eyes widened. "Atylem, too?"

"Aye, Atylem their chieftain, too. Thou must swear to spare them all, to grant them citizenship in Gramarye." Brom shook his heal in mock despair. "A most strange alliance, by my troth!"

"Very." Rod frowned, tugging at his chin. "I assume this news came by Elf Express?"

"Aye."

An ugly gleam grew in Rod's eye. "And would the elf, by chance, have spoken directly with Kernel?"

"Nay, most certainly not." Brom grimaced. "The elf spoke only to Yorick—that great, grinning lummox of a lieutenant."

"Lummox?" Harold's head snapped bolt upright. "Yorick?"

"Aye, lummox," Brom snorted. "A wall of flesh with half a brain! He will bespeak matters of most grave import as pleasantries in heavy-footed peasant terms; and when he doth, perchance, speak of matters of state, 'tis with a grin and jest—if he doth not forget to tell thee of them, cold!"

He cocked an eyebrow at Rod. "He ha' missed his calling; for he should ha' been court fool."

Rod shook his head, eyes narrowed. "Don't let him put you on, Brom. I have a strange feeling that jester front hides a very shrewd brain."

"Scarce half a brain, more like," Brom growled, turning back to the fire. "Belike a brain scarce larger than an apple. It must be so; his skull is thick enow."

Rod noticed, out of the corner of his eye, that Harold was looking thoroughly scandalized. Rod frowned mentally, decided to file the datum for future consideration. "I take it none of your spies have caught sight of Kernel?"

"Nay. Oh, and Yorick hath ever had most excellent explanations of his master's absence; but the sum and whole of it is, Kernel will not show himself."

"And your elves haven't tried for an occasional, uh, unofficial look at him?"

"Oh, they ha' tried, much good may it ha' done for them. Kernel must suspect their presence; for he ha' stopped each mousehole, each nook and cranny within his lodgings, in the mountains where he now doth dwell. And when he ha' come forth for raids, his face is masked, his form is cloaked, and naught of mine elves may say what is his semblance." He cocked an eyebrow at Rod. "Thou must needs take him on faith, if thou takest him at all."

"I'm a little low on faith just now, Brom."

The dwarf sighed, turned back to the brazier shaking his head. "Yet he doth seem to fight our fight, Rod Gallowglass; and, in truth, it may be he, and he alone, who marks distinction 'tween success and failure in this our venture. What sayest thou, High Warlock? Wilt thou have his aid?"

Rod's clasped hands twisted, till the knuckles whitened, as he glowered at the fire.

"Thou must choose, and soon," Brom growled, "for thou knowest that the King will, in this, be guided by thy council. 'Tis warlock fighting warlock in this battle-work; thou knowest that for truth. The troops are but for show in this. Therefore, Warlock, thou must tell us: shall we trust this warlock Kernel?"

Slowly, Rod looked up at Brom. "All right, damn it! Take him up on it. We hit the beach, attacking from the front; he attacks from the back and, hopefully, takes the High Cave." He raised a shaking forefinger. "But I intend to be in on that attack on the High Cave myself, Brom, if I can. Not that I'm mistrustful, you understand—just in case. Besides, I have a sneaking suspicion it'd be a little healthier if it was someone from our side who took care of the Kobold."

"Just in case," Brom murmured.

Rod nodded grimly. "I won't feel at all safe unless I chop that damned wooden idol to bits with my own two hands."

"Yet thou wilt trust the Kernel."

Rod shook his head slowly, smiling sourly. "Just because I ally with him, Brom, doesn't mean I have to trust him. Just the reverse, in fact. No, I'll never trust him. Never."

"Aye, that he doth know, Lord Warlock."

Rod's eyes snapped over to Puck. *"What?"*

Brom nodded. " 'Twas the other final word that Yorick sent: their Kernel sends to tell thee that he is, and knows he is, the only man in all the universe that thou wouldst never truly trust."

It was cold below decks, too, where sailors huddled around a glowering brazier.

"Spring doth come betimes," muttered an old sailor, shivering, wrapping his cloak tighter about him. "Then it leaves betimes, and winter cometh again."

"Nay, 'tis not that winter comes," said the lean sailor, his long moustaches swaying as he shook his head. " 'Tis we who have come to winter." His eyes kindled, becoming a little wild. "Such things were not done in our youth, ere these witches came to govern in Gramarye. Men rested content in their homeland, and fishermen did not sail far beyond the sight of shore. But, now that the High Warlock ha' come to reign supreme—"

" 'Tis the King who reigns!" cried a young sailor, shocked at the treason in the lean sailor's words. "The High Warlock is only the King's councillor."

The lean man smiled sourly. "That is good saying, boy; 'tis well that youth should speak thus. Nay, I remember me of a time that I, too, had faith in a King. But that was a King without a High Warlock to govern him. Nay, be not deceived!" he cried, overriding the young man's protest. "The High Warlock doth rule the King; and as a punishment for this foul rule hath God set these beastmen to fight witch-war upon us!"

"Yet the Wee Folk ally with the witches," said the young sailor uncertainly, "and the Wee Folk would never have traffic with evil. Forever have they been of the Good."

"Indeed," purred the lean sailor, "and hast thou spake, then, with the Wee Folk?"

"Oh, nay, to be sure," the young man said hastily.

"But thou hast heard talk." The lean man smiled sourly.

"So have we all, we all have heard talk—but that is all! And none knows where the talk started. *I tell thee*"—his voice cracked, finger spearing out at the young man—"this talk began with the witches!"

The sailors shuddered and huddled in on themselves, muttering.

"Have any seen the Wee Folk in converse with witches?" The lean one's eyes glittered; he had a hungry look. "Have any seen a Wee One riding upon the High Warlock's shoulder? Nay!"

"Be still!" growled a graying, potbellied man, shivering inside his robe.

"I will not be still!" the lean sailor roared, his fist striking the deck. "Too long have men of good heart and good will held their peace! Too long have we kept silence as evil forces overtook our nation! And what have we bought with our silence? This, this war which you see! This war, which will keep us from those we love till—we return to them maimed—or part us from them forever, in death!

"This war must end!" he bellowed, then slammed fist into palm and hunkered down, glowering at the brazier.

The cabin was death-still about him, every eye riveted on him.

He lifted his eyes slowly, seeking out individual faces. "We may not rise up against the King," he breathed, " 'twould be an act ungodly; aye, that I will own.

"But we may destroy these witches!"

"Nay, but how?" an old sailor spread his hands in consternation. "For mere mortals to go up against witches means death!"

"But how would we do it?" said another sailor. "We are but a handful here; how should we go against witches?"

"We will wait until they cannot fight us." The lean sailor smiled savagely. "The beastmen shall be our allies in this; for, when the witches are locked in their foul circle's stillness, hands joined in unholy multiple union, the weight of the beastmen's Evil Eye on their souls—then shall we strike, in the thick of the battle! We shall strike out upon them, when the Evil Eye drags at their power, and they can spare but little of their evil strength for the battling with us! Then shall we strike—and, in the Lord, shall we be victorious!"

"Heart trouble?"

"Huh?" Harold looked up, startled.

Brom and Puck had gone to loose the dogs of confusion

in Beastland. Harold had immediately lapsed into numbed silence, staring at the fire.

"Greta?" Rod prodded. "That what's got you down?"

"Oh, hell, no!" Harold swore, then turned thoughtful. "Maybe that's my basic trouble—that she hasn't. But, no. . . ." He shook his head, jaw firming. "No, Major, she's in the past, now."

Oh, yeah, sure! Rod thought, biting the inside of his cheek.

"No," Harold said, staring pensively at the fire again, "what's got me down is Lord O'Berin."

Rod's eyebrows shot up. "Brom?"

"Yeah." Harold's mouth tightened. "Kind of disillusioning, you know?"

"Yeah." Rod didn't.

Harold chewed at his lip. "I've got a high enough opinion of Brom to take anything he says pretty seriously; if his information is correct, his opinion probably is, too. And you can't beat personal experience for information. But . . ."

"But?" Rod raised an eyebrow.

Harold sighed. "But he comes up with this business about Yorick. And . . . well, like I say, I've got too high an opinion of Brom to just throw out anything he says."

Rod lifted the other eyebrow. "You have some reason to believe Yorick's anything but what Brom says he is?"

"Yeah." Harold nodded, looking scrambled. "Ever since I was a little bitty kid, I thought Yorick was a Class A Number One silver-plated superhuman hero. And now Brom comes along, and from what he says, Yorick's really a grinning idiot who spends his time cracking bad jokes."

Rod nodded judiciously. "Sounds like a pretty good thumbnail sketch. . . ."

"Yeah." Harold shook his head, resigned. "This time-travel business can get very disillusioning, Major. Funny how your boyhood idols turn out to be human. . . ."

Rod nodded heavily, silently commiserating with the loss of a childhood ideal; he'd been through it himself a few times. . . .

He let the silence run a few minutes, then asked tentatively, "Uh, Harold . . . you said you'd always thought Yorick was a great big fat hero. . . ."

Harold looked up, frowning a little. "Yeah."

"Uh, well . . . where'd you get this idea? Your school-book history lessons?"

Harold's face set like cast iron.

Then, slowly, it thawed into a look of self-disgust.

He turned to the fire, shaking his head. "I'm one hell

of a great agent, aren't I, Major? Giving away everything I know, without even being asked—and setting up a few potential time paradoxes, just by the way."

"Oh, a little slip now and then is excusable," Rod said slowly, controlling the wince at the thought of a few that he'd made in his time. "Now, of course, Captain, I wouldn't want you to break security, or anything like that, but could you tell me if . . . maybe . . . Yorick . . . belongs to the same organization as you? Or would that be giving away a little too much?"

Harold glanced at Rod out of the corner of his eye.

"Think it over," Rod said quickly. "After all, I wouldn't ask you to tell me anything you shouldn't, uh, would I?"

"Yes." Harold smiled sourly. "That's why the history books have you down as being such a good agent, Major. You seem to have this knack for finding out just about anything you want to know."

"Uh, yes." Rod watched the leap of the flames. "Well, Captain? What do you say?"

Harold's lips pressed in against his teeth. He turned to the fire, clasping his hands. "Well, Major . . . I can't tell you all that much, at this stage of your career. . . . But I guess I *can* tell you that Yorick's organization is in sympathy with SCENT."

"Oh?"

"Yeah. They're both working to further democracy."

"Hm." Rod turned away. " 'In sympathy,' huh?"

"Yeah." Harold frowned slightly.

"Which, of course, means that Yorick doesn't belong to SCENT; that he belongs to another organization. . . . Which means there's at least one more time-travel organization than I thought. There's the totalitarians from the future, whom Skolax is probably working for; and the anarchists from the future, whom Shaman is probably working for; and now there's a third group, democrats, whom Yorick, and probably Kernel, too, are working for. . . ."

"*Damn!*" Harold slammed a fist into his thigh. He turned to glower at Rod. "Major, you are a Class A bastard."

Rod looked up, surprised. "Why, thank you, Captain. I haven't had a compliment like that since the last diplomatic conference. What did I do to earn it?"

"I gave you one item of information," Harold groused, "and you turn it into a major disclosure." He surged to his feet, stood glowering down at the brazier. "Oh, I'm a real great agent, just telling you anything you want to know —aren't I?"

"Why, yes," Rod said, smiling faintly. "From my viewpoint, anyway."

Harold left shortly afterward, still smarting under the effects of his own naïveté, and Rod sat staring at the brazier, ostensibly talking to himself.

"Personally, I can't think of any other place they could've come from," he said, with a touch of exasperation. "I mean, sure, I know the old argument about the humanoid shape being the shape for intelligence, that evolution on any planet will eventually come up with something bipedal, erect, with upper limbs ending in manipulative members— but that evolution on any other planet could come up with something that looked exactly like the Terran Neanderthal? Isn't that straining credulence just a tiny bit?"

"It is also stretching coincidence almost beyond the limits of credibility, Rod," Fess answered from his stall in the hold far below.

Rod interlocked his fingers, turned his hands inside out, and stretched, cracking the knuckles. "Yorick and his kin come from Earth . . . and, therefore, Kernel, too. Somebody discovered a group of Neanderthals that happened to have a mutant talent for projective telepathy. . . . But why didn't they just leave them on Terra? Why'd they have to bring them here and make trouble for us?"

"That, Rod, was obviously the intention. The most likely motive of whomever transported them to Gramarye was simply to cause trouble for the current regime."

Rod cocked an eyebrow. "You sure that's cold, dispassionate logic? Sounds a touch paranoid to me. . . ."

"Given the recent history of this planet, Rod, and the forces ranged against SCENT in this matter . . ."

"All right, all right," Rod grumbled. "But aren't you forgetting that Yorick's, and consequently Kernel's, organization, is in sympathy with SCENT—or weren't you eavesdropping on that last conversation?"

"I was, of course, paying polite attention to the discussion, Rod. . . . However, I might remind you that the data thus received are merely subjective opinions, and thus liable to distortion."

"Hearsay, hm?" Rod tugged at his lip. "Well, for myself, I'll buy what Harold says; I think he's still a little too naïve to lie convincingly. I'd bet the kid was telling the truth. So, if Kernel's organization is working to further democracy that means that, by pulling the Neanderthals off of Terra, Kernel was furthering democracy. Right?"

"It is logical," Fess murmured noncommittally. "However,

the Neanderthals' attempt to gain control of Gramarye for the Anarchists, as represented by Shaman, must certainly be viewed as action against democracy. . . ."

"No, you've got it backward. Actually, it's very simple, Fess. You see, Kernel is working to further democracy by getting the Neanderthals off Terra; and I have a suspicion that, left to themselves, the Neanderthals would have been very peaceful, under Kernel."

"But they *weren't* left to themselves. Shaman and Atylem came in, and they *are* working against democracy. . . . uh, Fess?"

The robot was silent.

"Fess, are you there?"

"I am, Rod," the robot said slowly. "I was merely wondering if *you* were; and I reluctantly admit that you are. I will further admit that that particular interpretation of the situation had not occurred to me. . . ."

"And you're not too happy about having to admit it's possibly right." Rod grinned, with triumph.

"I am not, primarily because of its close relation to the essential dichotomy of Christian theology, which is incompletely defensible from a logical standpoint."

"Huh?" Rod stared, pie-eyed. "What're you talking about?"

"The dichotomy of 'good' and 'evil,' Rod. That the essential force of 'good' is incapable of producing 'evil.' Any 'evil' resulting must, therefore, be due to the intervention, in subversive manner, of an agent of 'evil.' "

Rod frowned. "Oh, yeah! Sure . . . well, I do see what you're getting at. . . . And you must admit, there is some essential truth in the concept."

"Some," the robot admitted. "However . . ."

"However, it doesn't really have a whole lot to do with Shaman, Kernel, or the Kobold," Rod said firmly. "We were discussing fifth columns, remember? And just to make things a little clearer, Fess, can you think of any reason why getting these mutant Neanderthals off Terra would count as furthering democracy?"

"Why, it is self-evident, Rod." The robot's voice had a faint note of surprise.

Rod scowled. "So I'm dense. So?"

His earphone reproduced the effect of a metallic sigh. "Rod, we already have some grounds for asserting that the 'Evil Eye Culture'—for want of a better term—is, to some extent, paranoid."

"Well, if you mean they've got a grudge against anybody who isn't one of them—it's true, I suppose. But it's also true of all other primitive peoples, isn't it?"

"Not to this extent, Rod. In this particular case, the paranoia seems to be so well-developed that, with only a slight nudge from an exterior force, they will attempt to insure their own security by dominating adjacent social groups."

Rod's head lifted slowly. "In other words, all Shaman had to do was tell them the only way for them to be safe was to go out and conquer everybody in sight. And they did it. Or tried to. . . ."

"Precisely," the robot agreed. " 'Do unto others before they do unto you.' "

"I still don't see how this adds up to pulling the Neanderthals off Terra to protect democracy."

"Rod," said the robot, its patience only slightly exaggerated, "what would have resulted from the Evil Eye Culture being left in their original time-space matrix? And, when answering, please consider that they would have had all of human history in which to implement their policies, in addition to a considerable portion of human prehistory. What would the ultimate effect have been?"

"Well. . . ." Rod frowned, thinking furiously.

Then his eyes snapped wide, his jaw plummeting. "Ye gods, Fess!"

" 'Today the immediate area, tomorrow the world,' " the robot murmured.

"And with that much time to work in . . . Fess, they just might have made it!"

"And one single tribe, equipped with the Evil Eye, would have dominated the world," the robot murmured, "under what we may assume would have been an extremely strict despotism. And the Evil Eye power would, presumably, have been passed on to the Cro-Magnon descendants. . . ."

"If," Rod threw in, "there *were* any Cro-Magnon descendents. This time, the Neanderthals just might not have become extinct."

"A distinct possibility."

"And history would have been just one totalitarian government after another," Rod whispered. "Lord! And democracy would never have arisen!"

"Neither in Athens, England, or America," the robot agreed.

Rod shuddered. "Kernel was a little too lenient. If I'd been in his shoes, I wouldn't have dumped them on Gramarye. I would've picked some uninhabited planet—far, far away!"

"And if you had, Rod—what would the result have been,

when they eventually evolved a technology capable of producing interstellar travel?"

Rod went stiff.

"Especially," the robot bored on, "if their cultural paranoia had not diminished—and totalitarian and anarchist agents, through initiating certain aspects of the folk culture, could provide for the maintenance of such a state of the group-mind."

"They would have taken over the galaxy," Rod whispered.

"Precisely. . . . In brief," murmured the robot, "the Neanderthals of the Evil Eye Culture would have had to have been either exterminated or absorbed. And we may assume that Kernel is sufficiently ethical not to wish to commit genocide."

Rod nodded numbly. "True, true. . . ."

"We must also consider that the Evil Eye involves a form of telepathy, and that telepathy is vital to the future of the Decentralized Democratic Tribunal."

Rod's lips thinned. "All right, so they have to be absorbed culturally, so they'll lose their paranoia and won't be a threat, and they have to be absorbed genetically, 'cause DDT's gonna need every telepath they can get. But why Gramarye?"

Rod broke off, his eyes widening. "Oh. Yes, of course. Dumb, aren't I?"

"Occasionally, Rod, yes."

"No matter where Kernel put the Neanderthals, the futurians were bound to try to stir them up sooner or later, weren't they?"

"A valid hypothesis, Rod. Due to the presence of, or possible presence of, the futurians, the phases of contact preliminary to cultural absorption would have involved a distinct element of danger to any social group adjacent to the Evil Eye culture."

"Yeah." Rod frowned, musing. "And I suppose it was better to have them stirred up while they still had a primitive technology, wasn't it?"

"There would be a distinct advantage to the confrontation's occurring at such a stage of development, yes."

"And, if the goal of the game was to absorb the Neanderthals into a democratic culture—well, then, you'd better put them where someone's going to have an even chance against them when they go out conquering."

"The inevitable conclusion of such a line of reasoning, Rod, can only be . . ."

"Gramarye." Rod nodded. "We're the only ones in the galaxy who could stand a chance against them."

"I believe you were wondering, some short time ago, Rod, by what right Kernel dumped his projective-esper problem on Gramarye?"

Rod nodded, his eyes glazed a little.

"It would appear to be the right of necessity, Rod."

"I question your ethics."

"Nonetheless, Rod, if they had asked your opinion of the necessity of relocating the Neanderthals on Gramarye . . ."

Rod closed his eyes, nodding grimly. "What else could I say, Fess?" His eyes snapped wide. "But that *doesn't* mean I would have given my permission!"

"With all due respect, Rod—would that have made a great deal of difference?"

"No." Rod closed his eyes, sighing. "No, probably not. I couldn't guard the whole planet all at once. They would have snuck 'em in somewhere." He bowed his head, letting his shoulders droop.

He lifted his head slowly. "Fess, did you ever get the feeling you were just a pawn in somebody's game?"

"Never, Rod. I simply follow my programming."

Rod nodded dully. "I'm beginning to feel the same way. . . ."

"Lord Warlock!"

"Huh?" Rod looked around and, in spite of two and a half years on Gramarye, felt a moment of panic when he didn't see anybody.

"Down here, thou great lummox!"

"Oh!" Rod looked down. "Hello, Kelly. What's up?"

"We draw near to Beastland."

"Yes, we most surely do," Rod murmured, looking toward the western horizon. The fleet had run down its sails and thrown out sea anchors, waiting for darkness. A half hour's sailing would bring them in sight of Beastland.

Rod looked down at Kelly again. "Word from Brom?"

The elf frowned. "Why wouldst thou think that?"

"Why else would an elf come see me?"

"Mayhap for love of thy company," said Kelly acidly.

"That's a left-handed way of admitting I'm right, and Brom *did* send a message. Well, what is it?"

The elf gave a long-suffering sigh. "That I am assigned to thee for the duration."

"Huh?" Rod frowned. "Assigned to me? Duration of what?"

"The battle, thou witless wall!" the elf snapped. "Assigned to thee as liaison, or for any other work thou hast in mind!"

Rod nodded, lower lip protruding. "Well, that's wise, I suppose." He lifted an eyebrow. "You don't sound terribly happy about it."

Kelly's shoulders heaved with a massive sigh. "I had lief be adding my hammer to the fight," he admitted. "Still, at thy side, I shall see my share of the battling, I suppose. Yet shall I be but seeing it. . . ."

Rod shook his head, commiserating in advance. "Sorry, Kelly."

" 'Tis not thy doing." The elf's face took on a look of profound resignation. "What we must do, we must do."

"But you do have to take my orders, huh?"

The leprecohen glared furiously, then forced himself into a semblance of calm. "I can see His Majesty's reason in this," he grudged, "for he must needs have contact with thee in the battle. And, thou mayest ha' need of elf-magic aid."

"True," Rod agreed, thrusting his tongue into his cheek. "But, unfortunately, I've got another assignment for you."

The elf turned his head sideways, eyeing Rod with foreboding.

"I don't want Gwen unprotected," Rod said pensively, "and we've got the witches' cabin under heavy guard, but . . . well, just to be on the safe side. . . . As long as Brom was good enough to assign me an elf . . ."

"Nay!" Kelly wailed. "Master Gallowglass, thou wouldst not! I should see naught of the battle there! Not even see it!"

"I hope not," Rod said with the utmost sincerity. "But . . . just in case, Kelly, just in case . . . you see my point, don't you?"

The elf closed his mouth on a hot retort and turned away, muttering furiously into his beard.

Rod frowned. "How's that again?"

"Naught, naught," the elf muttered numbly. " 'Tis but mine own maunderings."

"Let's have it."

"Nay, nay." The elf shook his head with decision. "I will not air mine unwashed laundering and maundering in public."

"I'm public?"

"A point," the elf admitted. " 'Twas merely a few speculations regarding thine ancestry, Master Gallowglass, which I am sure thou dost not wish to know." He sighed heavily, adopting an air of resignation. "Well, I can see that it must needs be done; thou shalt fight the better if thou knowest thy wife to be safe as she can be, in battle. . . . What I must do, I must do," he growled, "and I will comply."

"Under protest, of course," Rod added.

Kelly's eyebrows shot up. "Why, certainly," he said, faintly surprised. "Wouldst thou look for any other form of compliance from an Irishman?"

The sky was clear, the stars drifted across the hours; but there was no moon this night. The Neanderthal village lay deep in gloom.

There are superstitions holding that the dark of the moon is a time conducive to magic, and not always pleasant, events. They are justified.

Watchfires dotted the plain locked within the semicircle of cliffs. Groups of beastmen huddled around the fires while sentries paced the shore. In the center of the camp, a large, long hut announced the location of the chiefs.

The beastmen were to remember this night for a long time, wishing they could forget. Looking back, they decided the defeat itself wasn't all that bad; after all, they fought manfully and well, and lost with honor.

It was the prelude to the battle that was embarrassing. . . .

While one of the small groups gathered around one of the fires were companionably swiping gripes, as soldiers always have, a diminutive shadow crept unseen between two of them, crawled to the fire, and threw something in. Then it retreated, fast.

The beastmen went on grumbling for a few minutes; then one stopped abruptly and sniffed. "Dosta scent summat strange?" he growled.

The beastman next to him sniffed—and gagged—gripping his belly.

The smell reached the rest of the group very quickly, and quite generously. They scrambled for anywhere, as long as it was away, gagging and retching.

That was one case. Let's take another.

Closer to the center of the camp, a dark, spherical object hurtled through the air to land and break open in the center of another group of beastmen. With an angry, humming sound, tiny black flecks filled the air. The beastmen leaped up and ran, howling and swatting about them with more motivation than effect. Little red dots appeared on their skins.

At another group, a series of short, violent explosions from the fire sent the beastmen jumping back in alarm.

216

At still another fire, a beastman raised his mug to his lips, tilted his head back, and noticed that no beer flowed into his mouth. He scowled and peered into the mug.

He dropped it with an oath as it landed on his toe, and jumped back with notable speed, holding one foot and hopping on the other as a small human figure scampered out of the mug with a high-pitched, mocking laugh.

The elf howled in high glee and scampered on through the camp.

Another beastman swung after him, mouthing horrible oaths as his huge club drove down.

A small hand swung out of the shadows and clipped through his belt with a very sharp knife.

The loincloth, loosened, wobbled a little.

In another two bounds, it had decidedly slipped.

The elf scampered on through the camp, chuckling, and a whole squad of beastmen fell in after him, bellowing, clubs slamming the ground where the elf had just been.

A small figure darted between them and the fugitive, strewing something from a pouch at its side.

The Neanderthals lunged forward, stepped down hard, and jumped high, screaming and frantically jerking leprechaun shoe-tacks out of their soles.

The fleeing elf, looking over his shoulder to laugh, ran smack into the ankles of a tall, well-muscled Neanderthal—Atylem, who growled, swinging his club up for the death-blow.

A leprechaun popped up near his foot, slammed him a wicked one on the third toe.

Atylem howled, letting go of his club (which swung on up into the air, turning end over end) as he grabbed his hurt foot, hopping about.

He hopped up, and the club fell down and the twain met, with a very solid and satisfying thunk.

As he went down, the fleeing elf (Puck, incidentally) scampered away chortling.

He skipped into a tent, shouting, "Help! Help! Spies, traitors, spies!"

Three beastmen dashed in from the nearest campfire, clubs upraised and suspicions fortunately lowered (sometimes innocence doesn't pay), as the tent's occupants swung at Puck, and missed him. Outside, a score of elves with small hatchets cut through the tent ropes.

The poles swayed and collapsed as the tent fabric enfolded its occupants tenderly. The beastmen howled and struck at the fabric, and connected with one another.

Chuckling, Puck slipped out from under the edge of the

tent. Within twenty feet, he had another horde of beast-men howling after him.

But the beastmen went sprawling as their feet shot out from under them, flailing their arms in a losing attempt at keeping their balances (which isn't easy when you're running on marbles). They scrambled back to their feet, somehow, still on precarious balance, whirling about, flailing their arms, and in a moment, it was a free-for-all.

Meanwhile, Atylem slowly sat up, holding his ringing head in his hands.

An elf leaned over the top of the tent and shook something down on him.

He scrambled up howling, slapping at the specks crawling over his body (red ants can be awfully annoying), executed a beautiful double-quick goose-step to the nearest branch of the river and plunged in over his head.

Down below, a water-sprite coaxed a snapping turtle, and the snapper's jaws slammed into Atylem's already-swollen third toe.

He climbed out of the water more mud than man, and stood up bellowing.

"Order! Rally! To me, men of mine, to me!"

He flung up his arms, shouting, and opened his mouth wide for the hugest bellow he could manage, and with a *splock* one large tomato, appropriately overripe, slammed into his mouth.

Not that it made any difference, really; his orders weren't having too much effect, anyway, since his men were busily clubbing at one another and shouting something about demons. . . .

Then the marines landed.

The Gramarye ships drove in, plowing up the beach, and ground to a halt. Soldiers leaped shouting to the sand.

Rod was the first one ashore. Fess leaped off the deck and landed galloping.

"No jets, Rod?" Fess murmured as he leaped up the beach toward the clamoring village.

"No; we don't want to worry the boys in the High Cave any more than we have to."

"But why will we not take part in the battle, Rod? Would it not be logical?"

"Yes," Rod said between his teeth, "but that would mean trusting Kernel alone in the High Cave, and that *isn't* logical—not from my viewpoint, anyway. Head for the trees, Fess. With the village such a mess, it'll be faster going around."

Fess obediently changed course for the forest. "You do not believe his claim of friendship?"

"I do not, no."

"You do not believe you have sufficient evidence of his loyalty."

"Since Kernel is never in evidence, I suppose you might say that, yes."

Behind them, soldiers' shouts tore the night as they charged.

The momentum of the first charge carried the soldiers into the middle of the Neanderthal camp. There the charge slowed and bogged; for, almost by reflex, the Neanderthals sought out individual soldiers' eyes, and held them in hypnotic stares.

All through the village, the Gramarye line slowed to a grinding halt.

In the cabin of the lead dragon ship, Agatha squeezed the hands of the witches to each side of her, squeezed her eyes shut.

The pikes, spears, and swords began to move again, slowly, gathering force to block the beastmen's swings.

The beastmen swung hysterically in the desperation born of superstitious fear.

The soldiers countered their blows, and the battle raged high and wild.

Then the soldiers began to slow.

In the cabin, witches grimaced in pain, shoulders hunching under the strain as a huge black amoeba strove to fold itself over their souls.

"Now is our time!" Skolax snapped.

His dagger thudded into the cabin roof.

He hissed, "Strike! For the glory of God!"

Six sailors leaped from the cabin roof. Their feet slammed into the backs of the guards' neck, crushing them to the deck.

Six other sailors, who had been lunging about the deck watching the battle, now whirled and chopped with belaying pins, just in case.

It wasn't needed. The soldiers were already limp, unconscious. One was dead.

Skolax howled victory as he leaped to the deck. He threw his shoulder against the door; three sailors leaped to help him. The door shuddered under the impact of their bodies, but the bar held.

Inside, the witches sat stiffly, hands locked, jaws clenched.

Here and there, one lay unconscious. The rest sat bathed in cold sweat, oblivious to the hammering at the door.

All but Harold.

His head jerked as he came half out of the trance; then, carefully, managing to split his mental focus, lending as much of his power as he could to the ring, he joined the two hands he clasped, kept his hold on them with his left hand, and slid his sword free with his right, turning sideways, readying himself to fight two battles at once.

On the far side of the circle, Greta sat frozen, eyes screwed shut.

Above the door, Kelly stood on the lintel, hammer in hand.

One of the brackets that held the massive door-bar, groaned, bent, tore loose; and, with a rending crash, the door slammed open.

With a shout of victory, two sailors leaped in.

With a howl of joy, Kelly leaned forward, lifted their hats, brained them both.

There was sudden silence outside.

Kelly cocked his head, frowning, at a spate of whispers.

A third sailor leaped through.

Kelly slammed his hammer on the man's cranium.

A hand lashed out, and caught his wrist.

Kelly bit, hard.

The sailor dropped him with a scream of pain.

Kelly landed on the deck, shouting triumphantly, "Thou fool! Didst thou think to hold a leprecohen with ought but a silver chain?"

And his hammer slammed down on a toe.

The sailors yelled rage, and charged.

They were every one barefoot.

And the doorway was narrow.

And Kelly was nimble.

He kept them hopping.

Rod and Fess galloped up the series of rock slopes that led to the High Cave, and found Brom waiting.

Rod reined in, frowning up at the dwarf, where he stood on a projection of rock a little above Rod's head.

"Didn't expect to find *you* here, Brom. I'm glad of it, though."

"Someone must see thou dost not play the fool in statecraft, in the hot blood of this hour," the dwarf growled. "I fail to see why thou wilt not trust these beastmen allies by themselves; but, if thou must needs fight alongside of them 'gainst the Kobold and, mayhap, against *them,* when the Kobold is beaten, I will fight by thy side."

"I'm grateful," Rod said, frowning. "But what's this business about beating the Kobold? It's only a wooden idol, isn't it?"

"So I had thought, till I came here," Brom growled. "But great and fell magic doth lurk on this hillside, magic more than mortal. Shaman is too slight a man for the depths of this foul power. I feel it deep in me, and . . ."

There was a yell up ahead of them, the clash of steel, and a chaos of howling.

"It's started," Rod snapped. "Let's go."

Fess leaped into a gallop as Brom hurtled through the air to land on the horse's rump. Rod whipped out his sword.

They rode into a mammoth cave, more than a hundred feet deep and perhaps seventy wide, coated with glinting limestone, columned with joined stalactites and stalagmites, and filled with a dim, eldritch, light.

Three Neanderthals lay on the floor, their throats pumping blood.

All about the cave, locked pairs of Neanderthals struggled.

But Rod saw none of this. His eyes, and Brom's went immediately to the dais at the far end of the cave.

There, on a sort of rock throne, sat a huge-headed, potbellied thing with an ape's face, concave forehead, bulging cranium. Its limbs were shriveled; its belly was swollen, as though with famine. It was hairless and naked, except for a fringe of whiskers around its jowls. Its eyes were fevered, bright, manic; it drooled.

Two slender cables ran from its bald pate to a black box on the floor beside it.

The spittle dribbled from its chinless mouth into its scanty beard.

Behind it towered three metal panels, keys and switches, flashes of jeweled light, and a black, gaping doorway.

At its feet, Shaman and a short, muscle-bound Neanderthal strained locked in combat.

Its eyes flicked to Rod's.

Icicles stabbed into Rod's brain.

The monstrosity's eyes flicked to Brom's, then back to Rod's.

Brom moved, slowly, like a rusted machine, and the Kobold's eyes flicked back to him. Brom moved again, even more slowly.

The Kobold's jaw tightened; a wrinkle appeared between its eyes.

Brom froze.

In the witches' cabin, all lay unconscious except Agatha and Harold. Her two hands were clasped to his left. His right still held his upraised sword; he knew Kelly couldn't hold the sailors forever.

And, finally, by sheer chance, a sailor's kicking foot collided with Kelly's midriff. The leprecohen slammed against the far wall of the cabin, howling more in rage than in pain.

Three sailors roared victory and burst into the cabin.

Harold's sword whirled, blocking the blows of their belaying pins and knives; but he could only spare half his mind for the battle, and his riposte was slow, much too slow.

Two sailors beat down his sword; a third struck the base of his skull, and he slumped, senseless.

Agatha sat, deep in the trance, clinging to Harold's hand, oblivious to her son's fate. A trickle of blood ran down from the corner of her mouth.

Skolax burst through the door with a shriek of holy fervor, caught up Harold's sword, and, screaming triumph, whirled it up for the coup de grâce.

The sword twisted, jerked, and disappeared from his hands.

Skolax found himself staring into a pair of cold gray eyes, a bearded old face rigid with rage.

The other sailors stood frozen in shock.

The moment was enough; Kelly had gotten his wind back.

He leaped to Skolax's shoulder, slammed his hammer against the skull just behind the ear. Skolax grunted, folded, and collapsed.

Kelly bounded to another sailor, lashing out with the hammer; but he slashed through the air, for Skolax and his sailors had disappeared.

Kelly stood a moment, stunned.

Then he whirled, crying, "Where didst thou throw them to, wizard?"

But Galen was kneeling, his hands joined to Agatha's. His shoulders hunched; his face swelled, purpling.

On the beach, the soldiers moved a little, slowly, then froze again.

Agatha's teeth bared in a bloody grimace of agony. Galen swayed on his knees, then regained his balance, his shoulders heaving up under a titanic load.

Kelly stood in the doorway, hammer in both hands,

ready. He knew something of mortals' magic, and knew that, in the stress of battle, Galen might not have been able to spare the energy for a very long "throw."

Skolax might be back.

The High Cave was silent, like some fantastic Hall of Horrors in a waxworks museum. An occasional whine or grunt escaped the Neanderthals, frozen body-to-body in combat, straining each against the other, Kernel's men to Kobold's guards, Shaman locked with the stocky, short apeman.

Rod and Brom knelt immobile, the Kobold's glittering, malevolent eyes fixed on them, holding its frozen prey in a living death.

There was agony in Rod's eyes. A drop of sweat ran down from his hairline.

Silence stretched out in the glimmering, ghostly elf-light.

In the village, the soldiers slowly ground to stasis, their muscles locking to stone.

The Neanderthals roared and swung their axes like scythes, mowing through the Gramarye ranks, victory song grinding high.

In the cabin, Galen bent low, the black weight pressing down, squeezing, kneading at his brain. The other soul was still there with him, around him, within him, blended with him, fighting valiantly, heaving with him against the black cloud.

And the High Cave lay silent.

A crowing laugh split the air, and a wriggling infant appeared on Rod's shoulders, straddling his neck, chubby hands clenched in his hair, drumming his collarbone with small heels.

"Horsey! Gi'y'up! Da'y, gi'y'up!"

Rod shuddered, his neck whiplashing, as the black mantle wrenched free of his mind.

He tore his eyes from the Kobold's, saw Shaman and the Neanderthal locked straining in the embrace of hatred.

Rod leaped forward, ducking and dodging through the paired, immobile Neanderthals, and sprang. His stiffened hand lashed out in a chop at the back of Shaman's neck.

Shaman stiffened, mouth gaping open, and slumped in the Neanderthal's arms.

The ape-man dropped the contorted body and lunged at the black box, slapping the main switch.

Slowly, the Kobold's eyes dulled.

Galen's body snapped upward and back.

His hands still held Agatha's.

For a moment, minds blended completely, point for point, id, ego, and conscience, both souls thrown wide-open as the burden they strained against disappeared—open and vulnerable to the core, for one lasting, soul-shivering moment.

They knelt, staring deep into each other's eyes.

In the village, the Gramarye soldiers jerked convulsively and came completely to life, saw the carnage around them, the mangled remains of friends, brothers, and leaders, and screamed bloody slaughter.

The steamroller was started. By sheer weight of numbers, the soldiers began crushing the beastmen.

Fess' hooves lifted, slamming down at the back of a Neanderthal's head. The beastman slumped.

Brom heaved at a beastman's ankles; the Neanderthal fell like a pole-axed steer, and Brom sapped him with the hilt of his knife.

They'd been working as a team as soon as the Kobold was out, whittling down the locked pairs of Neanderthals. Not knowing who was for Kernel and who was for Kobold, they'd played it safe by KO'ing both of each pair.

Rod had gotten in on the act as soon as he could. So had Magnus, slamming stones at skulls by TK, gurgling "Fun game!" And, as each stone thudded home, he crowed, "Tag!"

The stocky Neanderthal trussed up Shaman like a pot-roast and turned to join the battle; but, just as he did, Fess nailed the last beastman.

Rod mopped his brow as Magnus landed on his shoulders again, with an impact like a sponge-rubber club, and demanded, fretfully, "Gi'y'up!"

Rod reached up, plucking his son off his shoulders.

Magnus' eyes immediately went round and wide; foreboding entered his face. "Naw'y baby?"

Rod smiled, trying hard to look severe, and failing. "No, good baby this time. By accident, maybe, but still, good baby." He tickled Magnus' tummy; the baby chuckled, gurgled, and squirmed.

"But Daddy's busy now," Rod said, and managed to get the touch of severity in this time. "So baby go to Mommy, huh?"

Magnus put a finger in his mouth and nodded. "Huh!" he said, and disappeared.

"Where's the kid?"

Rod looked up, to see the short, stocky Neanderthal swaggering up to him.

"I sent him home." Rod's brow creased; something about this particular Neanderthal set him on edge at first sight.

"Doggone!" The beastman's mouth twisted with chagrin. "Wanted to thank him; he kinda saved the day, there."

"You might say that, yes," Rod said noncommittally.

"I might," the Neanderthal agreed. "Matter of fact, I already did. He really blew the Kobold's mind."

A connection closed in Rod's mind. "You're Yorick?"

A huge grin split the Neanderthal's face from ear to ear. "You heard about me already, huh? Hey, I'm famous!"

"Well, 'famous' wasn't quite the word I would have used. . . ."

"Comes to the same thing." The Neanderthal thrust out a huge paw, started pumping Rod's hand. "Well, gee, it was real great meeting you, uh . . . you *are* Major Gallowglass, I assume."

"Um. Not making much of a try at hiding your origins, are you?"

Yorick scowled. "Anything wrong with being a Neanderthal?"

Rod's mouth hardened. "Come off it. You know what I was talking about. And I know that you know."

"True," Yorick admitted, scratching behind an ear. He frowned at Rod a moment, then clapped him on the shoulder, leading him toward the mouth of the cave, "Well, gee, it was real great of you to stop by like that. We probably would have lost without you, Major. Hurry back, now."

Rod planted his feet obstinately and refused to be moved. "I'm not going anywhere."

"Oh, yes you are." Yorick grinned. "There's still a battle going on down in the village, Major. Had you forgotten?"

Rod turned, looking out through the cave-mouth to the village below. The roar of the battle came faintly to his ears.

"No, it's not quite over yet," Yorick said quietly. "Better get down there, Major; they're going to be needing your special talents."

Rod's eyes narrowed. "And leave you alone up here?"

"Oh, come off it! You can trust me!" And, as Yorick saw the retort rising in Rod's throat, his voice gained a sudden great urgency. "Go, Major, get! They need you down there! Get moving! I haven't lied to you yet, have I? Go!"

He turned to the unbound Neanderthals who had regained consciousness. "You too, boys! Go along with the *Major;* he might be needing you. Uh, and you too, O'Berin."

"Aye, most assuredly." Brom strode up to Fess, leaped up on the horse's rump. "Quickly, Rod Gallowglass! This battle may yet be lost!"

Rod wavered. "Well. . . ."

Yorick stepped forward, making shooing motions. "Go on. If you don't hurry, the party'll be over by the time you get there!"

"All right," Rod growled, and swung into the saddle. He turned, looked back over his shoulder, and saw all the unbound Neanderthals forming up behind him, shields and axes ready. He frowned, looking over their heads at Yorick. "Sure I can trust you?"

Yorick rolled his eyes up in exasperation and turned away to the Kobold. He ripped the leads out of the monster's head, tore the other ends out of the power pack, strode back to Rod, coiling the cables.

"Here!" He threw the coil to Rod. "That make you feel any better?"

Rod fielded the coil, glowered at it a moment, then nodded, and jammed them into his saddlebag. "Yeah, damnit, I guess so!"

"Go, go!" Brom trumpeted. "Shall mine elves taste of this battle, and I not?" And, when Rod still didn't move, "Come, leave this cave in this jester's care! I do indeed have some small trust in him!"

"Oh, all right." Rod turned away. "Okay, Brom. I'll go by his references." He swung his arm in an overhand circle, slamming his heels against Fess' iron sides.

The horse leaped into a canter, charging out through the mouth of the cave.

The Neanderthals loped after them, down the ledges toward the battlefield.

Yorick stood in the cave-mouth, hands on his hips, grinning, shaking his head.

He turned to the tall, spare, hooded figure that had emerged from the shadows of the cave. "I leave it in your tender care, Kernel. Got the gadget?"

A thin-lipped mouth smiled tightly from the shadows of the hood. The figure drew a silver chain from the folds of its robe.

Yorick took it, nodding. "Oughta do the trick. Be right back, Kernel."

The Neanderthal turned and sauntered away down the rock ledges, whistling and twirling the chain.

Just how much sincerity there was in Atylem must remain a matter of conjecture. Certain it was that he was playing a double game; but whose side was he really on is a topic for speculation only. He might have been fanatically loyal to Skolax and the totalitarians. Or it is entirely possible that, ultimately, Atylem was devoted only to the interests of himself. In either case, when he felt the Kobold's field collapse, and saw the slaughter of his Neanderthal army begin, and the battle started definitely going against Beastland, Atylem started shouting:

"Now! Now is our time! For Gramarye! For Gramarye, my men! Now fight we for Gramarye!"

"For Gramarye!" echoed three hundred Neanderthals, and turned on their comrades, slamming the flats of their axes against the heads of their shield-brothers, howling, "For Gramarye!"

"Truce!" Atylem bellowed, mowing down his own men. "Truce with Gramarye! We call for truce!"

The Gramarye soldiers hesitated, unsure.

"Treachery!" Tuan howled, cutting his way through the battle, his war-horse lashing out with its fore-hooves, clearing the path. "Treachery! Pay them no heed! I ha' foretold thee of this; heed now my words! 'Tis treachery they plan! For Gramarye, strike them down!"

Atylem and his men stared, appalled; then, Atylem cried, "To me! Hie now to me, my men! We are betrayed!"

His fellow conspirators howled and retreated to a circle around him.

A huge bellow rolled in from the west: "Strike down the false chieftain!" And Kernel's partisans slammed into the battle with Rod at their head.

It was all the main body of Neanderthal needed. With a bellow of rage, they turned on Atylem and his cohort.

Atylem saw Rod coming, saw Death and Nemesis riding down on him, braced his feet wide, swung his ax high, and chopped down straight at Rod's neck.

Fess convulsed.

Rod lurched forward in the saddle, the cantle slammed into his belly, and the razor-edge of the ax whirled by an inch from his head.

He dived from the saddle, rolled, snapped to his feet, to see the ax swinging straight at his eyes.

He stepped to the left; the ax missed by a hairbreadth, and Rod leaned in a lunge with every ounce of his weight backing the blade.

The rapier plunged into the Neanderthal's shoulder, lodged in the joint.

Atylem howled and fell, throwing his ax; it whistled past Rod's ear. The blade wrenched loose.

Atylem rolled, scrambled to regain his feet, and a score of war-axes slammed into his body.

The first slashed his throat; he could not even scream.

Kernel's Neanderthals wrenched their axes free and swung about, eyes outward, guarding Rod.

It was needed. Rod stood, sickened and trembling, staring at the raw, butchered meat that a moment ago had been human.

Atylem's men stared, frozen.

Then, "We are lost!" howled one, dropping his ax, throwing up his arms in surrender. "The Kobold is dead; I have felt it! Atylem is dead, I have seen it! Lost, we are lost!"

The cry "Atylem is dead!" echoed through the village, and cries of "We are lost!" "Mercy!" swept the field like a tidal wave.

Rod turned away, fighting nausea, and stumbling caught himself on Fess' saddle. He stood, trembling; then, slowly, his head came up. He frowned, then groped under the pommel for the reset switch.

Then, even more slowly, he raised his eyes, saw the village around him.

All about him, the beastmen had thrown down their weapons, holding their arms high in surrender.

He allowed himself a queasy smile; but his shoulders sagged as the tension abruptly lifted.

Harold lifted his head, slowly, and opened his eyes, even more slowly. There seemed to be black felt all around him; it was difficult to move against it. . . .

The felt began to thin; he could see light through it. It thinned, thinned—he began to be able to make out separate objects . . . they were coming clearer. . . .

Galen and Agatha, kneeling, hands joined, looking deep into one another's eyes.

There was vast wonder in those eyes; and there was something of a shyness about them. And more than a little fear.

A slow, tender, almost patronizing smile spread over Harold's face.

Then he remembered his manners, turned tactfully away.
. . .

And saw Greta spilled on the floor, unconscious.

The beastmen had been herded into a circle. They stood with arms upraised. The women and children had been herded in with them.

Rod leaned back in the saddle. "Well, Tuan, what'll we do with them?"

"Let them live," Tuan sighed. "Thou hast pledged clemency, hast thou not?"

"You'll be bound by my word?"

Tuan nodded, deliberately. "Thou art my minister, Rod Gallowglass. When thou speakest, it is with my voice; and, in thy place, I would have pledged as thou didst. They shall live."

"Good enough." Secretly, Rod smiled. Ordinarily, Tuan's stubborn adherence to an antique code of honor griped Rod more than a little; but there were times. . . . "I'm glad you support me, Your Majesty. I think it was an oath well-given; without Kernel's aid, we might not have won."

He looked out over the mass of captives, nodding slowly. "But we did make the bond with Kernel, and we *have* won, Tuan. We won."

"Provided," Fess' voice muttered in his ear, still a little bleary, "Kernel is trustworthy."

Greta swam up out of the murk and saw the light. It took on form and substance; it became a face—a face that strangely resembled Harold's except for the tender look of concern it wore. . . .

She blinked twice, her eyes widening in surprise, a surprise that deepened when she realized that it was not the hard wood of the decking that lay under her head and shoulders, but Harold's arm.

Her lips parted, trembling, eyes widening further.

He saw her eyelids flutter, saw them open, and widen. He saw the look of surprise on her face, and smiled bitterly. He recognized his own bitterness, recited a few ancient stoicisms in his mind, and let the smile mellow into sad cynicism.

Pain in her eyes, then, and she writhed out of his arm, threw herself to the cabin wall, well away from him, huddling there in the corner, hugging herself tightly.

Harold's smile disappeared. He frowned, with a trace of concern again.

A wail split the air.

Harold whipped about, to see Magnus hovering an inch above the unsconscious Gwen, tugging her hand and wailing for her to wake up.

A slight smile touched Harold's lips. He stepped over the fallen witch, touched the child lightly on the head. "Easy, kid, it's okay. It's all right; she's just asleep."

Magnus' tearful cries trailed off on a questioning note. He looked up at the towering man, saucer-eyed and wondering.

Harold knelt beside Gwen, fumbling in his belt pouch for a stick of smelling salts. He waved it under Gwen's nose; she shook her head tightly, made a sound somewhere between a sneeze and a gasp, and came awake.

"Here, now." Harold cradled the mother's head in his arm, lifting a flask of brandy to her lips. "Drink."

Gwen took a swallow, coughed, squeezed her eyes shut, waving the bottle away, and Magnus hit her with a bellow of joy.

Greta watched, from her corner, wonder and amazement coming into her eyes; and, as the mother cradled the baby in her arms, cooing soothing murmurs, the look in Greta's eyes turned to one of aching longing.

Slowly, she turned her head, singling out Harold with her eyes, and the strange light that came into her eyes was one whose definition has eluded many generations of very wise men.

Harold pulled out his smelling salts again, and started reviving the other witches.

Greta moved up silently behind Harold, that strange look still in her eyes, and touched him gently on the shoulder.

He looked up, saw her, and smiled weary cynicism again.

But she took his hands, looking solemn, and the light in her eyes had become very purposeful.

Harold drew back a little, entirely at a loss.

But not for long.

His arms were around her then, in a crushing, fervent embrace with all the tenderness of an affectionate boa constrictor.

Kelly stood in the doorway, watching Skolax's sailors; as he had guessed, Galen hadn't been able to spare the energy to throw them very far, only to the bow. They stood there in an uncertain, muttering knot, clustered around the unconscious Skolax.

Kelly noted their hesitation and decided to take the initiative. He scampered out to the mainmast, sprang up to the crosstree at the top of the sail, and shouted down:

"Belay, thou booze-stinkered blowfish! Dost thou not know a true elf when thou hast all but trod on one?"

They shied away, cringing at the sound of the voice, then looked up cautiously at the small figure high on the mast, muttering charms and making signs against evil.

Kelly's lips curled. "Charms against Evil! Dost thou truly believe them to have any weight 'gainst a leprecohen, a true elf of the sod, a creature of good, who hath ever sided with the Right?"

" 'Tis true, 'tis true," the sailors muttered to one another. "Aye, the elves were ever fighting for good." "Mischievous, assuredly, yet never malicious. . . ."

"Aye," said one, "and, when one single elf doth manage the holding at bay of eight sailors . . ."

"Assuredly," agreed another. "Evil could not so strengthen a poppet!"

"He must indeed be of the good," an older sailor nodded sagely.

"But, if he do be of the good," muttered one of the younger sailors, his brow knotted in fierce concentration, "then we who ha' fought him, fought then for the bad. And 'twas Skolax we fought for."

"And he, then," nodded the old sailor, "must needs be of the evil."

"Well said!" Kelly crowed. "Well said, and truly! And wilt thou let such evil run free?"

"Nay!" the sailors bellowed.

"I see that thou art of good heart at the core," Kelly cried, leaping to the deck. "Brave hearts, good lads! Most true, and honest good men! Now do what thou must!"

Kelly came strutting back into the cabin, twirling his hammer.

"Holla!" he cried. " 'Tis my pleasure and honor to bring great good news! The sailors have bound the evil Skolax and borne him away to Rod Gallowglass, there to tell all their tale and their crime to the High Warlock, and plead his intercession with the King! The days is ours, good . . ."

His voice trailed off as a silver-chain lasso snaked through the door, settled around the unwary leprecohen, and jerked tight. Kelly lashed out with his legs, struggling and tossing at the end of the chain, but it did no good.

The squat, bulky, chuckling form of Yorick followed the chain through the door, holding Kelly carefully at arm's length.

Harold whirled at Kelly's squall, leaped up, yanking at his sword; but it hadn't quite cleared the scabbard when Yorick's free fist slammed into Harold's chin, and the young warlock went down for the count.

Yorick whirled, grabbed up Gwen before she quite realized what he was doing, threw her over his shoulder, and leaped out the door with a chortle sounding in the midst of Gwen's frightened screams and Kelly's howls of rage.

The screams finally penetrated Galen's and Agatha's fog

231

of bliss. They whirled, dropping hands; Galen bellowed rage, and leaped to the door, then froze stock still, realizing there was very little he could do to the Neanderthal without risking hurt to both Gwen and Kelly.

Agatha saw her son stretched out cold on the floor, Greta clutching his head to her breast, crying, "Oh, my darling, my love!"

Agatha squawked and sprang.

She landed at Harold's side, felt a touch on her shoulder, snapped her head around to see Galen bending over her.

"Away!" she all but shrieked. "Or aid me to heal him! Our son lies . . ."

"He but sleeps," Galen said firmly. "To waken him from that sleep, thou and this child are more apt than I. Therefore, bide here and attend him, and come to me when thou canst; for I must to the High Warlock, to bear news that his wife is stolen away by a beastman."

"*Stolen?*" Agatha cried; but Galen had already disappeared.

Rod frowned, listening to the fearful sailors and looking down at the cocooned carcass of Skolax, who had come to; baleful eyes glared back at Rod.

"Rod Gallowglass!"

Rod looked down and nearly jumped out of his skin; old Galen stood by Fess' side, appearing out of nowhere. He sagged with weariness.

Rod leaned down, catching the old man's arm. "Galen! So that's how we won. . . . My thanks. . . ."

"Be still!" Galen gasped. "Thy wife . . . is lost! A beastman hath carried her off. . . ."

Madness stretched Rod's eyes.

He jerked back on the reins. Fess screamed, rearing and turning, then leaped into full gallop, toward the cliff wall, and the High Cave.

Galen stumbled back, knocked staggering into Tuan's arm as the young King leaned down, catching the old wizard around the shoulders, steadying him. "Our thanks, noble Galen," he said, "for this timely news, and for thy spell that won our battle this day. I regret that thy day's work is not done. Wilt thou accompany us to this High Cave?"

Galen drew himself up, his full dignity restored. "I shall," he said calmly, "and my son Harold with me; I go now to bring him. We shall be at the High Cave before thee."

He disappeared, the air whooshing into the space he had occupied.

Tuan bellowed commands and turned, swinging his arm for the charge; his horse plunged toward the cliff.

Eighty horsemen followed.

Ahead and above them, the tiny figure of the black horse soared toward the cliff, jets howling, and bore its rider into the gaping maw of the cavern.

Fess charged into the cave with his jets still thundering, froze as Rod sawed back on the reins, skidding to a halt.

The obscene monstrosity still brooded over the cavern with dulled eyes.

Rod's glance locked on it. His eyes widened in horror.

"No!" he whispered. "They wouldn't have, *couldn't* have done anything to her with *that!*"

"They didn't."

Rod whirled in the saddle, sword flashing out of its scabbard.

Yorick came toward him, grinning.

Rod saw Gwen over Yorick's shoulder, huddled against the cave wall, arms outstretched to him, face twisted in an agony of joy and relief.

He leaped from the saddle and ran to her, ignoring the Neanderthal, and swept her into his arms. She stood rigid in his embrace for a moment, then dissolved in tears, head on his shoulder.

Rod glared over her head at the beastman. "You bastard!"

"In truth, such a one could not have had a father," snapped a voice rigid with rage.

Rod turned his head, saw Kelly bound in a tidy bundle at the foot of a limestone column. The silver chain glittered in the eldritch light.

"Release me, thou great grinning oaf!" Kelly howled. "Thou hast thy wish; the High Warlock is here! Release me!"

Yorick shook his head regretfully, then smiled at Rod. "They're in A-One condition, Major, as you can see. A little shook, maybe, but completely undamaged."

"Scared half out of their wits," Rod growled, "and for what? Just to get me up here? All you had to do was ask, man! But I suppose that wasn't sadistic enough for you!"

"No. . . ." Yorick knit his brows, smiling reluctantly. "It just wasn't *private* enough. You would have brought five

233

score of guards with you, now wouldn't you? Or at least Brom O'Berin."

"And that's not secluded enough? What are you planning, a murder?"

"Oh, nothing like that," Yorick said hastily, then frowned. "Well . . . maybe *like* that . . . but there's a world of difference, Major."

"All right, I'm here. Can't you at least unwrap Kelly now?" Rod said dryly.

Yorick shook his head sadly. "Sorry, Major. I've got just a little too much respect for that elf. After all, anyone his size who can hold eight sailors at a door for a half hour . . ."

Rod frowned. "Kelly did that?"

"Aye, my lord," Gwen murmured, looking up at him. "He ha' saved our lives, all us witches."

"Well!" Rod's eyebrows went up; he nodded. "Great, Kelly. My thanks."

"Do not create too great a clamor in thy lauding of me," the leprecohen snapped. "Thou art in small danger of causing my pride to swell!"

"Yeah, that's a little unfair, Major," Yorick seconded. "After all, that's quite a feat for a guy that size. Aren't you a little amazed, at least?"

"No, not especially," Rod said, frowning. "After all, he's an Israeli, isn't he?"

"Hadn't thought about that," Yorick admitted, scratching behind his ear. "Well, he'll be a useful companion on your trip, Major."

Rod scowled. "I'm not going anywhere."

"Oh, yes you are," Yorick said cheerfully. He waved at the huge bank of glittering jewel-lights and the very black doorway beside them. "Through there."

Rod focused on the machine for the first time. "A time machine," he breathed.

"Chronomechanism, if you want to be a stickler," Yorick said helpfully. He took Rod's arm. "Right this way. . . ."

Rod's sword whipped around to the Neanderthal.

Yorick released Rod's arm, folded his own arms, and stood, smiling impassively.

Slowly, the sword-tip came closer, closer . . . it touched Yorick's throat . . . then stopped.

"We," Rod said between his teeth, "are going back down to the village. Now."

Yorick shook his head sadly, tender sympathy in his eyes. "Sorry, Major. Wrong again."

"And what," said Rod, "is going to stop me?"

"That I'm between you and the door, and I'm not moving. And you won't kill in cold blood. At least, that's enough for now."

Rod glared into the Neanderthal's eyes for a very long moment.

Then, slowly, he said, "Think you know me pretty well, don't you?"

"Right, for once." Yorick grinned. "Actually, that won't be enough to stop you when we get down to the nitty; it'll take something stronger then. But we'll worry about that when we come to it."

Slowly, Rod nodded. "I should have expected this."

"Right again," Yorick said agreeably.

"I never did trust you and Kernel," Rod growled. "I should have acted on it. But I thought your being on the side of democracy was my insurance."

"It is." Yorick's smile vanished, sincerity in every line of his face. "Everything'll work out all right, Major. You'll see. It'll just take a little while, is all. But GRIPE men don't fight their allies. Not much, anyway."

Rod heard the capitals in Yorick's voice, and frowned. "What," he said, "is GRIPE?"

"The Guardians of the Rights of Individuals, Patentholders Especially," Yorick amplified. "My organization." He flashed a cat-grin.

Rod shook his head. "Never heard of it."

"Oh, you will, though, you will. Right now, matter of fact. Briefly, we're an organization organized by Dr. Angus McAran, that is, to protect patent rights up and down the time line, see, and democracy has so far been guarding individual rights better than any other form of government, including patent rights—at least, it does while it's viable. . . ."

"Yeah, I've heard that before," Rod growled. " 'While it's viable.' But when a democracy starts to wane, and gets corrupt, it becomes a democracy in name only, and that means it's not really a democracy anymore."

"Right!" Yorick's finger jabbed out with a good deal more enthusiasm than the analysis warranted. Rod frowned, evaluating the slip, but Yorick was already rushing on.

"So it behooves GRIPE, you see, not only to preserve democracies, but to keep them viable, too. We're managing—uh, managed, that is; this time-travel bit gets a little confusing—to shore up the Interstellar Dominion Electorate —you know, the old Galactic Union—for an extra hundred years. So you see, we're on your side, Major. Almost more than you are, really."

235

"Yeah, I see," Rod said sardonically. "That's why you kidnapped us up here."

"Oh. . . ." Yorick scratched the base of his skull. "I wouldn't call it kidnapping, exactly. More of a very informal invitation, extremely hard to turn down." He paused in mid-scratch, his eyes suddenly on Rod again. "Besides, what've we ever done to make you think we don't like you?"

Rod stared for a moment, outraged by the Neanderthal's colossal brass.

"Well, come on, come on!" Yorick beckoned. "What'd we ever do to you?"

"Dropped a few thousand screaming Neanderthal projective telepaths on my planet, for one!" Rod snapped.

"Oh, yeah, *that*," Yorick interrupted. "But, well, there were extenuating circumstances, Major."

"I'm sure," Rod grated.

"Oh?" Yorick's eyebrows shot up. "Anything particular in mind?"

Rod paused, glowering at the ape-man; then he sighed and shook his head, half-smiling. "All right, you fugitive from a burlesque skit! How's this sound—the Evil Eye Neanderthals originated on Earth, in the Pleistocene, of course, and if you'd let them run wild, they would have taken over the planet, and democracy never would have arisen. So you had to move them some place where they could be integrated into a more peaceful culture. But the only culture that stood any chance against them was here, Gramarye. So you dumped them on us."

The Neanderthal nodded approvingly. "Not bad, Major, not bad at all." His brow quirked in a frown. " 'Course, you left out a few things."

"Oh?" Rod laid on the sarcasm. "Like what?"

"Well . . . like, the futurians, Major."

"Futurians?" Rod frowned.

"Yeah,' you know, Shaman and Skolax and the boys. The totalitarians and anarchists from the future."

"Oh." Rod frowned. "No, not really. I just hadn't gotten to them yet."

"Ah, ah!" Yorick shook a forefinger at him. "But they got into the picture a little sooner than you thought, Major. Right at the beginning, in fact."

"They did?" Rod frowned. "How?"

"By tectogenetics, that's how." Yorick jerked a thumb over his shoulder at the Kobold. "You may have noticed, they're pretty good at it. The future has worked up some dandy genetic engineering gadgets."

Rod nodded, still frowning. "All right, I'll buy it. So what did they engineer?"

"Evil Eye Neanderthals, that's what!" Yorick grinned triumphantly. "They cooked up a strain of mutant projective telepaths and planted 'em all over Terra. It would've made things a lot simpler for them, to prevent democracy's ever getting started."

"Of course!" Rod slammed his forehead with the heel of his hand. "Why didn't *I* think of that?"

" 'Cause you hadn't thought about tectogenetics," Yorick supplied. "It's still pretty much of a laboratory game, hasn't gotten much beyond mice. And even then you can't count on getting the same mutation twice."

Rod frowned. "But I don't see that it makes any difference, where the Neanderthals came from. It still boils down to your having to get rid of them."

"True!" Yorick's finger speared out. "But we *didn't* dump them on Gramarye! We do have *some* ethics, Major."

"You could fool me," Rod growled, puzzled. "So where *did* you put them?"

"On a handy little uninhabited Terra-type planet, of course." Yorick cocked his head on one side. "They're not all *that* rare, you know."

"Yeah, I know. So how'd they get *here?*"

"Why, Shaman snuck in when we weren't looking, of course. With an unregistered time machine—unregistered by GRIPE, that is—and arranged a nice little coup d'etat. Then they just followed him through the time machine to Gramarye."

Rod frowned. "Why here?"

"Can you think of a better place to scuttle democracy?" Yorick countered. "Without your telepaths, Major, DDT's days are numbered. And the number ain't all that high."

Rod nodded, scowling. "All right, I can see all that. But where'd Kernel come in?"

"Why, we couldn't let Shaman just go his own merry way," said Yorick, surprised. "It would've meant war."

"Like we just got done fighting."

"Well, yeah, but that was an accident. Anyway, soon as we found out about Shaman's little sneak play, we recruited Kernel. . . ."

"Recruited?" Rod frowned. "You brought him in specially? Why?"

" 'Cause he knew the territory." Yorick hurried on. "We recruited him, and sneaked him into Beastland here, and he fixed up a counter-coup, threw out Shaman and settled down to teach the Evil Eye-ers agriculture."

"I suppose he figured that if he gave them something else to learn . . ."

". . . they'd study war no more." Yorick nodded. "So he brought in maize—it'll grow just about anywhere—and . . ."

". . . they nicknamed him 'Kernel,' " Rod interjected.

"Right." Yorick nodded vigorously. "So they settled down to work at becoming civilized, and everything looked dandy."

"Then Shaman happened?"

"Yeah, he doesn't stay thrown out too good. He sneaked in somehow, sneaked the Kobold in with him—that wasn't in the original religion they'd dreamed up—and worked up a counter-counter-coup."

"How?" Rod demanded.

"We still haven't quite got that figured out," Yorick admitted. "But, roughly, he managed to sneak bootleg raiders out, all decked out in Viking rigs—that was his idea, I think he's a Wagner fan—to raid the Gramarye coast villages."

"Which, of course, got us mad enough to attack." Rod nodded grimly, cursing his own headstrong folly.

"Well . . . yeah," Yorick agreed. "Then, when you invaded, he played on the Evil Eye-ers' paranoia to turn them against Kernel, and . . . well, here we are."

"Yeah." Rod's mouth was a thin, hard line. "Here we are, with a little war and a lot of death thrown in."

Yorick spread his hands, shrugging. "What could we do, Major?"

"You could've stayed off of Gramarye, that's what!" Rod shouted. "When Kernel came in the first time, you could have shipped them back to their uninhabited planet!"

Yorick shook his head, serious for once. "No, Major. By that time, we'd realized that'd just put off their conquests for a couple of millennia. No." He shook his head, closing his eyes. "No, they had to be integrated into a healthy, sane culture. And Gramarye was the only possible choice."

Rod's eyes narrowed to needle glints. His voice was cold, and slow. "But who gave you permission?"

His voice rose. "No one, that's who! You had no right! No right, you hear me? And to prove it, I'm going to kick you and Kernel and all your Neanderthals off of Gramarye and out of this time!"

"My lord. . . ." Gwen touched his shoulder, pleading. Rod brushed her hand away.

But Yorick was shaking his head. "No, Major," he said. "No. You're the one who's going to get kicked out—through

238

the time-machine. That's what this whole kidnapping bit was for."

Gwen gasped, clutching at Rod's arm—and, he was sure, readying a spell. It was a reassuring feeling.

"How?" he breathed.

His sword flashed out, pricking Yorick's throat. "How are you planning to move me, ape-man? Without turning dead?"

The Neanderthal stood impassively, smiling. "You will," he said quietly. "You will. And Gwen, and Kelly, and Fess along with you. You will."

The sword-point pricked deeper. "How?"

"Willingly," Yorick said obligingly. "No coercion involved, Major. You'll go of your own free will."

Rod stared.

Then he laughed, hard and bitter, but his eyes staying locked on Yorick's.

When the long laugh was done, he calmed himself, regained his poise, then asked, very quietly, "Why should I want to?"

"Because," said a deep voice behind him, "this planet isn't big enough for both of us."

Rod whipped about, his sword up to guard.

He froze.

"Major Gallowglass," murmured Yorick, "meet Kernel."

Slowly, Rod relaxed, lowering his sword. He smiled sardonically, nodding slowly. "Of course."

Then he said, "I should have known."

"Yes," said Kernel. "You should have."

Gwen's eyes were round with wonder and total confusion.

Rod sheathed his sword and turned his head, smiling sourly at Yorick. "This is supposed to convince me that I should politely bow out and leave the field to him, hm?"

"No," said Yorick judiciously, "not particularly."

"Good. Because it doesn't. I'm not going."

"Oh, yes you are," said Kernel softly.

Rod gave him a hard, tight, one-sided smile. "Of my own free will? I'll choose to go?"

Kernel nodded.

"Why?"

"Because you're a major," said Kernel, "and I'm a colonel."

Something very cold seemed to lick Harold's face, and something warm and very moist fastened itself onto his lips.

He wanted nothing more than to stay in the sweet ob-

239

livion of sleep; but something seemed to be taking liberties with his own personal body, and he did sort of resent that. . . .

So, painfully, he forced his eyes open.

He saw Agatha bending anxiously over him, a damp cloth in her hand. But she was obscured; he was seeing her through a network of fine black lines.

He realized, suddenly, the black lines were Greta's hair; and, furthermore, the shapely young witch seemed to be diligently attempting mouth-to-mouth resuscitation.

He closed his eyes again, with a long, satisfied sigh. Then he remembered what had happened before he went to sleep.

With a sigh of infinite regret, he opened his eyes again, and gently disengaged himself from Greta.

He looked up, with a happy, satisfied smile, to find Galen standing just behind Agatha, looking almost as anxious.

"What's been going on?" Harold frowned slightly. "Last I remember, this beastman burst into the cabin, and then there were stars, and . . ."

"He ha' kidnapped the High Warlock's wife, and stolen her away to the High Cave."

"Ye gods!" Harold slammed to his feet. Greta gave a small cry of protest.

Harold kissed her, and Greta's arms clutched convulsively for one last hug; but she clutched empty air, for Harold had disappeared.

"I, too, must depart," Galen said sternly, but the look he gave the old witch was fond. "Bide here and await us."

He reached out to touch her hand briefly, and was gone.

Agatha stood a moment, then outrage swelled her face; her fists jolted up on her hips.

"Aye, oh, most assuredly we shall attend them! We whose power is no less than their own, who ha' sweated in battle this day alongside them—now are we to bide here, in maiden attendance."

"But what shall we do?" murmured Greta.

"Why, disobey them, of course," Agatha snapped, catching up her broomstick. "Child, let us fly!"

A moment later, two broomsticks, well-stocked with riders, shot up from the dragon ship toward the High Cave.

Harold and Galen materialized in the cave just as Tuan and Brom, with a large troop of cavalry, charged in—and froze.

Only momentarily, of course; the Kobold was shut down. But, even quiescent, it was a sight to give anyone pause.

A loud curse from the side of the cave brought them out of their trance.

"Damnit, no!" Rod slammed a fist against the rock ledge that currently served him for a seat.

Yorick grinned, exhaling a huge cloud of smoke from the stogie clamped between his teeth. "Why, what's wrong with it?"

"It's not true, damn it! Mankind just wasn't created by a huge milling mass of gods! Especially not a batch of gods that look like animals!"

Gwen sighed patiently, leaning back against the rock wall, gazing tolerantly but fondly at her husband.

Tuan finally found his voice. "High Warlock, if thou wilt pardon the interruption of a mere monarch—*may I ask the meaning of this?*"

"Huh?" Rod looked up, startled. "Oh! Hi, Your Majesty. How you been?"

"Extraordinary concerned for thy safety!" Tuan was beginning to redden. "I had thought to find thee in mortal combat, mayhap on the point of death—yet, here I find thee in ordinary converse with the enemy who ha' kidnapped thy wife!"

"Oh, yeah, that. . . ." Rod flashed an apologetic grin. "Well, he explained it all to me, and apologized profusely, Your Majesty. Seems he just wanted to invite us up here for a cup of wine, but he doesn't quite know our etiquette yet. . . . Yorick, this is His Majesty, King Tuan of Gramarye, and, Tuan, this ape's name is Yorick."

Tuan turned to Yorick with frowning, puzzled eyes under a slightly-knit brow. "Yorick . . . ?"

"Kernel's chief lieutenant," Rod explained. "Empowered to make treaties with you, if you're so minded."

Tuan's look turned to cold steel. "I am *not* so minded!" he rapped. "I will speak of treaties with Kernel himself, and one other! What! Shall the King debate with a servant?"

Yorick scratched at the base of his skull. "You see, Your Majesty, it's like this. . . ." He looked up. "Kernel's gone."

"Gone?" said Tuan blankly.

"Gone," Yorick confirmed. "When he brought my people here—Beastland, like you call it—he told us he'd stay with us only as long as we needed him. And, well, we don't need him anymore, so—he went."

Tuan scowled. "If there is truth in it, he must needs be the first king in all of history who ha' kept such a promise. How is it thou dost no longer need him? Thou art now conquered."

"Right," said Yorick cheerfully. "So we don't need Kernel to rule anymore. We've got you. By the terms of your alliance with Kernel—remember? We've all got citizenship . . . that is, assuming Your Majesty isn't about to go back on your promises. . . ."

Tuan straightened proudly. "Assuredly, I shall not."

"Yeah." Yorick grinned with a touch of relief. "Kernel didn't think you would. He said to wish you joy of us."

Tuan looked nonplussed for a moment; then his face went black with rage, which slowly lightened to a brown brood. He swung to Rod.

"Didst thou foresee such consequences to this treaty of thine?"

"Well, uh. . . ." Rod shuffled his feet, embarrassed.

Tuan's head nodded, heavy with irony. "I will someday learn to beware of thy counsels, High Warlock," he muttered.

He turned back to Yorick, sighed, shaking his head in resignation. "Well, 'twas the price of Kernel's aid; and even now, I think 'twas well paid. I am, then, thy King."

"But how of this?" Brom's voice growled.

The whole company turned, to see the dwarf standing in front of the Kobold, glowering thoughtfully up at its face.

"Aye," murmured Tuan, staring fascinated at the monster. "What of the false god?"

He tore his eyes away, turned to Rod. "What is this fell creature?"

Rod looked up at the monster. "A Kobold," he growled, face twisting with disgust and a touch of nausea. "Does it need any other name?"

"For you and for me, yes," said Harold.

"How about it, Major? What is it? A chimpanzee?"

"Its parents were." Rod turned away. "I can't see much in the way of surgical scars, so I'm pretty sure its parents were normal chimpanzees; but the normal strain might be quite a few generations back. It's obviously been genetically restructured; that's the only way you could get a monster like that." He turned back to the Kobold, holding his gorge down firmly. "Of course, I suppose you could say it's a tectogenetic masterpiece."

He turned his head and spat, then wiped his mouth with the back of his hand. "They doctored the chromosomes to make the poor beast into a converter—feed current into it, DC, I suppose, and out comes psionic energy."

Harold looked at the black box, frowning. He looked a question at the Neanderthal.

Yorick smiled, nudged the black box with his foot, nodded. "Atomic power pack."

Harold nodded, too, his eyes never leaving the beastman's. "Quite a primitive you've got there, Major," he said slowly.

"One of Kernel's best," Rod agreed.

Yorick was still looking at the power pack. "Wish I could figure out how to shut this thing off permanently."

"You mean it's liable to go on again?" said Harold nervously.

"Not unless somebody turns it on." Rod eyed the monster warily. "All the beastmen have surrendered, and Atylem's dead, and Shaman's tied up at the moment; so I don't think we have too much to worry about. . . . Say, by the way, Yorick, how is His Evilness?"

The Neanderthal rolled Shaman over, felt of the scarecrow's neck, then shook his head, clucking softly. "He *is* turned off permanently, Major. Guess you hit a little too hard with that chop of yours. Neck's broke."

"Well, I wasn't about to pull my punches just then," Rod said grimly. "At least we don't have to worry about him turning it on again."

"Still, it would be an almighty comfort if it was impossible from both sides." Yorick cocked his head on one side and closed one eye, squinting, looking the Kobold up and down. "I suppose it *is* a triumph of genetic engineering, if you look at it the right way. That bulging cerebrum can handle one hell of a lot of power. And no forebrain, did you notice that, Major? Prefrontal lobotomy in the womb. It can't do anything on its own. No initiative."

"And no soul," said Rod grimly.

"Well, yes, that too," the Neanderthal admitted. "Which may be just as well, come to think of it. We might conjecture what it would do if it had a mind of its own. . . ."

Rod shuddered, but Harold said, "It couldn't do much. Not with those atrophied limbs. All it can do is just sit there." Harold gulped, and turned away, looking slightly green. "That forehead."

"I agree," Rod said. "How can you just sit there and look at it, Yorick?"

"Oh, it's a fascinating study, from a scientist's viewpoint," the Neanderthal answered. "A real triumph, a great philosophic statement of mind over matter, an enduring monument to Man's ingenuity." He turned back to Rod. "Put the poor thing out of its misery!"

"Yes," Rod agreed, turning away, slightly bent over. "Somebody stick a knife in the poor bastardization!"

Nobody moved. Nobody spoke.

Rod frowned, lifted his head. "Didn't anybody hear me? I said, kill it!"

He sought out Tuan's eyes. The young King looked away.

Rod turned, catching Harold's eye. He, too, looked away.

Rod bowed his head, biting his lip.

He spun, looking at Yorick.

The Neanderthal looked away, whistling softly, eyes on the ceiling.

Rod snarled and bounded up to the dais, dagger in his hand, swinging up fast in an underhand stab.

His arm froze as he looked into the dulled eyes, looked slowly up and down the naked, hairless thing, so obscene, yet so . . .

He turned away, throwing down his knife, growling low in his throat.

Yorick met his eyes, nodding sympathetically. "It's such a poor, pitiful thing, when the power's turned off, Major," he said softly. "So weak and defenseless. And men have done it so much dirt already. . . ."

"Dogs!" roared Brom, glaring, "Stoats and weasels! Art thou all so unmanned as to let this thing live?"

He whirled about where he stood on the dais, glowering at the silent throng before him. He snorted, turned about, glaring at them all.

"Aye," he rumbled, "I see it is even as I have said. There is too much of pity within thee; thou canst not steel thyselves to the doing of it; for there is not enough pity in thee, to force thee to this cruel kindness."

He turned, measuring the Kobold up and down. "Yet must it be done; for this is a fell thing, a foul thing out of nightmare, and therefore must it die. And will no man do it this courtesy?" he bellowed.

No one moved.

Brom looked long and carefully, but found only shame in each glance.

He smiled sourly and shrugged his massive shoulders. "This is my portion, then."

And, before anyone quite realized what he was doing, the dwarf drew his sword, and leaped, plunging his blade up to the hilt in the Kobold's chest, in its heart.

The monster stiffened, its mouth wrenching open, face contorting in one silent, simian scream; then it slumped where it sat, dead.

The others stared, horrified.

Brom sheathed his sword, touched his forelock in respect where he stood on the arm of the Kobold's stone chair. "Good, lasting sleep, Sir Kobold," he said gravely.

" 'Twas an ill deed," said Tuan. "It could not defend itself." But he looked somewhat uncertain.

"Aye, but soulless it was also," said Brom. "Forget that not, Majesty. Is it dishonor to slaughter a hog? Or to stick a wild boar? Nay, surely not! But this thing ha' wrought death, and was now defenseless; and therefore no man would touch it."

"And therefore," growled a voice so low that only Brom heard it, "its death must be by a hand that was something more, and something less, than a man's."

Brom whirled, shocked and fearful. Rod Gallowglass alone among mortal men knew Brom to be King of Elves as well as King's Councillor; but it had not been Rod's voice in his ear.

It was the ape-man, Yorick, who stood grinning at his side.

For a moment, the two stood facing each other, looking deep into each other's eyes—Brom's wary, Yorick's gleeful.

"That blow was well-struck, my liege lord," Yorick murmured.

Brom's eyes widened under lowering brows, outraged—and a little fearful. "What manner of speaking is this?" he growled. "I am no lord of thine."

"Oh, but you are," said Yorick, with a deep chuckle. "After all, you're already King of Elves; why not be King of Goblins, too?"

Brom glared, appalled.

Then he wrapped a hand around the Neanderthal's negligible neck and yanked Yorick's head up to his own blazing eyes. "Who schooled thee in such loathsome folly?" he hissed.

"Why, Atylem," said Yorick, eyes wide and innocent. "He convinced all the beastmen that only the Kobold's killer could be our rightful king. Since he's dead now . . . and King Tuan has to stay in Gramarye, to rule there . . . after all, who else in Gramarye could pass for a Kobold?"

Then, raising his voice, he turned to the crowd, crying, "I am a beastman, one ruled by the Kobold, and I say that to the Kobold's slayer, to him and to him alone, will I kneel!"

And he suited the action to the word, dropping to one knee and bowing his head before Brom, shouting:

"Hail, my new King and liege lord!"

With a sinking heart, Brom saw a slow smile of delighted agreement break over Tuan's face; but before the dwarf could say a word in protest, a shrill voice screamed, "Aside!" at the cave-mouth.

"Make room!" it shrilled. "Let me pass! Nay, thou miscreants, thou spineless, water-blood men, be thou gone and away, step aside!"

The soldiers shrank back, startled, as Agatha elbowed her way to the front of the crowd, Greta in her wake.

"Harold, my son, thou art in no danger?" Agatha looked around in bewilderment; the bloody battle she'd expected was nothing but a bloody argument.

Galen came up to her and took her hand in a reassuring gesture, while Harold reassured Greta with a more passionate embrace.

Rod smiled at the family reunion, then looked up at Tuan. "And now, Your Majesty—what shall we do with these beastmen?"

Tuan's mouth was screwed up with suppressed laughter, his eyes on Brom. "Methinks Master Yorick has obtained a most excellent answer to that question, Sir Gallowglass." He threw out his arm with a flourish, gesturing toward Brom. "Behold the King of the Beastmen!"

"Nay!" Brom howled, backing away. "I have . . . I . . . but already, I . . . I cannot, I . . ."

He turned a piteous, pleading look to Rod; after all, he couldn't very well admit he didn't want the job because he was already King of the Elves. Only Rod knew his dilemma, and Rod was shaking his head ruefully.

"Sorry, Brom," he said. "I'm afraid they're right. You're the only man in Gramarye, qualified for governing, who has enough chutzpah and other sorts of magic, for the beastmen to accept him as King. 'Fraid you're elected."

And Yorick, the man who had gotten Brom into this, was off in a corner, in a huddle with Harold, Galen, Agatha, and Greta.

Which left Brom no one to glare at but Rod. And glare he did; after all, even a son-in-law should have enough filial respect to help his adopted father out of a tight spot.

"Oh, it won't be as bad as all that," Rod said soothingly. "I think this lummox here"—he nodded toward Yorick—"will make an excellent major domo. He can do the dirty work for you. . . ." He looked around. "Say, where is that lummox?"

The lummox looked up from the huddle in the corner. "You call me, Major?"

Brom looked the Neanderthal up and down with narrowed eyes while Rod decided the huddle looked suspicious.

"Aye," Brom growled, "he will do well. Down on your knees, worthless vassal! Kneel to thy King!"

Yorick leaped over to the dais and dropped to his knees, spreading his arms wide. "As my liege wishes, King Brom! Shall I kiss your foot?"

"What, only his foot?" Rod muttered; but Brom roared, "Guard thy tongue, knave! Or I'll kick in thy teeth!"

"Watch it, Yorick," Rod cautioned, "or he'll do it. And you know what medieval dentistry's like. . . ."

Yorick turned to Rod, incredulous. "This sample-size sovereign? Beat *me?*"

"Four falls out of three," Rod said, nodding sadly. "You should've seen what he did to me. Or better yet, you shouldn't."

Brom grinned, chuckling deep in his throat. "And therefore shalt thou mind thy master, knave. And now shalt thou lead me forth from this cave, presenting me to mine new subjects."

"Uh, if Your Minimal Majesty will grant me a moment's indulgence first," said Yorick, "I've got one small job to do before the Cornation."

"You mean, 'Coronation,' " said Rod helpfully.

"No I meant 'Corn.' You forget he's taking the Kernel's place." And Yorick hopped up and headed for the back wall, without waiting for Rod's grumbled, "Corn is right. *This* is a Prime Minister?"

"Master Gallowglass," said Tuan, "what is that wall of weird aspect, toward which the beastman goes?"

"Oh, that's a time-machine," said Rod, turning toward the back wall. "A warlock-thing. It's . . ." He stopped dead, because Harold, Greta, Galen, and Agatha were also heading toward the machine.

"*Hold*—it—right—there!" Rod snapped. "Where do you think *you're* going?"

"Why, home," said Harold, turning and grinning over his shoulder as he helped his parents into the dark doorway-cubicle. "Ready, Yorick?"

The Neanderthal punched a few buttons and nodded. "Ready."

"Wait a minute. Hold on. Whoa. Not so fast, there." Rod held up both hands. "Now, Harold, I don't know about you. But Agatha and Galen belong—here. This is their home. Right?"

"Wrong," said Harold cheerfully, and Galen said, " 'Tis late come upon us, Rod Gallowglass. . . . I have realized at last the truth of what this she-devil hath always spoke. . . ." He cut off Agatha's indignant squawk with a wink. "The long and the short of it is, Master Gallowglass, that this beauteous hag hath sworn love to me, and I to her; and"—

he gave Agatha a grimace that actually approached a lecherous leer—"our son hath sworn he shall take us to a land where we shall be made young again."

"But-but-but . . ." Rod rocked back on his heels, thunderstruck. "But I thought you were scared of women."

"Fearful, aye," began Galen, but Agatha cut him off. "I was ever mistook, Rod Gallowglass." Her old eye gleamed mischief at Galen. "This shriveled ancient was never truly a craven. He hath long known the trick of mastering his fear of unknowns (which, of course, was ever why he feared women), provided, of course, that the game was worth the candle. I had thought his soul founded on cowardice; but I see that I was mistook; for the base of his soul is licentiousness." She prodded Galen playfully in the ribs. "Be done with thy lustful looks, dusty ancient. I shall test thy courage and manhood most truly; aye, I shall have the groveling in gravel right soon."

"Mayhap I shall kneel before thee," the old wizard grinned, "but it shall not be from fear."

"Wait a minute, wa-a-a-it a minute!" Rod shouted. "You two are supposed to be too old for—well, that kind of thing!"

"Never too old for the intention," said Harold, grinning. "Of course, capability is another matter. But we've got mighty good geriatrics where I come from."

"Oh, come off it! It can't be *that* good."

"But it is, Major. We're far enough in the future to have a regeneration process. Oh, it's still pretty crude, of course; but it's safe. And effective. Very effective."

Galen chuckled deep in his throat.

"Oh, now wait a minute! That's impossible! You *can't* mean you're going to make them young again!"

"That he shall," said Agatha, darting a poisoned glance at Rod. "This our son hath promised us: we shall be twenty again."

"But you *can't!*" Rod squalled. "You're taking away half our available witch-power!"

"Oh, you don't need it now," said Harold placidly. "We've knocked out the Kobold for you. You've got enough psionic power to take care of anything else that should crop up—Gwen and the Royal Coven, you know. And Magnus, when he grows up."

"But you *can't!* It's illegal, it's immoral, it's . . . yeah, that's it!" Rod beamed with sudden inspiration, leveling a forefinger at Harold. "It's immoral! We've got first claim on them! What right do *you* have to them?"

"Right?" Harold frowned. "Major, are you crazy? I've got the best right of all to them!"

"Huh?"

"Sure, they're my parents, aren't they?" Harold smiled sympathetically. "Sorry, Major, but I've got first claim. After all, I have to insure my own birth, don't I?"

"You mean . . . ?" Rod sputtered.

"Yep. Going to take them into the future, Major, to eleven months before I was born."

"Uh, *eleven* months?"

"Two for regeneration treatments and nine for the pregnancy."

"*Harold!*" gasped Agatha, scandalized.

"Oh," Rod said weakly.

Harold's chin lifted stubbornly. "Anything wrong with that, Major?"

"Well, no, I suppose not." Rod frowned, puzzled. "It just seems incestuous, somehow. . . ."

Harold frowned. "You don't doubt my word, do you, Major?"

"Oh, no, no!" Rod said quickly. "You're . . . I mean, *it*'s conceivable." He glanced at Greta, questioningly. "You're going with them, of course?"

"Most assuredly." Greta beamed up at Harold. "I ha' waited overlong for the fullness of this man, Lord Warlock. I shall not relinquish him easily . . . ever."

Rod nodded, almost smiling. "It would seem that battles are very educational experiences. Thought this guy didn't come close enough to your idea of what was right in a man, Greta."

"I was in truth so foolish," Greta admitted, twisting her head so that she could look up into Harold's eyes. "Oh, he is not the man that I once dreamed he was, that is true—but I ha' learned that he is more."

"Will you jokers hurry up and quit yammering before I have to reset this thing?" Yorick griped.

"Sure, sure, right away!" Harold stepped further back into the cubicle, waving. "Well, bye, folks. It's been fun."

All four witchfolk waved. Yorick threw the key, and they disappeared.

"Your Majesty," said Rod, turning away from the machine with quite-evident relief, "shall we present the new King, now?"

"Aye," said Tuan, seizing gratefully on something he could understand. He turned and bawled over his shoulder: "Form for procession!"

"Oh, yes indeed, yes indeed!" burbled Yorick, hustling

to the front. "We must present the new King to my paleolithic kin!"

"Weird sense of humor on that one," Rod muttered, watching him go by.

They came marching out of the cave—first, the foot soldiers, marching in good order down the ledges to each side of the cave-mouth, forty soldiers on each side, trumpets blaring and sergeants barking.

After them came the four lords, two to a side, all mounted, looking stately, elegant and reserved in the false dawn.

Inside the cave, Rod looked out over the valley. He saw the entire Neanderthal population below him, at the foot of the cliff, ringed by the Gramarye army, lances at the ready, watching their foes of a few hours ago quite warily.

"Their numbers have shrunk a bit, haven't they?" Rod muttered grimly. "I wonder how many of the original five thousand are left. . . ." His jaw tightened with bitterness and self-contempt.

" 'Twas not so ill-done as that, my lord," Gwen murmured, her hand tightening on his. "Thou didst only what thou must needs do; thou didst not cause this war."

"No," Rod growled, "but I could have prevented it, if I'd been a little smarter."

"No man could ha' done that," Gwen said firmly. "And thou hast, at least, thy second nation."

"Yes," Rod sighed, "and we've got things set up so it'll be integrated with Gramarye, united under one Emperor, so that the tension between the two shouldn't ever come to outright war again."

Gwen murmured, "Before thou camest to Gramarye, 'twas ever petty warfare—'twixt a king and a duke, to make the duke mind; or 'twixt duke and duke, if the crown of the time was a weak one. Thou hast given this land future peace, my lord, and assurance the King will never prove a tyrant."

"Yes," Rod nodded heavily. "But the cost, darling."

"My lord," Gwen said firmly, "thy back will break if thou seekest to load all men's troubles upon it. No man can be a god."

Rod closed his eyes, nodding. Then he smiled gently. "It's been quite a while since you saw Magnus. Go on home; check and make sure he's okay."

As Gwen lifted into the sky, a throaty baritone bellowed outside the cavern: "My people, attend to me!"

Yorick stood with arms uplifted. "My people, the Kernel has left us, as he foretold!"

A startled murmur ran through the assembled beastmen below. Yorick let it pass its crest, then shouted:

"Yet he is with us! He has given us a new King, a most powerful, virtuous man! I am chosen High Councillor to this King, and I speak to you now for him!"

The crowd was silent; the air was tense.

"We have been conquered," Yorick went on, "and therefore our new King is vassal to the King who has conquered us! We are fortunate—for the King of our King is a wise, just, and merciful man! And the proof of it is, he has given to us the best and wisest of all his lords for our King! A King of a King is an Emperor," Yorick bellowed, and stepped to one side, throwing an arm out toward the High Cave. "Bow, Clan of the Kobold, to thy newfound ruler! Bow to Tuan, Emperor of Gramarye and of Beastland!"

Tuan strode forth, tall, proud, and handsome, hand on his sword-hilt.

A long moment of silence held the valley.

Then a thundering cheer rose from the beastmen.

"I am thy new ruler," Tuan called, "and will never forsake thee. Yet since I cannot abide here with thee, I give to you a new King. Thou hast called thyselves the People of the Kobold, and thou worshiped a goblin, calling him your god. This god was false, and the mark of it was, he demanded your homage. A false Kobold he was, false and evil, and the true Kobold slew him. It is the true Kobold I give you, for ruler and father. He is not a god, nor ever claimed to be; a man he is, a man only; yet withal, a man worth your respect, admiration. He is the true Kobold, the slayer of your demon! He has served me well many years; he shall serve you well many more. He can stand alone against any five of you, as he stood against the false Kobold, and slew it! In deed and in truth is he a king among men!"

Inside the cave, Brom winced.

"What's the matter?" Rod jibed. "Don't like the idea of living up to the reputation he's giving you?"

"That," Brom growled, "and the arrant falsehood of the words that he preaches."

"That's your opinion." Rod shrugged. "I would have said they were all true. For myself, I've found you to be a most excellent father-in-law."

"Be still!" Brom snapped, glancing frantically around the

cave. "Praise Heaven!" he sighed, relaxing. "She is not here!"

"No, she went to check up on Magnus; he needs a lot of checking up on."

"Aye," Brom agreed, chuckling proudly.

"I don't know why you won't let me tell her you're her father, though." Rod sighed. "I think she'd be proud."

"Mayhap," Brom said darkly, "and mayhap she might not."

Rod shook his head in resignation. "Being her father's something to boast about, Brom. I'm surprised a man should hide his true identity from his daughter."

"Oh, aye!" Brom eyed him sourly. "A man may hide the truth of himself from his father-in-law, though."

Rod stiffened, a chill on his spine. "Hide . . . his . . . uh . . . what are you talking about, Brom?"

"Oh, thou knowest, thou knowest well!" the dwarf all but roared. "Thou goest into this cave, and when I come, minutes later, thou hast gray hairs here and there in thy thatch, with new lines to thy face, in the space of a matter of minutes! And thy wife, thy wife my daughter, whose keeping I gave into thy hands, she also is aged! Oh, not so much, no, mayhap a year, or two years; but aged, aged most surely, in the space of minutes! Minutes! Nay, tell me, then; what man art thou now, Rod Gallowglass?"

Rod's head hung low, his eyes closed.

"Nay, then," said Brom, quieter, almost gently. "I know thee, thou art Rod Gallowglass, thou art mine own son-in-law. There could not be two with such a manner as thine; there could not be but one knew the most deep of my secrets, my fatherhood. Thou art Rod Gallowglass; but dost thou not owe, to a father and wife's father, the tale of the why of it?"

"I do." Rod raised his head, nodding, self-sick and weary. "I should have known, Brom. Anybody but you. Everybody else I could fool, but not you. You I should have told right away."

"That, I forgive thee," Brom growled, "provided that now, that shalt tell it me."

Rod nodded. "It starts a little while ago, Brom. Two years back."

"*Two years!*" Brom stared, thunderstruck.

"Yes, two years. And just an hour or so ago. Because there's wizardry in it, Brom, the kind that lets a man travel backward or forward in time.

"You see, an hour ago, Rod Gallowglass—a younger Rod Gallowglass, and a younger Gwen—came into this cave, and

252

met Yorick, and they talked for awhile, and . . . try hard to believe this, Brom. . . ."

"I ha' asked thee thy words; I will not doubt them," the dwarf said curtly, frowning. "Speak."

"Well, Yorick sent Gwen and me to a time more than a thousand years in the past, to a world far, far away, past the stars—Terra, where Mankind began."

Brom's eyes widened, but he held his tongue.

"There we met a—uh—wizard, named Angus, and Angus and Yorick told us that the beastmen had been brought to Gramarye two years ago, by Shaman, and . . . well, they convinced us that the beastmen had to stay on Gramarye—it was either that, or kill them all.

"But they also convinced me that I might be able to teach them peaceful ways. . . ."

"So thou camest to teach them," said Brom, still frowning.

Rod nodded. "Angus sent us back here, to Gramarye, and Yorick came with us—and we arrived here, in Beastland, two years ago."

Brom's scowl deepened. "Wouldst thou have me believe that for the space of two years, there have been two of Rod Gallowglass?"

"That's right," Rod said grimly. "Me, here in Beastland, and a younger me, in Gramarye. And for the past two years, I've been helping the beastmen build a settlement here.

"Before I could do that, though, I had to overthrow Shaman. . . . Well, it wasn't too hard to do, not for a SCENT agent. We wrapped it up quick, with a minimum of bloodshed, and I got down to teaching them the ways of peace. . . ."

"Peace!" Brom exploded. "This war, that hath fell on us out of nothing? This bloodflow, this maiming and dying, this . . ."

His voice trailed off as he saw Rod's shoulders slump under the guilt.

"That," Rod muttered, "at least was not my doing. Though it was perhaps my fault; I wasn't watchful enough. But I was on my guard, keeping an eye open for any sign of trouble—and I could have sworn there wasn't any monkey business going on. I never knew Shaman had come back, till the valley erupted in bloodshed and war, till the people he and Atylem had converted to the Kobold revolted against me. . . . We fled for our lives, Gwen and Yorick and I, and a few loyal beastmen; and we lived, we were lucky.

"And we've been fighting ever since, building our strength

and fighting, till today. Today, we came back, and our people are free of Shaman and the Kobold."

Brom still frowned. "But what of this other Rod Gallowglass? Where has he gone?"

Rod smiled sardonically. "To the past, Brom, to two years ago. You see, an hour ago, Yorick kidnapped Gwen, and the younger Rod Gallowglass came storming up here to find her, and met me. And I, ah, convinced him he could leave Gramarye in my hands, and go with Yorick, to meet the wizard Angus. So the younger Rod, and the younger Gwen, went back in time to meet a younger Yorick, who took them to Angus. And the older Gwen, and the older Yorick and, well, the older me—we stayed here, to keep an eye on Gramarye and Beastland.

"And here we are."

"And thou hast loaded thy kingdom onto my shoulders," Brom growled. "And, as thou wouldst have me believe it, the younger of thy two selves is two years in the past?"

Rod nodded. "The younger Rod Gallowglass is back there in yesterday, telling the beastmen they've finally found peace, teaching them ironworking so they can make plows, bringing them maize, teaching them how to plant it. . . ."

"Maize!" Brom's mouth dropped open, his eyes staring wide. "*Thou* brought them maize?"

Rod nodded, smiling sourly, his face tightening with irony.

"Then, *thou . . .*"

"Yeah. You guessed it, Brom. I'm Kernel."

ACE SCIENCE FICTION DOUBLES
Two books back-to-back for just 75c

06707 **The Blind Worm** Stableford
Seeds of the Dreamers Petaja

11560 **The Communipaths** Elgin
The Noblest Experiment in the Galaxy Trimble

13793 **Dark of the Woods**
Soft Come the Dragons Koontz

24100 **Flower of Doradil** Rackham
A Promising Planet Strike

27235 **Gallagher's Glacier**
Positive Charge Richmond

27400 **The Gates of Time** Barrett
Dwellers in the Deep O'Donnell

51375 **The Mad Goblin**
Lord of the Trees Farmer

52180 **Masters of the Lamp**
A Harvest of Hoodwinks Lory

76096 **The Ships of Durostorum** Bulmer
Alton's Unguessable Sutton

78400 **The Star Virus** Bayley
Mask of Chaos Jakes

81610 **To Venus! To Venus!** Grinnell
The Wagered World Janifer & Treibich

Available wherever paperbacks are sold or use this coupon.

ace books, (Dept. MM) Box 576, Times Square Station
New York, N.Y. 10036
Please send me titles checked above.

I enclose $.................Add 10c handling fee per copy.

Name ....

Address ....

City...................... State.............. Zip........
Please allow 4 weeks for delivery.   8

The World's Best Award-Winning Science Fiction Comes from Ace

03300 **The Atlantic Abomination** Brunner 60c

10410 **Children of Tomorrow** Van Vogt 95¢

13795 **Dark Piper** Norton 60c

17261 **Dune** Herbert $1.25

22811 **The Far Out Worlds of A. E. Van Vogt** 75c

33700 **High Sorcery** Norton 60c

73440 **The Rolling Stones** Heinlein 95c

79170 **Swords And Deviltry** Leiber 75c

80691 **This Immortal** Zelazny 60c

84000 **Uncharted Stars** Norton 75c

87180 **The War Against the Rull** Van Vogt 75c

91357 **World's Best Science Fiction: 1970** Edited by Wollheim & Carr 95c

---

Available wherever paperbacks are sold or use this coupon.
